Acclaim for
So Fey:
Queer Fairy Fiction

"*So Fey* is something more than a collection of short stories. Perhaps it's the connection with the faeries of folklore that causes this particular anthology to take on a little more depth, a little more meaning, a little more richness than are apparent at first glance. . . . Berman deserves congratulations, and if he wants to do another volume, it will find a ready audience here."

—Robert M. Tilendis,
Green Man Review

"Berman explores both meanings of the word fairy, using the age-old themes of folklore to tell stories relevant to gay and lesbian life today. . . . The twenty-two authors in this book have taken the threads of old folk tales and woven them into modern adult fairy stories about men who love men, women who love women, and mortals who love creatures of magic. The stories range from light to dark, whimsical to disturbing, introspective to erotic. Berman has mixed tales by talented newcomers with those by long-established, award-winning authors. A few stories are set in fairyland, or take us back in history, but most of the tales unfold in towns, cities, and suburbs much like our own, in places where fairy magic casts its glow on modern life. These are stories for all readers who have ever loved or desired what they've been told that they must not—whether that's men, or women, or stories of fairies long after childhood is done."

—Terri Windling,
Editor of *The Faery Reel*

NOTES FOR PROFESSIONAL LIBRARIANS AND LIBRARY USERS

This is an original book title published by The Haworth Positronic Press™, Harrington Park Press®, the trade division of The Haworth Press, Inc. Unless otherwise noted in specific chapters with attribution, materials in this book have not been previously published elsewhere in any format or language.

CONSERVATION AND PRESERVATION NOTES

All books published by The Haworth Press, Inc., and its imprints are printed on certified pH neutral, acid-free book grade paper. This paper meets the minimum requirements of American National Standard for Information Sciences-Permanence of Paper for Printed Material, ANSI Z39.48-1984.

DIGITAL OBJECT IDENTIFIER (DOI) LINKING

The Haworth Press is participating in reference linking for elements of our original books. (For more information on reference linking initiatives, please consult the CrossRef Web site at www.crossref.org.) When citing an element of this book such as a chapter, include the element's Digital Object Identifier (DOI) as the last item of the reference. A Digital Object Identifier is a persistent, authoritative, and unique identifier that a publisher assigns to each element of a book. Because of its persistence, DOIs will enable The Haworth Press and other publishers to link to the element referenced, and the link will not break over time. This will be a great resource in scholarly research.

So Fey
Queer Fairy Fiction

THE HAWORTH POSITRONIC PRESS™
Harrington Park Press®
Greg Herren
Editor in Chief

Mahu by Neil S. Plakcy

Echelon's End: PlanetFall by E. Robert Dunn

Slaves of the Empire by Aaron Travis

The Danger Dance by Caro Soles

Vintage: A Ghost Story by Steve Berman

So Fey: Queer Fairy Fiction edited by Steve Berman

Q-FAQ by Tom Bacchus

So Fey
Queer Fairy Fiction

Steve Berman
Editor

The Haworth Positronic Press™
Harrington Park Press®
The Trade Division of The Haworth Press, Inc.
New York • London

For more information on this book or to order, visit
http://www.haworthpress.com/store/product.asp?sku=5642

or call 1-800-HAWORTH (800-429-6784) in the United States and Canada
or (607) 722-5857 outside the United States and Canada

or contact orders@HaworthPress.com

Published by

The Haworth Positronic Press®, Harrington Park Press®, the trade division of The Haworth
Press, Inc., 10 Alice Street, Binghamton, NY 13904-1580.

PUBLISHER'S NOTE
The development, preparation, and publication of this work has been undertaken with great care.
However, the Publisher, employees, editors, and agents of The Haworth Press are not responsible
for any errors contained herein or for consequences that may ensue from use of materials or information contained in this work. The Haworth Press is committed to the dissemination of ideas and
information according to the highest standards of intellectual freedom and the free exchange of
ideas. Statements made and opinions expressed in this publication do not necessarily reflect the
views of the Publisher, Directors, management, or staff of The Haworth Press, Inc., or an
endorsement by them.

This is a work of fiction. Names, characters, places, and incidents either are the products of the
author's imagination or are used fictitiously, and any resemblance to actual persons, living or
dead, business establishments, events, or locales is entirely coincidental.

Cover design by Kerry E. Mack.

Cover art by Theo Black.

Library of Congress Cataloging-in-Publication Data

So fey : queer fairy fiction / Steve Berman, editor
   p. cm.
   ISBN: 978-1-56023-590-3 (pbk. : alk. paper)
   1. Gay men—Fiction. 2. Gay men's writings, American. 3. Short stories, American. 4. Fantasy fiction, American. I. Berman, Steve.

PS648.H57S6 2007
813'.0108358086642—dc22

                                                                          2007011844

To Holly, who I owe a tremendous debt
for she has brought so much enchantment
and wonder into my mundane world—
I could not ask for a better, truer friend.

Illusion is the first of all pleasures.

Oscar Wilde

Love is a cunning weaver of fantasies and fables.

Sappho

CONTENTS

Introduction

Once upon a time . . .

Since 1393, the term "fairy" involved supernatural beings, a myriad of shapes and demeanors. Some good-natured, some dangerous. Brownies and hobgoblins, pixies and kelpies. Elves that lure mortals away to live under the hills, never to be seen again. How extraordinary that gay men would come to be identified with these beings. Yet how fitting, as faeries have long been seen as handsome and eternally young, and so much of contemporary gay culture is linked to the cult of youth and beauty. And how many men have spied an attractive guy and known he was trouble? How many have had to leave home—disappearing, seldom seen again—in pursuit of their identity?

The first recorded usage of "fairies" as slang for effeminate gay men is in 1895, in the *American Journal of Psychology,* which reported a secret homosexual organization in New York City calling itself "The Faeries." What a wonderful notion: a secret cabal of limp-wristed plotters out for urban domination. The term homosexual had been coined only three years earlier. In his book, *Gay New York: Gender, Urban Culture, and the Makings of the Gay Male World, 1890-1940,* author George Chauncey offers that these proclaimed "fairies" had a sense of "otherness" among queer culture, defining their sexuality as different by adopting effeminate mannerisms and dress.

While lesbians do not have a similar link through slang to the fey world, modern writers of the fantastical have transformed the Queen of Elfland figure into a Sapphic icon. The Queen, with her regal pose and dominant sensuality, represents the allure of a mature woman, a blend of maiden's beauty and the crone's wisdom. For lesbians, Fairyland promises freedom from the restraints of society and the dominant patriarchy and holds the illusive possibility of acceptance.

The notion behind an anthology of queer fey tales is not entirely my own—I was inspired by a growing literature of queer speculative fiction stories involving the Fey Folk (I could use the term Fair Folk but they are rarely that in folklore). However, such offerings were scattered about the literary landscape, few and far between for readers. I decided to go on my own fairy hunt, seeking out stories—some old, but most new—that I felt best showed the vagaries not only of fairy demeanor but also of queer life—of romance and grief, of ageism and adolescence, of coming out and standing out. I am grateful that so many talented writers brought me a myriad of wonderful pieces.

The stories that follow offer a blend of queer sensibility with fairy-tale magic, and the pains of self-discovery, acceptance, and of finding and losing and finding love once more. Here are heroes and heroines seeking their own path, and at times when they stray or waylaid, the journey back is all the more interesting.

Legends tell that one should never taste the food or drink of Fairyland or else risk being trapped there forever. So, too, I hope that you find yourself trapped in the pages of this book. Though queer vocabulary has changed over the centuries, it is my hope that these stories will serve to remind readers of what faeries truly are.

Steve Berman
Winter 2005

doi:10.1300/5642_01

A Faun's Tale

Tom Cardamone

Christopher was about to make his first foray into the Ramble. He slipped out of the apartment while Barrett and Hector conspired in the kitchen. Pilfering an apple from a street vender in Union Square he leisurely strolled up Broadway as the sun set a florid pink fan down across the horizon. Reaching the park as the sky finally darkened, he hopped the low cobblestone fence bordering Central Park West and stood still among the nearest trees, their shadows wrapping around his ankles, enticing him further toward mystery.

He knew the general direction from the gossip of other fauns and set off on the winding path as the park's lampposts flickered to life, dim stationary fireflies held by rusty tethers, their low, constant electric rumble adding to the menace permeating the air. He knew that once he crossed either Bow Bridge or found the path above the boat basin he would enter the Ramble. A slight dread tightened in his chest. As the chill coming off the pond crept into the freshly brushed pelt of his thighs he stepped into the plaza woven around Bethesda Fountain. The moon's nimbus stung the clouds into bits of floating charcoal. The lilting laughter of unseen fauns in the distance comforted him. It was still too early for wolves to bay.

Steeling himself, he sprinted over the bridge. Almost immediately he felt a *difference,* a sexual energy, a tangible addition to the multiple layers of shadow expanding with dusk. Men stood within the thicket. He could not make out their faces, but he knew he was being observed. I'm here! Christopher thought, exuberant, frightened, and aroused. He decided to trot further down the path, deeper into the woods, worried that his budding arousal would prematurely attract attention—he wanted the night to last. Since entering faunhood he had entertained wild fantasies of sacrifice, invisible beasts tearing at him through impossible fields of darkness, biting his neck while ravaging his backside. Many a night he would wake up from such dreams panting heavily.

As he moved among the trees he sensed that the men within were *changing.* Beside the trunk of one massive gnarled oak a man squatted on all fours, having shed all his clothes. Christopher watched the man shiver in delight as blades of hair rose across his shoulder blades. In the moonlight he could see the man's emerging claws push into the earth. Hypnotized by this transformation, the spell suddenly broke as the werewolf returned his gaze with a primordial lust, eyes narrowing into silver canine mirrors reflecting an indifferent moon.

Christopher backed up slowly and took off down the path, his heart racing. He ran past shifting shapes, men groping wolves as they themselves sprouted new, black manes and long, sharp teeth. He nearly bolted over the bridge and out of the Ramble but paused, the edge of the park was in view, the neat silhouette of skyscrapers hovering far above the waving trees behind him . . . should he part the curtain and entertain the feast? The Feast. The Sacrifice.

Shivering, he held himself, feeling his slender bones beneath gooseflesh, imagining them snapping like twigs in the hanging jaws of some wolf gone mad. Christopher was startled as two frolicking fauns skipped past. Titling heads drawn close together in whispering, effervescent gossip, one with fur so white it shone silver in the moonlight, the other a complexion of rich chocolate, a fine, shaggy coat ending in a nimble, upright little tail. Each hand-in-hand swallowed by the Ramble. The black vacuum of their sudden arrival and departure left him cold. Then, instinctively, he knew. This was his true invitation. For after the feast as well as before, there is only darkness. Leaping back down the path Christopher knew that tonight he belonged to the Ramble.

doi:10.1300/5642_02

A Scent of Roses

Catherine Lundoff

> The night it is gude Halloween,
>   The faery folk do ride,
> And they that wad their true-love win,
>   At Miles Cross they maun bide.

Tam Lin, traditional ballad

Janet straightened her back against the persistent ache that filled her and wiped the sweat from her brow with a grimy hand. The sun was setting slowly, blinding her until she looked away. Time to leave the field and go back to the cottage. She grimaced at the thought. Tam would no doubt have been at the ale. He'd sit by the fire again tonight, singing that witch's tongue the Good Folk spoke and telling her tales about their country as if she cared to know.

With a groan, she picked up her hoe and her bag and began the weary walk home. Almost she wished that she'd not lain with him in the rose garden of her father's house at Carterhaugh. Almost she wished that her courage had failed at the crossroads marked by Miles Cross and that she had not saved him from the Fair Folk. But wishing would not take her back in time, nor restore their babe, sickened and dead in his cradle a year past. If he had lived, her father might have accepted Tam as his heir. Instead, he exiled her and her faery knight to a distant holding, little more than a cottage and a few rocky fields. She kicked at a rock in her path, wincing when it hurt her toes through her thin shoes.

"No longer so proud as you once were, I see."

The voice was cool and sardonic but it fell on Janet's ears like a burning brand. She spun around to face her tormentor but the words

5

caught in her throat. A lady sat on a great stone by the side of the path and her face Janet could never forget. "You!" She spat. "Have you not had revenge enough but must needs come back to mock me in my fall?"

The other woman tilted her head sideways like a bird, but no bird had eyes so fearsome and strange. Janet could not hold back a shiver and the Queen of the Fair Folk smiled to see it. "You fear me now, mortal? I was not so fearsome when you stole my knight away."

"Would your Majesty care to try and take him back?" Janet's fists clenched and her cheeks flushed red. She dropped her tools at her feet, bracing herself as if to box.

The Queen threw back her head with a merry tinkling laugh. "If I did not kill you then, why would I brawl with you like one of your fishwives now? You won him fair, Janet, and he is yours to mind and tend."

"Then why are you here?" Janet asked, her voice uncertain. "I've kine to tend and bairns and Tam to feed. You've naught to do with me."

"Do I not?" The Queen stood, her gown of green falling to her feet like a river of grass. She seemed taller than Janet remembered and she flinched away, as afraid now as she had been two years before. "There are no bairns, as you know well. Naught but my former knight waits for you and he sleeps before the fire, an empty cup by his chair."

Janet's blood ran hot again. "'Tis your fault! If you had not taken him, he would be an honored knight at the King's court! We should have had bairns aplenty and lands and . . ." Here her voice broke and she wiped savagely at her eyes.

The Queen reached out her hand, her skin glowing a pale green in the dim light. With one featherlight touch, she captured one of Janet's tears and brought it to her lips. She gave Janet a hard stare for a breath or two. Then her face softened in an odd smile, one that made her look a bit like any village girl watching her swain.

In a trice, she was gone, vanished like a dream. Janet stared at the spot where she had stood, one hand clasping the cheek those faery fingers had touched. Her skin burned pleasantly, sending a heat through her that she'd not felt in far too long. She took a deep breath and realized that the air around her smelled like nothing so much as the roses at Carterhaugh.

Torn between anger and something she dared not examine too closely, she picked up her hoe and bag and resumed her walk home. Now it was growing dark and the trees' branches twined an arch across the path above her head. All around her the evening was filled with small sounds: the cry of the hunting owl, the soft crackle of a deer's hooves on fallen leaves, and above it all, the distant silver tinkle of bells like those on a bridle. Would the Queen return for her? The thought made her flee for the safety of the cottage, shivering.

She slammed the door behind her and dropped the bolt in place before she turned to look around her, heart racing. Tam sat just as she knew he would: handsome sleeping face lit by the dying flames and an empty jug beside him. As she watched, he blinked and sat up, blue eyes puzzled as if he had dreamt of other times and places. Perhaps his dreams were full of eyes that had no color Janet could name.

Anger filled her with the thought, driving out the fear that held her silent in the doorway. "You drunken sot! Have you done nothing but lay here all day? Did you even go to the castle to see if Lord Edmond would have you as a guard?" She stalked toward the fire without waiting for an answer, for she knew there would be none that would please her.

"Ah Janet, lass, you know they'll have none of me up at the castle. Better I should come to the fields with you and work the soil at your side." He ran trembling fingers through his brown curls, leaning forward so his elbows rested on his knees.

"You cannot till the soil, and the cattle tremble when they see you. You are good for nothing but the sword and the lute and pleasing the Fair Folk's Queen until she saw fit to tithe you to Hell!" As soon as the words were spoken, Janet wished she could call them back.

Tam Lin gave her a look of pure agony, all cloudiness gone from the blue glory of his eyes for a moment. She felt his pain as if it was her own and she dropped a gentle hand to his shoulder as she went to stoke the fire. It was not all his fault that he was not raised to the farm and that the castle would not have him. Yet if he would try harder and drink less, they might yet make their living from this farm and the herd her father gave them as a parting gift. She sighed, wondering if she must fight the battle anew tonight.

Instead, he stood unsteadily. "I'll fetch the kine."

"No Tam, they fear you. I'll do it." She turned toward the door, remembering her earlier terror with a start.

He was there before her, wordlessly unbarring the door and vanishing into the darkness beyond. She started to follow him, then changed her mind and went to put on the remains of the morning's porridge for their dinner. Perhaps the beasts would grow accustomed to him with time. Unthinking, her hand caressed her cheek as if the Queen's fingertips were still there. She watched the fire for a span of breaths, seeing a beautiful face out of dream instead of her humble cauldron.

She was still standing there when Tam came back from stabling the cattle. He barred the door quietly and came up behind her to wrap his arms tight around her waist. She could feel his lips in her hair as he held her, desire stirring sluggishly inside her as if waking from a long sleep. She smiled at him over one shoulder, then swung the pot of porridge away from the fire before turning to kiss him. When they paused for breath, some impulse made her whisper, "Do you still dream about her?"

Tam pulled away from her as if stung. "Why must you ask these questions? You won me, heart and soul. Must you have all my thoughts as well?"

Janet gaped at him and stammered, "I only . . ." She stopped at his upraised palm and the shake of his head. Perhaps there had been too many words already tonight. Silently, she ladled the porridge into the wooden bowls and equally silently, they ate. Little more passed between them until Janet, weary of the silence heavy with unspoken thoughts, went to their bed alone leaving Tam to brood before the dying fire.

The dreams that came to her that night would have seen her barred from their humble church. The Queen rode through each of them, the bells jingling at her horse's bridle to signal her coming. Each dream began with her touch, sometimes her fingers on Janet's cheek, sometimes her lips. As the night wore on, her fingers and lips tasted Janet's breast and her tongue traced the outline of her belly. Then the curved roundness of her thighs. Janet started awake before that tongue could go elsewhere, sitting up to gasp for air and shudder at the burning in her loins.

Beside her, Tam slept like the dead, hearing and feeling nothing of her distress. She put out a tentative hand and rested it on his bare shoulder, then lay down at his side, pressing close against him. How could she want such things? Surely, this was the Devil's work and she was under a glamour. The Queen had tasted her tears. That must be how she did it. Tomorrow, she must go to the kirk and beg for shriving. Only that could save her soul. She lay awake, listening to Tam's heavy breathing and shivering under the burden of her thoughts until dawn.

"I must go to the priest," she told Tam when the cows were fed and they had eaten their meal. "Will you come with me?"

He shook his head but did not meet her eyes. "The damned fool will scrub all with holy water if he sees me. I cannot bear the stench of fear and hatred that hangs about the old man. Today I will feed the cattle and go to the field." His jaw was set and his face was grim when he described these simple tasks and Janet could not help letting a small sigh escape her lips. A quick and furious glare came hard on its heels to meet her eyes, then Tam caught up the tools and was gone.

She bit back the impulse to tell him not to lose the cows or burn down the cottage. It would do no good and was best left unsaid. At least it was better than that he should spend the day awash in ale. She was off to the kirk then. Still she found that her feet moved but slowly down the path despite her resolution. The old priest was foolish, just as Tam said. Perhaps he did not have the power to stand against a glamour like this. "Do you want him to?" The question whispered against her ear like a soft breeze carrying the breath of a lover.

Janet trembled against the words, the heat of strange longing filling her until she was near to feeling the Queen's lips against her own. She fought it with a howl more like an animal's than her own voice. "Yes!" When the word passed her lips, she dropped to her knees in the grass and prayed as she had never done before. Desperation lent her thoughts an earnest fervor that cooled her heated limbs and drove all dreams from her until she could stand and resume her walk. It would be enough. The priest would shrive her and there would be no more dreams, no phantom touches to give her unclean thoughts.

But the old priest was nowhere to be found when she reached the church. When she asked in the village, one had him at a deathbed in the Highlands, another at a baptism in a village some hours walk away. Discouraged, she went into the tiny church and knelt in prayer for a time. She could not say how long her head was bowed, how hard it was to send her thoughts toward heaven but when she stood at last, she swayed with hunger and the priest had still not returned.

She made her way out and followed the stream that ran through the churchyard away from the village. She walked until she reached a clearing ringed with berry bushes nearly past their full ripeness. These she added to the hard bread she had brought in her pocket and the water from the stream. Then she sat a time, watching the water flow past.

Her thoughts unbidden turned to Tam's tales of the Faery lands. Wild tales they were, full of a land in eternal spring, ever blooming and flourishing. There were green forests to ride through and clear streams to drink from and marvels to see with each passing day. The Queen's palace was made of silver and gems, flashing in the pale sunlight and all her folk were beautiful to hearts-breaking.

In all, he made it seem a paradise that she had kidnapped him from. Her jaw tightened with the thought. Once and once alone, he spoke of the other things he had seen there: the redcaps, the Jack-in-Irons with his clanking chains and the other nightmare creatures of fang and claw. They, too, dwelt in that fair land and haunted its corners and dark hollows, lying in wait for the unwary.

He spoke then too of the day he heard that the Court paid a tithe to Hell every seven years to keep them safe from the flames of God's wrath. The Fair Folk whispered that it must be he who went in place of them, for he had a soul and they had none. How he shuddered when he spoke of it! Janet herself shivered to remember it now, even in the warmth of the summer sun.

To drive the thought from her mind, she rose and went to the berry bushes. In the thicket was the biggest, juiciest berry she had ever seen and she reached for it, straining until her fingers clasped it. A thorn caught her then and she pulled her hand quickly from the bush as a bright red drop of blood spilled over her skin. She raised it to her lips only to feel the weight of another's gaze hard upon her. Janet whirled, heart racing, to find the Queen watching her from under a great oak tree a few paces away, a white horse at her side.

"Have you no servants, Madam, who can be trusted to spy on me but that you must do it yourself?" Janet asked when she caught her breath.

"Ah, but it pleases me to watch you. I stole Tam because he was brave and beautiful and bright with mortal promise, but you, you are something more." The Queen tilted her head as if considering what that might be.

Janet crossed herself frantically. If only the priest had been there to shrive her! She could not fail to notice that the gesture made the Queen smile and she shuddered, closing her eyes against desire and fear. Something caught her hand and she felt lips as tender as the dawn capture the blood welling from the scratch the thorns had left. All strength left her and she fell to her knees, heart pounding and flesh burning until her hand was released.

Then she forced herself to her feet and dragged her eyelids open. The Queen was far too close and Janet staggered back away from her, welcoming the bracing trunk of a giant oak at her back. The other's face had a glimmer of wonder in it. "You still resist me. Tam was mine for a fall from his horse into a mushroom ring, yet you can stand apart from me, despite what I have taken from you. I have never seen your like before, Janet. Can you still wonder that I come to try you myself instead of sending others?"

Janet shivered against the tree. "What glamour have you thrown on me, fiend?"

"I cast no spell. Come to me of your own free will, Janet, and I will show you all the wonders of Faery. Only come to Miles Cross to ride at my side on Hallows Eve." With one last near wistful smile, the Queen of the Fey vanished into the woods with only the faint jingle of bells and the frantic racing of Janet's heart left to mark her passage. Janet seized her bag and took to her heels, running toward the village as fast as she could, her long skirt tangling in her legs. Only when she staggered into the churchyard could she bring herself to look at the scratch on her hand. The flesh had begun to heal itself under a gossamer web like a spider's. Staring at it in horror, she fled into the church, the priest's name on her lips. Her words echoed into emptiness and she fell sobbing on her knees before the altar.

It was anger, finally, that drove her to her feet and onto the path that led back to their cottage. It seemed God's reward for saving Tam's soul was to put her own in danger. Bitterly, she cursed the impulse that had led her to Miles Cross and the night that she first spied the Queen of the Faeries in her bold, bright fury. Would that she had left Tam to his fate and born his bastard in the comforting concealment of her father's castle. He would have married her off to one of his knights and she could have continued a life free from want and desire alike.

Frowning, she imagined a life without Tam or the Queen. The thoughts sat heavy on her shoulders until the cottage came into view and she quickened her pace to reach it. Enough of might-have-beens. She made her choices at Miles Cross and Carterhaugh and there was no more to it than that. Now she had the kine to tend and the porridge to make. Her cousin had even promised her a chicken and a rooster before winter came. They would make their own ease and if she loved Tam a little less for the life they now led, it was not so different from other married folk.

Her back was straight and firm and her jaw set in resolve when she entered the cottage. The fire was cold in the hearth, but at least there was no silent figure in the chair, no empty jug on the floor. Tam must still be abroad in the field. Well and good, she must be about her own chores then. With a will, she set to setting the cottage to rights, starting the fire anew and placing the pot on the flames to boil. The floor was swept and the cobwebs in the corners cleaned away with scarce a shudder when Tam returned from the field.

He looked weary and red with the sun but she could hear the cattle outside. All was well and her lips curved into a welcoming smile as she kissed his cheek. He gave her a startled look and a shy smile in return and so they sat down to their stew at the table. "Did the priest shrive you then?" He asked after a few moments' talk.

Janet jumped in her chair, her hand going to her cheek as if the Queen's fingers still lay there. She made herself shrug as if it was no great thing, as if her fears and wants were like the washing and the mending. "No. He was away in the Highlands. I will go back another day for shriving." Tam nodded and returned to his stew, leaving her lost in her thoughts.

That night, they tried to recover some of what they had lost in the warmth of kisses and hot skin against skin until they fell asleep wrapped in each other's arms. No dreams about the Queen came to trouble Janet that night or the next or the ones that followed.

Instead, she began to see herself as she would be ten, twenty years hence when work on the farm had taken its toll. When she and Tam had no more love for each other but remained together from long habit and fondness. A great emptiness filled Janet when she woke from these dreams and more and more her fingers stole to her cheek or to her hand. She remembered the wild elation of Miles Cross, the knowledge that she alone had succeeded in defying the Queen of the Faeries. She remembered feeling alive and the dreams that she had now were repugnant to her.

More than once, she tried to speak to Tam of it but the harder he worked in the fields, the more silent he became. Sometimes she found him polishing his old sword and once she saw him fight an opponent that none could see but him. His dreams at night seemed as troubled as her own but she found no words to ask him what he feared. Nor did she tell him anything of the Queen, though once she tried to get him to tell her about his time at her Court. He gave her a sharp look and asked. "What have you to do with mushroom rings and those that dance within them?"

"Nothing. I but remember the tales you told me before." She stumbled over the lie and she could see that he knew it for what it was. He said nothing more, only reaching over to press her hand, a look of pity in his eyes.

It was but two mornings later that a well-dressed man rode up to their gate on a fine horse and spoke long with Tam. She heard none of their words and cared little more, thinking the stranger only a lost traveler. It was only when she came into the barn later to find Tam with his sword in his hands, his feet treading a measure with an imaginary opponent that she thought to ask, "Who was he? What did he say to you?" She sat on a pile of hay, admiring despite herself the sweep of the blade and the rusty grace with which he held it.

He spun, beheading a shadow before he rested the point of the blade on the dirt in front of him. "He came to speak to me of a fool's errand beyond the sea, of fighting and glory and all else that a farmer's life does not offer. He spoke of gold to be won, Janet, and a name to be regained." Tam did not meet her eyes, looking only at the sword in his hands. Even so, she could see that his eyes held a fire to them that she had not seen since Carterhaugh.

He put up the sword then, sliding it into its scabbard with an ease that his hands knew well. But she saw how his hand lingered on the hilt and she knew what his answer must be. She said nothing more, remembering with a start that tonight was Hallows Eve and Miles Cross was not so long a ride from the cottage. Her heart beat madly then for all she went about her work as though it was a day like any other. Tam, too, seemed lighter of heart but still they did not speak of their thoughts to each other.

And such thoughts they were! She shuddered at the tithe, bit back a wail at the thought of the monsters of Faery, of what she would leave behind. Still and all, what would she do with Tam gone, even if he sent back whatever gold he won? There was nothing for her here but to grow old and lonely and bitter until even the Queen of Faeries would have no use for her. But to live at the Queen's side, that would be worth the risks surely. Her thoughts ran round and round until dusk.

Her choice when it came found her running to the stable. She led their old plow horse out of the barn as quietly as she could. She had only just saddled the beast when there came Tam with his kit over one shoulder and his sword buckled at his side. They looked at each other for a long moment in the fading light until he spoke at last. "You go to her at Miles Cross, then?" He frowned, his hand reaching up to caress her cheek.

She held his hand there and kissed his palm. "And you away beyond the sea to fight?" He nodded and she smiled at him in understanding. Together, they released the cattle from the makeshift barn and doused the fire in the hearth. Together, they stood side by side looking at the cottage and the rocky fields around it.

Tam spoke first. "I loved you true, Janet, with no glamour to compel it. I will miss you." He pulled her close and held her tight. "Beware the tithe, love. If I may, I will come to Carterhaugh a year hence. If you need me, leave word for me there."

Janet wiped away a tear and smiled up at him. "Go well, love. May you be safe from all harm and find what you seek." Their lips met briefly in a final kiss. Then she mounted the old horse, glancing back to wave him on his way as they parted. Her heart almost failed her then and the night seemed full of secret sounds and whispers. Her hands trembled on the reins and she watched the shadows on either side. From far away, she heard music and laughter but she forced herself to stay on the path and closed her eyes so that she would not see whoever made the sounds. Still she rode on, turning neither to left nor right until the moon rose and the great stone cross appeared before her.

Then she had naught to do but wait for what seemed an eternity. When she had come to rescue Tam, she had hidden in the bushes, catching the Queen all unawares, but tonight she sat in full moonlight at the crossroads like a knight from a tale. Before she had her love for Tam and their babe inside her to buoy her courage, but tonight she had nothing but her dreams and the very longings that she feared. Almost she turned her horse back, almost she rode for her father's court to ask his forgiveness. Always something held her there, waiting.

It was nearly midnight when she heard the jingle of bells on bridles and saw the glow of riders through the trees. Her heart beat so fast she thought it would jump out of her mouth and the old horse fidgeted beneath her as he caught her mood. The faery knights came closer, the ladies of the Seelie Court on their heels and she could see that their eyes shone with colors that she could not name and that they were beautiful to hearts-breaking. All fell silent to see her there and the faery riders came to a halt at the edge of the clearing. She stared back at them, a wild excitement rising in her.

The Queen came riding through her courtiers and smiled to see her waiting there. Something broke inside Janet, like a river when the thaw comes and she laughed as she had not in years. The Queen rode closer and spoke, a victorious smile tilting her lovely lips, "Come and mount behind me, my Janet. My horse shall bear us both." Janet shook her head mutely and held her horse's reins all the tighter. The Queen looked amused. "Give me a kiss then and ride at my side."

She reached for Janet who did not pull away. The Queen's lips burned against hers until she broke away laughing, enchanted by a glamour all her own. Then, bright and full of mortal promise, she urged her horse into a gallop and rode into Faery with the Queen at her side.

doi:10.1300/5642_03

The Wand's Boy

Richard Bowes

1.

Mortals believe that the Fey always know what's coming. They have the Sixth Sense and the Foretelling, people say, and it's impossible to take the Gentry, as they call them, by surprise.

When I see some mortal or another half-breed waiting on a corner or looking out a window, I always think he's worried because dates are scarce that evening or she's anxious, wondering if her Lord will come out of the Hill tonight. Lives full of uncertainty.

That's how I remember my mother: standing at the front window of The Careless Rapture Café looking out at the old streets of the Maxee, the Mortal Quarter. It's exactly what I find myself doing on this January afternoon. As a half-breed, in this like a lot of things, I'm somewhere in between with enough foreknowledge to tantalize but not enough to make me sure of anything.

These tiny coffee houses and bars, these narrow streets are always awash in memory and rumor. Today, part of what's afloat is reminiscences of The Clathurin, how he came out of the Hill years ago and won the heart of the singer Athalia and the love of the population of the Maxee. It's also whispers about young Lord Calithurn, his son, and what he's been up to and why.

Evening still comes on fast in early winter. On the opposite side of the cross streets, I see pillow girls and dollar boys emerge from The Busted Straight Coffee House. They start to split up on the corner as they make their way to the condos and townhouses of their current patrons. And I know it's the blue hour, the time of assignation.

Behind me, the ones who spent the afternoon in here get up to leave. I let them hang out; linger over a beer or an espresso because business is slow in these cold months and because my mother never turned them away.

She was one of them, a refugee, an exile. Her story was theirs. In the Maxee the mortals love the Gentry for their beauty, their magic, the cold elegance of them. But no mortal has ever been quite certain what it is that the Gentry might love about her or him and whether it will continue or for how long.

It's understood that at the moment what the Fey find most attractive in mortals is their vulnerability, their perishable flesh. They seem to regard a little bit of wear, that first wrinkle beside the eye, the hairline's first retreat as piquant, enticing.

For a sex worker, it's really lucky that those first hints of age are not considered a drawback. They came to this calling, many of these men and women, after being raised for other things. They were athletes and pilots and actors, who found that none of that is worth much of anything in the demimonde. They are refugees with only their bodies to sell all vying for that invitation back to the Hill and the realm that lies beyond it.

Motorized traffic is mostly mortal vehicles; mongrel jalopies, tied together with wire, jitneys with coughing motors. But then, silently, its windows opaque, a long Faery car glides by afloat on a cloud of Glamour.

The new Wand strides down the sidewalk opposite me. I'd heard the mortals call him a cop and a rookie, which are close but not quite right. In fact, he's somewhere between an apprentice knight and a game warden.

Just assigned to the neighborhood, tall even for Fey, he steps into the intersection and looks up at the sky, sublimely confident he will not be hit. His cape of lights slowly changes from silver to blue then back again. Traffic stops.

The mortals call them 'Wands' because of the slender mace of magic each one carries. And for the sake of the double entendre. This one holds his so loosely in those long, tapering fingers that it's obvious only Glamour keeps it from falling on the pavement. He twirls it 360 degrees and quests all around him.

A Wand's quest is a mental probe, a quick scan of every mind in an area. He probes and mortals have no choice but to let him in. I deflect him. That's become routine in the short time he's been around. By now, no doubt he's been well briefed and knows where I got my legacy.

My father too was a Wand like the one across the street, the son of a noble house doing his service to the Realm. It was over at The High Peru Musique Room over in the Concourse that he met my mother. She'd made her way to the Maxee as an adventure in the demimonde; a thing humankind did in those days.

He took one look and that made him look again—right into her as the Faery do. He was attracted by her beauty and hooked by her mortality and her soul. She fell for him too, but she had strong reasons to go back to Gotham. He wooed her and bedazzled her and enticed her into staying. That's how it was done not so long ago when things were far more even between humans and the Gentry.

As a kid, I could stand on the Concourse on a clear day, look east and see the towers of Gotham waver like a mirage then look west to where the Hill sat and shimmered. And one was no stronger or more real than the other back before disaster struck their world and mortal visitors came not as adventurous tourists but as refugees.

Now, even on the clearest day the towers are no more. The routes from the mortal world are carefully guarded and only the most gifted and the most beautiful get through the checkpoints.

Even in the gloom of winter, though, the Hill looms just as green as and maybe a bit larger than ever. It beckons mortals. But no matter how far humans may travel, none will ever reach the Hill by themselves. Only a Faery can take them and that only happens if they have abilities the Fey desire.

"Jacky boy," my father used to say, with an emphasis on the second word, as amused and amazed as his kind ever get that I was such a human-looking kid. I favored my mother outwardly and emotionally. My Faery traits are hidden ones.

My father left us about twenty years ago when I was seven. Perhaps he was bored or summoned by some Sidhe command that a half-breed couldn't sense. Or maybe the legend he found himself enacting demanded that he leave his woman and child at that moment. What-ever the reason, he went off to the Forests of Avon with little warning and few words for my mother and me.

I inherited a couple of his abilities. Not the Watching and the Hearing, that ability to reach into mortal minds and bodies that the Gentry have. But I did get the ability to block any Faery who tries that with me. And I have traces of that sixth sense which they call the Foretelling.

My mother was unhappy when he left. But she didn't really begin to die inside herself until a year or two later when the towers fell. From her, when she was gone, I inherited this café. She also passed on a few of her tastes. Like her, I fall for Wands though they are rarely interested in me.

Everyone on the street was aware from the first that the new Wand liked boys more than girls. This evening I'm aware of him looking me over in the way of the Gentry, catching a glimpse of me by hooking into the mind of a passerby and looking through their eyes.

What he's doing isn't standard security and it isn't love. So I stare right at him, as no mortal would dare to do. Aware of my look he turns and moves away.

The very youthful looks, which I will probably have forever, are not in fashion among the Gentry. Nor am I Fey and well connected, which would win me a mortal boyfriend. So what I've had are a lot of overnight love affairs and a few protracted ones. But nothing much that caught me. Until a week ago.

2.

This part of my life in which I now find myself, began on that quiet night that always follows the Twelfth Night celebrations. We had closed and I came out of the back to make sure the door was locked when I realized there was someone sitting in the corner. He was tall, leaning back in his chair with a hat pulled down over his face.

"Last call is done, friend," I said and wondered how we'd missed him, how stoned he was, how much trouble it was going to be to get him out.

"Forgive me for laying in wait, Jack. My name is Cal. I've noticed you all through the holidays and wanted very much to talk." His voice was silver. He raised his head. His eyes were amber. He wore no trace of the Glamour, that small magic in which the Gentry dowse themselves.

He stood. I am a good height for a mortal but he was Fey and stood a head taller. His face was beautiful, long and V-shaped. He smiled and I was caught completely by him

The next several days were spent almost entirely up in my rooms above the café, without clothes, pausing only for bouts of sleep. Once or twice a Wand's questing swept through the bedroom. As I blocked it, I was aware of Cal beside me blocking in the same manner, at the same moment as I so we seemed as one. He was hiding I knew but he treated it as a kind of game.

Occasionally, I put on a robe and came down to The Careless Rapture long enough to make sure that everything was running as well as it needed to. The cook, the busboy, the waitresses were amused, sent me back upstairs. They brought up food and wine, knocked and left it on the landing. The name my mother had given the cafe made more sense to me at that moment than it ever had before.

The dollar boys and pillow girls when they boast about their protectors/lovers always talk of velvet tongues and cocks that know no rest and orgasms that ride on until you're hoarse with yelling. More than a little of that's the Glamour.

But some is real. A partner who can float above you and move the way you are about to move, who rests only when you want to and is ready to go again when you awake is magic enough that you won't ask questions or much remember that you have any.

I knew who he was, of course. And he was aware that I knew. The nickname, the absence of any sign of rank was like a reveler's mask, not a disguise so much as a sign that his identity was not to be mentioned.

When Cal had to leave, he promised to return very shortly. He said that and, as sometimes happens for me, I foresaw that he would climb through my back window at twilight which made me happy.

It was a bright, cold day when I got dressed and set foot on the street again. The Maxee was all on fire with disquiet and rumors of trouble in the Hill and in the mortal world. A street entertainer I passed sang a song I hadn't heard in years about a prince who walked the street and who could be yours for the price of a place to lay his wanted head.

Tales abounded of a quarrel between Lord Clathurin and his son and heir. The cook told me he'd seen fire in the sky that dawn and customers whispered that a great crowd of mortals had tried to force their way through the checkpoints and into the Maxee and been driven back by the guards.

Suddenly, large and clear in every mind, was an image, a figure huge in his ceremonial armor, striding in mid-air, wreathed in fire, hurtling down the Concourse. We saw him through the eyes of the Fey in charge of turning the undesirable, the sick, the ugly, and the ungifted back to the ruined, mortal world.

Coming out of nowhere, the assault took the Fey at the checkpoint by surprise. Their attacker ripped the images of what they saw from their minds and broadcast them throughout the Maxee.

They got knocked aside like hapless mortals. The armored figure removed his helmet. His hair was golden, his eyes wild. It was the heir-apparent Calithurn who, of course, I knew as Cal. He beckoned and the refugees surged forward, poured down the Concourse and into the Maxee.

Some of them tried to blend into the neighborhood, others ran like rats. A few looked more rat than human as I'd heard was sometimes the case now back in my mother's old world.

All that afternoon, flights of winged horsemen from out of the Hill galloped across the winter sky, swooped down when they spotted refugees. As night fell they were still out looking for strays. No one had any idea where Prince Calithurn had gone.

In fact, by then Cal was back upstairs beside me in my bed, allowing me to block the Wands who flooded the neighborhood. And when that was done, he was all over me inside and out. The sex was almost as good as the first time even though I now knew that he was here mainly as a means of hiding in the Maxee.

They say the cum of the Fey will keep a mortal young. And I know my mother half thought that's why she faded so fast when my father left us. I think it's the excitement of their presence that does it. Makes those they choose for their pleasures all giddy as children.

I knew I was supposed to be grateful that he had taken an interest in mortals in that distant, diffracted way of the Gentry. What I wanted to tell him was that his stunt that morning had done the refugees no good had in fact gotten a lot of them killed.

But none of that got said and before dawn this morning he was gone, kissing the back of my neck and whispering, "Until we see each other again, my love," then disappearing out the window. Again, I saw just how and where that would be.

Ten minutes later, a light flashed bright as the sun at noon, and a noise like a thunderclap awoke everyone in the Maxee. We saw him in an arc of light stride across the sky, a sign that the young successor had split and a way of making sure the Maxee would not soon forget that he'd been here. And that, I was sure, had been the most important part of this whole episode for him.

3.

The Wands are out in force this winter evening. I see a pair of them at the end of the block talking to the one who just walked past the Careless Rapture. I know that there will be repercussions and I wonder if Cal ever thought about that or cared about the trouble and danger in which he'd left me.

Without turning I sense Gentry behind me. I'd expected a visit from the authorities so it isn't a surprise. But it is a shock when a voice says, "Jacky boy," and gives the familiar pause between the words.

My father, when I face about, stands swathed in Glamour. The years have not changed him nor have they erased the amazement he feels when he looks at me. I wonder at whose behest and for what Faery plan I was produced.

"I am back in Maxee again," my father says like this must be the word I've been waiting for. He steps inside The Careless Rapture but I remain where I am. I know enough of Faery ways to be sure he won't think of mentioning let alone apologizing for walking out on my mother and myself or for his silence when she died and in the years since.

We stare at each other. It occurs to me that I'm more a mystery to him than he is to me. Then, over his shoulder, I see another figure in the doorway. Few among the Gentry are quite so tall as this one. And he looks right into my eyes instead of right through me like all the others including my father. Again I'm not quite surprised to see him but I am amazed by how much Cal resembles his old man.

"My Lord Clathurin . . ." I begin.

"Just Clathurin," he says and steps forward to shake my hand. The grip of those long, tapered fingers is firm, the smile is sincere. The ones who remember him in the old days when he lived for a time in the city between worlds said that it had seemed as if he was running for mayor.

Back then there had been great argument among the Gentry about what to do with the Maxee. The population of mortals was rising. Law and order, as they saw it, was breaking down. Many of them wanted to demolish this place. The Clathurin, the great lord, came out of the Hill and lived here in the Maxee, went out among the mortals and half-breeds.

If it had been a question of a campaign, he would have won in a landslide. Older inhabitants still speak of him with affection and reverence. The power of the Fey was extended right up to the very gates of Gotham. All this was years before the towers fell.

"Ah, Jack," he says. "Your father insisted on seeing you as soon as he arrived back here." And he smiles a bit ruefully. "It seems he and I are two fathers whose sons think badly of them. Maybe with some reason."

His charm is in this direct speaking. Ones who remembered him said you might think he had mortal blood. He doesn't let go of my hand, but draws me forward.

"I've appointed your father to a position we have just created for him. He will be the Knight of Wands." Here he gives an amused shrug. "Maybe Police Commissioner would be a better title."

My feet almost leave the ground as he turns me toward my old man who opens his arms to embrace me and says, "I'm going to need your help in this, Jack."

And I wonder for how long they've known, in the off-kilter way of the Gentry, that we would come to this moment. What do the prophecies say about the half-breed son he was so careful to propagate? What role was I created to play?

Outside, Wands have mounted guard around the café. My father gestures me to be seated at one of my own tables.

This is where I find out why these two think I was created. I will have to be braver than I feel and smarter than I've been to come through this intact. I've never felt my mortal side as strongly as I do right now. All I can think of is my mother gazing out the window and the poor refugees who died today.

The Clathurin sits opposite me and says, "My son and I have disagreed about many things lately, especially about what to do about the mortals and their world."

And it takes no gift of prophecy for me to know that my father will add. "We understand you and he got together recently. We know he'll be back to see you."

And I realize that with all their Sixth Sense and Foretelling, they don't know where Cal is or where I'm going to find him.

This part of my existence, the Careless Rapture, the Maxee, my life as a Wand's bastard son is about to end. My meeting with Cal will happen shortly in the ruins of Earth with both of us on the run. And though I fear it a bit, I would have it no other way.

doi:10.1300/5642_04

A Bird of Ice

Craig Laurance Gidney

It started with snow:

Ryuichi awoke with his feet tingling on the edge of numbness. The threadbare blanket did nothing to alleviate the chill that suffused the room. Reluctantly, he opened his eyes to the predawn darkness. His roommates were all deeply asleep, cocooned in their fuller blankets, yet they still shivered. Ryuichi noticed that the brazier's coals no longer glowed. With a sigh, he kicked off his blanket and sat up. He tried to spark the flint quietly—but Hideo, sleeping nearest to the brazier, groaned with annoyance. A spark jumped, bringing the coals back to life.

Ryuichi slipped into his sandals and silently padded out of the room, knowing that he would only toss and turn during the remaining hours of darkness. He went to the kitchen instead, and heated water for tea. The dark, herbal scent of the tea after it had steeped for three minutes coursed through his veins, warming him. He held the bowl between his hands, and thought of nothing. The day was a blank scroll, waiting for ink. All was sensation, and quiet (or, near quiet, as he heard the crackling of the hearth flames). Slow movement at the corner of his eye broke his trance, and he glanced out the window. Sparkling spirals of white drifted down from the darkened sky.

Ryuichi retrieved his robe and boots, and stepped out into the monastery's garden. It had been transformed. The soft, cold feathers mantled the trees, the flowerbeds, and the bridge. The dark water of the stream reflected the descent in reverse. The snow sculpted new shapes. A full moon peeked behind the clouds, illuminating the scene with silver brush strokes. The flakes kissed his cheeks, and landed in his hair. Soon, everything would be as white as a Noh mask.

Ryuichi smiled. It was moments like these where he felt the Calling. Enlightenment felt close. He remembered when his grandmother took him to the *torii* gate, when he was six years old. Snow had begun to fall then, too, transforming the earth.

"Stay by me," his grandmother had said. "One must always be careful when it snows. The lady of winter, Yuki-Onna, likes to snatch up little boys, and make them marry her. Then they live forever in a palace of ice, forever trying to get warm. . . ." Grandmother prayed to the *kami,* leaving a few coins at the feet of the fearsome statues. Then she would take him to a tea house, and slip him a bit of warm rice wine. Snow meant magic, as did his grandmother. He remembered the one time when they were walking to the gate, and saw a woman disappear into a silver mist. Both of them shared the secret visitation of the winter ghost.

He couldn't really say how long he stood in that nexus of white and peace. The scene began to change with the first blush of dawn on the horizon. Pink deepened into ruby slowly. He noticed that his tea was cold—that, indeed, he was cold. It would not be long before Yukio rang the bell, calling the monks to meditation. Ryuichi thought that he might as well be useful, even though he wasn't on kitchen duty today. He could bring out the rice for the morning meal from the storage shed. He started to move, when he noticed a shape in the dark pink sky. It was a large bird, painted by the light. The feathers drank the light, as if it were blood. It flew with perfect grace, its wings symmetry. Ryuichi gasped at its beauty.

The bird seemed to have heard him, for it changed its flight trajectory, and began to descend. Ryuichi stepped back, half in shock, and half in fear. The great creature seemed to be heading toward him. Ice and snow, feather and grace, the bird was a monstrous swan. With the precision of a jeweler, it landed on the snow-covered plum tree, and released a shower of packed snow that fell into the stream with force.

It looked as if the bird had expelled an enormous packet of excrement into the water. It was such an incongruous thought, that Ryuichi started to laugh. The swan, for its part, looked offended—or at least curious—at this new sound. It craned forward the porcelain vase of its neck, and peered through masked eyes through the shifting curtain of white. This movement upset its balance. The branch was apparently slippery, for the webbed feet lost their purchase. In a cosmic cough, the ethereal bird slipped off the branch, falling into the water with a splash.

Ryuichi laughed again, at its clumsiness. The swan emerged from the water dripping. It spread its wings, and with a thunderous clap, attempted to take flight again. It failed in that regard; it succeeded in swirling water in the stream into froth. Impulsively, Ryuichi put his tea bowl down on the ground, and walked toward the struggling swan. He stopped when he was three feet away.

The feathers were coated with the lightest dusting of frost. It looked like diamonds had been ground into them. Ryuichi looked around for a stick or something, to help the swan. He spotted a branch that the groundskeeper had neglected on the other side of the small bridge.

"I'll be right back," he told the frantic bird.

When he came back over the bridge with the stick in hand, he saw Yukio standing outside the kitchen, holding a broom. Yukio squinted at the peculiar scene through the snow. He glanced up, and saw Ryuichi.

He called out, "You are not going to help that creature, are you?"

Ryuichi paused at the foot of the tiny bridge. "What if I am?"

Yukio chuckled. "It is just that swans are among the meanest creatures in creation. Their beautiful shape hides their nasty disposition. They are one of nature's practical jokes."

"I am just supposed to leave it there to perish?"

Yukio shrugged, *What do I care?* and walked away, doubtlessly heading for the bell.

Meanwhile, the bird struggled, sending sprays of water everywhere. Ryuichi approached the swan cautiously.

He spoke in a low, and, he hoped, soothing voice: "Do not worry, I will get you out of there . . ."

Showered in coldness, he knelt on the ground about two feet from the water. He tried to ignore that and focused on the task at hand. Inch by slow inch, he moved the stick underneath the belly of the swan, whose sodden, partially frozen wings were curled against its body. When the stick was firmly underneath the swan, Ryuichi cantilevered the body out of its icy prison. The swan was surprisingly heavy, and it took effort to partly seesaw, partly pull him from the stream. He finally managed to get the swan out. A filigree of ice danced around the wingtips. Just as the morning bell began, Ryuichi removed his outer robe, and wrapped the now-stunned bird with it. Shivering, he carried his silent burden inside.

One of the younger monks was there, to start the cooking. One look at Ryuichi's strange companion caused a gasp. He jumped back skittishly.

"Don't worry, I'm just warming him up."

The monk still backed away, and left the kitchen in flurry, probably to get the abbot, who would doubtlessly chastise him. Ryuichi ignored his anxiety, and placed the stunned swan next to the hearth fire, maintaining a firm grip on the creature. He sang a song that his mother would croon to him whenever he had fever. Slowly, feeling and warmth came back to Ryuichi's bones.

The frost disappeared from the feathers of the bird, and its stunned look melted slowly. The swan made the first, cautious beginnings of movement. In the meantime, Ryuichi's feet fell asleep, due to the awkward squat-kneel he had positioned himself in. Icy needles pierced his soles and toes. In the distance, the hymns to the bodhisattva Amaratsu began, a familiar song about freeing the earth from the grip of the cold. Ryuichi thought: 'I would be just as uncomfortable there as here. My feet would have fallen asleep anyway!'

The coddled bird began to test its mobility even more. He could feel the tension of the wing muscles, the skitter of webbed feet on the wooden floor.

"Easy there," he began.

The swan ignored him, and gave into its animal franticness. It was like trying to hold air. Ryuichi gripped the robe that held the creature tighter. It slipped, as slippery as a whisper of silk, and the bird was free—sort of. The homespun robe was half on, half off the bird as it waddled madly about the kitchen. Ryuichi jumped up, and ignoring his painful feet, started to chase the swan. One of the wings broke free, and began knocking down things: a bowl of onions rolled to the floor, solid snowballs. The swan hopped-flew to the counter, upsetting dishes and cooking utensils.

Ryuichi swore. He stood still, as he watched the bird rampage through the kitchen, with attendant crashes and plops as things clattered to the floor. He started to laugh, as eggs and ginger root and herbs fluttered in the air.

"My, but you are a clumsy thing, aren't you?" He chuckled, even as he knew that he would be severely censured by Father Iido. "Yukio was right. You're as beautiful as a cloud, and as graceless as an ox!"

The swan stopped its meanderings. A sprig of mint gently fell on its head, crowning it. It turned one eye to Ryuichi, and glared at him.

"Now, that got your attention, didn't it?"

The graceful head looked away toward the closed kitchen door. It made a horrible noise, not unlike the sound of an untuned *koto*. Ryuichi jarred from the sound. "Now, you have decided to share your lovely singing voice."

A sharp jerk back of the head with its odd and askew crown of mint. A flare from eyes as yellow as Amaratsu's golden rays.

"Listen, if you will calm down, I will open the door for you."

For some reason, he wasn't completely terrified that the swan appeared to understand him. His grandmother had told him and his brothers of the *yosei* and the fox women, as if they were real. Both his father and his mother had humored her, while giving their sons firm instruction that she was speaking nonsense. And now, he was faced with this anomaly. As a monk, he was supposed to be open the workings of the supernatural world, the mysterious ways of the gods. Now, when confronted with such a wondrous manifestation, Ryuichi found it to be almost . . . ridiculous. Besides, he really didn't have time to ponder—there was a mess that needed to be cleaned up, and soon, before the other monks came back expecting a breakfast.

The swan ruffled its feathers. It shrugged at the indignity of being imprisoned in his robe. Ryuichi inched forward, making the universal gestures of peace and good intention, palms gently pushing to the floor. The swan stood its ground, and Ryuichi removed his imprisoning robe from the bird. In turn, the swan puffed itself up, and spread its wings in the kitchen. It shivered and trembled like water beneath new ice. A thousand droplets of water flew through the air, like flung crystals. They hit him, giving his nude flesh a gentle kiss of cold. Some of the droplets landed in the fire, which hissed. The swan stopped this when it was satisfactorily dry. The feathers stopped ruffling and lay inert. The sun eyes looked up at him, expectantly.

"Just a moment . . ."

Ryuichi ignored the eerie, alert tracking of the swan as he moved to the door. He opened it, letting in a blast of cold air. Another chant floated from across the garden. The swan regarded the door as if it were a puzzle.

Ryuichi gestured, and stepped away from the door. "You may go, brother, er, sister swan."

He saw the swan arrange itself for takeoff, the coil of yellow legs and narrowing of yellow eyes through their mask of black. It was sudden, as gravity was ignored. Feather became liquid became air. From ice to steam, the snowy feathers a shawl, it swam through the air to the door. It was the moon, shaped like a bird. It was pure in flight. Ryuichi felt it rush by him, and felt part of his soul go with it.

At the last moment, before it went outside, Ryuichi felt a tug on his face. The damned bird bit him! He ran outside, half nude, after it. But the bird had already sailed into the coral pink palace of morning clouds. Ryuichi watched as it shrunk into the distance, and his face began to throb where he'd been touched.

Evening finally came, and with it, the hour that the monks had to themselves. The past week had been a grueling one for Ryuichi. While not entirely humorless, Father Iido, the abbot, was strict, and wished to keep this a sanctuary of peace and quiet reflection. Ryuichi's encounter with the swan had disrupted that ideal, and he'd been punished accordingly. So, in addition to cleaning the messy kitchen, he'd been charged with extra chores, such as cleaning the massive temple floor, making sure that the statue to Amaratsu was gleaming, and preparing the evening meal for the sixty brothers and novices. This was on top of a day of devotions, and ministering to the poor in the nearby village. By the time Ryuichi got in his pallet each night, he fell immediately into the dreamless slumber of the truly exhausted.

This evening hour he finally had a little energy. He intended to use it and be productive. During the previous week, he had just lightly dozed, a sort of pre-nap before the big sleep. Now, he headed to the calligrapher's studio. It was empty, save for Hideo, who was concentrating on a mountainscape. He gave the briefest of nods to Ryuichi, and went back to scrutinizing the various shades of grey. Ryuichi set up his workstation, with brushes, inks, and rice paper.

He then sat before the empty canvas, and saw . . . snow and feathers. There were tiny whorls in the texture of the paper, like drifts. It was soft as down. He tentatively dipped a brush in black ink. Considered, then washed the brush. He picked one that was smaller, with a finer bristle.

A moon appeared on the page. It was lopsided. Ryuichi resisted the urge to crumple the paper, and convinced himself that he was merely exploring creativity, rather than producing something of significance. He crossed out the moon, and began the tracing the shape of a swan. But the ink wouldn't hold it. It smeared and defiled the grace. He put down his brush in frustration.

"Having trouble, brother?" Hideo looked over his shoulder. He'd finished his painting—his workstation was clean.

Ryuichi answered by sighing.

Hideo nodded in sympathy. Though he could be annoying, Hideo had some good qualities.

"It is still there," Hideo said. "Your kiss."

"It will not go away," Ryuichi found himself saying. The right side of his cheek had a red, inflamed bump where the swan had bit him. "Nothing Haruko tried has made it go away. No poultice or tonic. I guess I will have it forever."

"It gives you character. I guess." Hideo shuffled toward the door. "I bet that you wish you had never helped that beast."

"You know it. Next time I see that bird, I'll bite it back!"

Hideo laughed. "Don't be late for evening prayers," he said before leaving Ryuichi alone with his failed painting.

He sat staring at the meaningless smudges and smears for a good while, feeling his energy wane like the crossed-out moon on the rice paper. He began to clean up the work area.

Of course, the swan, its beauty and its clumsiness, still was on his mind. Ryuichi wasn't much given to portents like some of the other monks. He tended toward practicality. But that visitation had to mean something more than coincidence. The creature had seemed to understand him!

His grandmother, had she been alive, would have told him that the swan was a *yosei*, that he had been marked. For a stately woman given to mystical visions, she had been surprisingly tough. She would have told him, in no uncertain terms, that he was cursed. A feeling, like the warmth that came from drinking rice wine, rose up in him whenever he thought of her.

When inspiration struck, it sounded deep and resonant, like a gong. The gong calling the monks to evening prayer sounded. Ryuichi hurriedly dipped ink in the well, and hastily scrawled on the rice paper. He'd have time to clean up after services.

As he headed to temple, the sound of what he'd written resounded through his mind:

> 'A bird of ice flies.
> Clouds build a heavenly palace,
> As the snow drifts down.'

The snow had melted. Cold, icy mud lined the path to the temple. Ryuichi was the last brother in the temple. He sat on the very last mat available. Father Iido nodded, and sounded the gong starting the service. The *shinshen* of flower petals were strewn about the feet of the golden statue. She gleamed; there was a sparkle in her that underscored her joy. The rays haloing her head were especially gorgeous. He'd spent all week on her; Ryuichi couldn't help feel a swell of pride in his breast.

A few songs to her were sung, of her endless kindness, and the bounty of the heavenly rice fields that graced the land. Voices rose up, like the curl of incense at Amaratsu's side.

After the songs, the abbot announced that it was time to meditate. The divine serenity of the Buddha could be felt through Amaratsu's example. Sixty heads bowed down. Fifty nine minds went still, enfolding on themselves, reaching toward within.

One mind was restless. A thousand and one thoughts coursed through Ryuichi's brain, his mind a babbling brook. Behind the closed lids of his eyes, he saw the floor he'd swept all week, and the mats he'd shaken out. His legs began to ache, and he worried that they had fallen asleep. His tiredness began to get the better of him. *I could meditate better if I were lying down . . .*

No. He must still his mind. It must be free of mindless chatter. Ryuichi tried to focus on nothing. But Nothing eluded him, so on the screen of his mind, images appeared. Beautifully shaped *kanji* on fields of paper. The distant mountains wreathed in scarves of gold, mauve and lavender clouds—surely the most wonderful kimono there ever was. And, eventually, a white bird sailed amongst the embroidery. The bird in his mind landed gracefully beneath a cherry tree. Petals fell in snow showers, obscuring the bird. After the storm the gauze cleared and standing in the midst was a human face. There was a youth with skin of pale gold and hair the color of nothing. His hair, even the hair on his eyebrows and his pubes were transparent, like ice . . . the youth's long arms opened, beckoning him.

A scream broke the meditation. Sixty minds broke free of stillness. Ryuichi opened his eyes, jerked into reality. He heard a low rumble of chatter as he saw the monks talking and standing up. A group of monks looked in one direction: at the feet of the bodhisattva. There was a blur of movement as something small and white dashed back and forth.

Ryuichi gasped, thinking that it was the swan, returned. But then he noticed the curl of a tail, and the nude, shriveled face surrounded by snowy fur. A monkey had gotten into the temple. The temple was near the foothills of the mountains; this was hardly the first time something like this had happened. Occasionally, a stray monkey got into the compound before wandering off. There was a story about the time a monkey had entered the dormitory and reeked havoc, about twenty years earlier. The congregation watched dumbfounded as the creature galloped up and down the stage in agitated lines.

Someone giggled when the initial shock died down. The sound disturbed the monkey, and it screeched in frustration. It hopped on the altar, with its flickering candles and bowls of scented water, upsetting them with much crashing and banging.

Yukio burst from side stage, brandishing a broom. He chased the monkey around the stage and eventually into the audience. Groups of laughing and frightened monks parted like waves to allow the figures to continue their chase. Some of the monks began exiting the temple.

The monkey darted under retreating legs and hopped on startled shoulders, the man with the broom in hot pursuit.

Ryuichi took in this scenario with dulled amusement. See, strange things happen to everybody, he thought. Eventually, the monkey made its way back to the stage. Yukio got in some good swipes before the monkey scampered up the statue. Yukio cursed and swatted at the monkey. Unfortunately, his reach was just shy of hitting the monkey. It settled comfortably on Amaratsu's crown.

Yukio began hopping like a one-legged heron, and cursing with combinations of words that would shame a night-soil man.

Ryuichi laughed.

"What are you laughing at?" Yukio spun, and held the broom menacingly, as if he wanted to hit him. The monkey screeched, sharing his outrage.

Ryuichi got a hold of himself, and placed his hands out in a peaceful gesture.

"I . . ."

Yukio pounced like a leopard. "You think you can do better, eh? You were so successful with that swan!"

Father Iido stepped forward, "Now, Yukio, just calm down . . ."

"I will not calm down! This—mooncalf is laughing at me. I am only trying to save this temple from an animal befouling it, and I am laughed at."

The abbot clapped his hands. "Yukio! Stop this at once."

Yukio sighed dramatically, dropping the broom. He stalked off the stage.

Father Iido sneered at the groundskeeper then turned to Ryuichi. He beckoned him forward. "Brother Ryuichi, it is true that you were laughing at Yukio."

Ryuichi bowed his head, studied his slippers and the floor around them. "I am sorry for that."

"You may look up. Good. Now, I want the two of you to work together to resolve this situation."

Yukio glared at him. "Yes, Father Iido."

The abbot moved away from the stage, and cleared the lingering monks out of the temple. The monkey watched the proceedings with confusion, yellow eyes darting back and forth between speakers. As the last of the congregation shuffled outside, both men moved toward the stage together. The monkey perked up, and scuttled back toward the fan of golden rays on the statue's head. Yukio picked up his bristle-crowned weapon.

"There's another broom in the closet to the side," said Yukio. His eyes were on the monkey. The monkey tracked his movements.

Ryuichi turned, heading toward the closet. Then he stopped. Inspiration struck him, like the poem had, as swift and sudden as lightening. "Put down your broom, Yukio," he said.

"Why? Are you crazy?"

"Let me try something."

The monkey was a living cloud of fur, floating above the ancient sun goddess. In a way, he belonged there, as one as her children.

"Go get some food. We can entice him."

Yukio gave a disgusted grunt. "Food? Why waste it on such vermin as him?"

"Yukio, please."

The groundskeeper left the temple, muttering under his breath. Ryuichi turned to creature, lodged like a snowball with eyes in the glorious crown.

He spoke to it, feeling vaguely silly. But then again, it had worked with the swan, hadn't it?

"Now, you don't want to stay here, do you?"

The monkey sat up, appearing to listen to him.

"I did not think so. It is quite boring. And besides, I cannot keep Yukio from you forever."

The monkey blinked in response.

"That's right. He's a sour old man. If you come down, I promise to give you something to eat."

The monkey seemed to consider it, taking on the pose of a wizened thinker, tail curled around its feet.

"At the very least, leave the statue of Amaratsu alone. Guess who will have to clean her up? The same person who has been polishing her all week!"

The monkey screeched and suddenly leapt from the crown of golden rays. Instinctively, Ryuichi opened his arms, and caught the creature. He heard a sharp intake of breath in the direction of the temple entrance.

"How in—" Yukio stopped speaking.

Ryuichi didn't answer. He carried his furry burden slowly to the temple entrance. From the periphery of his sight, he caught glimpses of the monkey's strange becalmed golden eyes. The soft fur warmed his cheek and tickled his nose. A scent of wildness wafted up, of glacial lakes, and pine trees, and the faint whiff of dung and urine. He felt a tiny heart beating against his chest. It was an eternity of careful steps. Ryuichi felt something stir in his breast. Awe? The supine figure against him exuded a trust that was absolute, almost human, as if he were carrying an infant. He felt the graceful eye of the supernatural on him. This was not normal; neither had the appearance of the swan been normal. He passed the opened-jawed Yukio, and stepped on the porch. The monkey pulled away from him a little, to survey its surroundings. He caught a glint from the golden eyes. Eyes as golden as skin in a storm of petals and snow, fur pale against indigo night, some of it dyed that color, as if it were transparent.

"You may leave now . . . Yukio! Do you have anything for our guest to eat?"

Yukio had become a stupid statue, holding a bowl of something in his hands. He stirred to life, like a marionette. "Put the bowl on the ground, like that. Good." Ryuichi addressed the monkey. "Now, you may leave, but please enjoy some sweet rice before you return."

The monkey calmly jumped from his arms, and inspected the bowl. Yukio jumped back hysterically like a startled mouse. The monkey scooped some rice into its mouth, and looked to Ryuichi, as if awaiting further instruction.

"Go on, now. Go. Before Yukio comes to his senses."

A tiny paw rose, as if in farewell. Ryuichi bent down. The monkey patted him on the face. Its paw was cool and textured, like icy leather. Then it bounded off into the night garden, over the low stonewall, heading toward the mountain.

The spot where he'd been touched was cool, as if he'd been kissed. The coolness spread out like ripples, starting from the point where he had been bitten by the swan.

The night was a restless one. Ryuichi felt every slat of wood beneath his body, and every thread of the blanket above him. He heard the snoring and rustling of his slumbering roommates, and the faint crackle of the brazier acutely. He could discern the fine gradients of light and dark in the room when he opened his eyes. His heart glowed with embers like a brazier. There was a delicious tension in the air, the shimmering pause before the explosive bouquet of the Emperor's fireworks display, or the displaced air after a woman's fan was snapped shut. There was no way he could sleep.

What will be next? he thought. *A heron at the dinner table? A white fox at the well?* Something haunted him, scrutinized him, for what purpose he couldn't tell. He, who was studious and practical, had caught the eye of something supernatural. His grandmother's tales of the *yosei* who shadowed mankind, performed acts of great kindness and mischief, and occasional evil came to his mind. He'd been marked. What could he do to be rid of them? His grandmother was long dead; he felt regret that he hadn't really paid attention to her wisdom. She believed in the old ways, before the mainlanders bought their religion to the islands. "How is 'enlightenment' going to save us from the natural world? The sun, the earth and sea all depend on us, on our worship . . . we are the children of the *kami*."

Suddenly, when he was in the path of a sword strike, she didn't seem like such a silly woman.

Oh, he was terrified. But Ryuichi was also thrilled as well. His childish sense of adventure was engaged. During his long training at the monastery, he'd never had the visions that others had. The long prayer sessions were tiring, and didn't lead him any closer to enlightenment than, say, his calligraphy and drawing sessions did.

These thoughts swam in his head, as the rafters above him blurred into fuzzy shades of blue and gray.

His grandmother had a special garden on the grounds that surrounded the house where he was bought up. She tended herbs, a few flowers, and a cherry tree. A bench sat beneath the cherry tree, which would explode with fluffy white clouds of petals for two weeks in the spring. When he was young, he loved this garden, with its beautiful flowers and its small statue to Uzume, the *kami* of joy. The stone goddess laughed at him as he played at his grandmother's feet. It was this inclination for dreamy idleness that marked him for the monastery, he supposed, rather than the more warlike route his elder brothers followed.

Ryuichi sat on this bench now, beneath the cherry tree. However, there were subtle differences in the vista that made him realize that this was not exactly his grandmother's garden. For one thing, his childhood home was missing. Instead, this garden was an oasis in the midst of a forest of towering black pines. The small, chuckling goddess was missing as well. Through the trees, he noticed the sky was a nude pearl color that never occurred in nature. It was like a translucent shield of rice paper, through which muted tones of lavender and blue could be perceived.

"So, I am dreaming," said Ryuichi aloud.

He felt, rather than saw the arrival of the expected guest. It was a whisper on water, or a stir of the wind, that suggested his appearance. The shimmering youth.

"So you are," the youth said in a voice like a reed flute singing words instead of notes, "and yet, you are not."

The youth was underneath the cherry tree, nearly as tall as it was. His skin was as golden as ripe pears. He was as finely muscled as any

young samurai. His hair drifted in an unfelt breeze, invisible filaments, like the whiskers of carp.

When Ryuichi did not reply, the youth continued, "I met you in
your world. I only thought it fair that you get to see mine."

"I see."

"Are you frightened? Please, there is no reason to fear. You must
have many questions."

Ryuichi could not look at him directly. It was disturbing. His face,
while human, had strange aspects of both the bird and the snow monkey—in the expressions, in its narrowness. It seemed to move like ripples in a pond. And, the youth was nude. "Indeed, I do. I saved you
the first time. Why did you come back?"

"Need you ask, my Ryuichi? When I first laid eyes on you, I fell in
love. Your beauty was so bewitching that I lost my sense of balance
and fell into the water. You deigned to save me, and I felt your warm
hands on my body, and heard your beautiful voice. Surely, you noticed when I kissed you?"

"Is that what that was? I thought you were attacking me."

The *yosei* seemed not to hear that; he continued on in his callow
way: "Your embrace stayed with me many days. I craved your touch,
I wanted to hold you, to hear your voice. So I had to return."

Ryuichi glanced at him now. His willowy limbs were too long to be
really human, he decided. He moved with a sprightly grace, like an
epicene noble.

"You caused quite an upset at the temple."

The youth stopped his pacing, and kneeling in front of Ryuichi, he
contorted his impossibly long limbs until he was face level with him.
"You are not mad with me, are you?"

Ryuichi found himself staring into gold eyes, with no whites or pupils. It was like looking into the sun.

"Not really."

The youth leapt up. He clapped his hands happily, and danced
around the cherry tree. Pale blossoms drifted down, embedding
themselves on his hair. Ryuichi noticed that he was no longer so tall;
he'd adjusted his proportions.

"I was really more annoyed."

That stopped his frolicking.

"So, you are mad at me!" Ryuichi turned toward him, looking at his not-human face. There was just the slightest shifting of muscle, an undoing of flesh as it became fur or feathers. His translucent hair was both or neither. Ryuichi looked away. It was hypnotic. It made him sick.

He felt the *yosei* behind him. A swathe of shadow fell across his lap. But the shadow was insubstantial: a whisper in water . . .

Ryuichi looked up. Through his shifting face he saw the structure of bone, and the coursing of blood.

The *yosei* spoke after a silence: "I should have listened to my sister. 'It never works out, between our kind and mortals,' she warned me long ago. 'Creatures of flesh and blood are finite and have decay built in the very bones of their being: we can only bring pain and confusion to them.' I did not listen to her; she had been a fox among foxkind for a long time. I thought her brains were addled by that experience . . .'"

When the *yosei*'s voice trailed off, his head bowed in sadness or shame, Ryuichi felt compelled to talk. "Your sister sounds like a wise woman—er, fox. Listen," he stood, "I am honored to be—admired by you. Really, I am. But you see, not only am I human and mortal, I am also a monk, who has dedicated his life to the way of the gods and the Buddha. Liaisons of any sort are looked down upon."

When the youth looked up, his pale, blurry face was streaked with tears. Even they sparkled, like liquid diamonds. "Am I never to have you, my Ryuichi?" His voice was deeper in timbre, as if it were a flute played under water. The sight of the tear-streaked avian-simian face was too much for Ryuichi. Before he knew what he was doing, he stepped forward and brushed the glistening streaks away. They were cold to the touch, like ice. The flesh was soft, like feathers. Improbably, it began snowing. Petals fell from the tree, and he embraced the youth who wrapped him in suddenly longer limbs. It was like drowning in a sea of feathers, or petals, or snow. Sudden kisses burned the snow away, and caresses returned the chill. Wind on white wings painted by the silver moon. Ryuichi soared. The thin ether of desire burned his lungs. Then, he fell, hurtled toward the earth, crashing into a bed of luxuriant fur.

The impact was intense. He awoke with a groan that vibrated in his eardrums. Ryuichi awoke to blurred rafters, threadbare blanket, cold room. This stinking flesh. No amount of kneeling and mumbling and singing could bring him closer to the divine.

Hideo was the first up. "Brother Ryuichi, what's wrong?"

"He had a nightmare about the monkey chasing him," said another monk, clearly annoyed.

Ryuichi found that he couldn't talk. He really didn't want to, either. He just wanted to be left alone. He'd been in the air, a spirit soaring above it all. And now he was here, with obnoxious and small-minded monks, chained to the cold earth. When he didn't speak, the others gradually settled back down to sleep. Ryuichi became acutely aware that his small clothes were soaked through. They began to itch. A black wave of shame engulfed him.

"What are you looking at?"

Father Iido had crept up behind him. Ryuichi scanned the horizon from his seat on the rock, watching the clouds roll in. The sunset was truly spectacular: pagodas of orange, crimson and cream, a bold slash of color where the sun liquefied, like a rotting fruit. It meant nothing to him. He looked at nothing; only waited. What costume would his *yosei* wear next, during his next visit?

"Ryuichi, I asked you a question." The abbot's voice buzzed in his ear like a bee.

"I am sorry, I did not hear you."

Last night, Ryuichi had slipped away from his bed, which was just as well. Sleep had been impossible for the past two weeks. He had stood on the bridge one night, in the late winter chill, waiting. He heard the gurgling river beneath him. He saw the dark clouds and the fingernail moon above him. He waited for hours. What good was a river that you could only look at? Surely, with the *yosei*, he could swim in its dark waters, plumb its depths. And the vastness of the sky, with the etched stars hidden behind the secretive clouds, its mystery would be revealed to him, only if—

A shadow had passed over the bridge, a low-flying shape. Ryuichi jerked himself alert, out of his sleepy reverie. He saw silver-spangled wings gliding. It was only an owl.

". . . seemed distracted," Father Iido bought him back to here-and-now. His white beard flowed in the cool breeze. Would he ever shut up? "Others have noticed. It is like your energy has been leeched away."

"I am sorry to disappoint you, Father."

Any moment now, he would come. A monkey or a swan. And Ryuichi would follow him. And he would be away, in the heavens, or beneath the sea. All of that would not matter, if he could be with the *yosei,* wrapped in his willow-long arms.

Father Iido slapped him in the face. It stung him. Ryuichi was no fighter, but as his father's son, he'd received slight training. Instinctively, he leapt to his feet, and made to attack the aggressor.

Iido laughed. "Finally, some life in you."

Ryuichi relaxed out of the position. Yet another distraction, yet another speaking decaying sack of meat.

"What is wrong, son? You used to be one of the most impulsive people I knew. Are you homesick? Are you rethinking your initiation to the order? Speak to me!"

Why couldn't the old man be quiet, and leave him to his waiting?

Ryuichi lied, "I am feeling a little ill, these days."

Father Iido clicked his tongue against his teeth. "No doubt because you've been wandering around at night. Do not think that I don't know about that."

Ryuichi looked at Iido's face, as withered as a dried fruit, with skin of leather. Humans were such vulnerable things. "I . . ." he began. But no words could explain how he felt. And it was shameful, to say it. *Remember that monkey that got into the temple? Well, he is really a creature of myth that has fallen in love with me. And I love him, too. I am just waiting for his return, to let him know how I feel. You see, he let me feel his world. And it is nothing like ours. Colors are sharper. Music flows through everything. You can hear the stars laugh, and smell fragrances that you never thought possible.*

Father Iido considered Ryuichi's silence. "You are ill. But it is with soul sickness. I have been here for over forty years; I know that look.

There is only one cure." Ryuichi waited patiently for the old man to finish. "Prayer. Meditation."

Ryuichi bowed, nodding his head.

That evening, the monks filed into the temple like silent puppets. Ryuichi sat on his knees and closed his eyes after the last gong resounded. More waiting. Maybe he would see the youth there, behind his eyelids. It was as good a place as any. An acolyte began a low humming chant.

Ryuichi waited for a sign. His entire body was tense with anxiety. Every coiled muscle in his neck and thighs waited for release. Through a profane act he'd been allowed to see eternity, to taste it. The sacred no longer held any allure for him. Surely, the spirit could hear his psychic cries for help, feel the wave of desire for union.

It began with a tingling in the pit of his stomach. A presence heard him and Ryuichi left his body behind. The room and the chanting all faded into the background. He was enveloped in cloud, caressed by it. He waited for the mist to clear, to see the weird, elongated face of the swan boy. His heart swam in anticipation of seeing the face, and his grandmother's garden.

The cloud refined, reformed, and reshaped itself. Wispy, translucent trees grew in the distance—a ghostly pine forest. A monstrous willow tree draped shredded white leaves over a lake of sapphire. He found himself surrounded by the lake, in a small island of cloud, with flowers sculpted of water, and lace bonsai trees. It was beautiful, this sanctuary, the perfect place to meet his strange lover.

Ryuichi stepped to the edge of the impossibly blue lake and found that it wasn't a lake at all but the sky. Birds flew below him and further below were the pitiful bottom dwellers—humanity. He'd left it behind, including his body, for a grander existence.

He turned around to survey the garden of cloud, and found that he was not alone.

She sat on an ornately carved throne, decorated with serpents of blue and green. If you looked closely, you could see them moving, slowly. Her kimono was the red of lava; it also moved with a molten grace. Blue-black hair framed her bright, golden face. He found that he couldn't look at it very long. It was like looking at the sun.

With a gasp, he knew who she was. Ryuichi hastily fell to the (white) ground, and bowed his head.

"Stand up, young man," she said. Her voice was imperious, but not without a sparkle of humor. "You will find that flattery gets you everywhere; however, it does get tiresome."

When he stood up, Ryuichi found that the throne and the lava dress were gone. In their place was an old woman, with hair as white as a cloud, wearing a simple robe of blue. She stood next to a wheelbarrow full of cumulous flowers with cirrus petals. In a distant corner of the sky, there was a glitter of movement: the serpents spun through the air like acrobatic eels.

"Divine Mother," he began.

She held up her hand, stopping him. "Enough flowery talk. You may ask any question you wish, but please, no more 'divine mother.'" She promptly bent down, and pulled another flower from the ground.

Ryuichi walked next to her, apprehensively. "Divine— please excuse me, but I can hardly call you, 'You, there.'"

She laughed, putting the flower into the wheelbarrow. "I always did like you, Ryuichi. You have a wonderful sense of humor. Or at least you did, before that creature had his way with you."

A cloud bubbled up behind her, and she sat down. She gestured for him to do the same. Ryuichi found that a similar 'seat' had appeared behind him. He sat down. It was as soft as feathers.

"So I am cursed by the *yosei*," he said, sighing.

She rolled her eyes. She was nothing like her image, which he had obsessively cared for over the past month. And yet, her divinity surrounded her.

"What is a curse?" she said. "Men curse themselves; they need no help. That particular *yosei* loves making mischief; he has a peculiar fetish for chastity and piety. Imagine the nerve of him, sitting on my head with his dirty behind!"

"You know him?"

"Who don't I know? Listen, let me let you in on a little secret."

Ryuichi leaned in close.

The Divine Mother whispered, "It's all the same. Demon and god. Earth and air. Snow and petal. Swan and monkey. The sacred and the profane. It's all a matter of perspective."

Ryuichi sat back. "I don't understand what you mean."

The bodhisattva leaned back, as if she were considering something. "Years ago, when I was much younger, and more foolish and self-centered, I had a bit of a conflict with my brother. He can be a bit, how shall I say, insufferable at times. He was flexing his muscle, exulting in his power, much in the way that warlords on earth do. You know the type, eh?"

Ryuichi nodded.

"So I went into hiding. I was as sulky and ill-tempered as that little groundskeeper man—Yukio—is. You see, I was a bit, how should I say, vain. As a result, the world and the heavens were plunged into darkness for many years. But I did not care about anything but my own rage and annoyance at my brother. Ah! And no one could lure me out of my hiding place. No one, that is, except Uzume. How I love her, my whirling sister!"

Ryuichi remembered the laughing stone woman in his grandmother's garden. She seemed to be the *kami* his grandmother liked the most.

"It all came together, through her nasty, lewd dances. Shaking her breasts at me, showing me her nether regions, she reached me where prayer could not." She paused, as if waiting for a response from him. "You see, carnality and the pleasures of the flesh—laughter—are not antithetical to divinity."

Ryuichi nodded, stupidly. He said, "To be honest, Divine Mother, I still do not understand."

She leaned forward, and gently patted his hand. He felt her nascent heat. "Do not worry, child," she said, "You will."

She stood and kissed him gently on the cheek, on the spot where he had been marked by the *yosei*. Ryuichi expected to be singed. And he was, but not on his cheek.

The heavenly isle melted, and he felt himself spiraling downward, toward reality. He caught a solar-flare glimpse of Amaratsu in her divine form. It burned his eyes as he fell through clouds as soft as fur, and petals as cold as snow.

Spring arrived two weeks later. Buds appeared on the trees and the ground sprouted young grass, green stubble on the black skin of the soil. Cautious birds appeared on the branches, and flowers rose from the earth. The days lasted longer, and the perfume of growth drenched all.

Like the world around him Ryuichi was revitalized. A new energy coursed through him, no doubt granted by the *kami*. He filled the hours with activity. Mornings he would help the surly Yukio with his yard work. After a while, the groundskeeper began to grudgingly accept his presence. He taught villager boys writing, and nights would be spent working at his beloved calligraphy. Meditation and prayer came easily to him; the possibility of another visitation was always there. Iido seemed pleased and pulled him aside after a service.

"You seem to have rededicated yourself to your life here. You are no longer soul-dead."

Ryuichi smiled and gave a slight bow. "I wish to thank you for your advice."

Iido nodded brusquely, and never bought up the subject again.

The secret light of the *kami* shone in everything. Every drop of water was a prism that reflected her in rainbow colors. The warmth of the air, the raw glory of sunset—all were reflections of the Way. For the first time in a long time, Ryuichi felt that he truly belonged here. He was not merely the dreamy younger son left here for lack of fortune.

Ryuichi walked to his room, full of joy. It had been a wonderfully full day. There had been a visit to the village to share food with the poor and infirm, followed by an intense walking meditation led by one of the acolytes around the foothills of the mountain. The families had been grateful, which he recalled as he heard birds singing brightly. Ryuichi remembered his grandmother, the walks that they would take together, down forest paths and by the sea walls. The warmth of the rice wine in his belly, the taste of spring on his lips. Her stately gait, his hand in her hers, held tight.

A flushed and glowing Ryuichi entered the darkened room he shared with the other monks, looking forward to a long and restful sleep. As he passed the threshold, he was hit with chilly air. Early spring nights were cold, but it was colder inside than out. The brazier was not lighted, which was odd. He stood for a few moments adjusting to the dark. Black became grey, and lumps became human bodies, huddled underneath covers. Arms and legs, rising chests. He moved through twilight to his own pallet, and saw the multiplicity of limbs and legs spilling from the others' beds. The silver hoarfrost of sleeping breath mingled about supine forms. Two to a bed, entwined against each other for warmth. Why don't they just light the brazier? And movement, the melding of bodies beneath the grey covers, the anguish-wracked faces. Ryuichi gasped. But of course, not everyone could resist temptation. It was a struggle, eternal, the sundering of body and spirit. Still, it was shocking, to see male lovemaking right in front of him. Ryuichi removed his clothes and sandals in the dark, and dressed in his sleeping clothes, steadfastly ignoring the pulsing forms in the pallet near him. He heard groans, and closed his eyes against them. Limb on limb, the curve of bodies, the hollows, the masculine scents, all blending in his vision, his ears, his nostrils. Ryuichi shivered.

"Are you cold?" Hideo's voice was at his ear. Ryuichi opened his eyes, and saw Hideo standing next to him, wisps of fog falling from his lips and nose.

"Yes," he whispered. "We can light the brazier."

Hideo nodded. "We could. Or, we could do this . . ."

Hideo leaned close, and kissed him on the lips. He held Ryuichi's shoulders, and lightly kneaded them. Ryuichi kissed him back, and explored the cave of his mouth with his tongue. It was cold. The teeth he lightly licked where icicles. He pulled back.

Hideo's face was *wrong*: the expression slack and malleable. It was as white as clay, and sugared with frost. Ryuichi moved back, away from Hideo. He now stood still as a statue. All color had been bled from him, the skin white. The color of—

Ryuichi looked around the room. Figures still writhed slowly underneath covers. Frost glittered here and there, like crystals. Ryuichi stepped back. He saw the cold brazier, the wooden slats of the floor, the moonlit window. He discerned every shadow in every corner.

"Show yourself," Ryuichi said. His voice shook slightly; he was chattering with cold. He repeated himself, a little more firmly this time, "Show yourself!"

In the dark left-hand corner of the room, the air coalesced and thickened. Squinting his eyes slightly, Ryuichi could make out a form there. A suggestion of wings, the stem of a neck. Etched on the darkness, a transparent bird. A bird of ice. The topaz beads of its eyes glowed faintly in that dark corner.

Ryuichi jumped—he felt Hideo's hands on his shoulder. Cold fingers dug into his shoulders. He felt Hideo press into him, fit the contours of his body to Ryuichi's. Ryuichi felt the pull of his answering lust.

It was hollow and cold. The bird of ice watched the two monks swaddled in the dark clouds. Ryuichi echoed inside. Hideo, or the *yosei*, unfastened his robe, and so, unfastened his soul. It was like a soft falling away. Of petals from a tree, of white feathers from a leaden sky. Of a woman vanishing into silver mist . . .

That day with his grandmother, coming from the *torii* gate came back to him. They'd stood together for long moments after watching her fade away.

After a while, his grandmother spoke. Her voice crackled with age and wisdom, like the beads of a merchant's abacus. "A ghost is a soul that is not connected to Nature. They have fallen off the path of *kami*. It is always very sad."

Five-year-old Ryuichi had looked up at her. He saw her hair, as white as the snow that fell around them, the wrinkles on her pale face. The child thought, *Surely, no one is more connected to Nature than my grandmother.* She broke the somber mood by taking his hand and leading him into the tea shop. She gave him a taste of sake that burned his fear away. "Now, don't you tell your mother about this!" she'd said, merriment in her eyes.

The glow of the sake, the leathery feel of her hand, he felt them now, even as the *yosei* stared on, as Hideo tried to arouse him. That glow spread throughout his body. It went from his belly, up his spinal cord, through his arms, up to his brain. It rested in his eyes. Ryuichi felt that he had drunk down the sun. He was warm with the love of his grandmother, the wisdom of Amaratsu, and his connection to the path. Surely, he glowed. He gave into it all—the ghost bird, the haunted monk, the caresses. It all had a place. Ryuichi smiled. The smile was a ripple, a current of warmth that reverberated across the room like an earthquake. The bird in the corner faded. Melted into shadow. The topaz eyes dulled, and Hideo's hands fell away from his body. Ryuichi watched as he trance-walked back to his own bed. His two other roommates separated, and sleepwalked back to their own pallets.

Left alone in the darkness, Ryuichi watched the sleeping monks. He still glowed inside.

A low gong signaled the end of the ceremony and Ryuichi opened his eyes. He stood and stretched, feeling oddly refreshed. As he headed out of the temple and into the night, Hideo stopped him at the door:

"Brother Ryuichi, the stain on your face is gone," he said.

He touched his cheek. It was still warm.

Ryuichi smiled. "You are kind to notice, Brother Hideo."

doi:10.1300/5642_05

Charming, a Tale of True Love

Ruby deBrazier
Cassandra Clare

It wasn't, Ivy thought, so much that she didn't want to get married *ever*. It was merely the method that she disapproved of. Her mother, Queen Arhianrhod, told her she was being silly—the Queen claimed that her marriage, preceded as it was by a contest in which brave knights from all over the realm of Fairy vied to win her hand, had been the most exciting time of her life, and that when Ivy's father had won the Third Task *and* Arhianrhod's hand in marriage, she had wept with happiness.

Ivy thought of her father, tubby, graying, his beard often smeared with honey, and wondered if this could possibly be true. She could well believe that her mother had wept; she just wasn't so sure that it had been out of happiness.

"There is no point making yourself miserable about things you have no choice about," Queen Arhianrhod opined as she bustled about Ivy's room, her arms full of clothes. "There are worse things than your very own charming prince, you know." Ivy didn't believe in charming princes. She ducked to avoid one of her mother's pixies, long sewing pins held in its miniature green hands. Two of them staged a mini-swordfight; Ivy grinned.

"A smile, that's what I like to see," Ivy's mother said, pleased, and held up another dress. It was the gorgeous color of a rosy dawn breaking over distant mountains. "What do you think of this one?"

"Pink," Ivy said. "I hate pink."

Arianrhod tossed the dress onto the bed. "So far you've rejected the cloth of gold as too yellow, the thistledown dress as too scratchy, the gown of moonbeams as too flashy, and the cloak of starlight as, if I recall correctly, 'too naked.'"

"You could see right through it," Ivy pointed out.

"So what do you *want* to wear?" Arianrhod asked, exasperated.

"I'd like to wear my deerskin trousers," Ivy said eagerly. "They're so comfortable, and the corset that goes with them doesn't crush my wings like the dresses do—"

"Wings," Arianrhod said crossly, as if they were Ivy's fault. "I do wish you hadn't taken after your aunt Eleftheria in that department. So old-fashioned." She sighed, and held up another dress, this one the color of pale green daffodil shoots in springtime. "How about this one?"

Ivy shrugged. "I guess," she said, and her mother advanced on her in a swirl of pins and fabric. Ivy could see herself in the polished silver mirror that hung over her bed, a small rebellious figure at the center of a storm of green silk, her face under its cap of russet hair screwed up in annoyance, her gold and russet wings fluttering angrily.

"You've got a bruise on your shoulder," the Queen observed critically. "You haven't been out on that pony of yours lately, have you? You know what I told you about that."

"I haven't ridden Pepperberry in weeks," said Ivy, who, like all fairies, could not lie, and as a result had become a master at manipulating the truth. Her mother only asked if she'd ridden Pepperberry lately, not if she'd borrowed her father's (enormous, black, snarling) war stallion from the stables and gone off riding around the perimeter of the Forest Court, where she'd happened upon a number of High Court fairies at revel in a valley. She'd spent all day dancing with them, especially a beautiful fairy girl with golden hair that reached to her ankles, wound all through with apple blossoms. They'd dallied all day in the fairies' pavilion, eating fruit and honey, dancing and laughing. Ivy had complained about her upcoming marriage and the other girl had been most sympathetic. "Sounds dire," she'd said. "I wouldn't go home at all if I were you."

"But I must," Ivy said regretfully. "It is a law in the Forest Court that the hand of the princess must be won in a contest of three tasks, otherwise the Court will fall into ruin."

"You could stay here with us," said the fairy. "We could dance and ride and laugh all day—who cares if all the Courts of the world fall into ruin?"

"I care," Ivy said stoutly. "They are my people and I owe them better than that."

The girl just smiled and swung Ivy into an energetic dance; hence the bruise. "I bumped into a door," Ivy said now, and her mother raised a golden eyebrow, but said nothing else. Just then a great noise sprung up outside the window—something between a crash and a howl of pain.

"My goodness," said Arianrhod, "what is that commotion?" But Ivy had already dashed across the room to the window, clutching with one hand at the swaths of silk that wrapped her.

A high white wall circled the palace gardens, lined on the inside with rose bushes that looked harmless until touched, when they sprouted hundreds of razor-sharp thorns. At the moment, the garden was still—in the distance Ivy could see the whole forest court at their revels below the hill, tiny lights strung together in rings through the tall oak trees. They were celebrating her upcoming nuptials; not that any fairy court really needed a reason to dance and drink themselves into a stupor.

She wondered who would show up to the First Task in the morning. Probably some slimy hangers-on, a few power-hungry fairy lords from distant courts and an old enemy or two of her mother's, just to upset her. She was just trying to decide which of those options was the worst when a second howl of pain came from the rose bushes. A dozen arrows flew from the guard on the roof. Ivy leaned even further out her window to try to get a glimpse of the action, but she was too far away. All she could make out was the thrashing of a somewhat stocky figure, grimly entangled in the rose bushes' attacking thorns. He was hacking fiercely at them, while trying to dodge the arrows which snapped through the bramble like angry hornets.

"Oh, what fun," said Arianrhod, joining Ivy at the window. "I wonder if the guards will hack him to bits?"

Ivy didn't reply. The more the stranger struggled, she knew, the tighter the thorns would bind until they cut like whips into his flesh.

Most of the arrows flew wide, whistling through the air around the thicket or between the tangles, but a few had struck the wood, splintering it. She heard the intruder give a cry of pain as the guards reached him. They surrounded the thicket with arrows notched.

"Drop your weapon!" cried Pryderi, the captain of the Forest Guard. The stranger complied. "And state your business here before we kill you, or feed you to the moat monster."

"Wouldn't that kill me?" the stranger asked. He had a low, husky voice.

"That," said Pryderi, "would depend on the moat monster's mood. But I can assure you it wouldn't be pleasant."

The stranger shrugged. "My name is Sir Blythe and I desire an audience with Her Highness the Princess Ivy Blossom."

"Your desires are irrelevant here, Sir Lithe . . ."

"Blythe," corrected the intruder, in a tone unusually patient for someone with an arrow in his arm and ten more at his throat.

"Of what court are you?" the captain demanded.

"I am unaligned."

"Of what purpose is your audience," the captain said sarcastically, "with Her Royal Highness?"

"To declare my love for her," Sir Blythe answered. Ivy almost smiled before she heard the guards snickering.

"You will get your audience, Sir Blythe the Unaligned, although you may regret it!" The captain pulled Sir Blythe from the thornbush with a ripping sound.

"An audience with you," the Queen marveled aloud. "He must be one of the knights, trying to gain your attention. An unorthodox approach, but . . ."

Ivy made a shooing motion. "Do get out of here, mother. I need to get dressed if I'm to give an audience."

Arianrhod swept from the room with bad grace, her pixies trailing behind her. The moment she was gone, Ivy tossed her gown onto the bed and slipped on her worn and comfortable deerskin trousers. When the knock on the door came, Ivy found Sir Blythe on his knees flanked by ten guards. He wore a silver helm, which covered most of his face, but she could tell that he was younger than she had thought.

He had a strong chin and a full mouth and the hair hanging below the helm was fair and cut bluntly at the shoulders.

"Ivy," he began, raising his head.

He was interrupted by the captain's boot in his back. "You will not speak until you are spoken to, Sir Loathe!"

"*Blythe,*" said the stranger in a muffled voice. "I told you already . . ."

Ignoring him, the captain turned to Ivy. "What shall we do with him?"

"Well, that depends," Ivy said. "Is he here for the contest?"

"I don't see what difference it makes if he is."

"If he is, than he is under the Forest Court's protection as long as he is on our lands. It's part of the proclamation. You know. 'Whosoever in the land wishes to sue for the hand of the Princess, blah blah blah.' It's meant to encourage those from other courts to travel here, knowing they can do so safely."

The captain glanced down at his prisoner. "Are you here for the contest?"

"Ofcorsmam," said Sir Blythe.

"Take your boot off him," Ivy suggested, and the captain did so. Sir Blythe straightened up.

"Of course I am," he said. "To win the hand of the princess, I have traveled many miles, fought through untold dangers, withstood unimaginable hardships . . ."

"He does run on, doesn't he?" said the captain disapprovingly.

Ivy sighed. "Take him to the dungeons and have someone tend to his wounds. Let him sleep there. He may vie with the others in the morning."

"Are you certain, Lady?"

Ivy nodded. She could have Sir Blythe killed in some humiliating public way, she knew, but he had said that he loved her. And he had such a pretty face—what she could see of it anyway. "I am certain."

The guard bowed to her and escorted Sir Blythe out. He went reluctantly, allowing the guard to pull him to his feet and turning his head to look at her until the last possible moment. Even after he had left, Ivy could feel the strength of his gaze on her as if it had been burning through the helm.

One thing was sure, she thought, whether Sir Blythe was a true knight or simply a spy, things were going to be a lot more interesting tomorrow than she had expected.

Five fairy knights were about to duel each other to first blood in the Forest Hall, and Ivy was bored. She was perched on a tree branch like the rest of the Court, a host of wickedly bright birds flashing their brilliant plumage through the dark green branches.

It turned out that with the exception of Sir Blythe, Ivy had done a pretty good job of predicting who would show up to fight for her hand. Lord Caradoc had arrived from the Meadow Court and given her mother a really disgusting smile before falling to his arthritic elderly knees and declaring himself. He was well armed, with a curved blade made of enchanted bone, and it was possible that his lifetime of experience with a blade would make up for his decrepitude. Ivy shuddered at the thought of him winning—seeing Lord Caradoc there made Ivy realize just why her mother had been so happy when her father had won the contest.

Lord Gronwyth of the River Court, already married but wanting to strengthen his ties to the throne, had sent his nephew, Orrin, a young knight who was clearly terrified. He had taken one look at Caradoc's sword and gone the color of his own green fish-scale armor. Who knew if he even wanted to be here, Ivy thought. He hadn't looked at her once.

Then there was Rival, a knight of the traveling Wind Court. He had arrived for the duel in a patchwork suit sewed together from unmatched stolen human clothing. Bands of flowered silks vied with rags and scraps of cotton, all festooned with trailing ribbons and all in bad taste. He bowed to the King with a flourish of his rapier, grinning through a trailing lace sleeve. When he stood up, he scanned the crowd carefully. Ivy gazed upon him enviously—it was rumored that he was a spy for the Wind Court. She had always wanted to be a spy for her own Court, but both her parents had refused to entertain the notion for a moment. She'd asked Rival about it once, but he'd only scoffed, saying girls couldn't be spies.

The fourth knight was Prince Geraint of her own Forest Court. Tall and handsome, with flowing black hair, Geraint radiated a wicked allure. He batted his eyelashes at the Queen as he straightened out of his bow, and the Queen grinned back.

Ivy knew that her mother favored Geraint—she was so fond of him that Ivy had gone so far as to suggest that if Arianrhod liked Geraint so much, *she* ought to be the one who married him. Arianrhod had looked so delighted at the suggestion that Ivy had begun to fear for the future of her own father, who had brought a hunk of honeycomb to the proceedings and was eating it with relish, oblivious of what was going on around him.

The problem was that Ivy hated Geraint, had hated him ever since she'd caught him torturing a helpless pixie one day in the castle gardens. She wondered if she'd rather marry a sadist, a dandy, or a walking corpse like Caradoc.

Lastly, there was the mysterious Sir Blythe. Broad-shouldered and straight as a feather staff, he bowed stiffly to the Queen and declared himself. "I am Sir Blythe, here to seek the hand of the Princess Ivy."

"You mean the Princess Ivy Blossom of the Forest Court," the Queen said sharply, taking offense at Blythe's over-familiar tone.

"I didn't realize there was another princess on offer," Blythe said.

The Fairy Court tittered.

The Queen frowned, her crown of silver-dipped thorns sparkling in a threatening manner. "And you are of what court? A knight? A prince? What is your position, sir?"

"My position is unimportant," said Blythe. "What matters is the love in my heart. The love I bear the Princess Ivy."

The Queen frowned. "Let the First Task begin," she said, rising to her feet. "Caradoc, you will duel Rival to first blood; Geraint, you will duel Orrin."

"But I have no partner," Blythe objected, sounding alarmed.

"You, sir Blythe, will fight each of the winners," said the Queen coldly. "Should you best them, you may proceed to the Second Task. Otherwise, you are disqualified."

Ivy heard a murmur run around the Court. Clearly, the Queen had taken a dislike to the mysterious young suitor, who would now have to fight twice, and win twice, just to stay in the contest. She glanced anxiously toward Blythe, but he merely shrugged his indifference as the Queen clapped her hands sharply for the Task to begin.

It was soon clear where the advantages lay: Caradoc, though experienced, was old, and wearied quickly under Rival's onslaught. Soon a bright flower of blood bloomed on the front of his white tunic, and he conceded the fight. Geraint, true to his nature, tormented the young knight, Orrin, the way that he had once tormented that pixie in the garden—lunging at him, then veering away at the last moment, prolonging the boy's anxious terror. Finally his sword slipped, piercing the green fish-scaled armor at the elbow, and the duel was done.

"Geraint!" the Queen cried, leaping to her feet in girlish delight as Orrin limped from the scene of his defeat, his arm streaming blood. As he passed the King's throne, Ivy saw Blythe reach out to lay a sympathetic hand on the river fairy's shoulder. There was something about that movement—something familiar—something that nagged at the back of her mind.

The second round of duels began, and now Ivy found herself leaning far forward on her branch, no longer bored. Sir Blythe, though small, fought with a passionate fervor she'd rarely ever seen before. Within moments he had disarmed Rival and nicked his wrist. Geraint, so much taller and heavier, proved a greater challenge.

The two fought back and forth across the meadow, churning up mud and flowers with their boots. When Blythe's sword finally cut a gash along Geraint's upper thigh, Ivy had to stifle a cheer.

"All three of you go on to the Second Task," said the Queen, sounding disappointed, as the knights approached the throne. She glanced at Blythe, her expression sour. "You fought well enough," she said.

"I would fight a hundred, a thousand knights, for the heart of Ivy," Blythe said, his clear young voice ringing through the air. "I would best a dozen dragons, swim a score of roiling rivers, brave the icy slopes of Mount—"

"Oh, do shut up," said the Queen peevishly. "You're giving me a headache."

"I merely speak my heart," said Sir Blythe in a mild tone.

The Queen shook her head before she replied. "Hearts have no place in a contest like this."

That evening, Ivy sat again by the window in her tower room, look-ing out over the wall and the meadows and the far-off mountains. In the distance, a plume of black smoke curled up behind the trees—probably the local dragon, Faustilian, out for an evening maraud. Faustilian had lived near their lands for many centuries, and when she had been a little girl she'd spent many hours in his lair, listening to him reminisce about the good old days when mortals respected drag-ons and offered them presents like tasty knights in crunchy armor and the occasional maiden on a stick. "Now," Faustilian would say, "it's important to remember to toast the maiden lightly so as not to give yourself indigestion." And Ivy would nod, busily burying the dragon's enormous horny claw under a sand pile of gold coins.

Though it had been at least a century since she'd last visited Faustilian, Ivy couldn't push back a wave of sadness at the thought of tomorrow. When her mother had announced that the next Task was to be a quest into the heart of the forest to the lair of Faustilian, the forest dragon, from which each suitor must return with one of the dragon's scales, Ivy had been certain that Geraint would return with the scale, and that Faustilian would be dead. It saddened her, but she could not change her mother's mind.

As she raised herself up on the windowsill, she caught a flicker of movement out of the corner of her eye. The edge of a wing? No, it was a scarlet ribbon, trailing across the top of the white wall.

She leaned farther out as the ribbon was joined by another, this one gold. A moment later, a gaudily patchworked figure swung itself up on top of the wall. Rival of the Wind Court stood silhouetted against the moon for a long moment before he dropped lightly into the gar-den. Ivy thought that perhaps he, like Blythe, was coming to pledge his love to her—but he avoided her window, creeping silently toward the small door at the garden's foot that led to the castle's lower levels.

And what are you up to, my fashionable friend? Ivy remembered his curt words to her, and her mouth curled. No one knew this castle better than she did, and that included any spy of the Wind Court. *Let's see how the spy enjoys being spied on himself,* she thought, and rose lightly into the air, her wings barely rustling the leaves on the oak trees as she darted down into the garden after Rival.

"All three?" Amazement was plain on the Queen's face. "All three suitors have returned with the dragon's scale? Well, that is . . . unprecedented."

The Court stared along with her, for there, on their knees before the Queen, were the three knights, each of whom held a green and silver scale in his hands. The scales were as large as supper platters and as thick. Rival was untouched, his coat and boots as clean as they had been yesterday. Sir Blythe's armor seemed darkened, as if by smoke, but his smooth skin showed no marks. Geraint was cut and bleeding in a dozen places. *Oh, poor Faustilian!* Ivy thought, hoping that the great serpent was still alive.

The crowd pushed closer for a view of the scales, glittering in the light. "Well fought, suitors," the Queen said. "Each of you has quested into the heart of the forest. Each of you has battled the great beast and returned, not just with your lives," she shot a suspicious look at Blythe, "but also with the dragon's scale. You may all . . ."

"That is not exactly true, mother," Ivy said loudly, rising to her feet behind her parents, who turned to stare at her in surprise. Sir Blythe's hands tightened on the scale he held. Ivy wondered what troubled his conscience.

"What do you mean," the Queen asked slowly, "by this outburst, Ivy?"

"Lord Rival did not enter the forest at all. The scale he holds was stolen from our own treasury last night."

The Queen stared first at Rival, then at her daughter. "These are grave allegations, Ivy. What proof have you that they are true?"

"I witnessed his crime myself. I saw him creeping into the garden last night and followed him to the treasury. He picked the lock with a Wind Key and stole the scale, as well as a large quantity of gold."

"Stolen?" the Queen echoed. "Our gold?"

"Indeed," Ivy said cheerfully. "You will find the gold not on his person but in the hands of his creditors, whom he met last night at the

Old Oak. They are mostly garment merchants, to whom he had given chits of debt in exchange for his expensive clothing."

Lord Rival had gone the color of milk after it had been soured by a brownie. "This is preposterous," he protested. "While it's true that this suit cost me well over a hundred gold pieces . . ."

"You were overcharged," murmured Sir Blythe.

Ivy stifled the urge to laugh. "Examine Sir Rival's scale!" she said, turning the fairy guards who stood at each corner of the pavilion. "You will find the Court's insignia engraved on the corner."

The Queen stood, gazing down at Lord Rival from a frosty height. "Lord Rival of the Wind Court," she said, "are these allegations true?"

Rival looked frantically from one side to the other, then drew his sword, tossed the scale at the Queen's feet and, turning on one heel, ran from the hall with his sword drawn. The crowd parted to let him go, watching his cowardly flight with open mouths.

Ivy picked up the scale and held it out to her mother, showing where the engraved symbol of the flowering tree caught the light. The Queen nodded, her lips tightly compressed.

"Well, all for the best," said the King. "It seems we now have but two suitors who have honorably completed the Second Task." He turned to Ivy. "Do you know of any reason why these two should not be allowed to proceed?"

Ivy looked at Sir Blythe, singed but without a single injury, and shook her head.

Ivy approached the thickly tangled branches, through which tendrils of smoke curled gently, and knelt at the entrance to the cave. Shifting her satchel of healing herbs so that it nestled carefully beneath her wings, she wriggled her way into the narrow tunnel that led to the dragon's lair.

As she neared the lair, the scent of smoke and burning increased. This could only be a good sign, Ivy thought even as her eyes watered—if Faustilian was making smoke, surely he was still alive? At last she reached the end of the tunnel and scrambled out into the lair, a high stone cave whose roof was greasy with a thousand years of soot, and whose stone floor was thickly carpeted with gold and silver coins, diamond rings and heaps of glimmering emeralds.

Sleeping in the center of the vast treasure pile was . . . "Faustilian!"

The dragon opened an enormous yellow eye and regarded her thoughtfully. Although Ivy was not nearly as small as when she had first met him as a child, she was always amazed at how big he was and how silently he moved. Faustilian was about the size of a mortal family's cottage and yet the coins he lay on barely rattled as he stretched his long tail comfortably.

"Princess," he growled, and his breath singed the edges of her hair. Ivy was pleased to see that he looked not at all hurt. "You are the second visitor I have had in as many days. I remember when there were none who would brave these woods for fear of my breath, so strong I was, and young, and my scales rippled like the wind itself as I breathed fire, great tracts of forest laid waste beneath my—"

"Yes, yes," Ivy said, interrupting him hastily. "Wait—what do you mean, second?"

The dragon yawned. "And you are as little as I remember, fairy, so tiny that I scarce would notice if you . . . what is that?" His eyes had strayed to the bundle on the ground at her feet.

"Healing herbs, O' Dragon," said Ivy, thinking fast. "A fairy knight came questing here, and if he still lived I would have healed him, but of course you are Faustilian, and nothing remains of his bones but a circle of ash."

"A knight indeed did come this way!" Faustilian said. "A charming fairy person, with manners such as I had not seen in years, and quite a knowledge of Dragon Lore. We shared the opinion that quests to kill my kind are foolish. No woman's hand is worth the life of an immortal being such as myself! I have lived so long that when the fairies were but upstarts in the forest I was many years a God! My great-grandfather—"

"Sir Geraint *talked* to you?"

"For many hours we . . . Sir who?"

"Geraint."

"No, this was another Sir. Name of Blythe. A most intelligent youth—"

"How did Blythe get one of your scales, Faustilian?"

"Why I gave Sir Blythe a scale! The time we had passed together was so pleasant—"

"You mean he sweet-talked you out of a scale?" Ivy's mouth dropped open.

The dragon toed the ground with one enormous claw. "No, no. I am a reasonable creature, you know. When Sir Blythe begged a scale that might be brought back to the Forest Court— I didn't see why not—I don't recall the details of your brief lives very well most of the time. You come and go in a mere age and I—"

"What about Geraint? Tall knight, dark hair?"

The dragon roared with laughter. "Oh, I saw him, all right, though he never came near my lair."

Ivy's stomach went cold. "What do you mean?"

"I heard him crashing about in the forest, running here and there as if a band of harpies were after him—knocking his head into trees and throwing himself face-first into bramble. I poked my head out of my lair and saw him take a scale out of his pocket, pretty as you please, and march back off toward the castle. Poor wandering lunatic . . ."

"Thank you, Faustilian, darling," Ivy said. "You've been a help."

The dragon winked a yellow eye at her. "Sir Blythe is quite fond of you," he said.

Ivy felt herself blush. "Yes, I know . . ."

"You could do worse, you know," the dragon pointed out. "Charming, brave, clever, practical—she's the only woman I've ever met who thinks to armor her midsection. You should see what most of them fight in. Little more than scraps of metal."

The satchel fell out of Ivy's hand and hit the floor of the cave with a dull thud. *"Sir Blythe is a woman?"*

"Why, yes," Faustilian said mildly. "Didn't you know?"

If Ivy hadn't known better, she would have sworn that the dragon was laughing at her.

It was dusk by the time Ivy returned to the castle. Lanterns had been lit along the corridors and feasts were being laid out in each room in honor of the successful completion of the Second Task. Ivy stalked through the Great Hall, where her mother and Geraint sat at table together, their heads bent together over clear goblets of wine. As she passed them, Geraint raised his dark head and dropped her a lascivious wink. Ivy shuddered.

She slipped past their table and found one of the palace guards. "Take me to Sir Blythe's quarters," she demanded. "I must speak with her . . ."

The guard raised an eyebrow.

"I mean, I must speak with HIM immediately."

"Yes, your Royal Highness."

She followed him, but instead of leading her up to the guest quarters he brought her down the staircase which led to the dungeons. They were narrow and spiraled down like a conch shell. The faint hum of Ivy's wings was the only sound as the noise of the party faded into the silence of beneath-ground and the ceiling became roots and dirt.

"How long has Sir Blythe been quartered in the dungeons?" she asked at last.

"Since you ordered him placed here, your Highness, on the night that he was caught attempting to breach the Garden Wall."

Ivy said nothing. They continued to descend until it seemed like they were deep in the earth. At last the stairs ended in a small arched doorway, through which Ivy could see a long corridor lined by cells. She pulled the hood of her cloak up to hide her face and went through, telling the guard to wait at the foot of the stairs.

The cells were all empty save one. Sir Blythe sat upon a narrow wooden bench, her wrist cuffed by a silver manacle. A chain ran from the manacle to a silver ring embedded in the wood. Her helm shone in the candlelight, but most of the cell was in shadow.

Ivy tapped her ringed hand against the bars, and Sir Blythe looked up. Ivy saw the circles of weariness under her eyes, where the gaps in the helm left the skin bare, but Blythe smiled anyway.

"It's not as bad as it looks," she said. The chain rattled as she indicated her surroundings with a sweep of her hand. "It could use a coat or two of paint in a lighter color, to be sure. And perhaps a velvet divan against that wall, there, for reclining."

Ivy did not smile back, but said merely, "I would not have told them to bring you to the dungeon, had I thought that they would leave you here all this time."

Blythe said nothing.

"Have they been feeding you properly?" Ivy asked.

"Are you concerned with my satiety?" Blythe replied softly.

"Have you been hurt?"

Ivy could sense Blythe looking at her in the dark. "No. They have tended my wounds. From whence this sudden concern, Princess?"

Ivy took a deep breath. "Why did you not tell me you were a woman?"

There was a long silence.

"Answer me, or I shall have the guard make you answer me," Ivy said.

Sir Blythe tried to get to her feet. "Believe me, I—"

"No! Why should I believe you when all you have done is deceive us all?"

"I hoped you would recognize me. I have loved you ever since we first met."

"I have never met you before," Ivy protested.

"You don't remember me?" said Blythe softly. "I remember a beautiful girl who danced all night in my arms, in a gold-draped pavilion beside a crystalline lake. She wept when she told me of a cruel fate which awaited her, a contest of Three Tasks and her heart promised to the winner. I begged her to stay with me, but she refused—and when she went, my heart went with her."

Ivy covered her mouth with a trembling hand. Though the helm hid the long golden hair, which had then been braided with apple blossoms, and the armor lent a square look to the strong and slender figure of the girl in the golden pavilion, some part of Ivy had recognized Blythe's true self in the kindliness she had shown to Orrin when he lost the duel. It was the same sweetness Ivy remembered, the same gentle hands.

"You do remember!" Blythe pulled at the silver chain until the links made a high tinkling sound, like bells. "You see now that I do love you, have loved you all this time. You are the cleverest, kindest, and most beautiful creature that I have ever known. If I had thought that I could have quested openly for your hand I would have done so . . ."

"You could have," Ivy said.

"But I am a woman," said Blythe, and looking at her soft mouth and downless chin, Ivy wondered how she could ever have thought otherwise.

" 'Whosoever in the land,' that's what the proclamation says," said Ivy.

" 'Whosoever in the land desires to win the hand of the princess'— so why not you?"

"But I thought . . ." Blythe began uncertainly.

"You thought I would not choose you if I knew who you were," said Ivy. "And what kind of trick is that to play?"

Blythe shook her head in protest, but said nothing.

"When I met you, I thought you were the loveliest person I had ever seen, and I wanted to kiss you a hundred times," said Ivy. "And when I thought you were a knight, I thought you must be the kindest and the cleverest knight who had ever lived. But now I find out you are a liar like Geraint and a coward like Rival. You are just like all the rest!"

"Ivy!" Blythe cried, straining toward the bars of the cell, but Ivy stepped back, pulling her hood around her face, and hurried from the dungeon. She nearly knocked down the guard in her haste to get away, Blythe's cry still ringing in her ears.

"I'm so glad you've come to your senses, darling," said Queen Arhianrhod. She was referring to the creamy gauze dress, which Ivy had worn mostly to appease her mother. Her wings were bound securely underneath. Ivy said nothing.

"This is the Third Task," Arhianrhod continued in a stage whisper, although there was no one Ivy could see in the corridor outside the hall who could have overheard. "You will choose a husband today, and I have faith that you will choose correctly. Now, remember to say the riddle as you have been taught."

" 'What is the most valuable thing in all the kingdom?' " Ivy parroted dully. She had been unable to sleep all night, the sound of Blythe's voice calling her name ringing in her ears like a bell.

Arianrhod smiled. "Very good. A certain someone, of course, may have been given a hint as to the correct way to answer."

Geraint. Ivy felt her heart drop. So this was it, the last day of the rest of her life. Well, at least she wasn't going to make it easy for Geraint, or anybody else for that matter.

She heard trumpets sound on the other side of the great doors. Ivy turned back to look at her mother and felt something heavy and sharp placed on her head. A crown of silver-dipped thorns and roses.

"There!" Arhianrhod beamed. "Now you look like a princess!" She ran to the back doors and slid through.

Ivy sighed. She felt like a doll of herself. She wondered if it would be her duty to the kingdom to feel like this forever.

When the trumpets faded away and the doors opened, Ivy stepped out into the hall. The branches were alive with banners and wings but the hall was quiet except for their rustling as she walked up to the dais and took her place next to her parents. From the crowd Sir Blythe and Sir Geriant stepped forward and knelt. The proclamation of the Third Task was read and there was scattered applause. Ivy looked into Sir Geraint's eyes, cocky and triumphant as if he were already there for his own coronation. She glanced at Blythe, but Blythe looked quickly away.

"The Princess will now ask her riddle," said the Queen.

Ivy stepped forward. "What . . ." she began, and Geraint smiled. Ivy raised her voice. "What, Sir Geraint, would you do if I chose you?"

Queen Arhianrhod's left eyebrow lifted nearly off her head. Geraint and Ivy's father exchanged looks. Sir Geraint cleared his throat.

"If you were to chose me for your betrothed, I would honor you, as the future Queen of the kingdom we shall rule together, for the rest of our lives."

How conveniently spoken, Ivy thought. No love promised, no care for her wants, and if she should die by some unspecified means he would not even be under the obligation to honor her after her death.

She turned to Blythe, who raised her eyes. There was no unspoken question in them anymore, only a sort of resignation. "And you, Sir Blythe?"

"I would refuse it." Blythe said simply. A murmur of shock and disapproval went through the Hall.

"I believe," said Arhianrhod, "that the choice is clear. Announce your winner, Ivy."

Ivy raised her chin. "I choose Sir Blythe," said Ivy.

The murmurs from the boughs became a low rumble, like the distant sea. Blythe rose and removed her helmet. Long flowing blonde hair came tumbling down around her silver armor, falling nearly to the floor. Her pale blue eyes looked at Ivy, and were sad. She laid the helm on the floor at Ivy's feet. She curtseyed low, first to the King, then to the Queen, then to the entire court.

"I am Lady Starflower Blythespirit, a Knight of the High Court of Fairie, and out of my great love for Ivy I give her the only gift I can — her freedom. I am sorry to have misled you," she looked at Ivy, "and I will take my leave."

"You most certainly will not, *Sir.*" Geraint drew his sword. "You are a woman, and therefore unqualified to even enter this contest—"

"I think if you consult the law you will find it says '*whosoever* in the land wishes to quest for hand of the Princess' not 'whichever *man,*'" said Blythe. Another murmur shook the boughs of the trees; the Court was enjoying this immensely.

"The law has not been fulfilled," Geraint protested, even more furiously. "The Princess must be married—"

"No, Geraint," said Ivy, almost feeling sorry for him. "The princess's hand must be won in contest of Three Tasks, that is all the law says. Sir Blythe has won fairly, and is free to depart."

Geraint's eye twitched, but he sheathed his sword.

Slowly Blythe turned and walked out of the hall, leaving her helm at Ivy's feet. Ivy watched her go through a blur of tears.

"Was that a *girl?*" asked Ivy's father, always a beat behind everyone else.

Ivy's mother leaned close to her. "Did she say 'of the High Court?'"

Ivy lifted the crown off her head, and placed it at her mother's feet, beside Blythe's helm. "I do believe the Forest Court is safe from ruin now," she said gently, and then fled for the door.

It was easy enough to follow Sir Blythe's progress through the woods. She had left an easy trail, as if she had been in too much haste to get away to take much care in covering her tracks.

Ivy reached Blythe's camp in the late afternoon. Sunlight was falling in patches through the green leaves. A flask of elderberry wine and a loaf of honey bread were set on a rock near a small fire. Blythe, slumped against a tall oak, stood up in surprise when Ivy rode into the clearing.

Tethering Pepperberry to a tree, Ivy leaped down from the pony and approached Blythe. Blythe was still wearing her armor, though her hands were bare and so was her face. Her golden hair showered down around her, damp at the temples with sweat.

"I hope you have not come to invite me to your wedding," Blythe said.

"I have," Ivy replied, laying her hand gently on Blythe's smooth cheek. "To the wedding of Sir Blythe and princess Ivy, which will be held in the spring of next year. If I am so lucky."

Blythe looked up and her eyes widened. "But your parents!"

Ivy laughed. "They will come to accept it, and if they don't, what of it? My responsibility to the Forest Court is discharged, and I am free to do what I like, thanks to you."

"All I ever wanted was for you to be able to choose," said Blythe softly.

Ivy placed her other hand under Blythe's chin and kissed her lips, twisting her fingers in Blythe's hair and pulling her close. Blythe put both her arms around Ivy and held her so long that when they parted the shadows had deepened around them.

"I should have known you were a woman from the beginning," said Ivy.

"And how is that?"

Ivy laughed. "Because you are so charming."

doi:10.1300/5642_06

Three Letters from the Queen of Elfland

Sarah Monette

When Philip Osbourne found the letters, he did not do so by accident.

Since the birth of their son, he had become worried about Violet. In the evenings, when they sat together, he would look up and find her staring at nothing, her hands frozen above her embroidery. When he asked her what she was thinking about, she would smile and say "Nothing." Her smile was the same lovely smile that had first drawn him to her, but he knew she was lying. At their dinner parties, where formerly the conversation had sparkled and glimmered like a crystal chandelier, there were now silences, limping faltering pauses. He would look around and see Violet watching the reflections of the lights in the windows, with an expression on her face that frightened him because he did not know it.

He had come to believe, in the fullness and flowering of his love for her, that he knew Violet's every mood, every thought; but now he seemed to be losing her, and this sense that she was drifting away, borne on a current he could not feel, made him angry because it made him afraid.

The first letter:

Dearest Violetta,

I have obeyed your prohibition. It has been a year and a day. I have not spoken to you, I have not come near you, I have not touched your dreams. It is my hope that you have changed your

"Three Letters from the Queen of Elfland" previously published in *Lady Churchill's Rosebud Wrislet* (November, 2002), Small Beer Press.

mind. My garden is not the same without you. My roses still bloom, for I will not let them fade, but the weeping willows have choked out the cherry trees, and all the chrysanthemums and snapdragons have become love-lies-bleeding and anemones and hydrangeas of the deepest indigo blue. You are missed, my only Violet. Return to me.

On that afternoon in late May, Violet Strachan had been in her favorite place beneath the oak tree, a cushion stolen from her mother's boudoir protecting her back from the tree roots. She was writing poetry, an activity her mother disapproved of. Happily, as Mrs. Strachan abhorred anything closer to the state of nature than a well-tended conservatory, she did not come into the garden. Her daughters, Violet and Marian, spent much of their time in the little grove of trees along the stream.

Violet was never sure what made her look up—a noise, a movement, perhaps just the faint scent of honeysuckle. Something tugged at her attention, causing her to raise her head, and she saw the woman standing barefoot in the stream. She knew immediately, viscerally, that the woman was not mortal. Her eyes were the deep, translucent blue-green of tourmaline; her hair, held back from her face with cunningly worked branches of golden leaves, was a silken, curling torrent that fell to her hips. Its color was elusive—all the colors of night, Violet thought, and then did not know where the thought had come from. Neither then nor later could Violet ever describe the inhuman perfection of her face.

Violet's notebook fell from her hand unheeded. She knew she was staring; she could not help herself. The woman regarded her a moment with a bemused expression and then waded delicately across the stream, saying, "Our gardens abut. Is that not pleasant?"

"Beg pardon?"

The woman came up onto the bank, her sheer silver-gray dress instantly dry, its hem lifting a little with the currents of the air. She flashed Violet a breathtaking smile and said, "We are neighbors. What is your name?"

Violet had known the neighbors on all sides of the family estate from infancy, and this woman could not be imagined to belong to any of them. Yet she found herself saying, "Violet. Violet Strachan."

"Violet," the woman said, seeming almost to taste the syllables. "A lovely name, and a lovely flower." The tourmaline eyes were both grave and wicked, and Violet felt herself blushing.

"What . . ." she faltered, then recklessly went on, "What am I to call you?"

The woman laughed, and the sound made Violet feel that she had never heard laughter before, only pale imitations by people who had read about laughter in books. "I have many names," the woman said. "Mab, Titania . . . You may pick one if you like, or you may make one up."

Her words were only confirmation of what Violet's instincts had already told her, but they were nonetheless a drenching shock. While Violet was still staring, the Queen of Elfland came closer and said, "May I sit with you?"

"Yes, of course," Violet said, hastily bundling her skirts out of the way. "Please do."

"I have not walked among your world for decades," the Queen said, seating herself gracefully and without fuss. "I cannot reconcile myself to the clothes."

"Oh," Violet said, pushing vaguely at the masses of cloth. "But you're here now."

The Queen laughed. "I told you: we are neighbors." Her long white hand reached out and touched Violet's, stilling it instantly. "Have you chosen what to call me, Violet?"

"I cannot," Violet said, staring at their hands where they met against her dark blue skirt. "I know of no name that suits you."

"You turn a pretty compliment," the Queen said. She sounded pleased, and Violet felt even more greatly bewildered, for she had not meant to flatter, merely to tell the truth. "I would tell you my true name, but you could not hear it if I did. 'Mab' is by far the simplest of the names mortals have given me, and I find it has a certain dignity to it. Why do you not call me Mab?"

"No," Violet said, struggling against the weight of embarrassment—and a queer, giddy feeling, as if her blood had turned to glowing champagne. "Nyx is closer." For surely the Queen's beauty was the beauty of Night.

The Queen was silent. Looking up, Violet saw the beautiful eyes staring at her, the perfect brows raised. She saw that the Queen's eyes were slit-pupilled, like a cat's. "You speak more truly than you know, lovely flower. Very well. I shall be pleased to answer to 'Nyx' from your mouth." And she smiled.

For a moment, Violet's heart stopped with the impact of that smile, and then it began trip-hammering. She could barely breathe, and the world did not seem wide enough to contain the Queen's eyes.

The Queen lifted her hand from Violet's skirt to touch the piled chignon of her hair. "You have beautiful hair, Violetta. But all those pins with their cruel jaws! Why do you not let it free?"

"I couldn't," Violet said, purely by reflex—she was so dazed that she only knew what she was saying when she heard her own voice. "Mother would have a fit."

"Your mother need not know," the Queen said, her fingers as light as moths on Violet's hair. "I assure you, I am skilled enough to replace these ugly dragons when the time comes." And then, leaning closer so that the smell of honeysuckle surrounded Violet, she whispered, "I dare you."

Later, Violet would wonder how long the Queen had watched her—weeks? months? years?—before she had made her presence known. Certainly it could be no accident that she had found so exactly the chink in Violet's armor, the phrase she and Marian had used since childhood to make each other braver, stronger, less like the daughters their mother wanted. By the time Violet caught up with what her own hands were doing, they were already teasing out the second pin. And then it seemed there was no going back. In moments, the pins were out, resting in a natural hollow in one of the oak tree's roots, and the Queen was gently finger-combing Violet's hair.

"Beautiful hair," she said, sitting back. "It is the color of sunset, my flower. I can feel dusk gathering in your tresses."

Violet had not had her hair down in the daytime since she was a child. The feeling was strange, unsettling, but the champagne in her blood seemed now to have twice as many bubbles, and, as she felt the breeze tugging against the warm weight of her hair, she was hard-pressed to keep from laughing out loud.

"Now," said the Queen, "I feel I can look at you properly. Tell me about yourself."

It was an invitation, but from the Queen of Elfland, even an invitation fell on the ear like a command. Violet found herself pouring out her life's history to the Queen: her father's quiet, scholarly preoccupation; her mother's ferrous dissatisfaction; her sister Marian; her friend Edith; the callow boys who came calling; Violet's own true desire to write poetry and have a salon and never to marry, except perhaps for love. And the Queen listened, her knees drawn up to her chin, her eyes fixed raptly on Violet's face, only asking a question from time to time. Violet could not remember ever being listened to with such care, such fierceness.

Only when Violet had done speaking, made shy again by those brilliant, inhuman eyes, did the Queen move. She sat up straight and gently pulled free a strand of Violet's hair that had caught in the oak tree's bark. Still holding the strand between her fingers, she said, "And you have no lover, Violetta? I find that sad."

"The young men I know are all boring."

"And one's lover should never be boring," the Queen agreed. She was winding Violet's hair around her fingers, being careful not to pull. "What about your friend Edith?"

"Edith? But Edith's . . ." *A girl,* she had been going to say, but the Queen knew that already. Involuntarily, Violet looked at the Queen; the Queen was watching her with pupils dilated, a cat ready to pounce. "We couldn't," Violet said in a thin whisper.

"It is not hard," the Queen said, releasing Violet's hair. She caressed Violet's cheek. "And you are made to be loved, Violetta." There was a pause. Violet could feel a terrible, immodest heat somewhere in the center of her being, and she knew her face was flushed. The Queen raised perfect eyebrows. "Do *I* bore you?"

"No," Violet said breathlessly. "You do not bore me." The Queen smiled and leaned in close to kiss her.

Philip waited for a day when he knew Violet would be out of the house. She made very few afternoon visits since Jonathan's birth, but he knew she would not refuse her childhood friend Edith Fairfield, who had been so ill since the birth of her own child. At two o'clock he told his clerk a random lie to explain his early departure and went home.

He was not accustomed to being home during the day; he was disturbed by how quiet it was. The housemaid stared at him with wide, frightened eyes like a deer's as he crossed the front hall. The carpet on the stairs seemed to devour his footsteps. He had climbed those stairs a thousand times, but he had never noticed their breadth and height, the warmth of the glowing oak paneling, the silken run of the banister beneath his hand.

He stopped on the landing. There was a bowl of roses in the window, great creamy-golden multifoliate orbs, seeming to take the sunlight into themselves and throw it out threefold. Their scent had all the sweetness of childhood's half-remembered summers, and he stood for a long time gazing at them before he turned down the hall toward Violet's bedroom.

Her bedroom was not as he remembered it. Standing in the doorway, he tried to identify what had changed and could not. The room, like Violet herself, seemed distant. It was the middle of the day—he thought of the torch-like roses—yet Violet's room seemed full of twilight and the cool sadness of dusk.

For a moment, like a man standing on the brink of a dark, powerful river, he thought that he would turn and leave, that he would not brave the torrent rushing in silence through Violet's room. For a moment he recognized, in a dim wordless way, that the name of the river bank he stood upon was *peace*.

But it was not right that Violet should have secrets from him, who loved her. He took a deep, unthinking breath and stepped into Violet's room to begin his search.

Later, Violet would recognize that the Queen had in fact enchanted her, that first afternoon by the stream. But by then she had come to understand the Queen of Elfland as well as any mortal could, and she was not angry. The Queen had done as she had seen fit, and the enchantment had not made Violet behave in ways contrary to who she was. It had merely separated her temporarily from inhibition, caution, guilt . . . so that the feel of the Queen's mouth on her naked breasts, the feel of the Queen's cool fingers between her legs, had brought her nothing but passion.

Only at twilight, as she was hastening up to the house, praying that her buttons were fastened straight and that there were no leaves caught in her hair, did it occur to her to wonder what had possessed her, to imagine what her mother would say if she were told even a tenth of what the Queen had taught Violet that afternoon. Her face was flushed with shame by the time she sat down at the dinner table. Luckily, her mother assumed her heightened color was due to sun, and therefore Violet received only a familiar diatribe about the quality of a lady's skin. She bent her head beneath her mother's anger without even feeling it, her mind full of the throaty purr of the Queen's laughter.

That should have been the end of it—the encounter should have been a momentary aberration, from which Violet returned, chastened and meek, to her senses—but the heat the Queen had woken in her would not be damped down again. She found herself imagining what it would be like to kiss Edith, or Marian's beautiful friend Dorothea, or even Ann the housemaid. At night she fantasized about the heroines of her favorite books, and sometimes her hands would creep down her body to touch the secret places the Queen had shown her. Two weeks after their first meeting, Violet went back to the spinney. The Queen of Elfland was waiting there, her hands full of roses.

Philip finally found the letters hidden in the back of a photograph of Violet and her sister Marian, who was now in India with her husband. He had never liked the portrait, had always wished Violet would get rid of it, but it was the only picture she had of Marian. He did not like the dark directness with which the sisters looked out of the frame. It seemed to him unpleasant—and most unlike Violet. That girl's face, remote and delicate and somber, had nothing to do with the woman he had married.

He picked it up, turned it over, pried loose the back with a savage wrench.

The letters fluttered out like great helpless moths and drifted to the floor. He dropped the portrait heedlessly and picked them up, his hands shaking.

There were three of them; he could tell by the ink, which darkened from the terrible crimson color of blood, through a rich garnet, to a red so dark it was almost black. The handwriting was square and flowing, elegant yet as neat as print. The paper was translucently thin, as if it had been spun out of the great richness of the ink.

He looked first, viciously, for a signature. There was none on any of them, only an embossed signet, the imprint of a linden leaf. It meant nothing to him.

He put the letters in order, darkest and oldest to brightest and newest, and began to read.

The second letter:

> Violet, my song,
>
> I dream of your breasts, their small sweetness. I dream of your thighs, of the nape of your neck, of your fragile hands. I dream of the treasure between your thighs, of its silken softness beneath my fingers, and its warmth. I dream of your kisses, my Violet, of the taste of your mouth, the roughness of your tongue. My truest flame, my mortal queen, I dream of the feel of your lips on my skin, the feel of your fingers in my hair. I dream of your laugh, of your smile, of your velvet-rich voice.
>
> You asked me once if I would not forget you. I could see in your eyes that you believed I would, that you thought yourself no more than an amusement, a toy with which I would soon become bored. I could not tell you then that it was not true, but I tell you now. I have not forgotten you. I will not forget you. You are more to me than you can imagine. Return to me.

After he had read them all, Philip crumpled the letters in his shaking hands and hurled them away as if they were poison. His brain seemed full of fire. When he bent, automatically, to pick up the portrait, he found another object wedged in its back, an elaborately woven knot of hair, as firm and soft as silk; its color seemed to shift with the light, from ink to ash to fog. It had to be the token the final letter spoke of.

He was standing with it in his hand, staring at it in a dry fury, when he heard the rustle of Violet's dress in the hall. As she came in, her face already surprised, his name on her lips, he shouted at her, "Who is he?"

She looked from him, to the crumpled letters, to the portrait, to the token in his hand. The expression left her face, as if she were a lake freezing over. She said, "No one."

"Who wrote you these letters, Violet?" he said, striving to keep his voice low and even. "You said you hadn't had suitors before me."

"I hadn't," she said. "I did not lie to you, Philip."

"Then what are these?" He pointed to the letters.

She looked at him, her eyes as dark and direct as the eyes of the photographed Violet lying on the floor. "Mine."

He was so jolted he took a step backward. It suddenly seemed to him that he was facing a stranger, that this woman standing here, her red-gold hair gleaming in the sunlight from the windows, was not his wife, Violet Strachan Osbourne, but some almost perfect replica, like a Madame Tussand's waxwork come to life. "But, Violet," he said, hating how feeble he sounded even as he said it, "I am your husband."

"Yes," she said. "I know."

"Then why won't you tell me the truth?"

"It would not help." She looked away from him, not in embarrassment or shame, but merely as if she were tired of thinking about him. "If you will leave me now, in an hour I will come downstairs, and it will be as if none of this ever happened. We can forget it."

He did not want to talk to this Violet, so cold and patient and indifferent. He wanted to take her offer. But . . . "I cannot forget. Who is he, Violet?"

She came into the room, picked up the letters and carefully smoothed them out. She came past him, picked up the photograph, returned the letters to its back. She turned to him then and held out her hand, her eyes level and unfathomable. He surrendered the token. She put it with the letters, then replaced the back of the frame and returned the photograph to its accustomed place. Only then did she say, "I wish you would reconsider."

"I cannot," he said, with greater certainty now. "I will forgive you, but I must know."

She looked into the distance for a moment, as if she were thinking of something else. "I do not think I have asked for your forgiveness, Philip."

"Violet—!"

She looked back at him, her eyes like stone. "If you insist on knowing, I will tell you. But I do not do so because I think you have a right to hear it, or because I want you to 'forgive' me. I do so because I know that I will have no peace otherwise."

"Violet . . ."

"You married me two months after we met. I was glad of it, even gladder when I became pregnant so quickly. I thought she would lose interest then."

"*She?*"

The look Violet gave him was almost pitying. "My lover, Philip. The Queen of Elfland."

In fear and fury, he erupted at her: "Good God, Violet, do you expect me to believe this nonsense?"

"No," she said, and the flash of her dark eyes went through him like a scythe. "I don't care what you believe. You may hear nothing, or you may hear the truth. I will not lie to you."

"I thought you loved me," he said in a failing whisper.

"I wanted to. And I like you very much. But she was right. I cannot forget her, though God knows I have tried."

It came to him then clearly, terribly, that she was not lying. Those letters with their strange paper and stranger ink, the knot of hair with its shifting colors, the fabulous roses—all those things forced him to face the idea that Violet held secrets from him, that there was something in her he had never even guessed at.

"She found me," Violet said, and he knew dimly that she was no longer speaking to him, "when I was eighteen. There was a spinney at the bottom of our garden with a stream running through it. Marian and I went there to read novels and write poetry and do other things Mother disapproved of. Sometimes we would talk of what we meant to do when we were grown. We would never marry, we told each other solemnly. I wanted to be a poet. Marian wanted to be an explorer and find the source of the Amazon. But that day I was alone."

It was another thing he had never known about her. He had never known that she wrote poetry at all, much less that she had dreamed of poetry instead of marriage. It was another fragment of her that he had not held, when he thought he had held everything that she was.

She had drifted across to the mirror, the massive heirloom cheval glass in its mahogany frame. She was running her fingers over the carved leaves and flowers; her reflection in the glass seemed like a reflection in dark water.

"I can't remember what I was doing. I just remember looking up and seeing her. She was standing in the stream. I knew what she was."

The eyes of her reflection caught his eyes. He watched Violet remember where she was and to whom she spoke; her face closed again, like a door slamming shut.

"She seduced me," Violet said, turning to face him. "We became lovers. At night I would sneak out of the house and cross the stream to her court. One week, when my parents took Marian to visit her godmother, I told the servants I was staying with Edith, and I spent the entire time with . . . with *her*. She begged me not to go back, but I could not stay. Do you understand, Philip? *I could not stay.*"

She seemed to see in his face that he did not understand, and the vitality drained out of her again. "The night before I married you, I asked her to let me go, to give me a year and a day to try to be your wife. She did as I asked."

"But then she began writing letters," he said, because he had to prove, to Violet, to himself, that he was truly here.

"Yes. I have not answered them. I have been faithful to you."

He held up his hands, palms out in a warding gesture, as if the bitterness in her voice were something he could push away. But he could not keep the reproach from his tongue: "You kept the letters."

"Yes," Violet said, her tone too flat to be deciphered, "I kept the letters."

❦

The third letter:

Violet, my only heart,

I know that your silence must mean you will not return, that you have chosen your other life. I could compel you to return, just as I could have compelled you to stay. I hope you understand that my choice not to do so is itself a gift, the only way you have offered me to show you that I love you. I do not know what there is in your life to treasure: your husband, as blind and senseless as a stone? Your fat, stodgy infant who will surely grow up to resemble his father? The mother whose love you cannot win, the father who has never noticed you? Your sick and clinging friend? The infrequent letters from a sister who thinks of nothing but her husband?

You know the wonders and joys I can offer you. You know that in my realm you will be honored as you are not in your own. Violet, it is pain to me to know how you are treated, how little those around you see you—much less recognize your beauties— even as they use you and destroy you. I know that you will not heed me; I feel in your silence that your mind is made up. You are better than the mortal world deserves.

I will give you three gifts then, since you will not let me give you more. Your freedom, even though you turn it into slavery; this token—I wish that perhaps you will wear it next your heart; my roses, that your house, too, may become a garden. And I give you, still, my hope that you will return.

The silence in the bedroom was as heavy as iron, heavy as lead. Philip could not find the strength to lift it. In the end, it was Violet who straightened her shoulders and said, with an odd, crooked smile, "Well, Philip?"

"You don't love me," he said.

The smile fell from her face. "No. I am sorry."

"What about Jonathan? Your *son?*"

The Queen's careless description, "your fat, stodgy infant," hung unspoken between them. Finally, Violet said, "I will do my duty by him."

"My God, Violet, I'm not talking about duty! I'm asking if you *love* him!"

"You are asking too much." The color was gone from her face; for the first time, he was forced to admit that the solemn photograph captured something that was really part of Violet. Before he could compose himself against that realization, another hit him: that he did not know her, that the sparkling, marvelous conversations, on which he had founded his love, had given him nothing of her true thoughts, nothing of her heart. He had worshipped her as her suitor; he had worshipped her as her husband. But until now, he had come no closer to her; truly, as he had thought earlier, she was a stranger to him.

In the pain of that revelation, he said, "You used me. You're *using* me and Jonathan." Then, with a gasp, "You're using my love!"

"I have given everything I have to give in return!" Violet cried. "Is this all there is, Philip? Have I no choice but to give everything to her, or to you? Either way, what is there left for me?"

"Violet—"

"No," she said, so harshly that he was silenced. "I see that I am like Ulysses, caught between Scylla and Charybdis. To neither side is there safe haven."

He looked away from the bitter anguish in her face. He still loved her. He did not think he would ever forgive her for what she had done, but her despair struck him like barbed arrows. "I am sorry," he said at last. "I did not realize I was asking so much."

"You have asked no more than any man asks of his wife." She sank down slowly onto the chair by the window, resting her forehead on her hand.

"I did not wish to . . . to crush you," he said, fighting now simply to make her hear him. "I did not know you were so unhappy."

"I am not unhappy," she said without raising her head. "I chose between love and duty, and I am living with my choice. I had not . . . I had not expected to be offered that choice again. That makes it harder."

"Will you go back to . . . *her?*"

"No. I cannot. Her love will destroy me, for I am only mortal, a moth, and she is like the sun. My poetry was immolated in her ardor, left in her garden with my heart, and I cannot sacrifice more to her." He thought for a moment she would go on, but she said only, again, "I cannot."

"Will you . . . will you stay with me?"

She raised her head then to stare at him; her face was set, like that of someone who looks on devastation and will not weep. "Have I a choice?"

"No, I mean . . . I meant, only, will you *stay?* With *me?*"

"You know that I do not love you."

"Yes, but . . ." He could not think how to express what he wanted to say, that he needed and loved her whether she loved him or not, and was forced to fall back, lamely, on, "You are my wife. And the mother of my son."

"Yes," she said, her voice inflectionless. "I am."

He said, in little more than a whisper: "Don't shut me out, Violet, please."

"Very well," she said. Her smile was a faded reflection of its former luminous beauty. "What is left is yours." She turned away, but not before he had seen the brilliance of tears in her eyes.

He wanted to comfort her, but he no longer knew how. He stood, awkward in the fading afternoon light, and watched her weep.

On the landing, the roses of the Queen of Elfland, as clamorous as trumpets, continued to shout their glory to the uncomprehending house.

doi:10.1300/5642_07

The Kings of Oak and Holly

Kenneth D. Woods

The Oak King grows. Sap surges thick and golden beneath his wooden skin and twin trunks lift skyward as branches burgeon with green. The sun rises bright and warm and a gentle wind caresses bough and leaf. Full of life and growth, this day is nearly enough to make him forget that the King of Holly lies dead upon the hill by the Oak King's hand. So too, he can nearly forget that his own time will come soon enough.

The Oak King shrugs away the thought with a rustle of leaves; he has work to do. For if the sun sings it is but an answer to his own song. Each Yule he is reborn and sings the Song of the World and the light once again grows strong. On Beltaine, this day, he sings once more. Sings for the passing of his brother, sings for the quickening of the world.

On rivers of light his song is carried, nourishing and healing the world. On the wings of his song hope takes flight. In his song he lives.

Danny McCaffrey paused beneath the boughs of an old oak. The tree had split at waist height and twin trunks curved away to form a narrow seat. Danny was new to the city, and drawn to the tree almost from the start. He'd never considered himself to be a tree hugger, but as he hitched himself up into the bole of the tree he ran the tips of his fingers along the warmth of its bark, and imagined he heard a song.

Danny hummed, and it seemed as though a presence gathered around him. The fine blond hairs at the back of his neck stood on end, and his skin prickled the way it did when he knew he was being watched. A strange buzzing filled his ears and he flared his nostrils, inhaling the heady scent of warm, damp earth. An odd, phantom taste of salt rolled across his tongue, and the feeling of being watched intensified.

For the first time since he'd begun spending time with the tree he felt uncomfortable, and couldn't shake the feeling that something wasn't quite right. Nervously, Danny hopped down from his perch and looked around. A few early morning joggers meandered along the paths of the park, but otherwise no one was about. No one watched. Shaking his head, he retrieved his backpack from the ground and hitched it up around his shoulders.

As he made his way along the paths, a light breeze tousled his hair, and it seemed as though someone whispered in his ear, "Stay."

❦

Danny hurried across the street to the little coffee house on the corner, glancing over his shoulder as he pushed open the door and plunged into the dimly lit interior. He blinked, giving his eyes a second to adjust, gaze roaming walls painted in lavender and violent orange. A couple of shabby, black leather couches lined one wall and stained commercial carpeting rippled like waves at uneven intervals across the floor where it was coming loose. Years of smoke permeated everything and its stale blaring pushed away the lingering, softer notes of the park. An unassuming place with the best coffee in the world, the coffee house's tawdry appearance kept the shirt-and-tie set out. That suited Danny just fine.

He ordered a house coffee from a girl with spiky green hair and hematite plugs the size of quarters in her ears. The girl was slow, but when she at last handed him his coffee, he thanked her politely and headed over to the coffee station. Danny preferred his coffee to be sweet and dumped two packets of fake sugar into his cup before swirling it with a little plastic spoon.

He'd hardly sat down and taken his first, tentative sip before the stranger was there, standing over him. He met the stranger's eyes over the chipped rim of his cup, heart skipping a beat and groin stirring as he made eye contact. Soft eyes like golden light filtering through a lush canopy stared down at him, and when the stranger grinned Danny thought he heard the rustle of leaves. Dark hair, wooly and wild crowned his head, and when the stranger extended his nut-brown hand, heat flushed the back of Danny's neck and he nearly overturned the coffee cup in his hurry to set it down.

"Hello, Danny," the stranger said. "I'm Jack."

"How do you know my name?" Danny stammered.

Jack laughed, rich and rolling and deep. "How could I not?"

Danny reclined on the sofa in his tiny little apartment, idly picking at a snag in the red and brown plaid upholstery. His head rested on Jack's chest, and he relaxed by listening to the soft rising and receding rhythm of the man's breath and the muffled, metronome beat of his heart. Danny turned, his bare feet dangling off the arm of the sofa. He looked up through the skylight that had sold him on the apartment, at the few stars bleeding through the city's penumbra, and idly played with Jack's fingers. Jack hummed a tune he didn't recognize.

"What song is that?" Danny asked.

"I don't believe it has a name. Or if it does, I've long since forgotten it."

"Sing it for me?"

"Of course," Jack said.

He loved Jack's voice, its rich, deep sound. He closed his eyes to enjoy the beauty of the melody and the words.

> There is a bonnie lad I know,
> His eyes they shine so bright,
> My bonnie lad he loves me so,
> Love, like silver light.

Danny squeezed Jack's hand as the last note fell away. "So if it's a love song why do you sound sad?"

"I'm sorry. I suppose I'm just a little melancholy tonight."

"Over?" Having to ask him troubled Danny. The past two months since meeting Jack had been the best of Danny's life. Since that first unlooked-for meeting at the coffee house they hadn't spent a single night apart, and for the first time in his life Danny felt like he was really, truly in love. The money situation was looking up as well. He'd gotten a job teaching summer classes in art appreciation at the community college, and it looked like they would keep him on for the fall term as well. He was even thinking about buying a car.

He smiled, imagining his first drive out to the country with Jack to meet his parents.

"It's nothing," Jack said. "Forgive me."

Danny sighed. No matter how hard he tried he couldn't get Jack to open up. He did know that Jack loved him, it was written plain across his face, and manifested in his touch. There were some things one just couldn't fake, yet. Jack had secrets. Danny knew there had been something very different about Jack the moment they'd met. Jack was a mystery Danny had been eager to figure out, but as one month turned to two, that eagerness had turned to frustration. Danny stood on the edge of the perfect life; he could feel it, if only Jack would let him in.

"Are you poz, Jack?" Danny asked suddenly. It had been a question that had been preying on his mind of late.

"What? No! Why would you think that?"

"Because you never make love to me," he said.

Which wasn't entirely true. They did make love, spending long hours kissing and pressing their naked bodies against each other, exploring, until bringing themselves to orgasm. But whenever Danny had pushed Jack for intercourse, Jack had denied him, always saying, "Not yet."

Jack grabbed him by his shoulders and lifted him away, standing. Danny leaned back against the couch while Jack paced before him. "Look, Danny, why can't you just let things be what they are? Why do you always have to push?"

"Because I love you, Jack. I want to have everything with you."

Jack stopped his pacing and headed for the door where he'd left his shoes, and thrust his feet into them. Danny wasn't going to let him get way that easily.

"Where do you go, Jack? When you think I've fallen asleep?"

"Look, Danny. I'm sorry, but there are some things I'm just not ready to talk about right now. I have to go." And then he was gone, slamming the door behind him, leaving Danny to sit bewildered on the couch.

What the fuck just happened?

❦

Over the course of the next month things changed between Jack and Danny. Danny still loved Jack, still saw him every night, but the easiness of the relationship was gone, and had finally led Danny to the dark paths of the park at 3 a.m., sneaking out behind Jack to finally see where it was his lover went each night. Of all the places he thought Jack would go, somehow the park had never been on the list. Jack had just never seemed like the whoring type.

The end of July was a miserable time in the city, and already the cotton fabric of his shirt clung damply to his skin. To his left, behind a stand of bushes, the sound of grunting and heavy breathing carried on the heavy summer air. In a way he envied whoever they were, envied their unbridled fucking. To his right, a man leaned up against the trunk of a large elm and rubbed his crotch as Danny passed. *In your dreams, buddy.*

He hurried past, keeping his gaze locked ahead on Jack's receding form. Moments later Danny rounded a bend in the path and stopped. Jack stood in front of an oak tree, the same one Danny used to come to when he'd first arrived in the city, before meeting Jack. Danny was just about to call out to him and ask him what he was doing when Jack took a step forward, and disappeared into the tree.

Rain fell in torrents outside, sheeting down the window and beating an intermittent tattoo against it with the aid of a fitful wind. Danny stood before his easel painting a portrait of Jack in shades of umber and sienna, capturing his essence in hues of brass and antique gold, accenting the work with subtle flashes of green like oxidized copper. He felt conflicted, unwilling to believe what Jack told him, and yet just as certain that what Jack said was true. He'd always known there was something different about Jack, but not even human?

"So my boyfriend's a fairy," he said with dark amusement, setting the brush down.

"We prefer the term 'sidhe,' or 'fey,' " Jack answered.

Danny didn't think he'd ever heard Jack sound so subdued before, so defeated. He turned away from the easel and looked to where Jack sat on the edge of Danny's bed with his hands clasped in his lap, looking like his whole world was ending. He tried to put himself in Jack's place. Would he have done any different had their situations been reversed? Probably not. So Jack wasn't exactly what Danny had expected. So what?

Danny felt something inside him give way. It broke his heart to see Jack like that, so small and drawn within himself. It was then that he knew that whatever Jack was, he loved him, and that was all that mattered. Tentatively, with his lips drawn up in a shy smile, he took the two steps to where Jack sat, and pulled Jack's head toward his stomach. Fingers played with Jack's thick dark curls. "Does this mean you will finally make love to me?"

Danny felt Jack shudder in his arms. The big secret was out now, so of all the things Danny expected Jack to say, "I can't," wasn't on the list.

The Laws of Faerie are clear. Never lie with a mortal. Oh, it's true enough that such things had been done in the past, but that was long ago. The world had changed since those days, and now fey essence and human souls were poison to each other. No one knew how it happened or why, only that it had.

Now the Seelie court knew. High summer had come and gone, and the Holly King had been reborn. The Oak King remained strong, but as the days shortened and the world plunged toward the fading days of autumn, he would be summoned to a meeting. The Oak King hadn't seen his brother since he'd slain him on Beltaine and was nervous. These first meetings were always the hardest.

Jack sat next to the Holly King on the lush grass of the hill beneath the boughs of the holly tree. The new king had only been reborn a month and had not yet reached full maturity but appeared as a boy of ten, a younger version of Jack. Only the eyes told them apart; the Holly King's gray as a winter storm.

"I have not fully shared myself with him," Jack said.

"And *that*," said the Holly King, "is the only reason why you still live."

Danny rose up in Jack's inner sight and he couldn't help but smile, despite the gravity of the situation. He thought about the touch of Danny's skin, the gentle warmth of Danny's breath on the back of his neck, and soft golden hair curling above eyes as blue and clear as the end of the world. The memories jangled with the discussion at hand, and he cursed the necessity of having it at all. Why couldn't they just be left alone?

Jack dug his fingers into the cool grass and twined them among its blades, fists clenching around them. "Who are you to chastise me? What gives Mab the right to decide what path the heart treads?"

"She is our queen, King of Oaks, and master even of you. It is for all of us that the law exists. Who will take your place if you persist in this folly? Will someone take your place?"

For all the storm in his eyes, the boy's voice held compassion and reminded Jack that this boy held the wisdom and memories of many lives within his small frame. He always forgot that at first.

Jack sighed and stood, unwilling to meet the Holly King's gaze. There were storms enough in his heart. "Your warning has been delivered, and the sun sets. I have somewhere else to be."

And suddenly all the long years piled atop him and crushed him with the weight of things let slip. The Holly King sighed behind him. A sigh is such a little thing, unless one is the Holly King. Then a sigh transforms into the howl of the wolf, and the deafening silence of snow fall. A sigh has the sharp crack of ice.

No, not a boy at all.

Jack stared out the window as he washed the baking pan. Looking out across the city, decked out in its autumn finery of gold and crimson, he couldn't help but sigh. The days shortened and soon it would be time for his reckoning with the King of Holly, time for the Little

Sleep. For the first time in centuries he regretted the cycle and chafed at the necessity of yielding to his brother.

Jack finished washing the round, metal pan and set it on the towel to dry, turning away to examine the cake on the table that he'd finished icing with butter cream only minutes before. While he hadn't done a bad job with the icing, somehow the cake had come out uneven, slanted to one side. It was his first cake, and he knew he would get better with practice, but it was Danny's birthday, and he wanted everything to be perfect.

He heard the opening and closing of the door and grabbed the little blue lighter, but fumbled for a moment before managing to light the candle. Danny entered the kitchen, eyes brightening as he tossed his backpack into the corner up against a cabinet.

"You remembered," he said, and walked over to Jack to hug him and kiss his cheek.

Jack blushed, feeling suddenly sheepish. "I'm sorry the cake turned out lop-sided."

Danny broke away from the embrace, yet kept an arm around Jack's shoulder. "It's beautiful," he said while kissing Jack on the cheek again. "Thank you."

"Well, don't just stand there. Make a wish and blow out the candle!"

Jack had done his homework and looked up the proper rituals on the Internet. As Danny leaned over to blow out the candle, Jack started to sing.

Danny blew out the candle, grinning like the devil as he turned back around. "What did you get me?" he asked mischievously.

Jack gestured to a large terra cotta pot on the floor. "Watch." Humming, he knelt down and thrust his hands into the dark earth. The late afternoon sun gleamed golden and warm through the window, and Jack gathered it around him, letting it spill down his arms. "Grow," he said.

As he spoke, two fragile green shoots pushed up out of the soil and began to wind themselves around each other as they grew, until a tangled sapling as tall as Jack rose up out of the pot. "It represents us; separate, but still growing together."

Danny clapped his hands once in delight and giggled. "Thank you, baby. That's the best present anyone has ever given me."

"You really like it?"

"I love it," Danny said, grinning. "Though, I think we're going to need a bigger house."

On All Hallows Eve, the Oak King was summoned to Faerie. Queen Mab chided him for his continued association with the mortal and cautioned him to think hard during the Little Sleep between death and rebirth.

"For We will not be so tolerant, upon your return, King of Oaks," she warned.

The trumpets blared, calling the Riders of the Hunt, and Mab went to join them. The Oak King turned his jeweled cup over on the stone table and vowed never to return. Golden wine spilled upon the grass.

Jack straddled Danny's thighs, just below his buttocks, and rubbed oil onto Danny's lower back. He pushed, kneading the muscles, moving his hands slowly upward. He was aroused, and, as he leaned forward, Jack's cock slipped between the mounds of Danny's ass. Danny gasped; his profile looked almost glacial in the gray-blue light cast by the street lamp.

Danny lifted his buttocks slightly and pushed back against Jack, and Jack lowered himself to rest his chest on Danny's back.

"Please," Danny whispered. Begged.

"I can't," Jack whispered back, letting all the longing of the world out in a ragged breath.

Danny pushed back more forcefully, and Jack's cock, well-oiled from friction with Danny's skin, slipped inside him. Jack inhaled sharply as Danny's heat surrounded him. Danny moaned and pushed back again, taking him in deeper. Jack's breathing grew more labored and suddenly he pulled away, collapsing forward and to the side. One arm hugged Danny across his back and he buried his face into the crook of Danny's neck.

"It's my choice," Danny said.

Jack squeezed Danny harder, and his whole body trembled as desire warred with what he knew to be right. Loving Danny was both the hardest and easiest thing he'd ever done. All these months of growing and sharing, but somehow never close enough. As he pushed his nose against Danny's skin to inhale the scent of eucalyptus and jasmine oil, Jack smelled the musky, salty scent of Danny's own need just below the surface.

This isn't how he'd wanted things to go. Not this last night of his current incarnation. Yet, Jack didn't know how he could have expected anything else. Was this their fate then, to always be the maddening, unobtainable object of each other's desire?

Danny turned to face him and shoved him on his back, quickly straddling his waist, pushing against him once more. Danny's fingers were soft as they traced patterns around Jack's nipples, leaving trails of fire in their swirling wake. Jack slapped Danny's thighs, and his hands moved across muscles covered with fine blond hairs soft as down. Danny rocked slowly, thigh muscles rippling beneath Jack as he teased Jack's cock. Jack groaned, fighting the urge to take him.

Danny suddenly leaned down and rolled his tongue along Jack's neck, up to his ear. "You taste like salt," he said. "Like love."

And then Danny pushed away, rising above Jack, his buttocks once more slipping around Jack's cock. "I love you, Jack," he said before plunging down on the shaft.

Jack cried out and grabbed Danny's thighs harder as he rode. All reason fled and Jack gave up trying to fight it. For so long he'd wanted this moment of joining. He opened himself up, releasing the part of him he'd always held back.

Danny leaned forward and Jack reached up, grabbing him by his hair, pulling Danny's mouth to his, kissing hard, then pulling back slightly, breathing his essence out into Danny's mouth. He breathed in a little piece of Danny's soul. For the fey this act was more than just a joining of bodies.

They were no longer two, but one. What one felt the other echoed, and as Jack neared his climax, he grabbed at Danny's cock and stroked furiously. Their bodies went rigid and they cried out with pleasure beyond any physical orgasm exploding through them. The force tore them with its wildness and threw them down into one other. Fey essence twined with human soul.

Jack never guessed there would be fire.

Later, Jack rose from the bed careful not to wake Danny. Quickly, he pulled on his jeans and fumbled for the black T-shirt that had somehow ended up under his pillow. Turning, he shoved his feet into his shoes and hurried out the door. Once outside, Jack hugged himself against the autumn chill. His strength waned as the year passed, and already he could feel the mortal thread of Danny's soul twining with his.

What have I done?

Even now he could feel Danny tossing and turning in his bed as the fever took hold, as the fire of Jack's spirit began its slow subsuming. Guilt wracked him like the leading edge of a storm and threatened to bring him to his knees. How could he have let this happen? How could he have been so weak?

And then the Holly King stood before him, a boy no longer but a man grown with a gaze hard as grinding ice. "The Seelie Court convenes. You are summoned Oak King."

Jack fought back tears. Must he endure this now too? What right did they have to judge him? Didn't they know he judged himself enough?

"Will you not answer?" the Holly King demanded. "Must I call the Hunt?"

Jack sighed and shook his head. Only minutes before everything had been perfect. "Tell them that I come."

Then the Holly King was gone, leaving only the bitter howling of the wind.

Jack took a deep breath and a slow step forward, gradually quickening his pace. As he neared the end of the block he felt Danny wake and rise from bed to frantically search for clothes.

You shouldn't follow me, Danny boy.

Danny's answer was the same response that Jack had once given to him. "How could I not?"

Jack stood beside Danny beneath the boughs of the old oak in the park. The branching arms of himself, bare of leaf, arched over them. Danny held his hand, hot, dry palm gripping tightly. Jack knew what came their way, even if Danny did not.

The Seelie Court marched in procession, nearly a score of fey heading toward them. They glimmered like soft silver or gathered strands of moonlight and starlight. Great standards, poles flagged with ancient crests and twined with bells tinkled in the predawn air. Mab headed the procession, a statuesque beauty in gossamer silk, raven hair billowing softly around her like a cloak. The Holly King followed close behind her. He held the Chains of Binding and the pain of iron etched his face.

"They're beautiful," Danny said, his voice filled with awe.

Beautiful and deadly. My doom comes.

Danny squeezed his hand tighter.

Mab stopped a pace away, and Jack stared unflinching into eyes black as the void. He felt repentant only for Danny's sake.

For all her beauty, Mab's voice was a harsh thing, like the croaking of ravens. "You have broken Our Laws, Jack O' The Woods, King of Oaks. What say you?"

"I have loved as my heart bid me," he said.

"Then you will die as We bid."

He was disappointed that there was nothing more said, that thousands of years of living and dying are dealt with in but a few moments. He wanted to plead with them, but knew it pointless. With their laws broken, they would hinder judgment. The fey had turned their backs on him and were marching away to leave only one of their number behind. Someone must carry out the sentence after all.

The Holly King stepped forward, and in his hands rattled chains, each link as thick as his wrist. "Will you fight me, or submit to justice?" he asked through gritted teeth.

"I submit."

"No," Danny cried.

"You have no voice here, mortal," the Holly King snapped.

Before Jack's eyes Danny slumped, his eyes staring sightlessly ahead, bespelled by the Holly King.

"I love you so much, Danny," he said and kissed his lover softly on slack lips once before releasing a hand that no longer held his back.

Jack moved to the tree and put his back against the oak. The Holly King wrapped the chains around fey and tree alike. The cold iron blackened Jack's skin. He writhed in agony.

Jack welcomed the punishment and pain. *Fey shall not lie with mortals.* He deserved this pain and so much more. Because of his actions, Danny would die as well. He was getting off far too easy, and he knew it. *I'm so sorry, Danny.*

How many Samhain mornings had the Holly King stood before him with the spear? How many Beltaine dawns had seen the Holly King raised on a gibbet? Too many to count, and no more after this.

The splinter of Danny's soul continued to grow inside him and diminished what made him fey, what allowed him to be reborn. For the first time Jack knew fear. Always there had been the certainty of the cycle and the comfort of the change of rule and seasons.

If only he could hold Danny one last time.

"I'm sorry, brother," the Holly King said as he raised the spear, but Jack heard only the snapping jaws of the wolf.

The Holly King stood over Danny in his kitchen. The mortal sat on the floor against the sink and next to a potted sapling and a portrait of the King of Oaks. It was Yule morning, and the Holly King had come to see that the cycle continued.

"I know you're there," Danny said.

The Holly King raised an eyebrow and let the Spell of Unseeing fall aside. "You should not have known that."

"Magick," Danny answered bitterly. "Have you come to gloat?"

The Holly King looked at Danny sadly. The mortal had wasted away in the weeks since Samhain. The part of the Oak King within him had nearly run its course, and all that remained of Danny was a husk of skin draped on a frame of bones.

"I take no pleasure in any of this, lad. I loved him too."

"But you killed him. Impaled him to the tree then cut him down."

"Mortal and fey cannot long survive each other," the Holly King answered. "Would you rather he'd endured this long wasting, growing colder while you burned? At least my way was quick."

"It's all my fault," Danny said. "I pushed him to it."

"Ah, lad. It's a fool's feeling, this guilt you hold on to. There is no blame in what was freely chosen by the both of you."

Danny looked away to glance up to the kitchen window at the beautiful day outside with its sky unmarred by clouds. The kind of day the Holly King liked to have on his own last days.

"What happens now?" Danny asked.

"The fey inside you will slip its bonds, and join with that sapling there. Before sunset Mab will come and breathe life into it and bring order to the wild magick. A new Oak King will be born this day as he's always been. He won't be Jack, and he won't be you."

"And my human part? My soul?"

The Holly King wished he knew. That knowledge might ease his own sorrow at the forever-passing of his brother. "Not even the fey know what happens on the twilight road," he said. "But if you see the Oak King on your way, tell him the Holly King wishes him a safe journey. Aye, I hope it may be so."

Danny's eyes burned with a golden light, and he reached out to touch the leafless sapling. A single green bud appeared on a branch. Then his hand fell and he sighed once before lying still.

A sigh is such a little thing, reflected the Holly King. Unless it is a clear day, a blue day. Then a sigh can fall away to a memory of green and gold.

doi:10.1300/5642_08

Detox

Elspeth Potter

Maria wipes crumbs from the doll-sized table and arranges two chunks of chocolate-cherry bread on a brown Wedgwood saucer. The shot glass of organic milk, skim, goes to the saucer's right, and a gold-plated dessert fork to the left. A sprig of rosemary in a bud vase adds a touch of elegance. Then she goes to bed.

The following afternoon, she wakes and stretches luxuriously before prodding her face. Her skin is taut, and last night's zit has vanished from her chin. She slides her hands down her thighs: firm, smooth, no visible veins. Her ass feels round and tight. Yesterday's fortyish sags—well, really, fifty-one, but who's counting?—are a bad dream. Her brownie deserves cake next time, perhaps even from Mrs. Tootsie's on South Street.

Not tonight, though. Mrs. Tootsie's is always jam-packed on Saturday, and Maria needs time to get ready. She slips into a lacy silk robe, pours herself a Campari and soda, and runs her bath.

Three hours later, she dries off with a heated spa towel and examines herself in the full-length mirror. She rubs her thick, newly dark hair with the towel and decides to wear spandex pants. Those are back in, for clubbing, if paired with a different texture on top. She'll go to the new place, with the weird name, Anubis.

It's a crisp autumn night and she's wearing a red sweater her brownie left for her once, made of gauze-light wool with a faint organic smell, like moss or lichen. The sweater never gets dirty or snags or stretches out; it clings like an aura. When the valet takes the keys to her Mercedes, his eyes never once lift from her breasts. Maria gives him a nice tip and sashays into Club Anubis.

Stench and heat and light and roar flay her to nerves. It gets worse every time. She needs a drink. Several drinks.

Girls appear on adjoining stools as soon as she sidles up to the bar and orders peppermint schnapps. She knows them, a hip young couple from the 'burbs. They're a tag-team act, shouting witty comments into Maria's ears; at least she pretends they're witty; really, they're inaudible.

The bathroom's quieter. All three of them screw in the handicapped stall while bass thumps in walls and floor and pussy. It's crowded and sweaty, and she can barely smell sex over stale cigarette pong, the broken toilet next door, and horrific cherry disinfectant. The sex is hot anyway. Maria revels in bending and twisting and grinding. She can bend over backward without a twinge. It's sordid, true, but only old people insist on comfort.

Yet again the girls want to go home with her. She'd like another fuck, but after sharing a cigarette with them, she says no. Her brownie needs time to fix her up, and they'll get over it. With her looks, and her sweater, she can pick them up again, or someone else, as easy as winking. Still, to be merciful, she gives them her cell phone number.

The car valet eats out her pussy in the back seat when she picks up her car, even after she explains she's gay and doesn't want to fuck him. He's good enough to make her come anyway, or maybe it's the magic. She goes home in the wee hours, floating on sex and schnapps and secondhand cigarette smoke. Giggling, she leaves out a cut of filet mignon the size of a half-dollar and a tiny glass of wine, and as an afterthought, the mysterious tab the valet (she thinks his name was Raoul or something) insisted on handing to her.

When she wakes up she feels soggy and hungover. It's been so long since she felt like that, it takes a few minutes to figure it out. She stumbles out of bed and peers into the mirror. She looks like a hag. Her hair is graying and scraggly like it had a bad tease job after a dip in Elmer's glue. Her thighs jiggle when she turns. She stares into eyes like fried eggs with catsup. Her head hurts too much for her to panic. She can panic after she's had a pot of coffee.

Only there's no coffee in the house. She stopped keeping it after her brownie came. She didn't need it any more. She wakes up every morning as fresh as a five-year-old. Except this morning. She thinks about hair of the dog and nearly vomits, so she struggles into a pair of old sweats and crams a floppy knitted hat over her horrific hair before going out to the local coffee shop. She doubts anyone will recognize her.

The coffee and a big glass of orange juice help. She remembers the pale blue tab she left out for her brownie the night before. Perhaps that wasn't the smartest thing she could have done. She didn't even know what the pill was. She'd put it out in the same spirit as drunken teenagers throwing rocks at buses.

She hopes she hasn't killed her brownie. When she gets home, she has a screwdriver made with the fresh orange juice she brought home, then checks all over the house and under the furniture for anything that looks like a tiny corpse. She doesn't know what it looks like, exactly. Her mental picture is something like a cartoon Keebler elf, only wearing brown, maybe like the little dresses the cookie-selling brownies wear, but with some of that *Queer Eye* stylish flair. She doesn't find anything like that, just a half-empty tequila bottle beneath the couch.

She hopes her brownie enjoyed its trip, but she has a pretty strong feeling it didn't, given the way she looks today.

That evening, she disguises herself and goes out again and buys food, mostly for her brownie, since she doesn't cook. She has a weird feeling she needs to make amends. She gets organic yogurt and one of those fresh juices with pomegranate and blueberry and other ultra-healthy ingredients, and some bread made with sprouted wheat and birdseed and such. A cookbook attracts her eye, and she picks it up. It has pretty illustrations, so she changes her mind and buys several. Shopping takes a while and makes her arms hurt from lugging groceries. She's too exhausted to think about her standing commitment to Margarita Night. She ignores the cell phone's repeated, insistent blaring of the "Hallelujah Chorus." Instead, she takes care selecting and arranging the food; she lays the porcelain dishes on a silk scarf, and pops a fragrant rose into a bud vase.

When she wakes up the next afternoon, she looks like Heidi. Latina Heidi, rosy and robust. It's not really her look but it's miles better than the day before. Maybe she'd go out tonight, there were always plenty of people in the mood for Happy Hour after the work week started.

She isn't in the mood for a decadent bath. She has a quick shower instead. While she examines her new, prodigious cleavage in the mirror—it's truly gravity-defying, perhaps her brownie's finest work—she thinks about Happy Hour later on and is surprised when the idea revolts her. She stays in, instead, not that unheard of; sometimes she needs a break after a weekend's hard partying. She remembers the tequila bottle under the couch and decides to clean the house; it's not something her brownie does, and lately she hasn't been cleaning, either. She's been too busy going out.

Then she bakes bread. She can't stop herself, and she doesn't even remember buying the yeast. It's freaky, but not as freaky as waking up in the body of a teenager every afternoon, so she gets over it.

She cooks all evening and, that night, finds herself putting out oatmeal for her brownie, oatmeal with raisins and a dribble of maple syrup and just one artistically placed dab of butter, along with a slice of her homemade bread. After a moment, she shifts the slice of bread a hair to the right, and shudders in artistic pleasure. It looks really nice, so maybe she'll look extra nice for the coming weekend.

The next afternoon, Heidi apparently had a facelift and a couple of tucks, because Maria looks and feels even better, but she still doesn't want to go out, except to shop. She buys a lot of groceries this time. She feels so much better, though, so much stronger, that she still has energy after she hauls the groceries home. She makes more bread, and cookies, and a fabulous lime chiffon pie, and lays it all out for her brownie and feels really, really good, high on endorphins.

Wednesday, she remembers to drop off her favorite clubbing dress at the dry cleaner's, but by Friday she still hasn't picked it up. It doesn't seem important any more, and anyway she left her cell phone at the grocery store or something—she can't remember when—so she hasn't been able to make any dates.

The week blows by and she hardly notices, she's so involved with new cookbooks. Saturday comes and instead of taking her fabulous new bosom out for a few spins, she's hand-beating egg whites for me-

ringues. In fact, according to the television, tuned to the Home and
Garden channel, it's actually a couple of Saturdays later than she
thought. She catches a glimpse of her reflection in the glass oven door.
Only then does she begin to suspect the tables have turned. But by
then, it's too late.

doi:10.1300/5642_09

From Asphalt to Emeralds and Moonlight

Aynjel Kaye

Aine and Fionn ride with the hounds of the Morrigan through the shadowed forests of the Otherworld, though neither of them is one of the lords and ladies of the hunt. Aine's stallion breathes mist and Fionn's breathes smoke, the air thick around them with shadow and sweat and steam. The Morrigan's thick-bodied hounds are muzzled—this hunt will not result in bloodshed—but this doesn't stop their howling cries.

Tonight the lords and ladies hunt neither the damned nor the saved, their lances of blue flame and shields of white light left behind. Tonight they hunt for a child of blood and fire, a child of the dance.

Maeve lies dying beneath the sidhe. Tonight, they hunt their new queen, and Aine and Fionn race with the hunt to see which of them will be the new king.

Tara Brady walks out of Venomous Crow Productions for the last time, escorted by security lest she walk out with more than belongs to her, more than what's in her head and the box of action figures and artwork that kept her cubicle from being drab and lifeless. They stand at her back as she walks down the steps, her boot heels clunking hollowly on the granite squares in the empty entry. For a moment, with the pair flanking her, she feels like royalty, and then she walks beyond the half-circle of granite and onto textured concrete, box tucked under her arm, and the illusion is gone.

Fall, and the air is crisp and damp, the streets empty this late in the evening, people chased away by the cold and the constant threat of drizzle. Even the buses seem reluctant to run, and Tara swears, continues walking down the street. Wind whips through the tunnel formed by corporate buildings shading the street, pulls at her hair and her coat, her scarf. She pauses at the stop for the Number 10 bus, rests the box of her entertainment against her hip and closes her eyes. So much for making on-screen magic happen; with Venomous Crow Productions letting her go, and the state of the industry, she is unlikely to get a job doing anything but simple digital editing any time soon.

᳠

"I saw her first." Fionn leans over his stallion's neck, wind pulling at hair and cloak. He's not dressed in the tight silks that the lords and ladies of the hunt wear, and he fairly glows with the wildness and color and streaming ribbons of a court princeling.

One of the lords of the hunt snorts, slows his mount, spidery fingers pulling lightly on the reins. He'll let the princeling have her if he can manage without unseating himself.

Aine is better dressed for the hunt, the sedate browns and greens of her cloak and tunic embroidered with golden leaves, and her hair is braided, but she is not so compliant as the other lords and ladies as Fionn takes lead. This is their hunt, hers and her brother's, and she'll be damned if she is going to let anyone else snatch their quarry and the throne from under her. She touches her heels to her mount's sides and the stallion stretches longer, digs up clods of earth with stone-sharp hooves. "You did not," she hisses.

The hunt lands stretch out in front of them, reaching for the buildings and pavement and asphalt, covering steel and concrete, hiding graffiti and swallowing electricity, making way for the hunt.

More wind and Tara shifts the box to her other hip, looks at the bus schedule, its plastic covering damp with the humidity in the air. She checks her watch, looks at the schedule again, and looks down the street. Wind pulls at her hair, makes the wild red curls lash her cheeks and lips and threaten her eyes. No bus in sight. Nothing in sight. Street lamps hum and go out in pairs, starting seven blocks away.

Tara takes a firmer hold of her box and walks. The streets have never felt so empty, not even on her latest nights at work. The shadows feel more frightening and she quickens her pace, pausing at corners to make certain no cars are coming, or perhaps to find a car on the street so she won't feel alone.

Sound of hooves and she stops, spins around, wind grabbing at her again, trying to pull her in the direction she was already walking. The evening is early enough for one of the horse-drawn buggies to be dragging lovers down the street, but the street remains empty, the shadows longer as streetlights continue to go out.

A dog howls, a long low truculent sound that raises goosebumps on Tara's arms and neck. She shivers, pulls her coat more tightly around her and continues walking, the clunk of her heels against the pavement mimicking the sound of horse hooves. The echoes mock her, bouncing off the walls of closed shops and the windows of executive towers. Even Starbucks is closed and Tara looks at her watch again. Nine fifteen. They should have escorted her out of the building earlier, but they wanted to get as much out of her on her last day as they could.

Two weeks of severance, she reminds herself. Two weeks to job hunt and rebuild her portfolio. "If I make it home tonight."

The lead hound howls, finally scenting what Aine and Fionn have already seen. The rest of the hounds of the Morrigan echo the cry of their pack mate one after the other as they catch scent of their prey. One of the lords of the hunt picks up his horn, blows a battle cry, a sighting. The antlered shadows of the lords' helmets stretch far in front of the hunting party, the moon ever at their backs.

Aine's heartbeat quickens as the horn's long note vibrates through her. Her thighs squeeze tighter and she glances at her brother. A cloud of starshine surrounds him, trails behind him along the length of his unbound hair and her breath catches; she couldn't possibly look so regal. Aine refuses to let herself ease up on her mount, won't let Fionn catch their prey no matter how beautiful he seems to her now in the moonlight, no matter how much like a king.

The glimmering shape at the edge of the forest is her prey as much as it is his and she has as much right to snatch it up as he does. More right, in fact, because she knows more secrets than her brother does. Aine knows the name of their prey.

Another howl and other dogs pick up the cry. And something
lower that makes Tara's heart pound. The sounds wash over her like
the wind, wild and whipping and she walks faster. She's halfway to
Madison Avenue when the rain starts. Wind makes the sharp stinging droplets fierce, the rain coming down like razors against her face
and hands.

Hooves and howling and Tara doesn't want to look behind her,
wants to get inside, get home, get into a hot shower to drive away the
cold that's weighing down her coat and making her skin ache. She'll
even settle for the bus with the old guy with the crotch ripped out of
his jeans, who sits there with his legs spread and the unfortunate
choice of nothing on underneath those jeans.

Lights go out over her head and Tara holds her box closer to her.
The cardboard feels flimsy, the rain making the sides warp, making
them less reliable. Where is the damn bus?

The scream of horses, wild shouts, and the echoing moan of a horn
fill the air and the shadows come to life, spread, weave together and
reach over the street like tree branches. Tara turns and drops her box
of distraction. Action figures spill onto the sidewalk, one figure's wing
breaks and skitters off the curb into the gutter.

Buildings no longer flank the street. The world is emerald and
shadow and threatens to swallow Tara.

"She's mine," Fionn says, pressed close to his stallion's neck, taking
his eyes off their prey for a moment to look at his sister.

Aine spurs her mount faster and reaches for Fionn's reins. "You
only wish, brother dearest." She snags his reins and yanks but Fionn's
stallion doesn't budge; Aine isn't in that saddle and their mounts
know better than to give in to the rivalry between siblings. The stallions are seasoned in the hunt while the princelings consider it a game
to be won no matter the cost.

Steam and smoke curl in the air, thick as the mist sinking from the
trees.

Their prey is lovely.

And frightened.

Tara runs, damns the heels on her boots. She clutches her coat tightly to her chest, but the wind pulls at the bottom of it, slows her down. Cold as it is outside, she shrugs out of the coat, lets it fall behind her the way she did on the playground as a child.

Her heart beats loudly in her ears and the air feels thick enough with water to choke her.

They're behind her, huge and dark and overwhelming, the moonlight making them indistinct shadows. Don't look again, she tells herself. Don't look. Just don't look.

The street doesn't exist in front of her anymore, neither does the city. The ground is nothing more than stone and twigs, grass stomped flat, crescent moon divots torn up from the earth, and leaves. The trees and their twisted branches block out the sky and the stars that should be above her.

Sauna heat blows up through her hair, lifts it from her neck. And then the heat blows against her neck as well, and against the backs of her knees. Snuffling, whuffling, howling, shrieking behind her, right behind her. Sandpaper-rough fur brushing her calf. If she had any breath left in her to scream, she would.

The Morrigan's hounds part like water around the girl and they race alongside of their prey, backs high as her hips, whip-sharp tails lashing the air, slaver dripping from their muzzles, teeth silver in the moonlight, gums blood red. They're hungry and the air is hot with it.

The stallions are hungry, too, their sharp teeth clattering against the bits. They're rarely allowed so close so quickly.

Aine shivers, inhales her stallion's steamy breath like sucking in summer or hell, tastes his hunger, feels the echoing of it in her own belly. Fionn looks wild as the hounds as he reaches for the girl.

This hunt victory will not be his. Aine won't let him have it. Only one of them can sit Maeve's throne when she departs and Aine will not let him have the advantage of bringing the girl back. She yanks her mount at his and the stallions both veer away from the girl, so close that she stumbles. The girl's hand touches the ground, her frantic run now staggering and flailing as she tries to keep from falling beneath the feet of the other stallions.

The lords and ladies of the hunt race by them and Aine pulls her
mount in a tight circle, back toward the girl. Fionn swears and fiery
comets of light explode in the air around him, spiral up into the trees
and down to the wet grass. The light matches the girl's hair.

Aine leans over her mount's neck and her brother is right beside
her. They both reach, stretch, and his arms are longer. He yanks the
girl up by the arm and she screams. Fionn's smile makes Aine sick to
her stomach, but this is *not* the end. She won't let it be the end.

Cries and cheers from the lords and ladies of the hunt follow them
back through the hunt lands, back into the shadows, down the pine-
needle road home.

"You rode well, sister dear." Fionn holds the girl across his saddle,
across his lap. Her hair curls at the stallion's shoulder like blood.

Aine searches for grace and patience but only manages to take hold
of one of them. "We shall see who is better-ridden by the time the
night is over." She spurs her mount past his, races hard for the stables.
There is still time, and there is so much left to do. Let him celebrate,
she thinks. Let him eat and drink and find complacency in the others
who will already be proclaiming him the next on the throne.

The night is not over. The stone has not spoken. He has not won.
Not yet.

Aine's stallion slows, stops outside the stables and she slides to the
ground, tosses the reins at one of the ladies of the hunt. She unbinds
her hair as she stalks toward the fountain.

"You thought it might happen this way."

Aine pauses, looks through shadow into Oona's eyes. "Of course."

"He's a better rider than you are."

"He'll not sit the throne."

Oona laughs. "Shall I tell him you said so?"

Aine cups Oona's cheek, tilts her head to one side. "Tell him what
you will. You always have."

Oona leans forward, brushes her lips against Aine's, a kiss like a
rose, a kiss like her brother's kisses, soft and sharp. "You know I prefer
you to him."

"Do I?"

Oona laughs like spring. "Let me bathe you and dress you and brush your hair."

"Fine." '

As they walk to the fountain, Oona's hair turns red, the straight blondeness becoming thick curls. "You mock me," Aine says.

"I tempt you, m'lady."

"Aye. You always have."

***

Oona sprawls across Fionn's lap in the great hall, he at the foot of his mother's throne and he pays Oona as much attention as Aine paid her earlier in the evening. Aine watches Tara, though. Wild emerald eyes and wilder red hair. She doesn't touch the food in front of her, as though she remembers the fairy stories told by her mother or grand-mother. This abstinence will not save her; the dance and the fire and the hunt are in her blood, and her blood will answer the call of them before the night is over. The Dannan is trapped inside of her and it *will* be freed. One way or another.

Oona uncurls from Fionn's lap as the harps begin, holds her hand out to him. "Dance with me, m'lord?"

Fionn shakes his head. "There is only one dance for me tonight."

Oona shrugs and looks at Aine, hand still outstretched. Aine shakes her head, unconscious mimicry of her brother's gesture. "I'm in no mood to dance right now. Perhaps later tonight." And she tries to put as much meaning into those words as she can, though she won't care to dance with *anyone* beneath the silks tonight if Fionn has his way. And if he doesn't, there will be only one dance for her and she will not waste that dance on Oona, no matter how lovely she looks to-night nor how much Aine once desired her.

Oona leaves them, picks a lording who will share the dance with her and Aine leans against her brother, brushes her lips against his ear. "She plays both of us, you know."

Fionn raises an eyebrow. "And why shouldn't she?"

Aine laughs low in her throat. "You tell me, brother."

He glances across the hall at the girl; he still doesn't know her name. He laughs equally low, cups his sister's cheek and their silver-black gazes meet. "She is already mine."

Aine smiles, says, "And if everyone saw you ride up with her across your saddle, why do you suppose Oona still plays us both as though the question remains unanswered?"

Fionn's laughter sours and Aine draws away from him. "She's a fool," he says.

Or she knows more than you do, brother mine. Aine sips her wine and watches the cloud settle over her brother's brilliant features; not even a kiss from his favorite hunt lord is enough to dispel that cloud.

They look like lovers sitting so close, sharing secrets and laughter, sipping wine from the same silver cup in the shadow of an ashen queen. Like lovers. Or twins. Tara wants to look anywhere but at them, but the rest of the hall is filled with more disturbing figures in midnight silks and starlight leathers so she looks at the plate in front of her: dripping-sweet fruits, flowers, leaves, all on a silver plate beside a silver cup filled with blue liquid shot through with something that glitters in the candlelight. Her mouth waters and her stomach grumbles. She skipped dinner so she could wrap up her project before they walked her out the door. The temptation to put something in her mouth is nearly overwhelming so she looks up from the plate, watches the raven lover twins across the hall.

The woman stands, leaves her lover/brother looking unhappy in spite of the lordling who strokes his neck and ear. She walks across the floor of the great hall, dancers spinning around her like starshine and snowflakes and she never has to stop, never has to step left or right. The music guides everyone on the floor, pulls them like they are puppets on strings.

She sits on the cushion across the table from Tara and Tara's world narrows, becomes the silver-black hair and nearly white skin of the woman across from her. And the woman's eyes. "You have a fortunate name." Her voice is nearly as mesmerizing as her presence.

Tara shakes her head, asks, "How would you know?" The first words she's spoken since she was yanked from the ground, as if this woman, in speaking to her, has somehow broken a spell of silence.

The woman laughs, leans forward. "It is in my best interest," she says. "And it is in my best interest that no one else knows it, so I hope you'll forgive my forwardness." She leans across the table, grabs Tara by the hair and kisses her.

Tara hears her name whispered in her head in the woman's voice. Hears another name, and another: Aine, Fionn, Oona, others. Flashes of faces to go with each of them, black hair, antlered half-crowns, pale sharp cheeks, but the image of Aine is the strongest flash, the one that burns the back of her eyes and brain, leaves her breathless. She leans into the kiss, discovers the flavor of Spring on Aine's lips, then the flavors of Summer, Autumn, Winter.

The lordlings guarding the girl should have stopped Aine, pulled her away. Neither she nor Fionn is supposed to touch her yet, and they'll have to bathe the girl again. They should have pulled Tara away from Aine before their lips touched, particularly if they were her brother's men, whether they suspected what Aine was up to or not. Perhaps he is not favored by as many of the lordlings as he thinks.

Aine drinks in the memory of Tara's name, savors it, swallows it and continues kissing her simply for the pleasure and novelty of tasting something mortal, something human.

Fionn comes across the floor like a storm, scattering dancers, disrupting the music. He takes Aine by the shoulder, pulls her back from Tara and Aine presses her lips tightly closed, swallows the last hint of Tara's name before she faces her brother. "Yes, brother mine?"

"What have you taken from her?"

Aine laughs, her fingers still tangled in Tara's hair; the girl hasn't moved. "I've stolen a kiss, nothing more." She looks at Tara; such a bewildered girl, so confused, and yet so accepting in her confusion. The Dannan knows, even if the girl doesn't, drags her through the night like a marionette. "I think she liked it." Aine draws Tara forward, fingers in her hair, nails pressing against her scalp. "Have you kissed another woman before?" Tara blushes, tries to look away and Aine tightens her grip on the girl's hair. "No, I don't think you have."

Fionn pulls Aine away, his fingers pressed tightly against her bare arm. He's so warm for someone so cold as he often is. "What *else* did you take from her?" His mouth is close to Aine's; his breath smells of starlight wine and berries.

Aine smiles. "Nothing she wasn't willing to give me." She reaches behind her, finds a piece of fruit with her fingers, the flesh slick and tender. "Fruit?" she offers, and before her brother can kiss her and steal the lingering hints of Tara's name from her mouth, Aine slips the sweetness between her lips, washes the last of the name out of her mouth and off of her tongue.

"I'll have it from your lips," Fionn says. "One way or another."

Aine laughs and shakes her head. "No you won't. I don't think you want to know what death tastes like."

Fionn loosens his grip on Aine's arm, turns away, but not quickly enough to hide his disgust from her.

Turning back to Tara, Aine asks, "Do you have any idea what's going on, precious?"

Tara shakes her head.

Aine smiles sadly and sighs. "He won't tell you, either." This time, the lordlings brush her hand away when she reaches for Tara, half-hearted effort, but she lets them, walks back across the hall and out into the moonlight.

Tara closes her eyes, touches her fingers to her lips. Did that count as eating? Was she damned forever to dance among these people? These beautiful, terrible strange people?

Something in her heart whispers to her, tells her that she was damned to that life when Fionn snatched her from the ground and carried her back to this place.

She licks her lips, tastes the lingering flavors of the seasons, watches Aine leave and then closes her eyes. The music starts again, harps, all harps, and yet it sounds like a whole symphony. Her fingers and toes itch, the palms of her hands and the soles of her feet. She wants to dance, though she never once got out onto the dance floor when her friends dragged her to the Vogue or convinced her to come to the Merc; she so out of place in those dark clubs with their darker music, clubs where she clung to the bar and drank rather than be embarrassed to be out among the raven-haired beauties.

And tonight? She draws a deep breath, retreats into the safety of habit, and drinks from the silver cup. Light explodes inside of her head at the first sip, a cascade of stars and galaxies born in the flavor of the liquid.

She drinks, drinks again, and then tastes the fruit. There is no salvation for her tonight.

The lordlings take Tara away when Aine returns to the hall; they lead the girl away, no doubt for another bath. Tara looks back over her shoulder and Aine meets her gaze.

Fionn sits stiffly beside Aine. The cloud over his features lingers, darkens his eyes, matches the tone of his skin closer to Tara's: peaches-and-cream rather than starlight. He's angry, in pain, and she caused both of them. The memory of Tara's name lingers, though the flavor is gone from her mouth. Chased away by wine and fruit, though neither was so sweet as Tara's lips.

"The night isn't over yet," Aine says, though whether she is trying to reassure herself, or her brother, she isn't certain.

He looks at her, brings a peach to his lips, darts his tongue over it and then nods. "Not yet." Challenge and resentment all in those two words. He'll walk with her into the dance, but only because it means that while they spin, he may be able to run faster than she can, that he may be able to reach farther and take hold of Tara, snatch her from under Aine's nose again.

Aine stands, steps backward toward the dance floor, holds her hand out to Fionn. "Dance with me, brother mine. Like when we were young." And they were young so very long ago, she wonders if he'll remember.

He stands, takes her hand, and the tempo of the harps changes.

The lordlings bring Tara to a room. She's been bathed again. Cleansed. They've taken Aine's touch from her skin, but they cannot take it from her memory. They take her to a room and take her clothes from her, leave her there alone with only the echo of the harps for company.

She walks around the emptiness, imagines furniture and fixtures, touches the things that aren't there, and then there's a voice behind her.

"I'll make you what you want to be," the voice purrs, salty and sweet against her cheek, over her ear. Somehow, in the emptiness, Fionn is there. His tongue follows his words and she shudders. "What I want you to be. What you can be. Everything you can be."

"What is that?"

He shakes his head, cheek rubbing against hers. "You'll find out."

And the question echoes in her mind, *But who am I?* In the quiet of the room, she's afraid. So afraid. Because she doesn't know who she wants to be or *what* she wants to be. Before that evening, she could have said. Could have pointed to the computers and the magic on-screen and said, "That. I want to be that."

But now? What does she want to be?

Loved? The air asks her.

Yes, she wants to be that. But by whom?

Fingers rake through her hair, whether in reality, or only in her memory, she doesn't know. But those fingers hold on tight, draw her back and expose her throat. A tongue plays against her flesh, and the hand-hold on her hair draws her back even farther. "Sit."

She has no choice. The chair is warm and liquid leather against her bare thighs.

"Be still," the voice whispers, a mingling of Aine's and Fionn's and she knows now that they are twins and lovers. Or were lovers, once, a hundred years ago, or a thousand, before Oona came between them. Before the dying queen came between them. Lovers and siblings and now rivals. "Be still until you can't help but move."

And then the hand is gone and she is free.

She wants to run, the terror from the hunt building again in her belly. Wants to scream, but she stays, heart thick in her chest. Slow. So slow.

Even more, she wants to run. Run away from the darkness. And when she can't stand it anymore, thinks she might go crazy with nothing but that smooth, soft leather beneath her thighs, a thin sheen of sweat making it slick, making her physically uncomfortable to match her mental discomfort, light comes on.

She winces away from it. Tiny candles, and where did they come from? She doesn't know. Doesn't want to know. There are so many things she doesn't want to know and so many questions begging to be answered.

Who is he?

And a voice says, in her head, *This isn't about him.*

Aine and Fionn dance, but it isn't a dance, it's a struggle. They touch each other like lovers or assassins, trying to please and hurt at the same time.

Aine fears one of them will not survive the night, and this isn't how it is supposed to be. If one of them was killed before this moment, the other would dance with Tara now, here on the floor in front of the lords and ladies.

Both their nails grow longer, their hair wild as a storm around them, hiding them from the eyes of the lords and ladies watching.

Aine would rather this dance go on without their supervision, but it must be watched.

It's not about me, Tara thinks. *It can't be.*

A figure appears. Smooth. Black. Draped in silver and black and burgundy gauze. She looks but can't tell if it is a man or a woman. The chest is flat, the waist waspishly thin. Face? It doesn't have one; just smooth silver-blackness. Featureless. Tara whimpers, cringes into the leather beneath her.

Everything you want to be. She trembles.

A long, slender arm stretches out to her, silver metal fingernails curl, beckoning with light-streaks through the dim air. Tara's seen that gesture before: Oona tempting Fionn and then Aine to dance with her.

There is only one dance tonight.

Tara shakes her head.

Everything you might be. It beckons again, flows closer to her.

Stay still until you can't help but move.

Tara prays for the leather to close around her, for the world to open up and drop her into her bed where she'll be safe from the genderless breathing mannequin in front of her.

The harps grow louder, more insistent. The candlelight dances with the music. How are the harps so loud when she is so far away from the hall where they must be playing still?

This isn't about them, that voice whispers again. Licking her mind, twisting through her thoughts with intimate familiarity. A lover. But it isn't Fionn. It isn't Aine, either.

Everything you might be.

But what am I?

"You took something from her," Fionn whispers against Aine's cheek. "Give it to me."

Aine laughs, spins across the floor, tempting him to follow her, to stay here instead of going there. "You'll have to take it from me, brother mine."

"Don't think I won't, Aine." He knows *her* name. They're twins. They share a name in their hearts.

Aine continues the dance, plays with fire. "Then catch me."

The figure stands in front of Tara, one slender foot posed between hers. Gauze brushes her calves, her thighs. Like silver. Like whispers, familiar intimate whispers. They match the voice in her head. And the figure's hand touches her cheek.

Something explodes inside of Tara, fills her with voices, color, light, heat. And she can't stop herself; she moves. Stands, and the figure's thigh nestles between hers.

Dance with me. Aine's voice. Fionn's voice. Oona's voice. Who is she dancing with?

Music and candles flicker. Sometimes there, sometimes not. And those whisper-caresses cover her. A hand closes around her right hand while the creature's other hand rests at her hip, those nails pricking like memory at the curve of her lower back.

Aching with a want she can't name, can't identify, she dances with the thing. Gauze wraps around her, hot, suffocating, sharp, painful, delightful. It winds around her arms, her thighs, swirls, draws wind like breath over her skin and holds it there.

More light. More music. And more intimate, breathy heat.

Stars flicker in the featureless face. Lips. She remembers kissing Aine, wishes for lips and presses her face against the formless thing in front of her. And it opens up to swallow her.

"Tell me her name," Fionn snarls, his teeth against Aine's ear.

Aine shakes her head. "Take it from me."

He lets go of her ear, spins her so she faces him. "I will, you know."

"You'll try," Aine whispers, but she's afraid. His teeth are like his stallion's, like the teeth of Morrigan's hounds. He's hungry and she has the key to the thing he hungers for.

Tara is pulled, twisted, torn, pushed. Like taffy, caught between who she was and who she might be. Caught between Aine and Fionn. They're there even though she's alone.

Fionn appears in her mind's eye. His voice throbs in her belly. Urges her, teases her, coaxes her like a lover.

But Aine is there, too, soft and liquid, swirling through her body, settling in her chest, between her legs, onto her lips. Like honey, like brandy, like chocolate.

Tara doesn't know who to listen to. Who to trust. because they are both so persuasive, so demanding, so intimate.

The change continues, tears her apart bit by bit, peels away layer after layer of who she was, exposes raw and tender places, the places that will make her who she might be.

Who she wants to be.

No. The throbbing voice in her belly denies her, demands, "Who *I* want you to be."

Aine and Fionn dance love and hatred, pull hair and gouge with dagger nails until they are both bloody and sweating. Darkness cloaks Fionn. The night isn't over and he wants it to be; Aine sees as much in his eyes, hears as much in her heart and her head.

She wants the night over, as well. This should have been a dance, not a battle. Maeve should not see one of them die at her feet: over a mortal, over the throne.

Oona watches them from the cushions where they sat earlier. She smiles. The night isn't over. Even when the dance is done, the night isn't over. Tara, or what is left of her, will come back to the hall.

Tara struggles, twists. And the gossamer gauze turns to wire, cuts into the tender places, tries to slice them away.

Please.

She dives into the liquid softness and the tenderness there coats the wires, soothes the ache, turns sharpness back to gauze, hurt back into tenderness. But the sharpness is still there, beneath it all, beneath the softness; beneath the beauty lives that terrible hurting, that horrible hardness, the thing that can destroy.

Then the pain, the liquid, everything floods back into her, swirls in her breast, her belly, between her legs, and she collapses, aware of the leather. So warm. Slick. Beneath her, cradling her.

And what am I now? she wonders.

She reaches up, her hand moving like something she no longer owns, no longer controls. She touches her face, feels high cheekbones: no longer round, sharp instead of soft. Her lips are tight instead of full. Fingers tremble and she opens her eyes. Long, slender fingers, with silver metal nails. So pale. White-pale. Silver-white.

She stands. Dizziness, like liquid through her head, swirling, disorienting. She closes her eyes, waits for the whirling in her brain to steady. Then, eyes open again, she steps slow toward the mirror. Reaches one hand out to touch it. So cold. So hot.

She wears clothes now. Somehow. Gauze. Spiked leather. They mingled, made themselves at home over her chest, her hips, at her waist. She feels her waist. So thin. If she tries, she might circle her waist with her long spidery fingers and long dangerous fingernails.

So flat. Her fingers splay, up her stomach, over her chest. So very flat. She shivers, closes her fingers at her throat.

The dance pauses. The battle lulls. The queen stirs on her throne, draws a slow breath that sounds of storms. Aine watches Fionn pause and she realizes that she is still as well.

Something has happened in that room on the far end of their shadow palace. Something has changed. The Dannan is let loose. The air is alive with it, prickling and tickling like feathers.

"Aine." Fionn whispers her name, a plea, his voice that of the boy he was so many hundreds of years ago. He reaches out to her, his fingers and palm covered with blood: hers, his, it was all the same.

Aine shakes her head. The night isn't over. Not yet.

Everything I might be?

She shakes her head, feels that taffy-pulling inside of her, everything stretching, settling. She will not be torn apart, will not be pulled in all directions. Silver light sparks at the tips of her nails.

Determined, she pushes past the lordlings and walks down the hallway, more certain in her steps than she has ever been.

Aine and Fionn stare at Tara when she pushes through silk and silver curtains and walks into the hall. They're children, now, so secure and so uncertain at the same time. She wants to laugh—at them, at her earlier fear—but now is not the time for laughter; the queen is nearly dead.

She walks to the center of the great hall and curtsies to the queen. Home. Her home. The Dannan in her blood sings at being returned to this place and this time. Maeve inclines her head, a gesture that takes more than a regal amount of time, and then Tara turns to the lover twins.

"Neither of you can be whole without the other." Tara holds her hand out to Aine. Cool fingers close around Tara's and she draws Aine close, kisses her, steals back her name. "That's mine," she murmurs against Aine's lips. "And there is no reason to hide it anymore." Then she holds out her other hand to Fionn.

He looks at his sister, looks defeated, but the night is not over and he takes Tara's hand. She draws him to her the way she brought his sister close. She kisses him, as well, tastes twilight and the hunter's moon, darkness and mist. She gives him the taste of her name as they kiss so he has it as well. "Don't forget it," she whispers.

"I cannot be whole without both of you. And neither of you can be whole without me." Tara draws the two of them together.

"The rock of kings has spoken." Maeve whispers the words, her starlight faded to midnight, her eyes nearly closed. Like ash clinging to bone, clinging to life to see this moment so she can bless it and then whisper of it to her beloved, already a thousand years gone.

There will be three crowns, and the other Dannan in the hall sigh relief like a storm. Gauze and silk drapes flutter with the greatness of it.

The old queen passes into a new queenship in a realm that the sidhe can't even guess at while Aine and Fionn and Tara hold hands and the lords and ladies sing remembrance and dawn.

doi:10.1300/5642_10

The Coat of Stars

Holly Black

Rafael Santiago hated going home. Home meant his parents making a big fuss and a special dinner and him having to smile and hide all his secret vices, like the cigarettes he had smoked for almost sixteen years now. He hated that they always had the radio blaring salsa and the windows open and that his cousins would come by and try to drag him out to bars. He hated that his mother would tell him how Father Joe had asked after him at Mass. He especially hated the familiarity of it, the memories that each visit stirred up.

For nearly an hour that morning he had stood in front of his dressing table and regarded the wigs and hats and masks—early versions or copies of costumes he'd designed—each item displayed on green glass heads that stood in front of a large, broken mirror. They drooped feathers, paper roses, and crystal dangles, or curved up into coiled, leather horns. He had settled on wearing a white tank top tucked into bland gray Dockers but when he stood next to all his treasures, he felt unfinished. Clipping on black suspenders, he looked at himself again. That was better, almost a compromise. A fedora, a cane, and a swirl of eyeliner would have finished off the look, but he left it alone.

"What do you think?" he asked the mirror, but it did not answer. He turned to the unpainted plaster face casts resting on a nearby shelf; their hollow eyes told him nothing either.

Rafe tucked his little phone into his front left pocket with his wallet and keys. He would call his father from the train. Glancing at the wall, his gaze rested on one of the sketches of costumes he'd done for a postmodern ballet production of *Hamlet*. An award hung beside it. This sketch was of a faceless woman in a white gown appliquéd with leaves and berries. He remembered how dancers had held the girl up while others pulled on the red ribbons he had had hidden in her sleeves. Yards and yards of red ribbon could come from her wrists. The stage had been swathed in red. The dancers had been covered in red. The whole world had become one dripping gash of ribbon.

The train ride was dull. He felt guilty that the green landscapes that blurred outside the window did not stir him. He only loved leaves if they were crafted from velvet.

Rafael's father waited at the station in the same old blue truck he'd had since before Rafe had left Jersey for good. Each trip his father would ask him careful questions about his job, the city, Rafe's apartment. Certain unsaid assumptions were made. His father would tell him about some cousin getting into trouble or, lately, his sister Mary's problems with Marco.

Rafe leaned back in the passenger seat, feeling the heat of the sun wash away the last of the goose bumps on his arms. He had forgotten how cold the air-conditioning was on the train. His father's skin, sun-darkened to deep mahogany, made his own seem sickly pale. A string-tied box of crystallized ginger pastries sat at his feet. He always brought something for his parents: a bottle of wine, a tarte tatin, a jar of truffle oil from Balducci's. The gifts served as a reminder of the city and that his ticket was round-trip, bought and paid for.

"Mary's getting a divorce," Rafe's father said once he'd pulled out of the parking lot. "She's been staying in your old room. I had to move your sewing stuff."

"How's Marco taking it?" Rafe had already heard about the divorce; his sister had called him a week ago at three in the morning from Cherry Hill, asking for money so she and her son Victor could take a bus home. She had talked in heaving breaths and he'd guessed she'd been crying. He had wired the money to her from the corner store where he often went for green tea ice cream.

"Not good. He wants to see his son. I told him if he comes around the house again, your cousin's gonna break probation but he's also gonna break that loco sonofabitch's neck."

No one, of course, thought that spindly Rafe could break Marco's neck.

The truck passed people dragging lawn chairs into their front yards for a better view of the coming fireworks. Although it was still many hours until dark, neighbors milled around, drinking lemonade and beer.

In the back of the Santiago house, smoke pillared up from the grill where cousin Gabriel scorched hamburger patties smothered in hot sauce. Mary lay on the blue couch in front of the TV, an ice mask covering her eyes. Rafael walked by as quietly as he could. The house was dark and the radio was turned way down. For once, his greeting was subdued. Only his nephew, Victor, a sparkler twirling in his hand, seemed oblivious to the somber mood.

They ate watermelon so cold that it was better than drinking water; hot dogs and hamburgers off the grill with more hot sauce and tomatoes; rice and beans; corn salad; and ice cream. They drank beer and instant iced tea and the decent tequila that Gabriel had brought. Mary joined them halfway through the meal and Rafe was only half-surprised to see the blue and yellow bruise darkening her jaw. Mostly, he was surprised how much her face, angry and suspicious of pity, reminded him of Lyle.

When Rafe and Lyle were thirteen, they had been best friends. Lyle had lived across town with his grandparents and three sisters in a house far too small for all of them. Lyle's grandmother told the kids terrible stories to keep them from going near the river that ran through the woods behind their yard. There was the one about the phooka, who appeared like a goat with sulfurous yellow eyes and great curling horns and who shat on the blackberries on the first of November. There was the kelpie that swam in the river and wanted to carry off Lyle and his sisters to drown and devour. And there were the trooping faeries that would steal them all away to their underground hills for a hundred years.

Lyle and Rafe snuck out to the woods anyway. They would stretch out on an old, bug-infested mattress and "practice" sex. Lying on his back, Lyle'd showed Rafe how to thrust his penis between Lyle's pressed-together thighs in "pretend" intercourse.

Lyle had forbidden certain conversations. No talk about the practicing, no talk about the bruises on his back and arms, and no talk

about his grandfather, ever, at all. Rafe thought about that, about all
the conversations he had learned not to have, all the conversations he
still avoided.

As fireworks lit up the black sky, Rafe listened to his sister fight
with Marco on the phone. He must have been accusing her about getting the money from a lover because he heard his name said over and
over. "Rafael sent it," she shouted. "My fucking brother sent it." Finally, she screamed that if he didn't stop threatening her she was going to call the police. She said her cousin was a cop. And it was true;
Teo Santiago was a cop. But Teo was also in jail.

When she got off the phone, Rafe said nothing. He didn't want her
to think he'd overheard.

She came over anyway. "Thanks for everything, you know? The
money and all."

He touched the side of her face with the bruise. She looked at the
ground but he could see that her eyes had grown wet.

"You're gonna be okay," he said. "You're gonna be happier."

"I know," she said. One of the tears tumbled from her eye and shattered across the toe of his expensive leather shoe, tiny fragments sparkling with reflected light. "I didn't want you to hear all this shit.
You're life is always so together."

"Not really," he said, smiling. Mary had seen his apartment only
once, when she and Marco had brought Victor up to see the Lion
King. Rafe had sent her tickets; they were hard to get so he thought
that she might want them. They hadn't stayed long in his apartment;
the costumes that hung on the walls had frightened Victor.

She smiled too. "Have you ever had a boyfriend this bad?"

Her words hung in the air a moment. It was the first time any of
them had ventured a guess. "Worse," he said, "and girlfriends too. I
have terrible taste."

Mary sat down next to him on the bench. "Girlfriends too?"

He nodded and lifted a glass of iced tea to his mouth. "When you
don't know what you're searching for," he said, "you have to look absolutely everywhere."

The summer that they were fourteen, a guy had gone down on Rafe in one of the public showers at the beach and he gloried in the fact that for the first time he had a story of almost endless interest to Lyle. It was also the summer that they almost ran away.

"I saw grandma's faeries," Lyle had said the week before they were supposed to go. He told Rafe plainly, like he'd spotted a robin outside the window.

"How do you know?" Rafe had been making a list of things they needed to bring. The pen in his hand had stopped writing in the middle of spelling 'colored pencils.' For a moment, all Rafe felt was resentment that his blowjob story had been trumped.

"They were just the way she said they'd be. Dancing in a circle and they glowed a little, like their skin could reflect the moonlight. One of them looked at me and her face was as beautiful as the stars."

Rafe scowled. "I want to see them too."

"Before we get on the train we'll go down to where I saw them dancing."

Rafe added 'peanut butter' to his list. It was the same list he was double-checking six days later, when Lyle's grandmother called. Lyle was dead. He had slit his wrists in a tub of warm water the night before they were supposed to leave for forever.

Rafe had stumbled to the viewing, cut off a lock of Lyle's blond hair right in front of his pissed-off family, stumbled to the funeral, and then slept stretched out on the freshly filled grave. It hadn't made sense. He wouldn't accept it. He wouldn't go home.

Rafe took out his wallet and unfolded the train schedule from the billfold. He had a little time. He was always careful not to miss the last train. He looked at the small onyx and silver ring on his pinkie. It held a secret compartment inside, so well hidden that you could barely see the hinge. When Lyle had given it to him, Rafe's fingers had been so slender that it had fit on his ring finger as easily as the curl of Lyle's hair fit inside of it.

As Rafe rose to kiss his mother and warn his father that he would have to be leaving, Mary thrust open the screen door so hard it banged against the plastic trashcan behind it.

"Where's Victor? Is he inside with you? He's supposed to be in bed."

Rafe shook his head. His mother immediately put down the plate she was drying and walked through the house, still holding the dishrag, calling Victor's name. Mary showed them the empty bed.

Mary stared at Rafe as though he hid her son from her. "He's not here. He's gone."

"Maybe he snuck out to see some friends," Rafe said, but it didn't seem right. Not for a ten-year-old.

"Marco couldn't have come here without us seeing him," Rafe's father protested.

"He's *gone*," Mary repeated, as though that explained everything. She slumped down in one of the kitchen chairs and covered her face with her hands. "You don't know what he might do to that kid. *Madre de Dios.*"

Rafe's mother came back in the room and punched numbers into the phone. There was no answer at Marco's apartment. The cousins came in from the backyard. They had mixed opinions on what to do. Some had kids of their own and thought that Mary didn't have the right to keep Victor away from his father. Soon everyone in the kitchen was shouting. Rafe got up and went to the window, looking out into the dark backyard. Kids made up their own games and wound up straying farther than they meant to.

"Victor!" he called, walking across the lawn. "Victor!"

But he wasn't there, and when Rafe walked out to the street, he could not find the boy along the hot asphalt length. Although it was night, the sky was bright with a full moon and clouds enough to reflect the city lights.

A car slowed as it came down the street. It sped away once it was past the house and Rafe let out the breath he didn't even realize that he had held. He had never considered his brother-in-law crazy, just bored and maybe a little resentful that he had a wife and a kid. But then, Lyle's grandfather had seemed normal too.

Rafe thought about the train schedule in his pocket and the unfinished sketches on his desk. The last train would be along soon and if he wasn't there to meet it, he would have to spend the night with his memories. There was nothing he could do here. In the city, he could call around and find her the number of a good lawyer—a lawyer that Marco couldn't afford. That was the best thing, he thought. He headed back to the house, his shoes clicking like beetles on the pavement.

His oldest cousin had come out to talk to him in the graveyard the night after Lyle's funeral. It had clearly creeped Teo to find his little cousin sleeping in the cemetery.

"He's gone." Teo had squatted down in his blue policeman uniform. He sounded a little impatient and very awkward.

"The faeries took him," Rafe had said. "They stole him away to Faeryland and left something else in his place."

"Then he's still not in this graveyard." Teo had pulled on Rafe's arm and Rafe had finally stood.

"If I hadn't touched him," Rafe had said, so softly that maybe Teo didn't hear.

It didn't matter. Even if Teo had heard, he probably would have pretended he hadn't.

This time when Rafe walked out of the house, he heard the distant fireworks and twirled his father's keys around his first finger. He hadn't taken the truck without permission in years.

The stick and clutch were hard to time and the engine grunted and groaned, but when he made it to the highway, he flicked on the radio and stayed in fifth gear the whole way to Cherry Hill. Marco's house was easy to find. The lights were on in every room and the blue flicker of the television lit up the front steps.

Rafe parked around a corner and walked up to the window of the guest bedroom. When he was thirteen, he had snuck into Lyle's house lots of times. Lyle had slept on a pull-out mattress in the living room because his sisters shared the second bedroom. The trick involved waiting until the television was off and everyone else had gone to bed. Rafe excelled at waiting.

When the house finally went silent and dark, Rafe pushed the window. It was unlocked. He slid it up as far as he could and pulled himself inside.

Victor turned over sleepily and opened his eyes. They went wide.

Rafe froze and waited for him to scream, but his nephew didn't move. "It's your uncle," Rafe said softly. "From the Lion King. From New York." He sat down on the carpet. Someone had once told him that being lower was less threatening.

Victor didn't speak.

"Your mom sent me to pick you up."

The mention of his mother seemed to give Victor the courage to say: "Why didn't you come to the door?"

"Your dad would kick my ass," Rafe said. "I'm not crazy."

Victor half-smiled.

"I could drive you back," Rafe said. He took his cell phone out of his pocket and put it on the comforter by Victor. "You can call your mom and she'll tell you I'm okay. Not a stranger."

The boy climbed out of bed and Rafe stuffed it with pillows that formed a small boy-shape under the blankets.

"What are you doing?" the boy asked as he punched the numbers into the tiny phone.

"I'm making a pretend you that can stay here and keep on sleeping." The words echoed for a long moment before Rafe remembered that he and Victor had to get moving.

On the drive back, Rafe told Victor a story that his mother had told when he was little, about a king who fed a louse so well on royal blood that it swelled up so large that it no longer fit in the palace. The king had the louse slaughtered and its hide tanned to make a coat for his daughter, the princess, and told all her suitors that they had to guess what kind of skin she wore before their proposal could be accepted.

Victor liked the part of the story where Rafe pretended to hop like a flea and bite his nephew. Rafe liked all fairy tales with tailors in them.

"Come inside," his mother said. "You should have told us you were going to take the car. I needed to go to the store and get some—"

She stopped, seeing Victor behind Rafael.

Rafe's father stood up from the couch as they came in. Rafe tossed the keys and his father caught them.

"Tough guy." His father grinned. "I hope you hit him."

"Are you kidding? And hurt this delicate hand?" Rafe asked, holding it up as for inspection.

He was surprised by his father's laugh.

For the first time in almost fifteen years, Rafe spent the night. Stretching out on the lumpy couch, he turned the onyx ring again and again on his finger.

Then, for the first time in more than ten years, he thumbed open the hidden compartment, ready to see Lyle's golden hair. Crumbled leaves fell onto his chest instead.

Leaves. Not hair. Hair lasted; it should be there. Victorian mourning ornaments braided with the hair of the long-dead survived decades. Rafe had seen such a brooch on the scarf of a well-known playwright. The hair was dulled by time, perhaps, but it had hardly turned to leaves.

He thought of the lump of bedclothes that had looked like Victor at first glance. A 'pretend me,' Victor had said. But Lyle's corpse wasn't pretend. He had seen it. He had cut off a lock of its hair.

Rafe ran his fingers through the crushed leaves on his chest. Hope swelled inside of him, despite the senselessness of it. He didn't like to think about Faeryland lurking just over a hill or beneath a shallow river, as distant as a memory. But if he could believe that he could pass unscathed from the world of the city into the world of the suburban ghetto and back again, then couldn't he go further? Why couldn't he cross into the world of shining people with faces like stars that were the root of all his costumes?

Marco had stolen Victor; but Rafe had stolen Victor back. Until that moment, Rafe hadn't considered he could steal Lyle back from Faeryland.

Rafe kicked off the afghan.

⌗

At the entrance to the woods, Rafe stopped and lit a cigarette. His feet knew the way to the river by heart.

The mattress was filthier than he remembered, smeared with dirt and damp with dew. He sat, unthinking, and whispered Lyle's name.

The forest was quiet and the thought of faeries seemed a little silly. Still, he felt close to Lyle here.

"I went to New York, just like we planned," Rafe said, his hand stroking over the blades of grass as though they were hairs on a pelt. "I got a job in a theatrical rental place, full of these antiqued candelabras and musty old velvet curtains. Now I make stage clothes. I don't ever have to come back here again."

He rested his head against the mattress, inhaled mold and leaves and earth. His face felt heavy, as though already sore with tears. "Do you remember Mary? Her husband hits her. I bet he hits my nephew too, but she wouldn't say." His eyes burned with unexpected tears. The guilt that twisted his gut was fresh and raw as it had been the day Lyle died. "I never knew why you did it. Why you had to die instead of come away with me. You never said either."

"Lyle," he sighed, and his voice trailed off. He wasn't sure what he'd been about to say. "I just wish you were here, Lyle. I wish you were here to talk to."

Rafe pressed his mouth to the mattress and closed his eyes for a moment before he rose and brushed the dirt off his slacks.

He would just ask Mary what happened with Marco. If Victor was all right. If they wanted to live with him for a while. He would tell his parents that he slept with men. There would be no more secrets, no more assumptions. There was nothing he could do for Lyle now, but there was still something he could do for his nephew. He could say all the things he'd left unsaid and hope that others would too. As Rafe stood, lights sprung up from nothing, like matches catching in the dark.

Around him, in the woods, faeries danced in a circle. They were bright and seemed almost weightless, hair flying behind them like smoke behind a sparkler. Among them, Rafe thought he saw a kid, so absorbed in dancing that he did not hear Rafe gasp or shout. He started forward, hand outstretched. At the center of the circle, a woman in a gown of green smiled a cold and terrible smile before the whole company disappeared.

Rafe felt his heart beat hard against his chest. He was frightened as he had not been at fourteen, when magical things seemed like they could be ordinary and ordinary things were almost magical.

On the way home, Rafe thought of all the other fairy tales he knew about tailors. He thought of the faery woman's plain green gown and about desire. When he got to the house, he pulled his sewing machine out of the closet and set it up on the kitchen table. Then he began to rummage through all the cloth and trims, beads, and fringe. He found crushed panne velvet that looked like liquid gold and sewed it into a frockcoat studded with bright buttons and appliquéd with blue flames that lapped up the sleeves. It was one of the most beautiful things he had ever made. He fell asleep cradling it and woke to his mother setting a cup of espresso mixed with condensed milk in front of him. He drank the coffee in one slug.

It was easy to make a few phone calls and a few promises, change around meetings and explain to his bewildered parents that he needed to work from their kitchen for a day or two. Of course Clio would feed his cats. Of course his client understood that Rafe was working through a design problem. Of course the presentation could be re-scheduled for the following Friday. Of course. Of course.

His mother patted his shoulder. "You work too hard."

He nodded, because it was easier than telling her he wasn't really working.

"But you make beautiful things. You sew like your great-grand-mother. I told you how people came from miles around to get their wedding dresses made by her."

He smiled up at her and thought of all the gifts he had brought at the holidays—cashmere gloves and leather coats and bottles of per-fume. He had never sewn a single thing for her. Making gifts had seemed cheap, like he was giving her a child's misshapen vase or a card colored with crayons. But the elegant, meaningless presents he had sent were cold, revealing nothing about him and even less about her. Imagining her in a silk dress the color of papayas—one he might sew himself—filled him with shame.

He slept most of the day in the shadowed dark of his parent's bed with the shades drawn and the door closed. The buzz of cartoons in the background and the smell of cooking oil made him feel like a small child again. When he woke it was dark outside. His clothes had been cleaned and were folded at the foot of the bed. He put the golden coat on over them and walked to the river.

There, he smoked cigarette after cigarette, dropping the filters into the water, listening for the hiss as the river smothered the flame and drowned the paper. Finally, the faeries came, dancing their endless dance, with the cold faery woman sitting in the middle.

The woman saw him and walked through the circle. Her eyes were green as moss and, as she got close, he saw that her hair flowed behind her as though she were swimming through water or like ribbons whipped in a fierce wind. Where she stepped, tiny flowers bloomed.

"Your coat is beautiful. It glows like the sun," the faery said, reaching out to touch the fabric.

"I would give it to you," said Rafe. "Just let me have Lyle."

A smile twisted her mouth. "I will let you spend tonight with him. If he remembers you, he is free to go. Will that price suit?"

Rafe nodded and removed the coat.

The faery woman caught Lyle's hand as he spun past, pulling him out of the dance. He was laughing, still, as his bare feet touched the moss outside the circle and he aged. His chest grew broader, he became taller, his hair lengthened, and fine lines appeared around his mouth and eyes. He was no longer a teenager.

"Leaving us, even for a time, has a price," the faery woman said. Standing on her toes, she bent Lyle's head to her lips. His eyelids drooped and she steered him to the moldering mattress. He never even looked in Rafe's direction; he just sank down into sleep.

"Lyle," Rafe said, dropping down beside him, smoothing the tangle of hair back from his face. There were braids in it that knotted up with twigs and leaves and cords of thorny vines. A smudge of dirt highlighted one cheekbone. Leaves blew over him, but he did not stir.

"Lyle," Rafe said again. Rafe was reminded of how Lyle's body had lain in the casket at the funeral, of how Lyle's skin had been pale and bluish as skim milk and smelled faintly of chemicals, of how his fin-

gers were threaded together across his chest so tightly that when Rafe
tried to take his hand, it was stiff as a mannequin's. Even now, the
memory of that other, dead Lyle seemed more real than the one that
slept beside him like a cursed prince in a fairy tale.

"Please wake up," Rafe said. "Please. Wake up and tell me this is
real."

Lyle did not stir. Beneath the lids, his eyes moved as if he saw another landscape.

Rafe shook him and then struck him, hard, across the face. "Get
up," he shouted. He tugged on Lyle's arm and Lyle's body rolled toward him.

Standing, he tried to lift Lyle, but he was used to only the weight of
bolts of cloth. He settled for dragging him toward the street where
Rafe could flag down a car or call for help. He pulled with both his
hands, staining Lyle's shirt and face with grass, and scratching his side
on a fallen branch. Rafe dropped his hand and bent over him in the
quiet dark.

"It's too far," Rafe said. "Far too far."

He stretched out beside Lyle, pillowing his friend's head against his
chest and resting on his own arm.

When Rafe woke, Lyle no longer lay beside him, but the faery
woman stood over the mattress. She wore the coat of fire and, in the
light of the newly risen sun, she shone so brightly that Rafe had to
shade his eyes with his hand. She laughed and her laugh sounded like
ice cracking on a frozen lake.

"You cheated me," Rafe said. "You made him sleep."

"He heard you in his dreams," said the faery woman. "He preferred
to remain dreaming."

Rafe stood and brushed off his pants, but his jaw clenched so tightly
that his teeth hurt.

"Come with me," the faery said. "Join the dance. You are only jealous that you were left behind. Let that go. You can be forever young
and you can make beautiful costumes forevermore. We will appreciate them as no mortal does and we will adore you."

Rafe inhaled the leaf-mold and earth smells. Where Lyle had
rested, a golden hair remained. He thought of his father laughing at

his jokes, his mother admiring his sewing, his sister caring enough to ask him about boyfriends even in the middle of a crisis. Rafe wound the hair around his finger so tightly that it striped his skin white and red. "No," he told her.

His mother was sitting in her robe in the kitchen. She got up when Rafe came in.

"Where are you going? You are like a possessed man." She touched his hand and her skin felt so hot that he pulled back in surprise.

"You're freezing! You have been at his grave."

It was easier for Rafe to nod than explain.

"There is a story about a woman who mourned too long and the specter of her lover rose up and dragged her down into death with him."

He nodded again, thinking of the faery woman, of being dragged into the dance, of Lyle sleeping like death.

She sighed exaggeratedly and made him a coffee. Rafe had already set up the sewing machine by the time she put the mug beside him.

That day he made a coat of silver silk, pleated at the hips and embroidered with a tangle of thorny branches and lapels of downy white fur. He knew it was one of the most beautiful things he had ever made.

"Who are you sewing that for?" Mary asked when she came in. "It's gorgeous."

He rubbed his eyes and gave her a tired smile. "It's supposed to be the payment a mortal tailor used to win back a lover from Faeryland."

"I haven't heard of that story," his sister said. "Will it be a musical?"

"I don't know yet," said Rafe. "I don't think the cast can sing."

His mother frowned and called Mary over to chop up a summer squash.

"I want you and Victor to come live with me," Rafe said as his sister turned away from him.

"Your place is too small," Rafe's mother told him.

She had never seen his apartment. "We could move, then. Go to Queens. Brooklyn."

"You won't want a little boy running around. And Mary has the cousins here. She should stay with us. Besides, the city is dangerous."

"Marco is dangerous," Rafe said, his voice rising. "Why don't you let Mary make up her own mind?"

Rafe's mother muttered under her breath as she chopped, Rafe sighed and bit his tongue and Mary gave him a sisterly roll of the eyes. It occurred to him that that had been the most normal conversation he had had with his mother in years.

All day he worked on the coat and that night Rafe, wearing the silvery coat, went back to the woods and the river.

The dancers were there as before and when Rafe got close, the faery woman left the circle of dancers.

"Your coat is as lovely as the moon. Will you agree to the same terms?"

Rafe thought of objecting, but he also thought of the faery woman's kiss and that he might be able to change the course of events. It would be better if he caught her off-guard. He shouldered off his coat. "I agree."

As before, the faery woman pulled Lyle from the dance.

"Lyle!" Rafe said, starting toward him before the faery could touch his brow with her lips.

Lyle turned to him and his lips parted as though he were searching for a name to go with a distant memory, as if Lyle didn't recall him after all.

The faery woman kissed him then, and Lyle staggered drowsily to the mattress. His drooping eyelashes nearly hid the gaze he gave Rafe. His mouth moved, but no sound escaped him and then he subsided into sleep.

That night Rafe tried a different way of rousing Lyle. He pressed his mouth to Lyle's slack lips, to his forehead as the faery woman had done. He kissed the hollow of Lyle's throat, where the beat of his heart thrummed against his skin. He ran his hands over the Lyle's chest. He touched his lips to the smooth, unscarred expanse of Lyle's wrists.

Again and again, he kissed Lyle, but it was as terrible as kissing a corpse.

Before he slept, Rafe took the onyx and silver ring off his own pinkie, pulled out a strand of black hair from his own head and coiled it inside the hollow of the poison ring. Then he pushed the ring onto Lyle's pinkie.

"Remember me. Please remember me," Rafe said. "I can't remember myself unless you remember me."

But Lyle did not stir and Rafe woke alone on the mattress. He made his way home in the thin light of dawn.

That day he sewed a coat from velvet as black as the night sky. He stitched tiny black crystals onto it and embroidered it with black roses, thicker at the hem and then thinning as they climbed. At the cuffs and neck, ripped ruffles of thin smoky purples and deep reds reminded him of sunsets. Across the back, he sewed on silver beads for stars. Stars like the faery woman's eyes. It was the most beautiful thing Rafael had ever created. He knew he would never make its equal.

"Where do you get your ideas from?" his father asked as he shuffled out to the kitchen for an evening cup of decaf. "I've never been much of a creative person."

Rafe opened his mouth to say that he got his ideas from everywhere, from things he'd seen and dreamed and felt, but then he thought of the other thing his father said. "You made that bumper for the old car out of wood," Rafe said. "That was pretty creative."

Rafe's father grinned and added milk to his cup.

That night Rafe donned the shimmering coat and walked to the woods. The faery woman waited for him. She sucked in her breath at the sight of the magnificent coat.

"I must have it," she said. "You shall have him as before."

Rafael nodded. Tonight if he could not rouse Lyle, he would have to say good-bye. Perhaps this was the life Lyle had chosen—a life of dancing and youth and painless memory—and he was wrong to try and take him away from it. But he wanted to spend one more night beside Lyle.

She brought Lyle to him and he knelt on the mattress. The faery woman bent to kiss his forehead, but at the last moment, Lyle turned his head and the kiss fell on his hair.

Scowling, she rose.

Lyle blinked as though awakening from a long sleep, then touched the onyx ring on his finger. He turned toward Rafe and smiled tentatively.

"Lyle?" Rafe asked. "Do you remember me?"

"Rafael?" Lyle asked. He reached a hand toward Rafe's face, fingers skimming just above the skin. Rafe leaned into the heat, butting his head against Lyle's hand and sighing. Time seemed to flow backward and he felt like he was fourteen again and in love.

"Come, Lyle," said the faery woman sharply.

Lyle rose stiffly, his fingers ruffling Rafe's hair.

"Wait," Rafe said. "He knows who I am. You said he would be free."

"He's as free to come with me as he is to go with you," she said.

Lyle looked down at Rafe. "I dreamed that we went to New York and that we performed in a circus. I danced with the bears and you trained fleas to jump through the eyes of needles."

"I trained fleas?"

"In my dream. You were famous for it." His smile was tentative, uncertain. Maybe he realized that it didn't sound like a great career.

Rafe thought of the story he had told Victor about the princess in her louse-skin coat, about locks of hair and all the things he had managed through the eyes of needles.

The faery woman turned away from them with a scowl, walking back to the fading circle of dancers, becoming insubstantial as smoke.

"It didn't go quite like that." Rafe stood and held out his hand. "I'll tell you what really happened."

Lyle clasped Rafe's fingers tightly, desperately but his smile was wide and his eyes were bright as stars. "Don't leave anything out."

doi:10.1300/5642_11

How the Ocean Loved Margie

Laurie J. Marks

Margie had a lot of practice keeping secrets from people. She had taught high school English in Somerville, Massachusetts, for nearly fifteen years without anyone, not even her cappuccino buddies, suspecting that she was a lesbian. When she arranged for a year's sabbatical no one, not even her mother, knew that she was pregnant by donor insemination. And when she disappeared abruptly shortly after the last day of school, no one except she herself suspected that she had gone mad.

Going mad was a very English-teacher-spinster-Victorian-melodramatic thing to do. If she were going to do it, she should have worn a flowing white nightdress with a tucked bodice and ruffled hem. She should have done her hair up like a Gibson girl, with tendrils wisping fetchingly down upon her neck. Then, if she had run down the rocky beach and flung herself into the cold Atlantic someone might have noticed and pulled her out again. But Margie went mad in a pair of blue jeans nearly white with age and an oversized T-shirt that declared Parkfield, California, to be The Earthquake Capitol of the World. It was very undramatic. It was, in fact, pedestrian. She did not hear voices or believe she was Catherine of Aragon or want to kill the president. She simply felt an irresistible compulsion to go to Maine. With her dreams and her every waking thought filled by a restless desire such as she had never before felt, it had taken all her strength to finish the school year. Yet, because she was a woman of more discipline than imagination, she had toughed it out to the last day, cleaned out her desk and filled out her forms, graded the last papers and

---

"How the Ocean Loved Margie" was first published in The Endicott Studio/The Journal of Mythic Arts (n.d.).

turned in her library books, canceled her newspaper subscription and paid all her bills before finally filling her car with camping gear and getting on the Interstate.

She had gotten pregnant out of simple loneliness. Turning forty turns a woman invisible, and forty more years of being dismissed as insignificant by her students, and of having people see her just enough to keep from walking into her began to seem unendurable. For certain, she'd had her last lover, though at the time she hadn't realized it. "It's not shame," she had insisted. "I just don't want to lose my job."

Now she had crossed the Piscataqua River and was in Maine. "Now what?" she said irritably, addressing the creature that swam like a seal in the harbor of her womb. Surely this compulsion was all the fetus's fault, some kind of new psychosis brought on by pregnancy, or a strange kind of toxemia that had altered the chemical balance of her brain. Her answer came only in the form of psychic shocks of overwhelming anxiety that made even stopping at a roadside service area almost unendurable. She continued northward. For more than an hour she felt an easing of tension, but after she had driven through Portland she began to feel wretched again. The psychic shocks drove her eastward to where the coast of Maine frays away into tattered shreds of land.

By sunset, she had been driven to the remote tip of one peninsula, Pemaquid Point, where a lighthouse overlooked the harsh ocean writhing under a red sky. A lobster boat puttered past, the lobsterman standing in the bed of the boat, rhythmically bending and rising to toss his traps overboard. A cold sea wind made Margie wish for the barn jacket left in the car, but she could not go back for it. Waves crashed on the tumbled black boulders of the shoreline, throwing threatening fans of white spray. Suddenly, the Pemaquid light began to flash, and the tourists who had gathered to worship the most photographed lighthouse in the world started clicking their cameras.

Only Margie continued to gaze out to sea. The fetus wanted her to continue eastward, even though it meant throwing herself into the water. This was not the tame Pacific, into which people might light-heartedly fling themselves for pleasure. On her trip to the West Coast several years ago, Margie had been astounded by the fearlessness of

California swimmers, for she was accustomed to this bitter northern sea, which was not far, relatively speaking, from the Arctic. Yet Margie's mad desire drove her down onto the rocks, until cold spray slapped her cheek and she stepped back in horror. She wrestled herself into the car, and drove west as far as she could endure, which was about a mile and a half.

Ever since she became pregnant, she had been craving seafood. She bought herself a lobster dinner in New Harbor and ate outside on the wharf where, unfortunately, the cold did not deter the mosquitoes. A small boat-tour company had a boat leaving at 9 a.m. for Monhegan Island, but when Margie looked at her AAA map, she knew that the island was too close to the mainland. If she took the boat there, she would only be driven into the sea again.

She cleared away the emptied husk of the lobster and studied her map. Nearby, a dog barked at the edge of a noisy crowd that gathered around the open-air bar. When Margie looked up from her useless map, the dog had taken up a position near her, expectantly, as if it were her duty to give him the inedible remains of her lobster.

"Don't give nothing to the beggar," a man advised. Darkness had settled in, and the wharf's lighting was less than impressive. She could hardly see the map anymore.

"That map's no good," the man said.

"What?" She looked up with a schoolteacher's automatic glare. "But it's a triple-A map."

"Don't matter how many A's it's got. Half the islands are missing. It doesn't show the Duck Rocks or the Thread of Life Ledges. And look here, the map just ends as if there weren't nothing out here." His blunt forefinger poked the table beyond the map's edge. "As if it was the end of the world. But it's still Maine out here, you know."

Margie restrained her impulse to correct his double negatives.

"Beyond the edge of this no-good map of yours, is Skerry Island, where I come from," he said. "And after Skerry there's truly nothing else, just open sea, until you reach whatever's on the other side of the ocean—some part of Europe, I guess. Now what you need is a good nautical chart, and you'll see every single island, clear as day."

He just happened to have a chart folded up in his pocket, and Margie's silence seemed a sufficient invitation. With his friends grinning and nudging each other over at the bar, he unfolded his chart in the lobster juice. He wore a flannel shirt and jeans. Besides the beer, he also smelled like diesel exhaust and fish. On his chart, the mainland was merely a blank shoreline, but numbers and geometric shapes cluttered the usual empty blue of the open sea. The man's forefinger touched a flake of land some twenty miles due east of Pemaquid Point. "See what I mean?" he said. "Skerry Island. But according to most maps it don't even exist."

Margie sighed, as a profound relief washed over her. "That is the place I'm looking for." Or perhaps it was the fetus who had spoken, for her words were garbled and distorted, as if they had been spoken under water.

The man continued, "Well, it was settled by Scots and they named it after an island about the same size, in the North Sea. A cold, lonely place, hardly more than some rocks sticking out of the water."

Margie didn't ask or care which of the two islands he was describing. "Can I hire you to take me there?"

She had awakened early to a chilly June dawn and had checked out of her hotel before sunrise. Now, her camping gear jostled the boxes of mundane groceries that filled the bed of Joe's lobster boat, and Joe stood at the wheel. A striped buoy was pierced on the radio antenna. By morning light, Joe was a man without mystery; as interesting as a car mechanic with a hangover. He wore the same clothing as the night before and had not shaved. Margie supposed he had slept in his boat. The calm ocean shone like polished aluminum until they entered a fog bank. Wearing the barn jacket over her sweatshirt for warmth, Margie perched on the edge of the boat, sipping sour coffee poured from a thermos.

The water below, suddenly gray and dark, writhed with shadows. The ocean was full of illusions. Margie had become used to them when a sleek figure as long as a woman but shaped like a torpedo swam by just under the water's surface. She did not realize that it was no illusion until it broke the water's surface and peered up at her, solemn and incurious. Then it was gone and she was on her feet, startled, with a swimming, spinning sensation deep in her belly. If she had not known the sensation's source was that restless slave driver in her womb, she might have mistaken the feeling for joy.

"You have seals here!" she shouted, so Joe could hear her over the engine.

He slowed the boat. "Eh?"

"You have seals so far out?"

Joe looked oddly displeased. "You saw a seal?"

"They swim so far from land?"

"Depends on what you mean by land. There's a bit of rock not far from here, where they lie around and holler at each other." Some time later, he slowed the engine again, so Margie could hear the seals barking in the fog. They sounded like a pack of dogs just barking to hear the sound of their own voices, but the seal that had peered into Margie's face had not seemed like an animal at all, but like an intelligent alien.

Skerry Island appeared slowly rather than suddenly, a gray shape in the fog bank that gradually formed into a steep, forested mountaintop. The island's seven houses, each of which had to be at least a hundred years old, clustered near the small harbor on the sheltered western side of the island. A dirt track wound perhaps half a mile uphill from the landing, between the houses, which were mobbed by blooming lupines and walled in by lobster traps. Margie helped Joe unload the groceries and camping gear from the boat into a truck, the island's only vehicle. Joe had been in New Harbor the night before because it was his turn to travel to the mainland for supplies, and now he drove from one house to the next, delivering boxes of groceries directly into people's kitchens. The ancient, weather-beaten front doors had no locks. In one house, three children of various ages worked on correspondence-course lessons, supervised by a woman who gave Joe a loaf of bread hot from the oven. They all stared at Margie as though they had never set eyes on a stranger before. At another house, Joe chatted with an old man rooted in a rocking chair on his porch. No one else was at home; Joe said they were out in their boats.

The road ended at the tiny, unkempt cemetery, where Joe did a U-turn and took Margie back to his house, which was a seeming derelict with sagging roofline and peeling paint. He'd lived there alone for twenty years, he said. She turned down his offer of supper, bed, and assistance in finding a good campsite, insisting that having a guide would take the adventure out of her vacation. In fact, she was worried that the longer she spent with him the more likely he was to notice that she was pregnant, which no doubt would make him feel entitled to interfere when she just wanted to be left alone.

She promised to let him know when she needed more supplies, picked up her backpack and sleeping bag, left the rest of her gear on his porch to come back for later, and set out to explore the island. Within her, the fetus swam peacefully in its sea, home at last.

Margie had been camping near the shore for six weeks before it finally felt like summer, warm enough that when the sun was shining she dared leave camp without even a jacket, though she always carried a heavy duty, bright pink plastic bucket bought at Costco years ago, along with a fishing knife and a small pamphlet on foraging. The bucket's unnatural color guaranteed that she could find it again no matter where she laid it down. Most of the time she simply carried it with her because she never knew when she might stumble across something to eat. Although she had brought a fishing pole, Skerry's entire shoreline was too inhospitable and dangerous for fishing, except in the small harbor, which she avoided. She organized her day around the tide table, so that low tide would always find her at the rocky shoreline, wading through cold water in search of sea urchins, blue mussels, and periwinkles. She would then fill her bucket with whatever else she could find that her foraging book told her was edible: Irish moss and kelp from the water's edge, chickweed, beach peas, and wild strawberries from the windy cliffs and rocky headlands. When her bucket was full, she would go back to her camp and cook and eat whatever it contained; then she would gather and chop wood for her next meal, and go foraging again. She had very little spare time.

It was impossible to get lost, for the ocean surrounded her, and she merely had to follow the sound of the crashing waves to find herself again at the shore which, if she followed it, would inevitably bring her back to her campsite. Though the island was thick with trees, she had set up her camp beyond the edge of the woods, for mosquitoes swarmed in their damp shade. Instead, she camped in the wind, among huge stones that helped to anchor her tent on stormy days. At night, the nearby sea went crashing through her dreams: cold and wild, atangle with wrack and the threatening shapes of stone and shore. In her dreams she lived in those waves, twisting powerfully through the forces that should have crushed her, at home in a body that was designed to slide gracefully between the waves. When she awoke, sometimes she was gasping for breath, and the infant swam wildly inside her, as if it shared its crazy mother's dreams.

The fetus had ceased to torture her, but her days were not as fearless as her nights. Her watch, without which she could not have kept her appointments with the sea, told her that it was mid-July, and that she was six months pregnant. Impregnated in the bitter chill of January, she was due in early October, when, as far as her foraging book was concerned, there would be nothing on this entire island for her to eat.

Sitting on her wild cliff with the ocean wind tugging at her hair, she had a vision of herself, unable to see the ground around the vast swelling of her abdomen, searching desperately through her foraging pamphlet. Because she was mad, she accepted that she could not leave the island until her child was born, but she could not accept that she would starve to death first. Many weeks had passed since she used up the last of her flour, potatoes, and cooking oil, and her ability to hunt shellfish decreased as her belly swelled. This, she thought, was why human females could not bear their children in solitude. Yet she couldn't bring herself to walk to the settlement and give Joe or one of the other lobstermen a shopping list and a couple of traveler's checks, for she doubted that even this insular community would continue to mind their own business once they recognized she was pregnant.

The blackberries and blueberries began to ripen, and between tides she wandered the woods like a wild animal, eating every berry she could find. Still, she lay awake at night, with her stomach growling and the voracious infant twirling joyously in its little sea. The child took from her whatever it needed; she, on the other hand, went hungry.

Then, one day, the ocean threw her a fish. Having gathered periwinkles until the tide turned, she stood in the water, captivated by the glorious sunset. If she wasn't so hungry, she thought, she might almost be happy. Then a fish, a big fish, went flying through the hectic light of the setting sun, flashing silver red-gold, and landed in a frantic, thrashing splash, practically at her feet. She snatched it up and nearly lost her grip on it, but hung on with one hand while she grabbed a rock with the other, and bashed its head in. It was a mackerel, her foraging book told her later: iridescent green by the light of the fire, easy to filet. She had no oil to fry it in, so she poached the filets in sea water, surrounded by her favorite seaweed, the one called Irish moss. The summertime mackerel run must have begun. Her book said that during a mackerel run you could catch a fish a minute. But this same book told her that mackerel can't be caught from shore because the schools of fish avoid land.

The next morning, it happened again. And again, in the evening. Twice a day the ocean tossed her a mackerel, as though it knew she was there, waiting, and didn't want her to go hungry. It was ridiculous, declared Margie in her schoolteacher voice, but that didn't stop her from eating the fish. One day, standing ankle deep in water at low tide, she called out, "I don't suppose you can spare some potatoes?"

The next day the ocean gave her five pounds of potatoes. They didn't come flying through the air like the fish, but she found them at low tide, half sunk in shallow water, where she hardly could have missed them. On subsequent days, the ocean gave her a tub of margarine and several pounds of flour, tightly sealed in a Ziplock bag, and a half-dozen onions, so that she could make fish chowder. When the ocean gave her a box of saltines, she had something on which to spread her sea-urchin roe, which she could only bring herself to eat if it was served like caviar.

She didn't have to work anymore, except to gather edible plants on her way to and from the low-tide potluck. The ocean gave her whatever she needed. Suddenly, almost overnight, she became enormous, and the infant began to struggle inside her at night, as though it were beginning to feel a bit cramped in its rapidly shrinking little sea. She set her watch alarm and dozed between tides with her swollen feet raised on a rock. For the first time since her arrival at Skerry, she had time to read the paperbacks she had tucked into her backpack: *Jane Eyre, Sense and Sensibility*. No one ever has a pregnant heroine, she realized, not even the women writers, but she could vaguely remember a pregnant heroine in one of the old ballads, saving her man's life by, as she recalled, simply hanging onto him no matter how ugly he got. "Not me," she said out loud. "I'd have let him go."

"Uh," someone said.

She sat up too fast. Head swimming, she stared at a square, blurry shape, which resolved itself slowly into a person. Joe. "Shit," she said. He stared at her in blank astonishment, a picnic basket dangling from one hand. "Hello," she said. "You startled me." She had not seen or talked to another person in two months, and she honestly couldn't say that she felt like she had missed out on anything.

"You're, uh, pregnant."

She quelled any number of possible rude replies. "Yes."

He sat down upon a stone. "Well." He looked around himself rather desperately. "Nice camp. Neat." Silence. "I expected to hear from you by now about supplies, so I thought I'd better check on you."

"I'm doing fine."

"Uh." His gaze skittered around her gravid shape, managing to avoid direct eye contact. "Shouldn't you, uh, be seeing a doctor?"

"Do I look sick to you?"

"I never heard of a pregnant woman camping before."

"Back on the mainland, it's all the rage," she said, before she could stop herself.

Joe gazed at her, humorless and dull as a used hubcap. "You should have told me."

"I didn't think it was anyone's business but mine."

"But I'm the one who gave you a ride out here."

Margie could not quite follow the logic of this statement. Maybe Joe's assumption of responsibility for her welfare was like some peoples' for their invited houseguests. Though Margie had invited herself to Skerry Island, she couldn't have gotten here without him. So now he felt like whatever happened to her would be his fault. She needed an excuse for being here that had nothing to do with him.

"Actually, I'm doing some research," she said. "It's for a novel about a pregnant woman who gets stranded on an island. My doctor said it was OK."

Joe looked skeptical.

"Besides, this is my last chance to be alone for at least eighteen years. I'll be an old woman by then."

Joe raised his eyebrows. "And the father?"

"A syringe."

"A what?" Some people, Margie supposed, might not understand the mechanics of donor insemination, but Joe looked not so much puzzled as sickened. "Fine," he said, backing away. "You want to be alone, that's fine with me. Just do me a favor and stay away from the water. No one who ever fell into the ocean has gotten out alive."

He stalked away, still carrying his basket. Belatedly, Margie realized that the basket must have contained a picnic lunch that Joe had planned to share with her: fried chicken, maybe, and chocolate chip cookies. The man had lived alone for twenty years, and Margie surely was the only marriageable woman to come his way for some time. No wonder he had been so disconcerted.

Low tide that day came right on the cusp of the late sunset, and she stood there, vaguely worried, as the red sky turned a deep, translucent blue which slowly darkened to black. Her pink bucket was empty, and the tide had long since turned.

Surely the ocean, so kind until now, wasn't jealous? She abruptly shouted, "I don't want him, or his fried chicken! I sent him away, didn't I?" She stopped, feeling much more foolish than she had when she asked for potatoes the first time. The waves crashed, startlingly close, for in the darkness, the danger of the rising tide had crept up on her unobserved. "The hell with you," she muttered, not sure who she was talking to. She turned toward the safety of the shore.

The bitter ocean mugged her from behind. Off-balanced, Margie went down, and the water sucked her away from the stability of shore. She thrashed herself up to her knees, but now another looming black wave fell onto her, like a shower of black crockery. She breathed water, and envisioned herself battered to death upon the rocks, and no one but she would know it was a lover's quarrel. Another cold wave loomed. She struggled feebly, but the stones rolled underfoot like marbles. Then, a new force jerked her forward, out of the crashing waves' grasp, and again, out of the writhing water and onto stones, like a sack of wet laundry. She lay on her back, coughing, retching, with the stars starting to come out overhead in a sky of midnight blue.

"The ocean will not give you up so easily. Get on your feet now. You're not yet safely on dry land."

She rolled onto her side, and the same hand that had jerked her out of the ocean's grasp hauled her briskly to her feet and supported her as she walked away from the water's writhing edge. Safely out of the range of the tide, she collapsed onto a boulder, still gasping, starting to shiver now in her soaking wet clothes and the chill wind of evening. Her eyes burned with salt but through the haze and twilight she thought she saw another woman, utterly naked but carrying some kind of heavy clothing under her arm, stride through the shallow, starlit water and bend over to pick something up. She came back and the thing in her hand resolved itself into Margie's pink bucket.

"You'd better get those wet clothes off," the woman said. "That wind's not so cold, but it's cold enough to give you hypothermia if you're not careful." She tossed the bucket and her own armload of wet clothes onto the rocks, safely out of the ocean's reach. Self-conscious, Margie took off her shirt and pants. "Come on," the woman said, and helped her up. "I'll come back for our things."

Margie went with her, shivering, her knees rubbery from shock. She could not tell where they were going, and even though she thought she knew this shoreline pretty well, soon she had entered in an unfamiliar place, starlit and filled with the shapes of great, looming stones, with the trees sighing nearby as the wind flowed through like the tide, and the sound of the crashing waves far enough away that Margie's fear began to ease. A door creaked open, a lantern was lit, and she found herself indoors, sitting in a chair crudely cobbled together out of driftwood, wrapped in a Hudson Bay blanket. The naked woman knelt before a rusty old wood-burning stove and blew energetically on the tinder within until it burst into flame. And then she was gone, leaving Margie alone in the faint, warm light of the crudely furnished shack. Its walls seemed to be made of rimed planks salvaged from the sea, with the gaps and knotholes filled with mud and grass. The cushions on the furniture were handmade, with bits of the grass that stuffed them poking through the seams. Blankets lay unfolded in one corner; the bed appeared to be the floor, where an unlikely pile of oriental carpets lay several layers deep. An open doorway led to a dark second room, which seemed to be for storage; Margie could see cardboard cartons, and clothing hanging from hooks.

On one wall, near the stove, an Olympic gold medal hung from a nail, its ribbon faded with age.

The door opened, and the woman came in, hauling a tangle of wet clothing and what seemed to be a substantial wetsuit, which she hung in the storeroom. Calmer, warmer, Margie took a good look at her this time as she pulled on a worn pair of jeans and a faded flannel shirt. She had a swimmer's big shoulders, and had a layer of fat to insulate her from the cold water. Her hair was already starting to dry, and in the firelight it seemed almost red, but her eyes were dark, almost black. She turned and looked at Margie, as though she felt her stare. She had to be forty years old, or close to it, and her face had the closed-off look of one who had lived long enough to lose all her trust of the world.

"Abigail Macauley?" said Margie in disbelief.

The woman gazed at her for a moment, then glanced at the gold medal. "I never could figure out what to do with that thing. For God's sake, don't call me Abby, like they kept doing on T.V. It's Gayle."

"It's not every day a pregnant woman gets rescued from the sea by an Olympic gold-medal swimmer."

"I suppose not." Having finished buttoning her shirt, she added wood to fire, which started to forth a welcome warmth, and put on a pot of water to boil. "Some tea will warm you up."

"I've been here two months and never realized I had a neighbor."

"I rinsed your clothes with fresh water." Gayle hung Margie's clothes by the stove to dry.

"You swim in that ocean? Even in a wetsuit—"

Gayle smiled suddenly. Her crow's feet pleated like the folds in a paper fan. "I'm no more crazy than you are," she said.

Margie eased herself back into the grass-musty, crackly cushions of the driftwood chair. The scratchy, stiff blanket smelled salty as the sea. The sea really did love her, Margie thought, sleepy in the aftermath of having almost drowned. After weeks of giving her everything she needed, it had tried to kill her in a jealous rage, but then had regretted it and sent instead this island hermit, rising up out of the wave to save her life.

I am insane, Margie thought, waking up a little.

Gayle's kitchen included an ice chest, a small but sturdy table, and a wooden box of kitchenware. Waiting for the water to boil, she took a knife from the box and opened the ice chest to remove a mackerel. Dumbstruck, Margie watched her filet the mackerel with one brisk swipe of the knife. Gayle turned the fish over and did it again, then tossed the remains out the door for the seagulls. She poured the water for tea and brought Margie a cup with the teabag still in it—peppermint, the same brand the sea had given her last week.

Margie said, "Do you swim all the way to land for supplies?"

"Now who would sell groceries to a naked woman carrying a wetsuit?" Gayle seemed utterly serious. "I've got a boat over at the harbor."

Gayle was accustomed to silence, of course, and as she rolled the filets in cornmeal and sliced some peaches while the fish fried, Margie felt no pressure to engage in idle talk. There was a question she had to ask, but she had a feeling the answer would not be simple, and perhaps there would be no answer at all, but just a reproving look from a woman who clearly placed great value on her privacy. Once, that woman had been a slightly fat girl with big shoulders who swam to fame on television one hot summer's day between Margie's sophomore and junior years in college, twenty-three years ago. If Margie let go of her assumptions about how the world worked, their meeting like this began to seem too inevitable, not the result of a mysterious accident, but a choreography. Margie was comfortable in this chair, and to be handed a plate of hot food that she had neither gathered nor cooked was a great luxury. She did not want to risk losing this sudden comfort by asking paranoid questions.

So she finally said, "Thank you for helping me."

Gayle managed to seem preoccupied with her food, but when she looked up she was still a little flushed. She didn't pretend like she thought Margie was referring to saving her from drowning. "You looked a bit hungry," she said. "But it seemed like you wanted to be alone."

They never directly mentioned the subject of the food from the sea, but that was because Margie thought she knew everything she needed to know: that Gayle had and would continue to feed her, and that she would not otherwise interfere or intervene with Margie's life. When Margie's fear lifted, as she sat eating the mackerel filet, she realized how afraid she had been, for much longer than just two months, how, in fact, it had been out of fear that she got herself pregnant in the first place. Now she knew that she would not die of hunger, or give birth alone.

Gayle offered Margie another slice of bread, and gave her a shirt and socks to wear, and asked if she should buy Margie some larger maternity clothes the next time she took her boat to the mainland. By eleven o'clock, she had heard with apparent equanimity the entire story of Margie's secret madness, and had commented, as though it were only common sense, "I guess your baby wants to be born here."

About herself she volunteered nothing, and it seemed only courteous not to inquire how a champion whose face had once appeared on cereal boxes had wound up in a cobbled-together shack on an island so remote it didn't appear on auto club maps. But when Margie cautiously mentioned Joe's visit to her campsite that day, Gayle's occasionally expressive face hardened. "Joe's the kind of man who'd strip off and incinerate his own skin if he thought it would make him more like everybody else."

Years, perhaps even a lifetime of bad blood, lay behind that bitter declaration. In Somerville, a city of apartments, people stayed for a few years, and if anything irritated them, they simply moved on.

Margie had forgotten what hatred was like. She managed to say, "Well, I hardly know him, of course, but he just struck me as being rather dull."

"Yes," Gayle said venomously. "Exactly. Pathologically ordinary, that's Joe."

"Is he the reason you don't live with the others, by the harbor?"

Gayle said after a moment, "No, I can deal with Joe. But I'm just too queer for the island folks. I don't belong with them anymore."

The mattress of layered oriental rugs was much more comfortable than Margie's air mattress, which lately she had found difficult to inflate, since the breathlessness of late pregnancy had set in. She awoke at dawn and went out to pee in the rocks, and as soon as she got a good look at the shoreline she knew exactly where her own camp lay in relation to Gayle's. But she felt no desire to rush back to the increasingly awkward cook fire, the tent she could just barely crawl into, the sleeping bag she could no longer zip up. She stood in the cold wind, thinking, but she did not have to think for very long. The shack was all but invisible even in plain sight. A simple comfort waited behind its camouflage. Margie went back inside, and shut the door.

Gayle stirred among the blankets, with her red-brown hair in a tangle and her shirt rucked up to her armpits. Margie put her hands on bare skin and stroked up to Gayle's lush, flannel-framed breasts. Gayle caught her breath and mumbled, her words thick with sleep, "You don't know what you're—"

"Oh god, your skin!"

"My skin?" she repeated, groggy and strangely startled.

Her skin smelled like the ocean, but she was warm and soft and quickly ceased her incoherent protests. Her hair had seaweed in it, and her whole body tasted of salt. Margie tasted the length and breadth of her. Between them, the infant rested peacefully in its little sea.

That day, Gayle helped Margie to collapse her tent and pack away her camping gear, and Margie moved into the shack. Neither one of them had ever lived with another person, but Margie found she could put up with almost anything if that meant she could lie on the cushions of the simple driftwood bench with her feet up. The energy of early pregnancy had evaporated, and Margie found the smallest effort exhausting. Gayle went to the mainland and returned with desperately needed larger-sized maternity clothing and some ice cream, which had stayed firm in the ice chest on the long journey from the grocery store, and a fresh supply of batteries for the radio, and a half dozen more classics in paperback. She wouldn't take Margie's money.

Gayle spent almost every day from dawn to dark making her solitary living from the sea. She gave her catch to the bread-baking woman's husband, who, during the mackerel run daily hauled everyone's fish to the mainland in his big boat, in exchange for a portion of the take. Sometimes, though, when Margie woke up in the morning, Gayle's wetsuit would be gone, and Margie knew that Gayle was in the sea, not on it.

On one of those days, Margie awoke from a long nap to the bizarre sensation of the baby practicing a flutter-kick against her ribs. The small, windowless room was faintly lit by a red light, which seeped in between the boards. The battery-powered radio murmured news of a world so distant Margie could hardly make any sense of it. Margie got awkwardly and heavily to her feet and opened the door. The loud crashing of the waves told her it was high tide. There was a chill in the air, and when she glanced over at the nearby woods, she saw a hint of red among the leaves of the sugar maples. Was that just the red sunlight, or was autumn already so close? What was the date? What had she done with her watch?

The waves crashed. In the moment of silence that followed, Margie thought she heard a voice calling. She started hastily down the narrow path. Gayle was not usually so late on the days she went swimming. There was another silence, and she heard the voice again, calling, "Margie!" But it was not Gayle's voice. More slowly and more carefully now, for the pregnancy had utterly confounded her sense of balance, Margie made her way down to the shore. At a distance, a square figure wandered the rocks, shouting her name.

"Joe!" she yelled. "What the hell is the matter?"

He heard her, and turned, and hurried toward her. "Thank God," he said. "Your tent was gone and—I didn't know what to think."

"I moved my camp," she said. "I told you, I need to be alone." He looked at her, taking in her dramatic shape, her backward tilt, her legs, straddled like a sailor's upon an unreliable deck. "How far along are you, anyway?"

Margie gazed at him, baffled. He had become as incomprehensible as the radio news. "How far along what?"

"How many months? When are you due?"

"What? Oh." After a bit of effort, she managed to get her hands into her pockets. She should have brought her jacket out with her; she was standing in a cold wind. "I've kind of lost track, I guess." Then she realized how strange that would sound to someone who was accustomed to pregnant women brooding over every week of development, hauling ultrasound pictures around to show their relatives, reading baby books and pasting yellow duckies on the bedroom wall.

Joe's face was suffused with hectic light. "You can't have your baby on the island."

"Why not? You were born here, weren't you?"

He looked at her blankly for a moment, as if her simple question were too convoluted for him to answer. Then he said, seriously, "There's things an outsider don't know about this place."

"Such as what?" she asked impatiently. Joe reminded her of nothing so much as a sixteen-year-old trying to explain why cruising around all night had been more important than writing an overdue paper on *Hamlet*.

"The seals."

The waves thundered suddenly, close by, and wind-carried spray chilled Margie's skin. Gayle had told her that the seals never come ashore on Skerry Island because they remembered having been hunted long ago. Gayle often made statements that suggested she had a rather eccentric view of the world, but Margie was hardly in a position to criticize. Joe, on the other hand, was the last person she would have expected to turn superstitious. Margie said, "In evolutionary terms, seals are just dogs that learned to swim."

"I'm talking about a different evolution," Joe said. "I'm talking about the seals that followed the Scots across the sea when they settled here. The kind that ought to be extinct—"

There was a silence. Margie said briskly, "Well, I really don't see the relevance—" Then she noticed his face, and stopped. She had only before seen an expression like that on a witness to a recent gruesome auto accident. "What is the matter with you?"

"Gayle," he said.

Margie turned, and saw that Gayle had risen out of the ocean like Aphrodite, and stood knee deep in water, naked, with her wetsuit under her arm. "Well, hello, brother," she said. "What brings you to this end of the island?"

"I'm not your stinking brother!"

"Stinking cousin, then," she said amiably.

Joe seemed to lean toward her, like a dog about to bite, while simultaneously recoiling from her nudity. Riveted, Margie struggled not to laugh. "You did this to her!" he shouted.

Gayle said mildly, "I got the girl, if that's what you mean."

His head jerked, and he turned on Margie the horrified stare she had always feared. Folding her hands across the belly, she felt the baby give an idle kick. "Yes," she confirmed, and felt a giddy rush of euphoria.

"But you don't know," he said. "You don't know what she is—"

Margie said, "I do strongly suspect that she might be a lesbian." The waves crashed.

Gayle uttered a snort of laughter. "There's not a thing you can do here, brother—cousin. Go home to the house you stole from me—go home to your warm, safe little fire and your two television stations. You've gotten everything you ever wanted, so go home and enjoy your little life."

Breathing heavily, as though her contempt had struck him a physical blow, Joe stood swaying. Then, he turned and said weakly, reaching for the arm that Margie hastily snatched out of reach, "Come with me, please. You have no idea what she's capable of."

Gayle was a dark, still figure, her shape defined by the writhing, vivid sea.

Margie said, "Don't be ridiculous." She saw him give up, a physical movement, almost like collapse. He walked away.

Without speaking, Gayle and Margie watched him travel toward the little bastion of house and harbor, where even the boats were anchored. Margie felt an impulse to make a joke, but Gayle's silence was too profound, too strange. Her shadowed face had an unsettling expression: not angry or distant, but simply alien; an expression utterly undomesticated.

Margie said, "Let's go in." She wanted the light of the lantern, the interplay of clever voices on National Public Radio. "We'll have some corn and peaches with our fish."

Gayle nodded, distant. From across the restless water, voices seemed to call: Gayle, Gayle, Gayle. She turned and looked out to sea. "A storm is coming. Do you hear the seals?"

"I'm afraid I haven't really listened to the weather reports."

Gayle abruptly took Margie's hand; her skin was cold and wet, but she did not seem chilled. "Corn and peaches," she said. "Sounds good."

When Margie's contractions began, Gayle was out in the ocean. Margie went down to the beach to look for her, and got herself trapped there, lying among the frosty stones as the contractions washed over her like the sea washing over the beach. October had arrived all of a sudden, and now a bitter wind blew across open ocean, all the way from the Arctic. The trees crowded beyond the beach, shivering in their scarlet costumes. The ocean crashed into shore, and the spray seemed to freeze in the air, suffusing the light with glowing particles of ice. Margie felt lifted out of the cold, out of herself. The ocean drew back, then came rushing forward again, and drew back, now leaving behind a half dozen visitors to land. The seals undulated out of the water, humping their bodies across the stones. More arrived behind them. They surrounded her: gray as salt-aged cedar, speckled with bits of white and black, earless, with deep, human eyes. They enclosed her and ended her solitude, making her one of them. She lay fearless in their midst as the tide of contractions washed over her.

On a bitter beach, surrounded by the seals, Margie felt the baby break free of its harbor. The seal beside her rolled onto its side and Gayle emerged naked from its belly. The living flesh that had enveloped her fell slack, like an empty costume. She carried the seal skin into the rocks where it would be secure, and returned a woman, though her eyes were still the eyes of a seal. She sat beside Margie, holding her hand as the contractions, nearly continuous now, rolled across her like waves herded before a storm wind. She told her a story:

> Many years ago, an island girl found an injured seal in the harbor, and she began to feed him fish stolen from her father's nets. The island people had long since forgotten that the fin folk were their kin, but still, the selkie came to trust the girl so that he dared to drop his skin, and the girl came to love him, so that one day she turned up pregnant. When her child was born a selkie, she would not give her daughter to the sea, even though the father came for her. Out of revenge, perhaps, he seduced the island girl's sister, and she also bore a selkie child. Both mothers hid their children's sealskins away, and the entire island conspired to forget that they were selkie children, though I suppose that in their dreams the old ones still remember. The two children grew up in the same house, both of them loving the sea, and—this is the part you know—the girl became a competitive swimmer for a time. Still, her heart yearned for the island, and she felt that part of her was missing, though she did not fully understand why, until one day she came home for her mother's funeral and found the sealskins hidden away in the attic.
>
> By then, she and her half brother were the last of their family alive. She put on her skin and went home to the sea, but he built a bonfire on the beach and burned, not just his skin, but his soul to ashes. He hates me because he hates himself, and I hate him for his cowardice. So we have been enemies for twenty years.

But the choice I made was a lonely one, Margie. The seals do not remember that they once were human, and the humans don't remember that they once were seals. Me, I am alone in both worlds: on land or in sea, I am the only selkie. I know now what moved my father to get his children on these island women: human sperm will not kindle in me, and with seals I am fertile but only to bear seals. In one of my many skins, I am a man, and I thought what I did would be no different from what a sea urchin does, when he sends his sperm out upon the waters, to find an egg or die. Margie, I am your baby's father.

Margie uttered a shout, for the seal child was emerging: sleek and soft, with ancient, gentle eyes. As it broke loose from her, her old English-teacher self enveloped her. Smothered in this heavy and unyielding skin, she struggled, but she fit the skin so easily and it felt so safe and familiar that she quickly succumbed to it. I am myself again, she thought, and saw the seal child in Gayle's embrace, and she screamed with horror and could not stop screaming.

Going mad and running away to a remote island for five months, pedestrian though it had seemed at the time, began to seem rather lurid and romantic in retrospect. Like with most lurid romances, the appeal of it was a mystery to outsiders. So Margie, now an outsider to herself as she lay in Gayle's shack recovering from childbirth, considered the past months with a bewildered embarrassment. What in the world had come over her? Periwinkles and sea lettuce for breakfast? She could not imagine how she could have been so contented in this shabby and most unsanitary shack. And as for Gayle, had she always been so reserved?

Gayle scarcely left the shack. She kept the fire burning, produced food, changed diapers, and heated water for baths. Margie slept, nursed the red-haired baby, and sang to her sleepily, a lullaby Tennyson had embedded in a longer poem:

> Wind of the western sea,
> Low, low, breathe and blow,
> Wind of the western sea!

When she was awake, she talked about the spare bedroom in her apartment, which she'd paint and fill with baby furniture, now that she was herself again.

Gayle was cooking the laundry on the stovetop, stirring it with a wooden spoon and said, almost inaudibly, "There is so much you don't seem to remember."

Of course, the entire birth was a haze to Margie now, a hallucinatory memory that included peace and fear but not pain. Gayle had been there, though, she remembered that clearly, putting the baby into Margie's arms, saying, "Look, there's nothing wrong with her; she's perfect. Let's get you both inside."

There had been something wrong with Gayle's face, though. Margie shook her head, unable to remember what had been wrong. "It's a blur," she admitted. "But it's over now, and everything's fine."

The baby uttered a squawk in her basket by the fire, and Gayle bent over and picked her up. "What, hungry again?" she said to the baby. Her face seemed unutterably sad.

"You will come back to Somerville with me," Margie said. "I've got plenty of room, and I'll help you find a job—"

Gayle said, "I think you should name her Ianthe."

Margie was surprised; she would never have expected that Gayle would be versed in Greek mythology. "Because she was born on the beach?" she said.

"Because she is a daughter of the sea," said Gayle.

Margie said, "Isn't it best if we return to the mainland as soon as we can, before the winter storms? I'm sure I should bring her to a doctor, get a birth certificate. . . . And I should call my mother, for heaven's sake—she probably thinks I've dropped off the face of the earth."

Gayle said, "But a nor'easter is bearing down on us right now, and it'll be a few days before it'll be safe to make the crossing." Gayle brought the snuffling baby to Margie. Gayle's eyes and the baby's eyes were the same: a blue so dark the iris almost disappeared. The sperm donor also had blue eyes and red hair; Margie had chosen him specifically for that unusual coloring, and because he was an athlete. It was indeed remarkable that Margie's prepartum mania had brought her to this island, to be befriended by this woman who looked so much like the child.

Margie said, "Why are you so sad?"

"I'm not sad," Gayle said. "To have a child is such a gift. How could anyone be sad?"

At dawn on the day they would be leaving, Margie awoke to a strange sensation of emptiness and silence. Their gear lay in a pile by the door, covered with a tarp lest the storm wind blow rain in through the cracks as was its habit, ready to be hauled to where Gayle's boat waited in the harbor. Sunlight gleamed in the cracks; the sun was well risen. Margie sat up in bed and called, "Gayle?"

The ocean, still turbulent from the storm now passed, crashed upon the stones. The baby made no sound in her basket. Margie crawled over to the warm place by the stove, and found the basket empty, except for Gayle's Olympic gold medal, laid there deliberately like a payment or a message. Besides the baby and Gayle's wetsuit, nothing else was missing, not even the baby's blanket or the box of disposable diapers.

Panicked, Margie dressed in haste and went out into the cold sunlight, but no voice returned her shout, and no one moved among the trees or along the shore. Inside the shack again, she threw a few things into the pink bucket: diapers, the baby's blanket, a first-aid kit. She set off, almost running, along the shore to the harbor, but she tired quickly and soon could scarcely walk. In the hour it took her to follow the island shoreline to the settlement, Gayle had surely journeyed far out to sea, and the baby would get hypothermia in this bitter wind.

She found Joe down at the harbor, working on his boat in dry dock. He didn't have to look at the cluster of bobbing boats moored offshore to be able to answer Margie's question. "No, she ain't been here. Her boat broke its mooring during the storm and washed up on the rocks." He pointed at the lobster boat that lay crazily tilted upon the shore near the harbor entrance, deposited there by the strong winds and storm tide. "It might still be seaworthy, but it'll take the whole town to get it back in the water."

"Joe, she's taken the baby."

Joe said, "And now you're surprised."

"She must still be here on the island, somewhere."

"She took her skin with her, didn't she?"

"She's not swimming with a baby! In this rough sea! Unless she's stolen a boat, she's still on the island."

Joe looked as shocked as Margie's students would have looked if she had uttered an obscenity at the chalkboard. "Steal a boat? Steal a boat?"

"Are you going to help me find them or not? For god's sake, Joe, I gave birth not six days ago."

Joe put his hands in his pockets and looked grimly out to sea. "All right. But you listen, Margie . . ."

She wasn't listening, though. She was a high school English teacher; she could tune out almost anything. Later, she would try to remember what he had said, and to what she had consented, but her memory was like a muted television show. She could see Joe's mouth move, but no sound came out. Instead, she heard her own impatient thoughts: Why had Gayle walked out on her like this, and what did she want with the baby? What was she planning to feed her; with what would she diaper her? If she had some kind of problem with raising the child in a fully furnished room equipped with modern electricity, why hadn't she simply said so? What did Gayle want from her? Surely Gayle had not expected Margie to remain mad forever.

It was a gorgeous day, but cold. Margie managed to trail Joe halfway around the island, though she could no longer manage to climb the rocks, to cling to their slippery surfaces while the ocean covered her with its bitter rain, peering over and around the places where ocean meets stone, searching for some sign. Why Joe was so convinced that they would find Gayle and the baby here at the water's edge, Margie couldn't imagine, but she finally gave up the argument when he turned on her and shouted, "Do you think I don't know my own cousin's queer ways? Do you want my help or don't you?" Margie sat beside the trail, which was scarcely wider than a single foot, and waited for Joe to come back. She had never in her life waited for a man before.

She felt a dull pain in her heart. Her breasts ached, and she knew that more than enough time had passed for the baby to freeze to death. Numbly, she waited, and Joe came, and they walked some more, then he went down to the shore to search again, and she waited again. The sun was setting, and here on the windward side of the island the cold cut to the bone.

Once, she had almost loved this stalwart, ungenerous island, but she could not remember that now, no more than she could remember how the sea had once courted her favor. She only knew that she had been a fool, and perhaps had been made a fool of. Oddly, she longed for a policeman, though it surely would be mortifying to have to explain what had happened.

On this side of the island, the wind-driven waves crashed into unyielding stone with shattering explosions of sound. Numbed by cold and misery, Margie was slow to notice the sound of voices, almost inaudible beneath the crash of waves. She came to her feet and ran confusedly through the rocks. Was that Joe's voice, or Gayle's? Or was it the barking of seals carried on the wind? And then she teetered above the shoreline, thwarted by an impassable ledge.

The light of the setting sun set the maple leaves ablaze behind her, and the ocean aflame before her. Despite all this garish light, the long shadows of encroaching night lay across the shoreline, and the writhing shapes in the water shifted and changed so that Margie could make no sense of them. Perhaps that was Joe, gesturing grandiosely, knee deep in water. Perhaps that was Gayle he struggled with, or perhaps they were only senseless shadows. Perhaps they were seals, all of them, and there was nothing human down there at all. Perhaps that was a gun shot, or perhaps merely a wave crashing. And now the sky went dark, and the dark shapes she might have seen, flailing or fleeing or spasming in death, were gone. The waves drew back, the ocean gave a sigh, the seals fell silent, and nothing was left.

doi:10.1300/5642_12

Isis in Darkness

Christopher Barzak

She called herself Isis, though her real name was Iris, and her last name was even worse. Smith. Nothing doing. How do you wake up with a name like that and be happy for the next sixteen hours? Add a crooked front tooth, a habit of chewing your fingernails, a falling-down drunk father, and an uncanny inability to flunk tests. It couldn't get worse, or else it could. She tried not to think of what might be worse.

So Isis it was once she reached the city and found herself sleeping in an abandoned church with several other squatters: Lola, Meph, and Rem. They were all kids, really. Isis at sixteen was the youngest. Lola and Meph were a few months older, but Rem was nearly eighteen and that first day he saw her as she stepped down from the bus, he had noticed the strands of light surrounding her, fine filaments of magic. She was an Orphyn, he realized immediately, and although Isis did not know what it meant to be an Orphyn at that moment, she had felt the effects of being one her entire life.

"You know it's bad luck to look like that around here," Rem said as he approached her. Isis looked from side to side. *Are you talking to me?* written across her eyes, her cheeks, her trembling bottom lip. "Yeah you," said Rem. He extended his hand.

Isis looked at it for a moment, but didn't shake. She felt no obligation to exchange pleasantries with a stranger. Especially one who came at you as if you already knew him. "Look like what?" she said instead. And before Rem could answer, she added, "Who the hell are you anyway?"

He liked that she knew enough to cop a front, but she was an amateur. Hustlers and pimps would have been on to her from that first exchange. "Like a farm girl lost in the city," he said, and she made a face.

"For your information, I'm from Columbus," said Isis, nose and eyebrows turned up. "Not farm country, I'd say. But that doesn't mean anything."

"Strike two," said Rem.

She nodded sarcastically. "I know, I know. I shouldn't tell you where I'm from, but it doesn't matter. You're not out to get me."

He grinned sly and stayed that way. Jutted his chin out, very macho: "You up for something to eat?"

"Famished," said Isis.

"Rem," said Rem.

"Isis," said Isis. "Nice to know you."

He picked up one of her bags and said, "This way."

They did not speak about the strangeness of their names. No explanation was necessary. Isis might look like one of the young ones who arrived without a clue about where they came from, but she had figured out enough on her own to realize she needed a new name.

Rem was impressed. He considered her over the rim of his water glass. She was talking about a father, a mother, vague figures with ominous auras surrounding them. She didn't look beat up, but sometimes—most often—a person is broken and bruised inside, not out. He suspected inside. When she smiled, she didn't show her teeth.

He could have remembered her, but he decided to let her tell him what she wanted, when she wanted.

"So," said Isis. "It was nice meeting you and all, and thanks for the coffee, but I've gotta fly."

"Where to?" said Rem.

"Still have to figure that out." Isis raised her eyebrows and blew a strand of hair out of her face. "I need to find a place to crash. What about shelters? Are they cool here?"

Rem shook his head. "I've got something better. You can squat where I live."

Isis winced. "I don't know. I wouldn't want to impose. Plus we barely know each other. You could be a creepy serial killer for all I know." She arched one thin eyebrow in mock suspicion.

"But you know better," said Rem. He held her stare.

She nodded, then looked down into her cup to hide her smile. Their waitress approached, slapped their bill on the table and walked away. Rem dug into the pockets of his army jacket. A moment later he pulled out a few dollars to pay.

"All right," said Isis. "I'll see what's up. No promises though."

"Never any promises," said Rem.

Here is the church, here is the steeple. Open the doors and here are the people.

Isis nodded as Rem introduced her to Lola and Meph. Even though she was scared, she forced a tight-lipped smile. Rem already felt good to her, and Lola appeared fairly normal—hair pinned up with blonde tendrils falling around her ears, black diamante glasses, denim jacket, knee-ripped jeans and worn-down kicks—but Meph was off center, just a little. He stood back from Isis by several feet, head lowered, hands stuffed in his pants pockets. His skin looked sweet and creamy, a caramel color. When she held her hand out to him, he jumped backward, almost losing his balance and falling. He caught the side of an empty pew, though, and pulled himself back up. As Meph grabbed hold of the pew, Isis noticed his hands were wrapped in dirty bandages, all the way up his fingers, like a mummy. She felt a hand on the small of her back. It was Rem's. His look told her, "Later."

"This is Isis," Rem told the others. "She's going to crash with us for a while."

"Hey, Isis," Lola smiled. "I like your name."

The church was on the corner of Martin Luther King Jr. Boulevard, backed up against an abandoned warehouse. "We tried getting in there, too," Rem told Isis. "But it was already claimed."

"By who?"

"Ghosts," said Rem. "There was a fire there. About ten years ago. The folks working on the third floor were trapped inside."

The church had faded lettering above the arched front entry outside, which Rem said never to use. St. Peter and Paul's blah, blah, blah. The stained-glass windows were mostly still intact. Rocks or gunshots or fists had busted a few out, though. The pews still lined up straight across from each other; an aisle carpeted red stretched to the altar. The walls and ceiling were water-stained brown and yellow, molded over in dark corners. On the wall behind the altar, someone had spray-painted the words, "Orphyn Grove," in an almost calligraphic style. "Lola," said Rem. "She's good with graffiti."

"Why does she spell Orphyn that way?" Isis asked. "With a 'y' instead of an 'a'?"

"We all do that," said Rem. "That's how we spell it. 'Cause we're not regular orphans. You know that."

"You mean not straight," said Isis. Rem nodded.

"Yeah. There are women and there are womyn. There are boys and there are bois. Girls and grrls. Same here. We're orphyns, not orphans."

Isis shrugged.

Rem shrugged her shrug off. "It helps sometimes," he said. "When you're feeling alone."

Isis said, "Whatever works. But I've always been alone, except for my father."

"Your mother?" asked Rem.

"Long gone," said Isis. "I can still remember her face, though."

"Good," said Rem. "Don't forget that."

Rem showed Isis where she could crash. It was a small room in the basement, one of the old Sunday school rooms, with low wooden bookcases built along the perimeter of the walls. Except for dust, the shelves were empty. Isis beamed when she saw them. She wished she could have brought her books with her, but they would have only weighed her down in her flight. She told Rem as much.

"You like to read?" Rem asked, a hint of incredulity in his voice.

"I love to read," said Isis. "It's where things are best."

"Yeah," he said. "I know what you mean. I wish sometimes I could live in books."

"You can," Isis said. "At least for a little while."

They stared at each other, not saying anything. Then Rem snapped their silence by telling Isis about Meph. "It's his hands," said Rem. "He can't touch people with them. They hurt people."

"How do you mean, hurt?"

"I mean, their skin might burn, or open up. Like deep cuts."

"Are you for real?" said Isis.

Rem narrowed his eyes and snorted. "Are you? Come on. You know you're not the only one."

"I don't know what you're talking about," said Isis.

"Yes you do. You know perfectly well. You're not weird here, Isis. You don't have to be afraid."

She shook her head, though. "I don't know what you're talking about."

Over the next few days, Rem helped her get settled. They stole pieces of discarded carpet from the dumpster behind the remnant store, carried home furniture left out on sidewalks. A trip to the Salvation Army provided Isis with more clothes—nothing special, but warm and wearable, very practical: old sweaters and a jacket and pants. Rem gave her street pointers, who to talk to, who was a Nobody, how to avoid the cops. "What do you mean, a Nobody?" asked Isis.

"You know," said Rem. "Nobodies. Stay away from them, or they'll make you a Nobody too."

"Someone has been following us for a while," said Isis.

Rem nodded. "He's a Nobody," he said, daring to look at the guy who stood on the sidewalk on the other side of the street, brandishing stares at each other like nine millimeters. "Best to stay away from him," said Rem, his face suddenly closing.

"Why?" Isis asked.

"He's straight," said Rem.

"Straight?"

"You know," said Rem. "Not Orphyned."

Isis said, "There's more you're not saying, but that's alright. I'll leave it."

"Good," said Rem. "Thanks for that."

Before the end of the week, her room looked like a room, like someone real and alive was living there. No longer a musty room in a church basement where children once sat, answering questions by rote: "Who made you?" said the Sunday school teacher. "God made me," they would repeat. Isis remembered that. She remembered how

it had always felt wrong to her. *Who made me?* It was a tricky question.
You wanted to say, God made me, and feel the truth of it. She tried.
She tried to fake it even. But a dark guilt crowded her body whenever
she pretended to those origins. Finally, after years of feeling wrong-
souled, she had relented. "I don't know who made me," she had said
to her image in her bedroom mirror. She had been eleven. She had
cried, "I don't know who made me," and sobbing, melted to her
knees, covering her face with her hands.

It doesn't matter, she thought now. She didn't need to know where
she came from anymore, what to believe. Only to believe in herself.
Her mother had left her and her father years and years ago, when Isis
was eight. She had packed while her husband was at the bar and told
Isis to be good and go to sleep. She tucked her in. "Where are you going, Mommy?" Isis had asked.

"To get Daddy. I'll be right back."

But her father returned later without her mother. Between the two
of them, they figured out that they had been abandoned.

At fifteen, Isis had quit school and started running drugs with her
boyfriend, Howard, who was twenty-three, beautiful, and arrogant.
When Howard was arrested for trafficking, Isis decided to leave him.
She felt safe to leave him while he was locked up. Several months
later, after waiting tables for tips only, she realized she had been leaving a lot of things and decided it might be a good idea to leave town as
well. When she looked out at the streets, at the low buildings of the
college campus, a place she'd never be except as a panhandler maybe,
she thought she'd have better luck in a city. In a city, she could lose
herself in the dark of its streets. No one cared who you were or what
you did when there were too many people to keep track of.

And now here was Lola, helping her to arrange things real nice.
The rocking chair in the far corner, the rug cuttings thrown into a
pyramid pattern on the floor. "But these walls," said Isis. "It'll be like
living in a vanilla box."

"Oh," said Lola. "That's no problem. What color are you thinking
you'd like?"

"Why? Do you know where we can pinch paint?"

"No," said Lola. "We don't have to steal anything."

"Blue," said Isis. "Midnight blue. Maybe some yellow and white to make some stars. That would be cool."

Lola said, "Yeah, I like the way you think," grinning, and casually slid her hands over the white walls, continuing her banter. As she moved around the room's perimeter, the walls began to change from white to light blue, to deep midnight. "I've always loved celestial patterns," said Lola, circling the room once more, patting each wall with her fingertips. Yellow and white stars bloomed beneath her touch. When she was finished, she said, "Do you like?"

Isis nodded, in awe of Lola's quiet magic. "Yes," she said. "It feels right."

"Hurray me!" said Lola. "Meph is always complaining that our room never looks the same."

"The two of you are together?"

"Yeah," said Lola. "For a year now. We were both living under the Carson Street Bridge before that. Before we met Rem."

"Ugh. That sucks. I mean, living under a bridge."

"You do what you have to," said Lola. She crossed the room and stopped in the doorway. "If you need anymore help, just give me a shout out."

"Thanks," said Isis, and Lola left. She had had a moment of wanting to reveal some of her secrets to the girl, but Lola hadn't seemed interested. Back when she was with Howard, when he had found out, he had made constant use of her. "My security alarm," he bragged to his cohorts. And when the police busted him, he had shouted into empty air, "You little bitch, you set me up!" Isis had been standing on a nearby rooftop, out of sight. After this she disappeared quickly, quietly, to another side of town, before leaving town altogether.

When Isis arrived, it had been summer. But as she moved into the Orphyn Grove and became acclimated to her new home, weeks passed, and before she knew it, autumn had come to the city, changing the leaves from green to red and yellow, just as Lola had changed the white walls to a night sky. The wind held an earthy scent, sweet and smoky. Night came earlier. October's bittersweet lullaby whispered through the streets.

In her basement room in the abandoned church, Isis shivered a little. She had enough blankets, but the cold seeped in and stayed the night. Rem "found" two small space heaters, but they had no electricity, so the next item to seek out, they all decided, was a generator, or maybe kerosene heaters. They needed heat. "What did you do last year?" Isis asked.

"We burned wood in a barrel," said Rem. "But the smoke brought notice and, after a while, cops came to check it out. We had to split up and go to shelters for a few weeks. Some of the shelters make you call your parents or give them personal information. Busybodies, you know, trying to put you back where you're trying to get away from. We have to find another way this year."

She liked the way his hair fell over his eyes, brown and floppy. The way he'd lift his right hand to push it away from his face. The way he moved smoothly across a room, never hesitating, unlike poor Meph, who often jerked and jigged his way from one point to another. Rem had an uncanny ability to understand her, and when she spoke he would listen. Really listen. He would hold her stare like he had the first day she met him, and her words seemed to flow in direct connection, without any loss of meaning. He rarely argued with her. Sometimes she wanted him to argue with her. Mostly because arguing was what she'd gotten used to. But here was Rem, listening without undermining her thoughts on her own life. And he never pried. On the streets, private knowledge remained sacred. You shared it at your own risk, and when someone opened up to you, it was a gift. An unexpected invitation to intimacy in a world where intimacy might be your undoing. "Never share your real name," Rem had told Isis. "Except for with the people who prove to be family."

She had not told anyone her real name yet, not even Rem.

She panhandled with Lola. She'd never done it before. She didn't like doing it. But she didn't have an address, so couldn't apply for jobs. She didn't have any money to bring herself up either, and even if she did, she was sixteen. A noncitizen. She couldn't rent a room even if she'd had all the money in the world.

Meph and Rem played hunters; Isis and Lola, the gatherers. They would return sometimes with stereo equipment, and once a car, which was gone the next day. Isis didn't ask where they'd gotten it, or to where it had disappeared. None of my business, she told herself. Better to not know. Ask strangers for money and thank you, thank you, thank you. Tell them they have helped a poor soul.

The money she and Lola collected went toward buying necessities. Food, clothing, blankets, a used futon mattress for Isis, who had been sleeping on carpet remnants for a month and a half. The money didn't go far, but they spread it as thin as possible. The money from Rem's and Meph's "finds" helped to buy two propane heaters, and a store of fuel. "No shelters this year," Rem told them. "This year we all stay together."

Toward the end of October, Rem announced they were all going to a party. Lola clapped like a little girl and said, "Just in time, just in time. I thought I would die of boredom." Meph hugged her from behind, lacing his arms around her waist, resting his chin on her shoulder.

"Is it a Halloween party?" Isis asked.

Rem said, "Something like that." He grinned but played coy.

"What should we wear?" Isis asked. "I mean, is this a costume party?"

"No," said Lola. "It's a come-as-you-are. That's the thing. That's the great thing about this party, Isis. Come as you are. Us? We don't need to dress up, right?"

Isis nodded politely. She wasn't sure how to take their avoidance of her questions. It was just a *party,* she thought. What's the big deal? Why all the mystery?

But mystery she was to Rem and Lola and Meph. Since she had moved into the Orphyn Grove, she had not revealed anything personal about herself, except for a few remarks about an old boyfriend, drugs, her father, the missing mother, and how she liked to read. Nothing spectacularly intimate. Just the facts, thank you. In return, the others reserved their own private stories. They did not dole out friendship lightly, although they would come running to help Isis with even the smallest details of her new life.

On the night of the party, they collected at the front of the church, near the altar, and together left from there. Rem led them through the city streets, through alleys and through the subway system. At various places—a bathroom on Lexington; a phone booth on Broadway; a bulletin board in a Laundromat—they found clues to the place to which they would next proceed. "Rave codes," Meph murmured to Isis in the laundromat. It was one of the few times he'd ever spoken directly to her; she turned to him and nodded appreciatively.

They arrived at a building in the Warehouse District and climbed the steps of a docking platform, facing the riverside. The city gleamed on the other side of the river. An inverted image of yellow city lights glimmered on the slow oily surface of the water, the shadows of skyscrapers etched into the darkness. Music boomed on the other side of the warehouse door. Rem knocked. A slit slid open. Two eyes looked out. A hoarse voice said, "Password."

Rem said, "Going home."

The door opened and the man who stood behind it welcomed them inside. He was large everywhere, muscles ballooning his black T-shirt and jeans. He wore a goatee but he was bald on top, gleaming. He handed the four of them glow sticks on rope cords and told them to have a good time, to not cause trouble. "No problem, Mac Daddy," said Rem, and they filed past him.

They came out into a large open area where once machinery of all sorts had hummed, producing tubing. Now the room was empty of industry. Now it was full up to its catwalks with people dancing to the beat of a trance-y techno, their glow sticks the main source of illumination. Isis asked, "Who are all of these people?"

Rem looked down at her and said, "Orphyns. It's All Hallow's Eve, Isis. Welcome home."

They danced. They ran around the warehouse like kids in an amusement park, saying hello to those they knew from the street. Noise numbed their eardrums. Voices came at them from every angle, muffled, as if they were underwater. Lola disappeared for half an hour, then reappeared on the dance floor with a broad grin on her face. She gestured for the others to follow her to the bathrooms, shaking her hips as she led the way. They followed. In the bathroom, with the music and noise thudding on the other side of the door, she held her hand out, palm up, producing six round tablets with smile faces imprinted on the flat sides. Rem said, "I hope you didn't pay too much for those."

"I've been saving," said Lola. "It's on me. Don't worry. It's Christmas."

"It's Halloween," said Isis.

Lola rolled her eyes. "Come on, Isis," she said. "You know what I mean."

Rem plucked his pills from the stash and swallowed them down with water from the sink faucet. Meph and Isis followed. They left the bathrooms together and entered the fray of dancers once more. Leaving the bathroom, Isis had to readjust her eyes again to the dark of the dance floor. The glow sticks lit the warehouse with an eerie greenish-blue light. Someone else, another Orphyn, glowed too. Her whole body surrounded with a soft yellow light. Her hair was white. Her hips were round and she curved in all the right places. She smiled with all of her teeth. Isis thought she looked like an angel. It reminded her too much of her own body. She had been dancing with Rem, but then she wasn't. She had stopped as she looked at this girl lit up by the light of her own body. "What's the matter?" Rem's voice came to her.

"Who is she?" Isis asked.

He looked around until he figured out who had caught Isis's gaze. "Pearl," said Rem, his voice flattening.

"She's beautiful," said Isis, and Rem's hands were on her hips, pulling her back to dance with him. She looked up into his dark eyes. "She's beautiful," she repeated.

"She's pretty," said Rem.

"I wish I looked like that," said Isis.

"Like what?"

"Like a goddess."

"You do," said Rem. He kissed her forehead and her cheeks.

Isis blushed but shook her head. "No, I mean pretty, Rem."

"But you *are* pretty," said Rem.

"Not like her," said Isis.

"No, not like her," said Rem. "You're a different kind of pretty."

"How?" Isis asked, laughter covering up her fear.

"You know," said Rem. "Pearl's pretty like you'd touch her and she'd disappear. You're different," said Rem. "You're solid."

She wasn't sure if that was a good thing or not, but she took it as a compliment, laughed and said, "Sure," and lay her head on his chest. The music beat fast, and so did his heart, but they moved slowly. Suddenly, something melted inside Isis's chest, her head, her heart, and she was up again, and so was Rem, and the music entered them, spreading through their bodies like tea from a bag. Their bodies moved without direction; the music, puppeteer strings controlling them. Lola and Meph danced a few feet away in the sea of half-lit faces. "Oh wow," said Isis. Her flesh hummed.

Rem said, "Am I losing you?"

"No, I'm here," she said. "This stuff is powerful. Wow," she said again. "Lola doesn't mess around, does she?"

Rem laughed, his head swaying to the rhythms, his hips rolling. He moved like a fish in water, fluid, darting this way and that.

An hour later, exhilarated but feeling a little crowded, they decided to leave the warehouse. Lola and Meph remained behind to dance the pills off together. As Isis left the dance floor, she saw Lola kiss Meph's bandaged hands as they danced in a dark corner, placing each cloaked fingertip against her lips. In the center of the dance floor, Pearl spun, a white-hot essence.

"Beautiful," Isis said, and then they were outside in the October night chill. The cold air hit Isis hard. The pill heated her insides, but her skin was more sensitive than ever. Goose bumps shivered all over her body. Rem draped his army jacket over her shoulders, slid his arm around her waist. She let him keep it there as they walked, dropping into a lazy rhythm.

Halfway home, though, she felt him tense as they came out from the underground. The man who Rem had warned her about—the Nobody, the straight, he had called him—stood on the corner opposite. He stepped down from the curbside and Rem whispered, "Turn around, we're running the opposite way."

Isis nodded. Slowly they turned, then both took off in a sprint. Isis looked over her shoulder once. Rem ran a few steps behind, looking over his shoulder also. Beyond Rem's shoulder, she saw the Nobody giving chase. Isis turned a corner, then another, and another, making sure Rem was behind her every so often, monuments and buildings and brick and mailboxes blurring beside her, until she was out of breath and heaving and lost, she was sure, and hoping that Rem would say they didn't need to run any longer.

He caught up to her a moment later, breathing hard. Their breath fumed, plumes steaming. They bent at their waists, hands braced against their thighs like runners. For a while, neither of them said anything. Finally Isis looked around and said, "Where the fuck are we?"

Rem looked around too, licking his lips. "Almost back at the docks," he wheezed.

"Did we lose him?" asked Isis.

Rem nodded. He pushed hair out of his eyes.

"All right then," said Isis. But she hesitated. She was going to say, "Start talking, Rem. Who was that guy?" Now she had the right to ask. Her life had been endangered due to some obscure past Rem shared with the man. But she couldn't bring herself to demand such knowledge when she had shared so little of her own.

Rem lifted his chin a little, said, "What? What were you going to say?" She shook her head.

Suddenly a phone rang. Rem looked around to find its source. The ringing split the misty night air, echoing through the alleys. He spotted the phone booth across the street and laughed at his being startled by it. "Let's go," he said, waving to Isis, and she shook her head again, no, nodding toward the phone.

"Answer it," she told him.

He squinted, puzzled by her insistence. When he realized she was serious, he jogged lazily across the street. The phone rang in its booth, but the phone itself hung limp on its cord, dangling. He picked it up, placing the receiver next to his ear.

"Hello? Rem?" a voice came through crisply. It was Isis. Rem looked across the street. She stood on the street corner, leaning against a brick wall, her hands stuffed deep into the pockets of his army jacket. Her mouth closed. "It's me," she said. "It's Isis. This is what I can do, Rem. This is what I can do."

He nodded, still holding her stare. Then he said, "He was this guy I once tried loving. But he's not comfortable with my memory, so he wants me gone."

"I know that already," said Isis.

"I know you already know," said Rem. "I wanted to tell you myself though."

"How did you know I knew?" Isis smiled, their wordplay on the phone now a game, an honoring of her revelation, and of his.

"Because I remembered when you figured it out," he said. "Just a few blocks ago, you figured it out. I just remembered you did that."

"What do you mean?"

Rem said, "That's what I can do. Remember. Other people's memories, not just my own."

"Then you'll always know the past. Even mine."

"Yes," he said. His voice grew quiet. "But only after the fact. When it's too late to do anything."

"That's like knowing nothing about nothing," said Isis.

He nodded. The receiver was starting to warm against his ear.

"That's okay," said Isis. "I can talk through doors, phone booths, even to air and rocks and water, and what good does it do me?" She laughed, but her mouth didn't open enough for the laughter to really live. "What good does changing the color of her hair, or her clothes, or the walls of my room do Lola? What good are Meph's hands? Nothing," said Isis. "We're a whole lot of nothing, and it's okay, right, Rem?"

Rem shook his head. "Let's go back to the church," he said, and hung up.

"First things first," Rem said as they entered the front room of St. Peter and Paul's. He lit a few half-melted candles on the altar. Then he sat down with his legs stretched in front of him. He gestured for Isis to do the same. "Right across from me," he told her. Isis sat, stretching her legs out like Rem. They placed the soles of their feet against one another and lay on their backs looking up at the darkness that filled the vaulted ceiling. Every so often, a drop of water fell from above, landing near Isis's ear.

"What are we doing, Rem?"

"Be quiet," he said. "And remember."

As he spoke, another drop fell from the cavernous dark above. Isis followed the path of its descent. White light trailed behind it, like the tail of a comet. A falling star, thought Isis, and as the drop landed, an explosion rang in her ears. A bright light flashed in the darkness, blinding her. When her vision returned, she saw her mother holding a baby. Then she *was* the baby, looking up into her mother's face, the high cheekbones, the earrings dangling, catching the light. She reached out with a chubby fist to hold the light, but it melted in her hands. Gathering itself into a tendril, the light slithered up the side of her arm and neck, then snapped backward like a whip and entered her right eye. There was no pain. When her vision cleared again, Isis stood in a circle of robed figures, hoods shrouding their faces in shadow. All around her, a city loomed. But this was not the city she knew. Not the one in which she now lived, nor the one she'd left behind. The buildings of this city rose out of the earth like slabs of stone, as if they had always been a part of the landscape. Like mountains, they looked as if they'd been grown. Soft yellow-white lights lit the streets, like luminous pearls, the source of their power a secret of the air itself. The figures surrounding Isis whispered in unfamiliar tongues. They sound sad, thought Isis. But she revised her initial reaction. No. Not sad. Serious. They were doing something important here. Religious maybe. Mystical even. She tried on as many words as she could think of, but none completely fit the feeling, and all seemed only partially right. She sighed in frustration and the robed figure sitting next to her put his hand on her shoulder. Isis flinched. She turned and the figure turned to face her. He pulled back his hood. It was Rem. He spoke in the same tongue as the others. She watched his lips move, his tongue flicking behind his teeth. His nostrils flared. Then he placed his hands on her ears and his words filled her.

"This is the circle where you were born, a long, long time ago," Rem began. "It is the circle of your ancestors. This is the circle your mother was born to, and you to your mother, and so will be your sons and daughters. You are not a lost thing. You no longer have to live in the dark. Look. Around us, you see the city where our people began. Behind you is the Cathedral of Stones, where we worshipped our gods and elders. Before you is the Sea of Ageon, where we fished and crossed to the Northerlands. It was in the Northerlands that our people separated. There we found the way into the world we now live in, and the group of our people who crossed over could not find the way back. We are still looking. Even now our people look for the way home. We call ourselves Orphyns, and so we are without fathers and mothers, but we were not abandoned. We have lost our family, but only because we could not find our way back. Here are the memories, the circle of life that waits daily for our return, the fire that burns in the center, warming their hopes that we will find our way back, and so we shall. As we find each other, we find our way home."

He leaned in and kissed her, filling her mouth the way his words filled her body. She kissed back, and as she pulled away said, "My name is Iris."

"My name is Michael," he said, "though here they call me the Rememberer."

She wrapped her arms around him and he leaned into her.

"Thank you," she said.

Then darkness crept in at the city borders. Within moments it devoured the streets, the people, the Cathedral of Stones, the circle. Rem's face gold leafed by firelight was the last thing Isis saw before darkness consumed her.

She woke to the sound of someone shouting, and her vision returned. She sat up from the cold floor, but Rem was already gone. "Rem?" she shouted. Outside, an explosion rang through the streets. Gunfire. Isis could distinguish that from similar sounds without any effort. Running drugs with Howard had prepped her so a gunshot no longer disturbed her. Before she would have flinched in fear. Now she simply got up, looking for a hiding place, an escape route.

A moment later, her senses gathered, she ran to the front of the church and peered out a hole in one of the stained glass windows. In the street outside, Rem kneeled, holding his side. A man fled around the corner with a gun gripped in his hand. The Nobody. The man Rem had tried to love. The Normal. He had found them after all. Isis wondered what could have transpired between them that could possibly make someone who loved you want to destroy you. It didn't make sense. But then she thought of her mother, her father. What could make a person who loved you leave? She had done it. She had left her father, a drunk—harmless and in need of care—and she had not looked back.

"Help," she screamed. "Meph! Lola! Someone! Rem's been hurt."

Before she reached him, Rem had slumped down on the street, curled into the fetal position. At his body, she knelt down and touched his shoulder. His face was turned away.

"Rem," she said, her voice a ragged whisper. "Rem, say something. Are you all right?"

He didn't respond, so she grabbed him by his army jacket and pulled him over so that he lay on his back. A groan escaped his grit-covered lips. His eyes remained closed. She saw the hole in his jacket then, stained black with blood oozing from where the bullet had entered. She pulled the jacket open, and tears sprang to her eyes. It was bad. He needed more help than she could give him.

She reached out, searching the wind and telephone wires and satellite signals in outer space and the thrum of electricity coursing beneath the surface of the city, until she found a connection with a woman answering calls for 911. "Someone's been shot," she told the woman, and gave the address of St. Peter and Paul's. "Hurry," she said. "He needs medical attention." The woman asked her to stay on the line, but Isis said, "I have to go. I'm sorry. I have to go."

She slipped her voice out of the woman's ear and returned it to her tongue. For a moment, she considered doing exactly what she had told the woman. Going. Leaving the scene. There would be questions she couldn't answer. They would return her to her father, put her in juvenile detention. They could find Meph and Lola and take them too. The whole family she had built. The whole family, she thought, would be separated. She couldn't bear it. Better to run away than be run away from.

But she swallowed that impulse, rejecting it. Rem needed her. Her mother had run away from her and her father. She had run away from her father and Howard and God as well. She felt bad about running away from her father, not bad at all about leaving Howard, and God? She felt on equal ground with Him. He'd done the same as she had. Run off and left everyone to their own devices. God was a runaway, too, she thought. Just like anyone. Just like everyone, thought Isis.

But she would not abandon Rem, she decided. Not like this. Not after she had found a place for herself, a space where she could recognize the people around her, and herself among them. She waited for what seemed like hours, but no help came. She imagined this was because the neighborhood she'd told them to come to was a lost section of the city where only the poor, the wretched, and the homeless lived. Things left behind. No need to hurry.

So she would do what she could to help keep Rem in this world, such as it was. Fumbling with the buttons of his shirt, she pulled back both sides and placed her ear against his chest. His heartbeat came back weakly. She slipped her voice into his head, calling. "Rem," she called. "Rem, are you there?" But the only thing that came back was the slow hum of his neural pathways. A flat line of thought.

Since Rem's voice could not be found, she spoke inside his body. She spoke to his cells, to the sinews of his muscles, to the artery the bullet had grazed. "You have to get better," she told the artery.

"I'm working on it," the artery said.

"Remember how you fit together," she told his body. "Remember."

And the body worked slowly but surely at trying to keep Rem inside. Isis kept her voice steady, filling him with her words as a guide. When he woke again, she'd be waiting. The only people she'd run from now would be those who would keep her from him. She needed him. The Orphyns needed him. To remember for them. There would be Orphyns until the world ended, who needed those stories. Until we find home again, she thought. Until it was safe to forget again, she'd stay.

The sound of an ambulance approaching grew loud in her ears.

doi:10.1300/5642_13

Touch

M. Kate Havas

"I dare you to kiss that tree." Chelsea giggled, her cheeks tinted red from alcohol and firelight as she crouched down among the discarded aluminum. A nearly dead cigarette burned between her fingers. "Like, with tongue."

Shrieks of "That's too easy!" and "Eww, gross!" came from the other five players, all reclined in various states of dress around the fire pit. Shadows flickered over skin, illuminating a mixed company of young faces.

"Come on, Chels, she'll catch something!" This set off a new chorus of laughing protests over Chelsea's lack of imagination and disregard for hygiene.

"Just have her get naked." There was a thud as Trinny McAlister, the recipient of the offending dare, smacked at a nearby boy with a dirty baseball cap emblazoned with their high school mascot. She got to her feet with all the grace of a birthing elephant, too buzzed on cheap brew to care.

"S'okay." Trinny flipped her dark hair over her shoulder, placing a hand on her hip in a mockery of bravado. The flamboyant gesture set her off balance and she tittered. "Wait . . . which tree again?" She bit back a grin, crushing a knuckle childishly against her teeth.

Chelsea shrugged. "Doesn't matter."

Trinny tottered over to an inviting-looking candidate, one mostly free of the Spanish moss and poison ivy so omnipresent in rural Georgia, and she slid an arm around the trunk then drew up a leg to rest on the base. The oak tree was so large she could barely extend her limbs around the trunk's girth. Trinny tilted her head against the bark, feeling it scratch her skin. "Just so y'all know, I think this is really really dumb."

"Kiss it." Chelsea ordered, rocking forward onto her knees and scraping out a cigarette on the sandy dirt.

"Pretend it's Ryyyannn." One of the other girls mocked, and Trinny stuck her tongue out, wagging it a little to make her point again. She supposed she should be grateful she didn't have to do anything more embarrassing. Trinny knew better than to ever pick Truth. She guessed her friends figured her choice a reflection of personality: up for anything, love for the spotlight. What they didn't know was that she just didn't want to answer questions. She could just imagine it:

"Okay, Trinny, what's your deepest secret?"

And, bound by a teenage sense of the sacred trust of Truth or Dare, as well as a liberal dose of Gentleman Jack, she would have to answer: *"Well, guys, Ryan's nice and all, but I think I'd really rather kiss girls."*

Which would go over like the Titanic and the iceberg. Trinny sighed, then gave her best impression of a sultry gaze and brought her free hand up to stroke the bark. She leaned in and pressed her lips against the rough surface, feeding off the laughter and catcalls from her friends urging her to make it a performance.

"Hey Ryan, the tree's getting more action than you do!"

"Yeah baby, do it like that!"

From the corner of her eye she could see her boyfriend look a little abashed, not watching her spectacle, as if embarrassed by her actions. Just to spite him, she renewed her attentions, then paused, her head suddenly swimming with something richer than alcohol. A strange prickling sensation began at the back of her neck, like fingernails scraping that sensitive flesh, and Trinny thought for a moment that she heard the trill of a pipe vibrating through the woods and into her head. She shivered and wanted to step back, but before she could pull away she felt the bark grow warm against her lips and there was the unmistakable sensation of being kissed *back*.

Trinny was so startled she stumbled backward, tripping over a root and landing hard on her denim-clad ass. Her black-rimmed eyes stared at the tree, the pupils dilated like dark marbles. She didn't even hear the reaction of her friends as she watched the tree, the knots of bark that curved under the wood flesh, the gentle sway of leaves and lichen. They seemed to sway toward her, like hands reaching to pull her back into an embrace. When she finally took a breath, she tasted dirt and honey.

"Trin!" Ryan bent over her, one of his large hands curling around her bicep. "Hey . . . you okay?"

Trinny still watched the tree carefully, half afraid it would move down to kiss her again.

"I told you not to drink so much." He continued scolding as he grabbed Trinny's chin and forced her to look up at him. She blinked a few times to focus; the world was dizzy. Maybe Ryan was right.

"If she's going to sit there on the ground then put her to some use!" The friend who had earned a smack earlier made a lewd gesture toward his crotch. Chelsea tittered at Scott's action, but Ryan only scowled as he brushed the dirt off of his girlfriend.

"Okay, Scott." Trinny drawled, taking Ryan's arm to haul back to her feet. "Since you seem so keen to play. . . T-Truth or dare?"

෧

Rough fingers roamed over her skin, leaving a delicious tingle where they scratched, running through her hair, down her spine . . .

Trinny's lips parted slightly as she rolled over in the truck bed to rouse a little as the ridges of the bed liner pressed her body uncomfortably. Her eyes fluttered open, and she could hear Ryan's low and soft snoring beside her, mixed in with the rustling leaves and night birds. It felt invasive to have him so close and she sat up, letting the sleeping bag fall around her waist. The sun remained a vague gray light to the east, and though the air was chilly and the sky vast Trinny felt flushed and claustrophobic. Her coltish legs kicked the sleeping bag until free of it and she slid down off the tailgate, wincing as the metal bumped against her bruised rear. As soon as her bare feet touched the earth Trinny felt dizzy. Her feet and calves ached as if she had been running a marathon rather than sleeping. She couldn't quite remember everything that had happened after the game, and her stomach lurched. Maybe she needed more sleep. She began to turn back, but the prick-

ling sensation on her skin returned. If the trees surrounding her had
once beckoned before, now they demanded, ordering her to surrender
into the dark.

She took a few steps before a loud noise ripped her back to reality
like a cold shower: a sick retching in the rustle of leaves, then sputter-
ing coughing gags with a sour smell carried on the wind. She watched
as Scott emerged from behind a tree, wiping his mouth on his flannel
sleeve as best he could before spitting out the last of the taste. He saw
her and made a face. His breath drifted upward, visible in the
morning chill.

"What are you doing up?" Even his words sounded sour as he contorted his mouth further.

"I . . . uh . . ." Trinny suddenly could not remember what she had
been doing up or why she was walking toward the black forest. "I
have to pee."

Scott shrugged and lumbered off. Trinny stood, dazed, unsure why
she felt as if she had forgotten something terribly important.

"Stop it," Trinny ordered, turning her head away from Ryan's insistent kisses so suddenly that his tongue left a trail of saliva along her
cheek. He tried again, this time nuzzling her jaw. She gave him a light
shove. "I said get off."

His gaze darkened and his palm slammed against the concrete wall
of the school courtyard. A few nearby classmates glanced over, now
curious, and Trinny huddled against the wall, embarrassed and irritated. Her arms crossed her chest and her eyes studied the gum and
patches of weeds littering the pavement.

"What is with you, Trinny? You've been acting fucked up ever
since we got back from that camping trip. Did drinking kill what
brain cells you had left?"

She didn't reply; all Trinny could think of was how the bend of the
weeds and the dandelion flowers reminded her of the forest. Her heart
felt wrapped up in those little curls of green.

"You've shown up every morning weird-eyed and you look like
you've been slugged and drug through the woods." He ran a hand
through his hair, huffing. "Trin . . . those bags under your eyes,

this . . ." He grabbed her forearm and yanked her sleeve up, revealing scratches in her pale skin. She yelped at the sudden invasion. "If you're on some shit, I need to know."

Trinny wished the bell would ring, even though a glance at the clock told her she still had twenty minutes before class started. There was no way of explaining to Ryan. Why had she ever put up with how clumsy he was, how overly warm his skin was, the irritating way he grabbed at her ass like he owned it? Even to pretend being normal . . . she had been so foolish. Now she knew better, and wanted to spit out the very taste of him. Trinny turned away and searched the courtyard for a savior. A flash of red hair by the picnic tables caught her eye. Chelsea. Abandoning Ryan, she ran over to her best friend, grabbing Chelsea's arm and linking it with her own. Chelsea's smooth skin felt welcome after Ryan's rough fondling, and Trinny smiled brilliantly, expecting to see the sentiment reflected in her best friend's eyes. Instead, she noticed confusion.

"You're, um, energetic today, Trin." Chelsea began. "Why is Ryan looking at us like we just shot his dog?"

Trinny forced her voice to sound light. "I don't know. He's just in a bad mood today."

"He's been a bad mood a lot of days this week."

Trinny shrugged, not really caring. "Look, Chelsea, I have to tell you something. Something amazing, like a dream . . ." Her voice trailed off. Perhaps she shouldn't tell Chelsea exactly everything, but it seemed selfish to keep so much to herself.

"Dreams? Trinny, you're about to lose your boyfriend from being freaky, and you want to talk about dreams? Look, you're going to have to—"

Strands of dark hair covered Trinny's lips when she shook her head and smiled like a geisha. Why could they not see how wonderful her life had become? All Chelsea and Ryan could think of was that she looked bad and didn't want to kiss a boy who didn't know the first thing about how it should be done. Maybe she should ask if Chelsea could come along next time. After all, she owed her friend for all of this and wanted her to understand.

"Trinny, are you even listening to me?" A note of despair hung in Chelsea's voice, one Trinny had never heard before and she offered a smile she hoped was reassuring.

The bell rang, interrupting whatever Chelsea intended to say next. Impulsively, Trinny leaned over and kissed Chelsea on the cheek, close to her mouth. The act felt so natural, bringing her closer to that pleasant other world. Her friend jumped back as if suddenly burned.

Ryan didn't attempt to talk to her again, and Scott walked right past her locker as if he didn't notice her standing beside it. By mid-afternoon most of Trinny's daze had lifted, and as yet another former friend passed her with just a whisper and giggle, she felt her stomach clench. Ryan must have told everyone about their fight . . . or else those who had open eyes and active imaginations had drawn their own conclusions. She had always imagined coming out would be like this and right now she wasn't even sure what she had done to earn her the cold shoulder from everyone. Had someone somehow read her mind? After everything that had been going on, she wouldn't have doubted it. She slipped into the bathroom, fingers sliding along the grimy tile as she turned to avoid another whispering figure, this time a girl she hadn't even realized knew her.

A quick check in the bathroom mirror convinced her she did, in fact, look like shit. How had she left home without realizing? Under each eye hung bags, dark like blackberry stains, as if she hadn't slept all week, and her cheekbones protruded sharply. She noticed along her neck a smudge of dirt and remembered waking up stiff and sore and finding soil in her bed. There was more . . . dancing. . . .

But before she could question herself further, Trinny glimpsed in her reflection sprigs of bluebell caught in her hair. The sight made her smile, all concerns spirited from her consciousness. She sat there, entranced, a palm pressed against the smudged glass for long minutes. She no longer heard the whispers of the other students as they filed out of the bathroom.

"Hey."

Trinny felt herself being shaken, and she turned her head slowly because it felt as if weighed down with sandbags. Her eyes widened;

through a veiled gaze she thought she saw her mistress, all angular features and rich hair like the night sky. But she wasn't so lucky; it was Chelsea, not the product of her wishful thinking. The girl's face was stern, with her brows drawn together and her chin thrust forward. Trinny had never seen her look so severe.

Chelsea pulled Trinny down, crouching between a cracked porcelain sink and the ancient pad dispenser. Trinny could not bring herself to return her friend's intense gaze, instead studying the patterns on the tile floor left by dirty wedge heels and sneakers. The tracks resembled tiny roads stamped out in mud. She wondered if she could walk upon them, follow them back to the woods.

"Look, we are staying right here until you tell me what is wrong with you," Chelsea said with gritted teeth. She then wiggled her fingers in Trinny's face forcing her to focus. "Honest, whatever it is, I'm still your friend. I may even already know if it's . . . if you're . . ." Chelsea dropped her hands into her lap.

Trinny wanted to tell everything right then, but she suddenly felt overcome by a wave of panic. She couldn't stand the way Chelsea was looking at her; her friend's gaze was accusing, and the way she was leaning close made Trinny's heart pound as if she were being trapped. She didn't like the concern she saw in Chelsea's eyes, didn't want Chelsea to think there was something wrong with her like everyone else seemed to. In an attempt to relieve that pressure, Trinny jumped up, nearly stepping on Chelsea's hand in the process. The other girl gave a squeak of protest and followed, whacking herself on the tampon machine in her haste and getting a rusty scratch on her jacket for the trouble. Her string of curses broke some of the tension, and Trinny tried not to giggle. She took both Chelsea's hands in hers, giving the other girl an elfin grin. Chelsea looked frightened, and Trinny stroked the back of her hands like a child would a whimpering puppy, roughly, but with good intent. She took a deep breath.

"If you want to find out, come spend the night at my house tonight. I can't tell you, but maybe I can show you."

"I . . . I really don't think *showing* me is what . . ." She was stuttering again, so Trinny cut her off with a strange trill of her tongue that made Chelsea's voice stop with its foreignness. They looked at each other without speaking, and Chelsea sighed again. "Please, Trinny. Tell me."

So Trinny did her best to relate the story, the faeries, the magic, her beautiful mistress and the wonderful ways they danced and played. Her body began to sway instinctively as she called up the pipe melodies in her mind, and Chelsea's expression changed from determined and scared to pure confusion. She stopped midsentence as her friend's forehead wrinkled and Chelsea opened her mouth to interrupt. Trinny saw Chelsea's fingers tapping against her thigh, a nervous gesture Trinny recognized.

"So Ryan's right." Chelsea's tone was low. "You really are on drugs."

The derision in her voice hurt, and Trinny drew her arms across her chest. She and Chelsea had been best friends since elementary school, and her simple disbelief hurt far more that Ryan's earlier display of anger. She had to find a way to prove to Chelsea that she wasn't strung out or crazy, and that she had found something wonderful. She had to let Chelsea see, and let her share.

"*No.* Please. Just come over. I told you I can't really tell it right." Her voice sounded desperate, even to her own ears, and she watched Chelsea's hand relax against her leg.

"Fine. I'll be there. But if you're lying to me about the drug thing, Trin . . ."

"I'm *not*! It's nothing like that at all. Trust me, after tonight you'll thank me. I promise, cross my heart."

Despite the sincerity of Trinny's protesting, Chelsea looked unconvinced. She didn't answer, and Trinny watched as she turned and stalked away.

They sat cross-legged on Trinny's canopied bed, both so close together that Chelsea's breath touched her lips. She could smell the soap and slight alcohol sting of acne wash on her friend's skin. The sheer fabric had been drawn around them, as they had often done as children playing games of princess.

"Now you have to trust me," Trinny said, "and do everything I say." She noticed the nervous flush to Chelsea's cheeks and reached over to pull up a strap of her friend's nightie that had fallen down over a freckle-tinted shoulder. Chelsea trembled slightly. "Close your eyes."

Trinny had promised not to tell anyone, it was different with Chelsea. Chelsea was so sensitive Trinny felt sure she would have no problem seeing the night folk, and she even had a faint hope that Chelsea would be taken in as completely as she was. Then Chelsea would be able to see that Trinny wasn't on drugs, or crazy, and that she had found something wonderful. Besides, there was just something right about wanting to share this with her best friend. It would be the same as it was when they were little, with all their secret codes and stories. She had to find a way to open Chelsea's eyes to the other world. It would be unthinkably selfish to keep it to herself.

With that thought in mind, Trinny leaned forward and pressed her lips against Chelsea's. She slipped only the very tip of her tongue into Chelsea's mouth and tasted the warmth and toothpaste as she willed every bit of magic granted her to rub off onto her friend. When Trinny pulled away, Chelsea looked so very red, her face matching the flame-scarlet of her hair.

"I knew it." Chelsea's voice remained low as her words flowed together, something about Ryan and being confused, her breath punctuated by little sighs and "I still love you, but's." Trinny could not understand why Chelsea didn't want to share something so special.

"Let's just go to sleep." Trinny interrupted, making a big show of fluffing her pillow and yawning. The sooner Chelsea saw what a privilege Trinny had been granted, she would drop all the nonsense about getting help and how much she had changed.

Chelsea's eyes darted from Trinny to the space beside her. She made no move to lie down.

Trinny knew what Chelsea must be thinking and it was so shocking her mind went momentarily sober. What did Chelsea think, that she was going to rape her? First the drug accusations, now this . . . it was like her friend didn't know her at all.

"Fine, sleep on the floor if you're scared of me now." She took the spare pillow and threw it to the ground, turning her back on Chelsea and burying her face in cotton-covered down. Trinny felt the light pressure of Chelsea's fingers on her shoulder.

"I think we should talk."

"Go to sleep."

Trinny felt cold when Chelsea grabbed a sheet and dragged it to the floor with her. She let out a slow breath of air and stared up at the canopy. Her stomach was bubbling with worry now. What if her attempts to share the magic didn't work, or worse, cost her her own trips in the night? She could lose everything in one action. Trinny rolled onto her side and clenched her fist against her bedcovers, silently praying that everything would work out despite Chelsea's closed mind. Now more than ever Trinny felt they needed this, to cement their friendship beyond any question of trust. She lay there, listening to Chelsea's muffled breathing with her eyes squeezed shut and her body tensed. She was so anxious that every sound made her twitch in anticipation of the summoning, each bump or whir of the ceiling fan causing a twinge of hope and then disappointment. When she finally felt the beginning touches of magic brushing against her she went limp with relief before being spirited away.

"Wake up. Come on Chelsea, wake up!" Trinny pulled at her friend, but the redhead slept stubbornly, as if she was curled on a comfortable bed and not a pile of rocks. She was going to ruin her night clothes if she didn't stop lying on the ground, Trinny thought with irritation as her gaze flickered around the foggy clearing. It seemed despite her best efforts to bring Chelsea into this magic her friend wasn't going to wake up to share. She hadn't even stirred when they had been summoned and the magic had surrounded them so intensely. It always felt like a jerk from strong hands to Trinny, but Chelsea didn't even crack an eyelid. Trinny supposed she should be grateful that the magic had pulled Chelsea along with her . . . at least her friend was here, which showed that at least some of her worry was unfounded.

"What troubles you, my darling?"

Trinny's eyes fluttered as her mistress came up behind her, a pale and perfect hand coming to rest at the girl's waist, another lifting to stroke her throat. The touch rendered her immobile and unable to speak. The faery's cheek brushed against Trinny's own as she peered over her shoulder at Chelsea.

"Well, I must say that I am very surprised you disobeyed me." The hand at her waist tightened, clawlike fingernails digging into her skin.

"She's my friend," Trinny muttered, feeling suddenly childish with her protest.

The faery made a sound low in her throat, a warning noise that made Trinny shiver. "But we are your friends, are we not?"

Trinny turned around to face the carnival that had entertained her for the past six nights. Creatures with hideous masks and graceful bodies whirred together in dances that required more joints than a human possessed. A table dripped with fruits, chambered like labyrinths and gleaming skins like jewels. A fountain of fresh spring water poured from midair. Beyond all these things was the beauty of her mistress. Her brown skin resembled mahogany; her hair fell like a shower of willow leaves beneath a curtain of foxgloves.

Her offer was not true friendship, Trinny realized, but still generous beyond measure. Trinny let her eyes flick back to Chelsea, still curled tightly on the ground and slightly snoring. The faery drew her attention back with a sharp tug.

"Don't think on her overmuch." Her mistress' lip curled upward. "After tonight, I won't have you worrying with *that* world."

Trinny nodded, as was expected, and even though she heard the tenderness around the words there was something about the phrasing that set off a vague twisting of worry within her stomach. The nervous feeling couldn't quite make its way to her brain, however, and she sunk down beside Chelsea's still body.

"Don't wake her." Then the faery disappeared in a cloud of sweet perfumes.

Trinny reached over and brushed Chelsea's arm, her lips quirking. A glimmer of gold caught her eye, one of the floating baubles that lit the oak base in a soft glow. She smiled and stretched out her hand, letting the little spell flicker over her fingertips. When it died, she looked back over at Chelsea, half expecting to see her smiling back. There was only silence.

Biting her lip she crawled back over, glancing between the sleeping body and the faery revels. Chelsea had to wake up. If she didn't, she would never know how wonderful this place was. Without seeing what Trinny had found, Chelsea would never be able to trust Trinny again. Her mistress would be upset, probably, but it was also true that it was easier to ask for forgiveness than permission. She reached over and lightly shook Chelsea's shoulder. No response. She shook harder, and Chelsea's face scrunched up to show she was coming around. Trinny gave her one more good shake, then rocked back as Chelsea's eyes opened and she sat up, her joints cracking with her stretch. For a second she appeared unfocused, but Trinny saw her eyes open wider and heard her suck in a breath. "Oh. you're awake." Trinny feigned surprise and grinned at Chelsea, whose mouth was open in a perfect 'o' of shock. "I told you."

"Trinny, this—"

"Isn't it beautiful?" Trinny sighed, hugging her knees to her chest. Her heart ached at the perfection of the faeries' revelry.

"Trinny," Chelsea's voice trembled. "Trinny, can't you see what this is?"

With her brows drawn together, Chelsea didn't look entranced at all. She looked pale and scared and a light sheen of sweat appeared along her hairline. Biting her lip, Trinny twined their fingers together. Chelsea winced. "You're so cold."

"You don't like it?" Trinny blinked, bemused. How could anyone see all this splendor and not adore it?

"We have to get out of here." Chelsea stood and then stepped into the shadow of the oak tree. "They've got you under some kind of spell." She reached out and grabbed at Trinny's arm, but Trinny pulled violently away.

"No! Chelsea, you just don't understand." Trinny crossed her arms and hugged herself. "They love me here." She reached up and touched her pale cheek, ghosting the movements her mistress often made. It made her shiver; no one in her world would dare to touch her so sweetly.

"Trinny, you have to try . . ."

Did Chelsea want to make her think *here* was bad as well? An anger fueled by helplessness welled up in her. "I'm tired of trying!" Trinny threw down her arms, her heart leaping. Her breath turned rapid and shallow. "I shouldn't have brought you here. You don't know what I have to go through every day . . ." Flickers of unease and disappoint-ment snapped against her charmed contentment, and her sentences were lost as she gulped for air. "I'm so sick of it." Exhausted, as if all the past days' effort struck her at once, Trinny would have collapsed had not Chelsea grabbed her. She hung there like a broken doll, her weight propped against her friend. She felt Chelsea's cheek against her hair and gave a defeated whimper.

Then her friend gasped and stiffened. Without even turning she sensed her mistresses' presence behind her and the eyes of all the dancers turned on them.

"Is this how you answer my kindness?" Her mistress pulled her away with a single hand. "I should kill you both for allowing my com-pany to be defiled by such ugly mortal eyes."

Trinny hung suspended, her eyes staring at the ground instead of the faery's anger. Her mouth moved in mute apology. She seemed to dangle for a short eternity, any words her mistress was saying lost in the pounding of her pulse in her ears.

Her mistress dropped Trinny then to loom over them. Her skin had darkened to the color of stained bark and her eye deepened to a black void. Trinny thought for a moment that her mistress would strike her, but instead the bony fingers traced her features as if to memorize them. Trinny was torn, wanting to flinch at the chill touch yet aching to lean closer for more affection. But she could hear Chelsea crying close by and the sound stopped her from being lost in the caress even as a prickling began against her skin. Trinny realized her mistress tried to repair the enchantments torn by human emotion. An other-worldly voice whispered in her mind, telling her how much she wanted to stay, how loved she would be. But the subtle violence be-hind the faery's touch, her thumbs jabbing against Trinny's temples and dragging slowly down, contradicted the sweet words. Trinny tried to protest, but her voice was stilled. She knew now what the mistress had dictated; she was to stay, for good. The thought, so tempting just minutes before, now terrified her.

Panic rose in her, punctuated by the hitches in Chelsea's frightened sobs. Even as the threads of magic began to weave around her, Trinny shrieked, pulling away from the net with all the will she could muster. For a moment she couldn't breathe as the spell tried to hold her, but the energy broke, and the ground trembled beneath them. Trinny continued shaking and thrashing even after the earth stilled. She could feel Chelsea's hands pressing into her back, clutching at her. Trinny breathed in deep and turned her face up to look at the faery, a little frightened of what she would see. Her mistress's eyes burned, and Trinny thought she saw a strange jealousy there. Silently, she pleaded to be let go. Chelsea had been right; now that she could see with clear eyes she knew this was no place for her. If she didn't leave she would go mad.

"If this is your choice." The faery's words hissed like wind through the Spanish moss, barely reaching Trinny's ears. A crystal orb appeared in her palm, which she threw down against the twisted roots of the oak. The jewel shattered into a dozen little sparkling shards that bounced into the air, and the sound left Trinny momentarily deaf. There were shocked murmurs from the crowd of fae, all wide-eyed and leaning forward eagerly as if they would love nothing better than to see fresh human blood on dirt. They were rewarded with a few drops from Trinny's palm, where a shard had cut. She pulled the little diamond from her skin. When she looked up again the faery had disappeared, and she was left sitting beneath the oak with Chelsea, holding what looked like a piece of dull beer bottle.

They hiked along the highway and found a gas station where they called Trinny's parents to come get them. The plan was to say that they had snuck out and ended up the victims of a prank—their friends abandoning them. It meant certain grounding, but right now Trinny liked the idea of lying in her room for a month.

The manager kindly gave them cheap coffee and a place to sit, and Trinny nursed the bitter concoction, letting the taste ground her. Chelsea half-dozed in her plastic chair, head tilted back against her shoulder. Uncomfortable, Trinny shifted her weight, crossing her legs, then uncrossing them. She turned each way experimentally, then sighed and threw her own head back. Even her own touch seemed unbearable and clumsier than ever. There were so many things she wanted to say to her friend, apologies, confessions, excuses. Her hand clenched convulsively around her wound. It burned as if scalded.

"Chelsea?" Trinny winced as her voice hit her own ears, the vocal cords raw. There was an answering 'hm?' as Chelsea's head lolled over, her eyes not opening. Trinny curled her toes, twitching a little. "I have to tell you something." There was another monosyllabic answer, which Trinny took as an invitation to proceed. "Chelsea, it wasn't just the magic . . ." Trinny found her eyes prickling wet from the stress and the confession. She hoped her friend would understand without needing any other prompting, but Trinny steeled herself for a rout. To her surprise, however, Chelsea didn't even open her eyes.

"Yeah, you're a dyke. I figured."

"You figured?" Trinny echoed, confused. That was it? "You're not going to . . . I dunno, argue with me?"

"Do you think it would make any difference?"

Trinny fidgeted, dragging her foot along the dirty laminate floor. "No."

"Then no." Chelsea opened her eyes and gave Trinny a crooked smile. It was a trifle as far as offers of acceptance went, but better than nothing. Trinny looked down at the gash on her palm. The burn in the flesh was starting to cool, the reddening lessening even as she watched. She let out a slow breath, hoping the pain would soon heal away to nothing.

doi:10.1300/5642_14

Dark Collection

Luisa Prieto

The unicorns had been good to him today.

Thank you all, Kenneth Reaves thought, feeding the *Enchanted Unicorn* slot machine a new ten-dollar bill. He set his hand over the buttons. Kenneth closed his eyes and envisioned the sigils he'd studied in his grandfather's book. Power flowed beneath his palm, lapping at the *repeat bet* button. Just a couple more spins and—

His surroundings pitched and rolled. The background noise and shining colors danced around him, making him nauseous. Kenneth slumped against the machine. He'd used too much magic tonight.

He hadn't won enough, though. Megan needed more.

Kenneth took a deep breath. He repeated until the room stilled, and then cast another surge of magic at the slot machine. The sigils altered probability in his favor. He only needed perhaps five minutes before five more unicorns pranced on the screen; not the jackpot but not earning much attention from the casino staff. Kenneth pressed another button and the payout slip printed out. He added it to the others in his wallet, and then rose slowly, testing his balance. The room remained steady.

After cashing out—"Four hundred and twenty-three dollars, congratulations, sir"—Kenneth headed for the exit. At the door, he savored the air-conditioning before stepping outside.

Though nearly midnight, a wall of August heat met him. He had been living in Las Vegas for nearly a year and he was still surprised that the asphalt didn't melt.

The taxi dropped him off at the old townhouse. Before he took out his key, he ran his fingertips an inch from the doorframe. He shuddered as the warmth drained from his body. Around the door, several red-gold half circles shimmered into life. The door clicked open. The sigils, a combination of his blood and magic faded. Cool, sandalwood-scented air rushed him from inside. He locked the door behind him.

"Hello, Kenneth." The voice was so soft that, for a moment, Kenneth wondered if he'd imagined it. He hoped so. It hurt his sister to talk.

"Hi." He walked over to the couch. Megan lay between the pillow and the couch arm, her small body twisted, as if she had tried to pull herself free.

Kenneth knelt and gently picked her up. Even as a doll, his sister was beautiful, with auburn chenille hair, button-shaped green eyes, and a soft, suede-like skin. "You okay?"

Megan's head tipped forward, sending a velveteen green hat falling.

"You don't like the hat, huh?" he said.

Megan's sewn red lips twitched, slowly curving up. A smile, for him. An ache grew in his throat.

"Bad day?" The words made the fabric of her sewn smile twitch side to side and then push out against the fabric as if something tried to escape. Then, her face stilled and she appeared nothing more than a fabric doll again.

"No," he said. "Good day. I won at the Gold Coast." Which, when added to the rest of their money, meant that they had enough for rent and food for the next two months. He could afford to focus on his magic.

"Wonderful."

"Yeah." Kenneth set her on a pillow and brushed the hair out of her eyes. "I'm going to go work on—"

Pain bit his fingertip, making him hiss. Kenneth glanced at his hand. Blood blossomed across the pad of his index finger.

"I'm so sorry," Megan said. "I never meant to hurt you. I wanted a weapon." Her chenille hair tumbled to one side, revealing the thin sliver of dark metal among the strands.

"What . . ." It looked familiar. "The needle from the cover of Grandfather's book." Perhaps if he ever closed the book, he would have noticed that it was missing.

"You mentioned something about iron."

Yes, though Kenneth didn't have the heart to tell her that it was too late to be carrying protection from fairies. "I'm going to go work on some spells before calling it a night," he said. Very carefully, he moved her hair back into place and then set her hat back atop her head. "Do you want to lie down or continue to watch television?"

"Television."

Kenneth's lips quirked. *Some things never changed.*

He went up the stairs to the landing-loft. From the closet shelf, he took five white candles and headed for the clear space in front of the bed. He sat cross-legged and arranged the candles in a circle around himself. One of his grandfather's books lay in front of him.

Kenneth turned to the pages about fairies and changelings. One page had an illustration of a wooden doll, something left behind when human children were stolen away. The drawing's eyes had the same half-life that Megan's sewn buttons possessed.

Deep breaths, he thought.

The candles trembled . . . and then rose into the air. Six inches. Seven. Warmth pulsed out of his skin. The air around the wicks wavered. Smoke rose like an uncertain dancer, and then red-orange flames leapt up.

Kenneth smiled. He was getting better at this. Soon he'd have the confidence to once more try to return his sister to flesh and blood again.

It had begun simply: a protective brother wanting answers from his kid sister about her latest boyfriend.

"So what's his name?" Kenneth had asked.

"Bastian." Megan headed for the answering machine on her nightstand. There was barely enough room in her dorm room for the two of them, but Kenneth knew that Megan didn't care. All that mattered was that she had the freedom to tour the different majors and occasionally borrow his car. "Isn't that cool?"

Kenneth thought it sounded made up. "It's cool," he said. "What's he majoring in?"

"He's not a student. He's a collector. He goes all over the world searching for stuff."

Kenneth frowned. *A collector?* "How old is he?" Megan sighed. "I'm a big girl, Kenneth. He's . . . a little older than me."

Ah, yes. He'd said that once, too. Right before he told their parents that he was gay. "How'd you meet him?"

"At the Ren fair. He was looking at the shops." Megan played through a couple of their parent's messages. "I'll tell him we should all get coffee together. I think you'll like him."

Kenneth doubted that. "Do Mom and Dad know about him?"

Megan snorted. "You know they'd flip. They . . ." Her shoulders slumped.

"You won't tell them, will you?"

Kenneth wanted to. He knew hiding things never ended well. When he was her age, he had been too frightened to tell his folks the truth.

At her age, though, he probably would've left town with an interesting, mysterious, handsome man simply because he'd asked him. The timing would've been good. At her age, his parents had asked him to leave.

But she wasn't him.

He sighed. She was smart. Perhaps age didn't matter. "No," Kenneth said. "I won't tell them."

After Megan's change, Kenneth had moved them to Vegas. He'd wanted to find a mentor. But Penn and Teller, Lance Burton, all the magicians showcasing the casinos, from the luxury towers on the main strip to the dingy holes somehow still open, were only good at sleight of hand. They didn't have enough magic to really make a girl float, let alone break a fairy spell.

He would have to learn the craft on his own. The knowledge in his grandfather's library only hinted at things, so Kenneth went to estate sales, flea markets, used-book stores, antiquarian shops, any place he could think of that might have some spell written that would help his sister.

At a neighborhood yard sale, Kenneth found himself drawn to the heap of crap atop one folding table. The woman behind it absently chewed on her stringy hair. His hands found underneath one pile a tattered book.

"Fifty dollars." Her voice suggested early-morning cigarettes.

"Fifty?" Kenneth opened the book. Its cracked spine barely held the pages together, but sparks flew as he turned them. He looked up; the woman seemed more intent on her split ends than the sale. "Fine." He'd have to return to the casinos later.

Nothing else registered to whatever sense guided him. He was heading back to his car when he passed one blanket covered with toys.

Stuffed animals bothered him these days, but Megan loved cows. He wandered along the edges of the blanket, until he saw one. The Asian woman standing nearby rushed over and handed it to him. She eagerly thanked him as he handed over three dollars.

"Cute cow."

Kenneth turned around. The man standing behind him was handsome, with short blond hair made paler by all the sun. He wore tourist clothes, not light enough for the Vegas summer, and expensive-looking.

"Yeah. It's for my sister." Kenneth wiggled the cow, making it nod at him, and then the man. The man chuckled. The soft sound lapped at Kenneth, making him smile. It had been a while since he'd exchanged words with someone that either didn't depress him or involved money, and it felt nice.

"I collect dolls, but they don't have any," the man said. "I'm Sebastian."

"Kenneth."

"So does your sister need her present now or could her brother step out for some coffee?"

Kenneth could not believe how forward the guy was, hitting on him after only a name exchange. But then, he had been out of the scene for too long. He almost accepted, but the last thing he needed—no, Megan needed—was a distraction, even an attractive one. "Thanks, but no."

Kenneth basked in the afterglow of an evening spent out. Out with friends, with music, sweet drinks, and the occasional fun grope. He'd didn't know if he would ever fall asleep again.

Then, as he turned the key in his apartment door, a soft voice whispered. He recognized his baby sister's voice immediately.

"Megan?" Kenneth went room to room, turning on every light. Nothing.

He found the voice's source a moment later: the kitchen. On the counter, the answering machine blinked the number two at him. He tapped the play button.

"Kenneth, it's Sean. How was—"

Next message.

"Kenneth." Megan. "Help, please help. It's Bastian, he's not human and—oh, oh no, Kenneth." He listened to the rest of her rushed words, writing down the address. He didn't recognize the street, but Megan had mentioned Bastian lived in a new development not far from campus. He'd hunt it down.

Dawn had edged the sky by the time he found Twilight Street. The house was dark like its vast neighbors. The driveway was empty. Kenneth crept up to the porch. He'd had a friend who lived outside Santa Cruz proper and rarely locked his door. Kenneth had always thought that it was an invitation to get robbed but if the habit affected other people—

No. Not this guy.

Kenneth went to try a window. Three windows later, he found an open one. He climbed inside.

Lit orange candles dotted the room. He wondered why he had not glimpsed their light from the street. The slender flames danced, weaving shadows across the plain walls and the black-and-white checkerboard floor. White sheets were draped over chair shapes on the white places.

"Kenneth."

"Megan." Kenneth turned. Her voice was soft, but close.

"Kenneth, please."

There. Under the white cloth three black steps from him. The bastard had tied her up.

Anger flooded Kenneth, followed by caution. He was breaking and entering. He was right to do so, but the important thing to do was get his sister out of there. He headed toward her. Before he took another step, a wave of nausea crept over him, making him stop.

"Be careful. The floor."

Kenneth paused. *The floor?* He looked down. One foot hovered over a white space. He set it back on a black square and studied the ground. The area he'd come in on was a black border. He'd moved from it to a black space.

Kenneth searched his pockets. Besides his keys and wallet, he had nothing to experiment with.

Which, he realized, might be a good thing. Bastian might still be home. Kenneth had to get his sister and run.

Black square by black square, he made his way to Megan. "It's okay," he said, pulling the fabric away from her. "We'll get out of here and—"

On the chair, a fabric doll stared at him. It was beautiful, with his sister's hair, her eyes, her smile.

Kenneth frowned. He'd been tricked. The son of a bitch had expected someone to come and—

"Kenneth." The doll's lips twitched and a slight voice crept from inside. "It's me."

A sound—a sigh, a whimper, he didn't know—escaped Kenneth. No. It couldn't be Megan. No.

"Kenneth." The doll's head shifted to look up at him. "Please. It hurts to talk."

Kenneth lifted the doll. Megan . . . Megan was . . .

"This is interesting," a sweet voice said behind him. "Usually when people break into my house, they head for the stereo."

A hot tongue slid up Kenneth's spine.

Sebastian, he thought, and for a moment he felt relieved. The man had been attractive, and nice, and was whispering things to him. He found him fascinating. Funny. He was alone too.

Warm, oiled pressure pushed into him. Kenneth arched back into a velvet-soft body. So long, it had been so long.

Warm lips nipped at his ear, hinting at sharp teeth.
"You can keep the doll," Bastian whispered. "I want you."
No.

Kenneth thrashed. Sheets twisted around him, and then he was free, he was falling. He hit the ground.

Shit, he thought. *Just a dream. Sebastian. Bastian. Sebastian, Bastian . . . paranoia. He's trapped. He's not coming after her again.*

He tossed the sheets back. The clock read 4:21 a.m. but Vegas never slept. He tried to think about unicorns and not elves as he dressed and headed downstairs.

Megan rested on the sofa next to the toy cow. Kenneth didn't know if she truly slept or drifted in and out of consciousness. He moved quietly, not so much for fear of disturbing her but rather not eager to explain why he was awake at such an hour.

Twenty minutes later, he crossed a wall of a hundred-and-two-degree heat and stepped into the Aladdin.

Kenneth sighed, letting the cold air envelop him. He hated the heat, and couldn't wait until winter came and it was a reasonable seventy degrees again.

A familiar chuckle lapped at him from behind. "One would think you've never had air-conditioning."

Kenneth turned. Sebastian smiled at him.

"I'm" —Sebastian. Bastian— "still not used to the heat."

Kenneth took a step back and studied Sebastian. He wore a green silk shirt over black jeans. The shirt looked soft and inviting to the touch. The material brought out the green in the man's eyes. Greenish-gold, the color of newborn leaves and sunlight. They shimmer—

No.

At a casual glance they could pass as normal. Hazel, though, did not glow in even indoor light.

It's him, he thought. Then; *no. Maybe just . . . someone like him.*

The resemblance was there, though. Kenneth gathered warm, tingling magic into his eyes. If Sebastian's appearance was an illusion, Kenneth could try to break through it.

His sight watered. Sebastian's face trembled—

"Kenneth?"

—and when it stilled, Bastian was there.

Panic filled Kenneth. *He's here. He's here. He's— Calm. He doesn't know you know.*

"Kenneth?"

"I'm sorry," Kenneth said. "I've just got a lot on my mind."

"I imagine." Bastian tipped his head to one side, his eyes thoughtful. Through the wisps of pale blond hair a hint of a tapered ear poked through. Subtle. Elegant. Fey. "Your eyes just did an interesting shimmering thing." Bastian smiled. "You look well."

"You look free."

Bastian let one shoulder rise and fall. "Faulty human construction. The glass broke."

"You're not getting my sister."

The elf chuckled. The sound reminded Kenneth of the man he had met at the yard sale. The man who touched him in the dream. He knew enough about magic not to believe in coincidence any more.

"I don't want her anymore," Bastian said. "She's rather dull."

"Then why did you change her?"

"I collect pretty things. In time her mind would fade like a spring flower and I'd be left with a pleasant poppet."

Don't argue with him. He's dangerous. Wait for him to get distracted and then make something heavy fall on him and run.

Bastian studied him. One beat of silence, two, and then he said, "I'm willing to let her go."

Kenneth had not expected that. "You'll change her back?"

Bastian's lips twitched. "So the mage hasn't been able to fix it himself?"

Kenneth frowned. He wasn't a mage, more like a novice. His last attempt to transform a plush frog into a living one ended with him having to kill the bleating, horrible creature. "Will you change her back?"

"For an exchange. I want you."

"You have to be joking." Megan was fourteen years younger than him. She was pretty. She was funny. She was a girl. Kenneth had thought Bastian liked those things.

"You surprised me." Bastian's voice grew soft. "It's been so long since anything has done that, let alone avoided me for so long. I can taste your magic from here. I want that." He smiled with sharp, uneven teeth. "I want to play."

"No."

Bastian chuckled. "I'll change her back." He waved one hand, and then frowned. "If you didn't have wards around her, she'd be human now."

Oh. Oh no. Kenneth wanted his sister to be human. To rebuild her life, learn how to trust again and one day fall in love. Birthday parties. Parking tickets. Everything. He wanted to give her that, and if all this guy wanted was him, then . . . it was fair. Kenneth had magic. He might be able to escape.

Bastian rose and held out a hand. The light glimmered along the tips of his long nails. "My car is outside. You can take care of whatever wards when we get to your place."

Kenneth rose. Megan. He did not want to touch Bastian. Megan would have a life. Bastian had sharp teeth. Megan—

He took Bastian's hand.

Bastian walked around the room. He was different than Kenneth had expected. Tall and thin, with pale hair and cool eyes.

"You must be the older brother." Bastian smiled. "So what brings you by?"

Kenneth held Megan close to his chest. "Coffee." He edged back to the window.

Bastian chuckled. "I see you found Marissa."

"Megan."

"Whatever."

"You son of a bitch." Anger swept through Kenneth, leaving him trembling and feverish. He felt so hot that his skin might burn. Calm, he needed to remain calm, to escape before—

Bastian motioned to him. Icy air swept over Kenneth, tossing his hair back. There was something there in the breeze, a sound—

Sleep.

And then whatever whispered to him had fled, taking some of the heat that had threatened to burn him.

Bastian raised an eyebrow. "Charming." He stepped onto a black square, and then another, slowly approaching him. "What else can you do?"

Mist ebbed out of one of the white spaces, circling Kenneth. Warm threads crept over him, tugging him forward. Kenneth twisted, fighting to stay on a black tile.

"Interesting."

Bastian stopped two feet from him. A smile lurked at the corners of his mouth. "It's been so long since I've encountered one of your kind," he said. "I thought you were all burned at the stake."

Burned?

The fog around him thickened and pulled him a step closer toward a white square.

No, he thought. *No.*

The fire within him pulsed across Kenneth's fingertips. It felt alive, and raw, and his. Mysterious. Magic.

Bastian stopped at the edge of a black square a foot away. "You'll be a wonderful addition, Kenneth. I'll protect you from—"

The heat in Kenneth's grasp burnt away the fog. Kenneth dropped low and, grabbing Bastian's right leg, pulled it out from under him.

Bastian fell back, hitting the ground with a thud. A sharp, howling wind erupted beneath him. Bastian struggled to rise, got up on one knee and was sucked into the white square he had landed on. The wind grew cold and tugged at Kenneth.

Kenneth turned and leapt diagonally to the next black space, and then the next. The wind stopped. Kenneth looked back.

A clear glass ball rose from the square that had swallowed Bastian. The sphere quivered and then rolled toward him.

Kenneth stepped to the side. The ball moved past him, hit the wall, and then came back to him. Something tumbled inside. Kenneth knelt and picked it up.

A furious Bastian, perfectly miniature, threw a tantrum against the sphere's walls.

Frowning, Kenneth shook the glass, forcing Bastian to fall on his ass. "We're going to find some wet cement," he said. "I'm going to bury you in it. I hope no one ever finds you."

Bastian remained on the sidewalk. Kenneth could feel the elf's stare at his back as he temporarily released the wards and went inside the townhouse. "Megan," he called out.

The doll's head slowly turned to him.

"Bastian's here."

Megan rose, slumped to one side, and then sat up. "He found us? Grab your books and go."

"Megan—"

"He won't go after you once he gets me. I'll talk to him."

"He said he'd change you back."

"Don't trust him," she said. "You can change me back."

Kenneth shook his head. The frog he'd tried to change . . . He could never risk her. "I don't think I can."

"You will."

"I don't know."

"He's lying. Why would he let me go?"

"I'm no longer interested in you, Megan," Bastian said.

Kenneth turned. Bastian stood in the entryway. The red-gold half-circles burned around him in the frame. The elf's face showed the pain of the wards. Bastian glanced at Kenneth. "Please undo one of your little marks."

Kenneth headed for the door.

"Kenneth, no," Megan said.

"He'll turn you back, Megan."

"I'm not worth this."

But to him she was. When his folks had thrown him out of their lives, his sister had never turned away. For a while, Megan was his only family. He needed her back.

Kenneth stepped up to the doorway and ran a thumb over a half-circle. Warmth pooled in his fingertip, making the oil in his skin blur against the blood and breaking the protection.

Bastian sighed, and then stepped into the room.

"No," Megan said, falling to the ground. She shifted, and then crawled forward.

"Well?" Kenneth asked.

"Hold on. This is interesting." Bastian knelt and watched Megan inch closer. "And to think, she's only human. I can't wait to see how you'll do."

"You lied to me." Magic pooled into Kenneth's fingertips, quick, hot, angry.

Bastian moved swiftly, grabbing Kenneth by the throat. "Pretty mage, I never said *when* I'd return the brat." Bastian forced him back and into the doorway. Pain erupted down Kenneth's back.

Bastian tsked. "Patience. First, she has to learn not to cross me. Then, she can run home and live her little life, remembering your screams."

Rage crept through Kenneth. Slow, subtle, alert. Kenneth reached back and blurred several half-circles in the wood. The ward had been broken, but the blood-ink remained behind. If he could gather enough of it perhaps something could be done.

"I've dreamed of this for months," Bastian said. He ran the tip of a curved fingernail down Kenneth's shirt. The black cotton fabric parted, revealing semi-tan skin.

Ward, Kenneth thought, feeling magic pool into his palm. *Protect*—

Bastian's fingers tightened around his neck, sending threads of pain throughout Kenneth. He could feel himself grow faint.

No, he thought, and the warmth in his hand faded. He blinked once, twice, forcing himself to stay conscious.

"Please," Megan said. "Don't—"

"Shhh." Bastian's fingertips moved down Kenneth's chest, trailing over a hardening nipple. "I want to hear *him*."

"Please." Megan sounded so close. Too close. If Bastian kicked her . . .

Kenneth grabbed at Bastian's arm and drew him closer. Me, he thought, focus on me.

Bastian chuckled, and then his fingertips crept down over Kenneth's stomach, his belt, his jeans, making Kenneth hard.

"My mage," Bastian whispered.

No. Yes. Megan.

Bastian suddenly jerked and the magic pulses stopped. Bastian's hand released Kenneth.

"You bitch." Bastian kicked at a small shape on the ground, sending it across the room.

The shape—Megan—smacked against the wall, and then slumped to the floor, her head falling to one side as if broken.

"Megan!" Kenneth moved around Bastian and had nearly reached her when something latched around his ankle. He fell to the carpet.

"Oh, no," Bastian said.

Kenneth looked back.

Bastian knelt. A dark sliver rose up through the elf's Italian loafer. *Megan's pin,* Kenneth thought.

The elf hissed when he touched the metal and tore it free. He looked past Kenneth to Megan. Bastian took a deep breath and stood. "For you, mage, I will make her death quick."

Kenneth found himself unable to rise, held by some unseen enchantment. He could not even speak. He needed that iron sliver or something to break the spell . . . Kenneth glanced at his right hand. He could see the faintest remains of the blood spell from where he'd touched Bastian.

Ward, he thought, trying to recreate the spell he'd had on the door. The red-gold ink billowed into the air above his palm like dust. *Ward.*

"Kenneth," Megan said. Only her voice came not as a whisper from a cloth sewn but fresh and heavy. Human sounding. He struggled and managed to turn his head. Bastian kneeled before a flesh-and-blood Megan.

Of course. Bastian wouldn't lie. Even if he wanted her dead, he'd honor his word and turn her human first.

Bastian gripped Megan by her long hair. A hand raised, nails looking like blades.

Stop him. The spell around his hand shimmered across the air, and the red-gold bled over Bastian.

Bastian trembled. "What—" His head was thrown back, then the rest of him. He skidded across the carpet like a toy, slamming through a sheetrock wall. Plaster dust fell around the hole.

"Kenneth?"

Megan crawled toward him.

Relief flooded Kenneth. She was all right, she was alive. He shifted and found himself free. He grabbed hold of her hand.

"Is he dead?" Megan asked.

"No." Kenneth didn't know for sure, but there was no way in hell he'd walk over to check. He'd seen enough horror movies to know that was foolhardy.

"We need to leave."

Kenneth nodded. Megan needed to leave, anyway. He'd made a promise and, however Bastian had twisted it, he would need to keep it unless he wanted Bastian going after Megan again.

I want to play. . . . Bastian had enjoyed being surprised. Kenneth suspected that he'd even enjoyed hunting him. Fine. If he wanted a game, then Kenneth would give him one. He would hide and, using whatever time he had, he would study and surprise Bastian again.

"Here." Kenneth handed Megan his keys. He rarely drove his car here but the last time he'd used it, it had been in good condition. It would get her far away. "If—" *When.* "—he comes after me, I want you to be safe."

doi:10.1300/5642_15

Attracting Opposites

Carl Vaughn Frick

For Randy.

First, a little family history. It is not uncommon for a faerie and a pixie to fall in love. Nor is it as unseemly as a pixie and an imp. Publicly, pixies look down upon imps as backward bumpkins, bumbling in dark and damp domains. Imps see pixies as uppity, giggly snobs, sniffing too many snootfuls of pollen. Both do agree that elves are much worse. Upon the odd dawn when a pixie awakes next to an imp in some flop of a fen, usually the blame falls on too much imbibing of the imp's home brew (imps excel at crafting fine, intoxicating liquors).

Formal faerie society is full of high falutin' court intrigue and mysteries beyond mere human minds, such as the curious and ancient faerie tradition of secretly trading human babies with their own offspring. Imps write this practice off as mere mystery for mysteries' sake, to mask any lack of depth, more faerie makeup to cover up their fear of being ordinary. The pixies all find this funny, and often try to exchange a faerie baby with a pig or a chicken. Considering all the layers of faerie glamour demanded by their obligations, it can take years for such a trick to be discovered. Once a faerie princess actually did marry a pig, but that is another tale involving much impish liquor.

Theodore Winkle was one such faerie changeling, transplanted one early August morning into the crib of a human family of Unitarians. Unitarians, of course, can embrace anything, even the utter mystery of raising a faerie child in the human world. Young Theodore Winkle was very creative and crafty, sensitive and mature beyond his base classmates, and possessed the ability to talk with the animals. Cats adored him. Ma and Pa Winkle accepted their son and were thankful that their God had so blessed them with this gift of diversity.

Theodore Winkle happened to be attracted to human males, partly desiring what he sensed he could never be. Faeries do sleep with anyone or anything, if that is what they want.

In the faerie fashion, to the outside world, Winkle showed himself as something he was not, which made many people desire him all the more. Humans too led lives veiled with fantasies. Theodore's fashion never appeared the same in the eyes of different humans, which led to much confusion when his name came up in circles of gossip. Winkle would flash his sharp little smile while gently munching on a fresh salad of nasturtium petals and other edible flowers, his favorite food.

At night he dreamed of summer shorelines lit by reflections of jewels the scale of mountains. He saw seabirds shaped in human form gliding across the warm waves, sea breezes sang vibrations passing through strange formations of coral. These dreams always made him feel lonely, to ache to walk through the jeweled sand in hand with a lover he had yet to find. As is said, beauty without the beloved is like a sword through the heart.

Out in the real world Winkle learned the trade of cosmetology, using his innate gift of glamour. An unsettling aspect of faerie illusion is at times you catch a glimpse of the true form out of the corner of your eye. This would bother his more sensitive customers; by nature people go to beauty parlors because they are already insecure with themselves. What made Winkle unique alienated him from the world around him. This is the human curse.

He nurtured friendships with quirky, artistic, neurotic outsiders, one of which told him about this thing called a faerie gathering. This friend, who named himself Barry Tone, trilled in a high falsetto about all the "faerie magic" he would see once he came to the gathering. Winkle was uncertain, as a similar ruse had been used years before to lure him into going to a Unitarian summer camp. It turned into Hokey-Pokey hell. Four dreadful weeks in the woods with a congregation who knew they were there, but didn't know why.

A plump and envious harpy at his work had caused endless trouble for Winkle. His boss knew he was the most talented cog in the salon, and that Winkle could make even a harpy look seductive, and just assumed Winkle needed some time off. So one sultry August Saturday Winkle and Barry drove to where the faeries came together. Barry assured Winkle that there would be plenty of flowers to eat. Winkle feared that to mean nothing but free-range dandelions. He brought along plenty of strong vinaigrette salad dressing

Where the faeries came was an old tumble-about farm situated in a small, secluded valley sequestered away from encroaching civilization. The bones of many hippy communal projects gone wild lay strewn about absorbing back into the landscape. The terrain was hot, dry, and dusty, and left Winkle sighing and realizing there would not be the promised flowers to nibble, maybe only a fate of warm iceberg lettuce.

The faeries represented there were of the odd human sort, a lot of tailings swept out from the mainstream gay world. Winkle feared that another round of the Hokey-Pokey awaited him in this strange place. A self-defined faerie wearing a stained smock who called himself Big Cuddle Bare strode up and greeted them with a sloppy, needy kiss that left spittle on Winkle's face. He smelled of garlic and sweat. Winkle started to fear this was going to be worse than the Unitarians. Being a true faerie that wore the face of desire in a place such as this, where he would be the new meat to ogle and grope made Winkle start to look longingly at his car.

Barry said he would be right back as he skipped off with another faerie named Black Hole, and that would be the last time Winkle saw him for the next two days.

Winkle found a glen of trees far away from the giggling and groping where he set up his tent. A lone crystal was strung up on the mossy branch of an old twisted maple tree next to his camp site. Sitting in silence, Winkle watched the goings of the forest creatures who shared his site at this strange place of giggling and groping men in stained smocks. A small brown lizard warmed itself on his left shoulder.

Winkle ached for the other who was yet to be a part of his life. The sun set behind the valley ridge casting the calming light of dusk. A chorus of crickets soothed his lonely heart. Then some idiot started screaming and pounding on a drum. In the dark Winkle began to explore. True faeries see fine at night without the aid of flashlights. The land hummed and glowed with activity and anticipation.

Weird and wonderful altars draped with bangles and relics dotted the domain. Through a landscaped garden full of statues and beads Winkle walked past a smoking circle that looked like a refugee camp, a refuge of beer cans and cigarette butts. Winkle kept his distance.

He entered a structure that appeared to have been a barn badly built by some committee of conflicting design, unfinished here while overwrought there. A chaotic kitchen set up inside was finishing serving up some rather grayish looking lentil stew. Even warm iceberg lettuce would have been better. Winkle found some granola stashed in a large bag kept in a garbage can as protection from the raccoons, and munched while watching. He was offered a hit of marijuana from a passing pipe, which he accepted. A tape of trance music played from a battered stereo system covered in red dust. A nymphet nearly naked lad danced, swirling a glittery shawl to his own internal rhythm.

"What's your faerie name?" asked a friendly faerie also watching the nymph now dancing dervishly. "I don't know my faerie name, my adoptive name is Theodore." Hearing himself say this surprised him, "adoptive" name? Who was he, really? Was this just the effect from the drugs?

From beside himself he heard "I'm Billie Holyday. For a moment there you looked like you were somewhere else." Winkle was somewhere else, he could still feel the warm jeweled sand between his toes. Winkle excused himself and walked back to his tent in the dark of the new moon, alone. Looking up to the sky, the clarity and expanse of the vaults of the heavens entrapped him in a sweep of eternity. The star sparkle reminded him of the glittery beach he would walk again tonight by himself. So many worlds, so many times. Winkle wept.

The whole next day Winkle shied away from the faerie humanity, hiking alone in the summer hills above the gathering. In the dark on the way back to the main meadow Winkle saw a lone figure switching around the stones of an intentional faerie circle that some human had arranged during a drug trip. Winkle crept up behind this individual that he could see was actually painting little faces upon the rocks using fingernail polish. "How pretty" said Winkle. The painter yelped then fell over, looked up to Winkle and said, "I'm caught! Want to join me in some fun?" Winkle noted he was painting in the dark, as the moon had yet to rise. This was no human. "My name is Morning Glory, or just plain Glory. They were serving up that fetid gray crap again for dinner, and I had to escape the coming storm of faerie flatulence." Winkle felt hungry, but not for that. "Want to go forage in the woods for something better to eat?" offered Glory. Winkle was dumbstruck. "Yes."

As the rising moonlight illuminated the forest, Glory found them some late summer flowers and berries to eat. Pixies always know where to find flowers. Later, in Winkles tent, they touched and kissed and loved each other. Winkle dropped his glamour with his clothes. Glory stood naked as a pixie. They embraced. The lone crystal that hung above the tent in the maple tree glowed with eldritch light.

The next morning, Glory told Winkle it was time for them to go. Time to leave this human world of Republicans and Cheese Whiz. In the dawn they walked together in early mist to the barn, where Winkle found Barry passed out with the dancing nymph. Planting a gentle kiss upon Barry's cheek, Winkle slipped a note in his pocket along with the car keys. Glory liberated the granola for the raccoons.

Glory and Winkle hand in hand walked to where they had first met the night before at the stone circle. In the dawn's light Winkle saw that what he thought were faces were instead glyphs and symbols of a sort alien to this world. Glory adjusted a few of the rocks, and together they stepped out onto a beach aglitter with every rainbow shade.

doi:10.1300/5642_16

The Faerie Cony-Catcher

Delia Sherman

In London town, in the reign of good Queen Bess that was called
Gloriana, there lived a young man named Nicholas Cantier. Now it
came to pass that this Nick Cantier served out his term as apprentice
jeweler and goldsmith under one Master Spilman, jeweler by appointment to the Queen's Grace herself, and was made journeyman of his
guild. For that Nick was a clever young man, his master would have
been glad for him to continue on where he was; yet Nick was not fain
thereof, Master Spilman being as ill a master of men as he was a skilled
master of his trade. And Nick bethought him thus besides: that London was like unto the boundless sea where Leviathan may dwell un-
noted, save by such small fish as he may snap up to stay his mighty
hunger: such small fish as Nicholas Cantier. Better that same small
fish seek out some backwater in the provinces where, puffed up by
city ways, he might perchance pass as a pike and snap up spratlings on
his own account.

So thought Nick. And on a bright May morning, he packed up
such tools as he might call his own—as a pitch block and a mallet, and
some small steel chisels and punches and saw-blades and blank rings
of copper—that he might make shift to earn his way to Oxford. So
Nick put his tools in a pack, with clean hosen and a shirt and a pair of
soft leather shoon, and that was all his worldly wealth strapped upon
his back, saving only a jewel that he had designed and made himself
to be his passport. This jewel was in the shape of a maid, her breasts
and belly all one lucent pearl, her skirt and open jacket of bright
enamel, and her fair face of silver burnished with gold. On her fantastic hair perched a tiny golden crown, and Nick had meant her for the
Faerie Queene of Master Spenser's poem, fair Gloriana.

"The Faerie Cony-Catcher" previously published in *Sirens & Other Daemon Lovers*
(1998), EOS.

Upon this precious Gloriana did Nick's life and livelihood depend. Therefore, being a prudent lad in the main, and bethinking him of London's traps and dangers, Nick considered where he might bestow it that he fall not prey to those foists and rufflers who might take it from him by stealth or by force. The safest place, thought he, would be his codpiece, where no man nor woman might meddle without his yard raise the alarm. Yet the jewel was large and cold and hard against those softer jewels that dwelt more commonly there, and so Nick bound it across his belly with a band of linen and took leave of his fellows and set out northward to seek his fortune.

Now Nick Cantier was a lusty youth of nearly twenty, with a fine, open face and curls of nut-brown hair that sprang from his brow; yet notwithstanding his comely form, he was as much a virgin on that May morning as the Virgin Queen herself. For Master Spilman was the hardest of taskmasters, and between his eagle eye and his adder cane and his arch-episcopal piety, his apprentices perforce lived out the terms of their bonds as chaste as Popish monks. On this the first day of his freedom, young Nick's eye roved hither and thither, touching here a slender waist and there a dimpled cheek, wondering what delights might not lie beneath this petticoat or that snowy kerchief. And so it was that a Setter came upon him unaware and sought to persuade him to drink a pot of ale together, having just found xii pence in a gutter and it being ill-luck to keep found money and Nick's face putting him in mind of his father's youngest son, dead of an ague this two year and more. Nick let him run on, through this excuse for scraping acquaintance and that, and when the hopeful cony-catcher had rolled to a stop, like a cart at the foot of a hill, he said unto him,

"I see I must have a care to the cut of my coat, if rogues, taking me for a country cony, think me meet for skinning. Nay, I'll not drink with ye, nor play with ye neither, lest ye so ferret-claw me at cards that ye leave me as bare of money as an ape of a tail."

Upon hearing which, the Setter called down a murrain upon milk-fed pups who imagined themselves sly dogs, and withdrew into the company of two men appareled like honest and substantial citizens, whom Nicholas took to be the Setter's Verser and Barnacle, all ready to play their parts in cozening honest men out of all they carried, and a little more beside. And he bit his thumb at them and laughed and made his way through the streets of London, from Lombard Street to Clerkenwell in the northern liberties of the city, where the houses were set back from the road in gardens and fields and the taverns spilled out of doors in benches and stools, so that toss-pots might air their drunken heads.

'Twas coming on for noon by this time, and Nick's steps were slower than they had been, and his mind dwelt more on bread and ale than on cony-catchers and villains. In this hungry, drowsy frame of mind, he passed an alehouse where his eye chanced to light upon a woman tricked up like a lady in a rich-guarded gown and a deep starched ruff. Catching his glance, she sent it back again saucily, with a wink and a roll of her shoulders that lifted her breasts like ships on a wave.

Nick gave her good speed, and she plucked him by the sleeve and said, "How now, my friend, you look wondrous down i' the mouth. What want you? Wine? Company?"—all with such a meaning look, such a waving of her skirts and a hoisting of her breasts that Nick's yard, fain to salute her, flew its scarlet colors in his cheeks.

"The truth is, Mistress, that I've walked far this day, and am sorely hungered."

"Hungered, is it?" She flirted her eyes at him, giving the word a dozen meanings not writ in any grammar. "Than shall feed thy hunger, aye, and sate thy thirst, too, and that right speedily." And she led him in at the alehouse door to a little room within, where she closed the door and thrusting herself close up against him, busied her hands about his body and her lips about his mouth. As luck would have it, her breath was foul, and it blew upon Nick's heat, cooling him enough to recognize that her hands sought not his pleasure, but his purse, upon which he pushed her from him.

"Nay, mistress," he said, all flushed and panting. "Thy meat and drink are dear, if they cost me my purse."

Knowing by his words that she was discovered, she spent no time in denying her trade, but set up a caterwauling would wake the dead, calling upon one John to help her. But Nick, if not altogether wise, was quick and strong, and bolted from the vixen's den 'ere the dog-fox answered her call.

So running, Nick came shortly to the last few houses that clung to the outskirts of the city and stopped at a tavern to refresh him with honest meat and drink. And as he drank his ale and pondered his late escape, the image of his own foolishness dimmed and the image of the doxy's beauty grew more bright, until the one eclipsed the other quite, persuading him that any young man in whom the blood ran hot would have fallen in her trap, aye and been skinned, drawn, and roasted to a turn, as 'twere in very sooth a long-eared cony. It was his own cleverness, he thought, that he had smoked her out and run away. So Nick, having persuaded himself that he was a sly dog after all, rose from the tavern and went to Hampstead Heath, which was the end of the world to him. And as he stepped over the world's edge and onto the northward road, his heart lifted for joy, and he sang right merrily as he strode along, as pleased with himself as the cock that imagineth his crowing bringeth the sun from the sea.

And so he walked and so he sang until by and by he came upon a country lass sat upon a stone. Heedful of his late lesson, he quickly cast his eye about him for signs of some high lawyer or ruffler lurking ready to spring the trap. But the lass sought noways to lure him, nor did she accost him, nor lift her dark head from contemplating her foot that was cocked up on her knee. Her gown of gray kersey was hiked up to her thigh and her sleeves rolled to her elbows, so that Nick could see her naked arms, sinewy and lean and nut-brown with sun, and her leg like dirty ivory.

"Gie ye good-den, fair maid," said he, and then could say no more, for when she raised her face to him, his breath stopped in his throat. It was not, perhaps, the fairest he'd seen, being gypsy-dark, with cheeks and nose that showed the bone. But her black eyes were wide and soft as a hind's and the curve of her mouth made as sweet a bow as Cupid's own.

"Good-den to thee," she answered him, low-voiced as a throstle. "Ye come at a good hour to my aid. For here is a thorn in my foot and I, for want of a pin, unable to have it out."

The next moment he knelt at her side; the moment after, her foot was in his hand. He found the thorn and winkled it out with the point of his knife while the lass clutched at his shoulder, hissing between her teeth as the splinter yielded, sighing as he wiped away the single ruby of blood with his kerchief and bound it round her foot.

"I thank thee, good youth," she said, leaning closer. "An thou wilt, I'll give thee such a reward for thy kindness as will give thee cause to thank me anon." She turned her hand to his neck, and stroked the bare flesh there, smiling in his face the while, her breath as sweet as an orchard in spring.

Nick felt his cheek burn hot above her hand and his heart grow large in his chest. This were luck indeed, and better than all the trulls in London. "Fair maid," he said, "I would not kiss thee beside a public road."

She laughed. "Lift me then and carry me to the hollow, hard by yonder hill, where we may embrace, if it pleaseth thee, without fear of meddling eye."

Nick's manhood rose then to inform him that it would please him well, observing which, the maiden held up her arms to him, and he lifted her, light as a faggot of sticks but soft and supple as Spanish leather withal, and bore her to a hollow under a hill that was round and green and warm in the May sun. And he lay her down and did off his pack and set it by her head, that he might keep it close to hand, rejoicing that his jewel was well-hid and not in his codpiece, and then he fell to kissing her lips and stroking her soft, soft throat. Her breasts were small as a child's under her gown; yet she moaned most womanly when he touched them, and writhed against him like a snake, and he made bold to pull up her petticoats to discover the treasure they hid. Coyly, she slapped his hand away once and again, yet never ceased to kiss and toy with open lip, the while her tongue like a darting fish urged him to unlace his codpiece that was grown wondrous tight. Seeing what he was about, she put her hand down to help him, so that he was like to perish e'er he spied out the gates of Heaven. Then, when he was all but sped, she pulled him headlong on top of her.

He was not home, though very near it as he thrust at her skirts bunched up between her thighs. Though his plunging breached not her cunny-burrow, it did breach the hill itself, and he and his gypsy lass both tumbled arse-over-neck to lie broken-breathed in the midst of a great candle-lit hall upon a Turkey carpet, with skirts and legs and slippered feet standing in ranks upon it to his right hand and his left, and a gentle air stroking warm fingers across his naked arse. Nick shut his eyes, praying that this vision were merely the lively exhalation of his lust. And then a laugh like a golden bell fell upon his ear, and was hunted through a hundred mocking changes in a ring of melodious laughter, and he knew this to be sober reality, or something enough like it that he'd best ope his eyes and lace up his hose.

All this filled no more than the space of a breath, though it seemed to Nick an age of the world had passed before he'd succeeded in packing up his yard and scrambling to his feet to confront the owners of the skirts and the slippered feet and the bell-like laughter that yet pealed over his head. And in that age, the thought was planted and nurtured and harvested in full ripeness, that his hosts were of faerie-kind. He knew they were too fair to be human men and women, their skins white nacre, their hair spun sunlight or moonlight or fire bound back from their wide brows by fillets of precious stones not less hard and bright than their emerald or sapphire eyes. The women went bare-bosomed as Amazons, the living jewels of their perfect breasts coffered in open gowns of bright silk. The men wore jewels in their ears, and at their forks, fantastic codpieces in the shapes of cockerels and wolves and rams with curling horns. They were splendid beyond imagining, a masque to put the Queen's most magnificent Revels to shame.

As Nick stood in amaze, he heard the voice of his coy mistress say, "'T'were well, Nicholas Cantier, if thou woulds't turn and make thy bow."

With a glare for she who had brought him to this pass, Nick turned him around to face a woman sat upon a throne. Even were she seated upon a joint stool, he must have known her, for her breasts and face were more lucent and fair than pearl, her open jacket and skirt a glory of gemstones, and upon her fantastic hair perched a gold crown, as

like to the jewel in his bosom as twopence to a groat. Nick gaped like
that same small fish his fancy had painted him erewhile, hooked and
pulled gasping to land. Then his knees, wiser than his head, gave way
to prostrate him at the royal feet of Elfland.

"Well, friend Nicholas," said the Faerie Queen. "Heartily are you
welcome to our court. Raise him, Peasecod, and let him approach our
throne."

Nick felt a tug on his elbow, and wrenched his dazzled eyes from
the figure of the Faerie Queen to see his wanton lass bending over
him. "To thy feet, my heart," she murmured. "And, as thou holdest
dear thy soul, see that neither meat nor drink pass thy lips."

"Well, Peasecod?" asked the Queen, and there was that in her musical voice that propelled Nick to his feet and down the Turkey carpet
to stand trembling before her.

"Be welcome," said the Queen again, "and take your ease. Peasecod, bring a stool and a cup for our guest, and let the musicians play
and our court dance for his pleasure."

There followed an hour as strange as any madman might imagine
or poet sing, when Nicholas Cantier sat upon a gilded stool at the
knees of the Queen of Elfland and watched her court pace through
their faerie measures. In his hand he held a golden cup crusted with
gems, and the liquor within sent forth a savor of roses and apples that
promised an immortal vintage. But as oft as he, half-fainting, lifted
the cup, so often did a pair of fingers pinch him at the ankle, and so often did he look down to see the faerie lass Peasecod crouching at his
feet with her skirts spread out to hide the motions of her hand. Once
she glanced up at him, her soft eyes drowned in tears like pansies in
rain, and he knew that she was sorry for her part in luring him here.

When the dancing was over and done, the Queen of Elfland turned
to Nick and said, "Good friend Nicholas, we would crave a boon of
thee in return for this our fair entertainment."

At which Nick replied, "I am at your pleasure, Madam. Yet have I
not taken any thing from you save words and laughter."

"'Tis true, friend Nicholas, that thou hast scorned to drink our
faerie wine. And yet hast thou seen our faerie revels, that is a sight any
poet in London would give his last breath to see."

"I am no poet, Madam, but a humble journeyman goldsmith."

"That too, is true. And for that thou art something better than humble at thy trade, I will do thee the honor of accepting that jewel in my image thou bearest bound against thy breast."

Then it seemed to Nick that the Lady might have his last breath after all, for his heart suspended himself in his throat. Wildly looked he upon Gloriana's face, fair and cold and eager as the trull's he had escaped erewhile, and then upon the court of Elfland that watched him as he were a monkey or a dancing bear. And at his feet, he saw the dark-haired lass Peasecod, set apart from the rest by her mean garments and her dusky skin, the only comfortable thing in all that discomfortable splendor. She smiled into his eyes, and made a little motion with her hand, like a fishwife who must chaffer by signs against the crowd's commotion. And Nicholas took courage at her sign, and fetched up a deep breath, and said:

"Fair Majesty, the jewel is but a shadow or counterfeit of your radiant beauty. And yet 'tis all my stock in trade. I cannot render all my wares to you, were I never so fain to do you pleasure."

The Queen of Elfland drew her delicate brows like kissing moths over her nose. "Beware, young Nicholas, how thou triest our good will. Were we minded, we might turn thee into a lizard or a slow-worm, and take thy jewel resistless."

"Pardon, dread Queen, but if you might take my jewel by force, you might have taken it ere now. I think I must give it you—or sell it you—by mine own unforced will."

A silence fell, ominous and dark as a thundercloud. All Elfland held its breath, awaiting the royal storm. Then the sun broke through again, the Faerie Queen smiled, and her watchful court murmured to one another, as those who watch a bout at swords will murmur when the less-skilled fencer maketh a lucky hit.

"Thou hast the right of it, friend Nicholas: we do confess it. Come, then. The Queen of Elfland will turn huswife, and chaffer with thee."

Nick clasped his arms about his knee and addressed the lady thus: "I will be frank with you, Serenity. My master, when he saw the jewel, advised me that I should not part withal for less than fifty golden crowns, and that not until I'd used it to buy a master goldsmith's good opinion and a place at his shop. Fifty-five crowns, then, will buy the jewel from me, and not a farthing less."

The Lady tapped her white hand on her knee. "Then thy master is a fool, or thou a rogue and liar. The bauble is worth no more than fifteen golden crowns. But for that we are a compassionate prince, and thy complaint being just, we will give thee twenty, and not a farthing more."

"Forty-five," said Nick. "I might sell it to Master Spenser for twice the sum, as a fair portrait of Gloriana, with a description of the faerie court, should he wish to write another book."

"Twenty-five," said the Queen. "Ungrateful wretch. 'Twas I sent the dream inspired the jewel."

"All the more reason to pay a fair price for it," said Nick. "Forty."

This shot struck in the gold. The Queen frowned and sighed and shook her head and said, "Thirty. And a warrant, signed by our own royal hand, naming thee jeweler by appointment to Gloriana, by cause of a pendant thou didst make at her behest."

It was a fair offer. Nick pondered a moment, saw Peasecod grinning up at him with open joy, her cheeks dusky red and her eyes alight, and said: "Done, my Queen, if only you will add thereto your attendant nymph, Peasecod, to be my companion."

At this Gloriana laughed aloud, and all the court of Elfland laughed with her, peal upon peal at the mortal's presumption. Peasecod alone of the bright throng did not laugh, but rose to stand by Nicholas' side and pressed his hand in hers. She was brown and wild as a young deer, and it seemed to Nick that the Queen of Elfland herself, in all her female glory of moony breasts and arching neck, was not so fair as this one slender, black-browed faerie maid.

When Gloriana had somewhat recovered her power of speech, she said: "Friend Nicholas, I thank thee; for I have not laughed so heartily this many a long day. Take thy faerie lover and thy faerie gold and thy faerie warrant and depart unharmed from hence. But for that thou hast dared to rob the Faerie Queen of this her servant, we lay this weird on thee, that if thou say thy Peasecod nay, at bed or at board for the space of four-and-twenty mortal hours, then thy gold shall turn to leaves, thy warrant to filth, and thy lover to dumb stone."

At this, Peasecod's smile grew dim, and up spoke she and said, "Madam, this is too hard."

"Peace," said Gloriana, and Peasecod bowed her head. "Nicholas," said the Queen, "we commence to grow weary of this play. Give us the jewel and take thy price and go thy ways."

So Nick did off his doublet and his shirt and unwound the band of linen from about his waist and fetched out a little leathern purse and loosed its strings and tipped out into his hand the precious thing upon which he had expended all his love and his art. And loathe was he to part withal, the firstfruits of his labor.

"Thou shalt make another, my heart, and fairer yet than this," whispered Peasecod in his ear, and so he laid it into Elfland's royal hand, and bowed, and in that moment he was, in the hollow under the green hill, his pack at his feet, half-naked, shocked as by a light-ning bolt, and alone. Yet before he could draw breath to make his moan, Peasecod appeared beside him with his shirt and doublet on her arm, a pack at her back, and a heavy purse at her waist, that she detached and gave to him with his clothes. Fain would he have sealed his bargain then and there, but Peasecod begging prettily that they might seek more comfort than might be found on a tussock of grass, he could not say her nay. Nor did his regret his weird that gave her the whip hand in this, for the night drew on apace, and he found himself sore hungered and athirst, as though he'd been beneath the hill for longer than the hour he thought. And indeed 'twas a day and a night and a day again since he'd seen the faerie girl upon the heath, for time doth gallop with the faerie kind, who heed not its passing. And so Peasecod told him as they trudged northward in the gloaming, and picked him early berries to stay his present hunger, and found him clear water to stay his thirst, so that he was inclined to think very well of his bargain, and of his own cleverness that had made it.

And so they walked until they came to a tavern, where Nick called for dinner and a chamber, all of the best, and pressed a golden noble into the host's palm, whereat the goodman stared and said such a coin would buy his whole house and all his ale, and still he'd not have coin to change it. And Nick, flushed with gold and lust, told him to keep all as a gift upon the giver's weddingday. Whereat Peasecod blushed and cast down her eyes as any decent bride, though the goodman saw she wore no ring and her legs and feet were bare and dusty from the road. Yet he gave them of his best, both meat and drink, and put them to bed in his finest chamber, with a fire in the grate because gold is gold, and a rose on the pillow because he remembered what it was to be young.

The door being closed and latched, Nicholas took Peasecod in his arms and drank of her mouth as 'twere a well and he dying of thirst. And then he bore her to the bed and laid her down and began to unlace her gown that he might see her naked. But she said unto him, "Stay, Nicholas Cantier, and leave me my modesty yet a while. But do thou off thy clothes, and I vow thou shalt not lack for pleasure."

Then young Nick gnawed his lip and pondered in himself whether taking off her clothes by force would be saying her nay—some part of which showed in his face, for she took his hand to her mouth and tickled the palm with her tongue, all the while looking roguishly upon him, so that he smiled upon her and let her do her will, which was to strip his doublet and shirt from him, to run her fingers and her tongue across his chest, to lap and pinch at his nipples until he gasped, to stroke and tease him, and finally to release his rod and take it in her hand and then into her mouth. Poor Nick, who had never dreamed of such tricks, was like to die of ecstasy. He twisted his hands in her long hair as pleasure came upon him like an annealing fire, and then he lay spent, with Peasecod's head upon his bosom, and all her dark hair spread across his belly like a blanket of silk.

After a while she raised herself, and with great tenderness kissed him upon the mouth and said, "I have no regret of this bargain, my heart, whatever follows after."

And from his drowsy state he answered her, "Why, what should follow after but joy and content and perchance a babe to dandle upon my knee?"

She smiled and said, "What indeed? Come, discover me," and lay back upon the pillow and opened her arms to him.

For a little while, he was content to kiss and toy with lips and neck, and let her body be. But soon he tired of this game, the need once again growing upon him to uncover her secret places and to plumb their mysteries. He put his hand beneath her skirts, stroking her thigh that was smooth as pearl and quivered under his touch as it drew near to that mossy dell he had long dreamed of. With quickening breath, he felt springing hair, and then his fingers encountered an obstruction, a wand or rod, smooth as the thigh, but rigid, and burning hot. In his shock, he squeezed it, and Peasecod gave a moan, whereupon Nick would have withdrawn his hand, and that right speedily, had not his faerie lover gasped, "Wilt thou now nay-say me?"

Nick groaned and squeezed again. The rod he held pulsed, and his own yard stirred in ready sympathy. Nick raised himself on his elbow and looked down into Peasecod's face—wherein warred lust and fear, man and woman—and thought, not altogether clearly, upon his answer. Words might turn like snakes to bite their tails, and Nick was of no mind to be misunderstood. For answer then, he tightened his grip upon those fair and ruddy jewels that Peasecod brought to his marriage-portion, and so wrought with them that the eyes rolled back in his lover's head, and he expired upon a sigh. Yet rose he again at Nick's insistent kissing, and threw off his skirts and stays and his smock of fine linen to show his body, slender and hard as Nick's own, yet smooth and white as any lady's that bathes in ass's milk and honey. And so they sported night-long until the rising sun blew pure gold leaf upon their tumbled bed, where they lay entwined and, for the moment, spent.

"I were well-served if thou shoulds't cast me out, once the four-and-twenty hours are past," said Peasecod mournfully.

"And what would be the good of that?" asked Nick.

"More good than if I stayed with thee, a thing nor man nor woman, nor human nor faerie kind."

"As to the latter, I cannot tell, but as to the former, I say that thou art both, and I the richer for thy doubleness. Wait," said Nick, and scrambled from the bed and opened his pack and took out a blank ring of copper and his block of pitch and his small steel tools. And he worked the ring into the pitch and, within a brace of minutes, had incised upon it a pea-vine from which you might pick peas in season, so like nature was the work. And returning to the bed where Peasecod lay watching, slipped it upon his left hand.

Peasecod turned the ring upon his finger, wondering. "Thou dost not hate me, then, for that I tricked and cozened thee?"

Nick smiled and drew his hand down his lover's flank, taut ivory to his touch, and said, "There are some hours yet left, I think, to the term of my bond. Art thou so eager, love, to become dumb stone that thou must be asking me questions that beg to be answered 'No?' Know then, that I rejoice in being thy cony, and only wish that thou mayst catch me as often as may be, if all thy practices be as pleasant as this by which thou hast bound me to thee."

And so they rose and made their ways to Oxford town, where Nicholas made such wise use of his faerie gold and his faerie commission as to keep his faerie lover in comfort all the days of their lives.

doi: 10.1300/5642_17

Exiles

Sean Meriwether

It is well after midnight when you leave Roger's apartment, but you opt to walk home, riding an amorous wave of invulnerability. Your new boyfriend's scent lingers on your clothes and you sniff yourself with a schoolgirl sigh, dance a love struck waltz, oblivious to the car trailing behind you. You gaze up at the moon with rose-tinted eyes, a little drunk and giddy, and blow the old boy a kiss. He stares back impassively; he gives you no warning before he slips behind a cloud ripe with rain.

You jump up and smack the street sign feeling butcher than thou, stumble into your future as iconoclast, lover, and champion of the written word. The public, at last, is about to find out just who the fuck you are. . . .

Rubber squelches on asphalt. Stark shafts of light snare you like a deer. Four doors slam open. *Yo, faggot.* Cold sweat douses your body; the icy drop of your balls. *You hear me cocksucker?* Your brain demands that you run, but your feet won't respond.

Five boys wall you in like a crowd. Metal bats slap palms with metronomic precision. *You wanna suck on this?* You shield your face with your arms but the gesture provides frail shelter. Metal bites into your flesh with a pronounced hunger, the uneven pattern of scuffed aluminum—variegated gray and silver—the last thing you see. Laughter, grunting, kicking. The concrete sidewalk cold comfort as the tornado of bats and boots funnels down. The hybrid odor of sweat and blood fades as you slip beneath the waterline into the darkness below.

You wake in the hospital, its antiseptic stench punching your raw nose. An invisible doctor pronounces you lucky to be alive, says you've been in a coma for ten days, cautions that there is little hope of saving your eyesight. You stop listening to the medical jargon detailing your cranial trauma; the loss, not being able to read or write . . . you stop short of complaining it isn't fair and hold your breath, try to block out the words of the doctor, deprive them of meaning.

Days later there is only quiet acquiescence when they remove the bandages and you find yourself mired in the mud puddle of your vision.

Roger is promptly dismissed, your relationship too fresh to be saddled with multiple operations and months of recovery. The police are of little use—unable to describe the assailants beyond number and approximate age, there are few details you can relay; no other witnesses come forward. The doctors and nurses only poke and prod, ask inane questions, force you to eat. You grow to loathe their staged optimism, roll away from their voices, accepting that you'd brought it all on yourself; being a fool in love, walking home at night, alone, on the wrong side of the sidewalk in the wrong part of town.

Jake, your oldest friend in New York, reads you stories from the paper to help cheer you up. The attack has made you an overnight local celebrity; a martyr to wake the community up to gay bashing. Your name inspires hope, disgust, and fear in equal measure, and becomes the topic of conversations held by other people in other rooms. You allow Jake to speak for you as proxy. He commits himself to his fifteen minutes—won by default—with quiet dignity. Still, your name gradually fades from the news, your first novel from the shelves, and the world shrinks back around you.

When the hospital finally discharges you, it is Jake who escorts you home. Your ground-floor apartment has been distorted into an alien landscape of obstacles and stale odors. You spend a week fumbling around, knocking things off tables and walls, until Jake removes everything you don't actually need. He rearranges your cabinets, stocks your writing desk with fresh paper and pencils, sweet talks you into taking walks outside. You shake your head, insisting you're not ready.

Over time, your external wounds knit and heal, but the internal scars fester and multiply. The stinging memory of the bats eclipses all others, playing in an endless loop against the black screen of your mind. You live in chronic fear of the next attack, the uncaught group of boys circling. You leave your bedroom only to use the toilet and shower; Jake patiently takes care of the rest, preparing your meals and paying your bills with checks from disability.

The rest of each day is spent in your chair, staring at the vague light of the window to the garden beyond. You try to recall the yard, adorned with fairy lights and interwoven rosebushes you planted when you first moved in—then the metal bats return, smashing the vision to bits.

This moment is no different, only the melancholy percussion of summer rain distinguishes it from the hourless rope of days. You feed the growing fear that Jake will soon grow bored of taking care of you and leave to spend his golden years chasing younger men with less baggage. You'll be left to twist in the wind until they push you out; then another group of children can finish the job. You blink at muted shades of nothing and nothing, see only boys with bats, acknowledge what fate has assigned you with a tight nod.

But then the memory fades, driven out by a single green dot. An absinthe fairy. You shake your head to jar it loose and return to your ominous thoughts, but the speck remains, strengthens in color, swells into a small bud. Doubting your sanity, you watch it shift and grow skeptically. The green ripens with each breath, uncoils like a blossom, spreads into a broad rectangle. White lines reveal themselves: a series of graceful sweeps and curls—more art than language. You laugh, a bubble of joy escaping chapped lips, the release like ejaculation. The message hovers, teases your hungry eyes, then snaps off. You reach out to recapture the vision, but your hands remain empty. The jarring loss shudders through you and you grip the worn arms of the chair to steady yourself.

Your labored breathing slows and quiets—beyond the darkness you hear a fire engine wail by, birds chattering about the rain, the dis-

tant rumble of thunder foretelling heavier showers to come. You rise
on the wave of an epiphany, open the window to the moist scent of the
garden. The wet blows in brisk gales, baptizing your face with clean,
fat drops. The garden takes shape before you: the cascade of rain on
the leaves, dance of branches in the wind, secret rush of some small
animal scurrying to his home. *Oh, you blind fool,* you chide yourself,
voice thick with snot, *it's all still there.*

In the morning you open the door and move into the garden, surround yourself with the familiar aroma of rosebushes grown wild.
When Jake arrives with dinner he is excited by this overnight change
in your disposition. You wave him away impatiently, his distraction
interfering with your vigilant search for the message. He retreats to
the apartment, puts on classical music that fills the air with tangible
notes.

When the vision reappears, the letters are already familiar, their
shape implying meaning like Japanese cuneiform—yet this language
is more foreign and elegant. You lean forward, the image growing
stronger. A transmission from somewhere . . . some*one.* You reach out
to run invisible fingers over the smooth lines, translating their essence
through touch, like Braille. *Entrance. Invitation.* You bark out a laugh
when you uncover each piece. Jake returns to say how good it is to
hear you laugh again; hugs you awkwardly. The message vanishes.

The alien invitation appears for days in a row; you look forward to
it the way you once enjoyed writing. At times the image is strong, the
words vibrant, strung tight like a piano. More often the message is a
pulsing signal—you reach out to it, strengthen it with your own will
until it swells to fill you with humming illumination.

Once, instead of snapping off like a light, the invitation fades
gently. Beyond the brackish gray light of the garden stands a man.
You sense him more than see him, his aura of dark green light flickers
like a flame. Tall and slender, a tower of sinewy muscle like a college
basketball player. You understand that the man allows himself to be
seen, just as the letters revealed their meaning. The man whispers, not

aloud but within your mind as if the thought were your own yet in his voice. *Come.*

You stand to face the green fire. The voice repeats, a quiet demand weakening. You keep your gaze fixed on the singular light as it leads to a corner of the garden. *Without your help. We die.* Cold crawls across your flesh. The world rushes over in a flashing wave of panic. The bats. You withdraw, spilling into your cool bedroom. Your skin clammy. You sprawl onto the hard floor, ding of pain echoing through you, shielding yourself from remembered blows.

Jake finds you cowering on the floor and asks what's wrong, what happened. You inch away from the door, afraid of him seeing the man outside, of losing that one true secret. Your friend helps you out of your sweat-soaked clothes into fresh pajamas, urges you to relax, soothes you with a tranquilizer and a glass of water. You take them both with hands that betray your fear. The boys and bats blare in your mind like a car horn, then wane. The vision of the man shines forth. *Come,* he had insisted, but you retreated like a frightened child. Worse. A grown man afraid of ghosts from the past.

Wet days drag by inside your apartment, and the vision of the man remains a disruptive memory. You ignore Jake's constant worrying and focus on the image burned in your mind. You run your hands over the finely tooled lines, revealing more of the message like fog burning off the landscape. *Trapped beneath the earth. Our story lost.* You understand these things the way you know the message is from the man in the garden, that he is not a man, not human, but alien, other, fragile. Wounded eyes stare at you from the void of your memory. You have seen him before, in the garden, *the thin man with the sad smile.*

A small fire lights in your mind, like hunger forcing you to eat—he is there. You jump out of your chair and test the wall for the French doors leading outside. You grab the doorknob, twist. Locked. Jake locked it after your recent fright. The green flame flickers in the garden; you're afraid he'll disappear before you can get to him. You throw your weight against the door, budging it slightly. You repeat—an endorphin rush propelling you—the doors fly open with a tinkling of shattered glass.

The thin man retreats. His green light turns and extends an arm, points to the corner, then fades with the scent of ozone. You rush forward, upsetting terra cotta pots and waterlogged plants, searching for him within the walls of the garden. You reach the corner, dig your fingers into the cement lines between mossy bricks, memorizing every inch in your search for the exit he used. There is nothing. You cry out, tilting your head to the vague gray of the sky, a muted square above your head.

The message flares in your mind, the lines shifting, altering the words, revealing a hidden meaning. You race your mental fingers over the letters, tracing out the new communication. *Entrance. Trust.* You think of the man, his wounded eyes staring out from the past; his breath fills your mouth. A word comes alive, taking on a sound full of ancient vowels.

A deep thunder, rocks tumbling, and a tunnel yawns before your outstretched arms. Your fingers lead you forward with a simple tug like a warm hand welcoming you home. You step down into the earth, testing the smooth walls with your fingers, tracing antique words near the entrance. The rock noise repeats and you are sealed into the humid air, thick with the dust of ages. There is no one around, but the fear of the boys, of those unseen, follows you underground.

The tunnel is a tributary leading to a larger one. Dozens of smaller passages wend off in other directions as the main tunnel curves down. You wonder which will take you to the green man. Your steps falter and silence looms.

You breathe in to sniff out your quarry. The dense air carries hidden aromas that wrinkle the nose: spoiled meat, unwashed skin, ripe bite of standing urine. *Something's not right.* You about-face and run back haphazardly, but are unable to remember which tunnel you came from, turning this way and that, winding yourself into the labyrinth. Your panting ricochets off the rounded walls. You dash into a large room, its size judged by the echo of your heavy breathing. You shrink by comparison.

At the other end of the hall, a flickering light, the man from the garden. *Finwë,* your mouth speaks his name. You rush toward him, hands outstretched, wanting to embrace the being who allowed you to see. *Come.* His image stutters, flares, and burns out. The floor beneath your feet tilts sharply and you slip, grappling against the slick surface. You slide off, float through rushing air, fold and roll across the dirt floor, intense pain as your legs rejoin the earth. Liquid panic grips you, thrashes your heart, steals your breath; you hyperventilate until white spots race across your mind.

A strong voice, your own, tells you this is no time for fear, you must stay in control. Surreal calm settles into you with the weight of deep sleep. Your breath slows, you cough, the stench burning into your lungs. You methodically check your legs; your left ankle flares and you bite down to stop from crying out. Quickly assess the situation: it is silent, the floor is uneven and tacky, the stench like a slaughterhouse, your ankle possibly broken. You build a shaky hope that you'll escape.

On all fours, you send your fingers out to map the sticky earth around you, counting off seconds to judge the distance. Ninety-three seconds from where you started, your hand lands on a slick surface. You slide fingers over its fragile concave shell into gaping holes, over teeth . . . your hand jumps back as if burned, refusing what it has discovered. You move in another direction, come across the tattered remains of another lost soul. Your hands fan out, uncovering an open grave beneath the earth.

Terror swells like fire, erupts in a scream, bulleting over the unseen dead, victims of this malevolent invitation. You collapse into the ground, the gummy earth against your face, imagining what it will be like to die here, alone in the dark, slowly starving to death. You claw at your neck, unable to breathe, vomit boiling in your throat. You sit up and tuck your head inside your shirt. The smell of your own sweat comforting through frantic hours of denials and accusations.

Stop. Clear your mind. You banish the boys and their bats, the creature's flickering image, even Jake's awkward embrace, and focus on the message. It had provided the password for the entrance in the garden, it must also offer an escape from this place. The letters melt, reshaping into crosshatched lines. They don't make any sense; random scratches in the green surface. You turn away from it, cry into your shirt, feeling more abandoned than that night of the attack. You'd survived that to end up here, buried alive in an unmarked tomb. The irony of the situation strikes you and you laugh, unable to stop yourself, hysterically joking that at least you'll have someone to eat. The laugh trumpets out of you, a huge noise in the cavern, giving you a strange confidence in the face of certain death. You wonder what Jake will do when he finds you missing. Would he be tricked below ground, joining you here in a marriage of corpses?

The thought of them trapping Jake freezes your blood. The uncontrollable laughter chokes off. You can't let that happen to him, not to anyone else. You sit cross-legged, the way you did in kindergarten, and formulate a plan. You have to navigate back to the surface and make sure the secret doors were closed forever, but first you need to get out of here.

You bring the message back into focus, certain that it means something. When you run your mental hands over the lines, they hum like silver strings. Some lines sound long and low, others pitched high and shrill. You touch one, then another, orchestrating a strange music like a child banging the piano. Slower, forming an atonal melody, changing nothing. One long line runs across the length of the message, ending in a fat bulb. The tone of it ranges from star singing to deep frog croaks. Dozens of other lines run perpendicular to it, each with their own range of tones, sweeping out into a bloodstream of little lines, a map of . . . you flash onto meaning, superimpose Manhattan over this musical version, Broadway running above the long line, ending here, at the great hall, the ball at the end.

Just to the side of the bulb, a thin line, barely a mark on the map, its tone so low that you can barely make it out. It wiggles its way north, joins another tributary, another vein, the end of the line a tinkling of bells.

You lie flat on your back, shut your eyes and focus on the skinny line, on the deep bass note. You try to hum it, match the tone in your throat to the one from the map. You clear your throat and try again, pitching down to that impossible note, the sound resonating in your head with a violent vibration. You cough harshly and try again, dropping your hum another octave, until your throat burns like whisky, using your entire body to force it out.

You fall back winded, ankle throbbing, unable to press on. The darkness bites down, fills your body with renewed lethargy, memory of the months spent in your chair. It would be so easy to let go and allow the earth to take what's hers. A creeping eternity is spent in thoughtless contemplation of death, your stomach grumbling impotently for food.

The remembered aroma of Jake intercedes; the smell of his body, his powdery cologne. The image of him rises in your mind, from that first time you met, the dapper gentleman with the crooked nose. How he had made you laugh, made you feel comfortable in the gangly body you once inhabited, attempted to get you to stand on your own. You'd never said thank you to the man who had been there all along, who had taken care of you when the world tossed you aside.

You swallow the lump in your throat, take a deep breath of squalid air, and drop your hum down as far as you can, holding that memory of Jake, his smell and his unique spirit, foremost in your mind. The note swells out of you, raspy and raw, but attained, growing outside of you. The ground drops a fraction and you dig your fingernails into the floor to prevent sliding off, but keep the sound going, filling the cavern with a deep bass. Your ear catches a sound, like the tumbling rock noise of the first gate, creeping open slowly. You crawl to it, forcing the hum through shuddering breath, face purpling, afraid of it closing before you can reach it. Your hands sweep the way clear, knocking the remnants of those who came before from your path, aiming for the sound. Stale air filters through the thick stench, funneling from a small space, wide enough for you to slip through. You wriggle through the tight enclosure, inch yourself to the small channel beyond.

At the end you tumble to the ground, wheezing from the exertion, but life ringing in your veins. You thank Jake for getting you this far, wonder how many have made it out of that graveyard. A reply from another voice, *You are the first.* It is the man from the garden. Finwë.

You pull yourself into a painful stand and limp, angry fingers searching the way, riding the sides of the tunnel. *Where are you, crea-*

ture? The tunnel curves dramatically to the right, and you follow it, confirming your progress against the map in your mind.

The vision of the man appears, flickers weakly. You jerk toward it, your ankle protesting the beating it receives. A small room opens off the side, a faint green light radiates from there. He is within, lying prostrate on a low bed. You rush at him, hands ready to choke. He speaks, his voice in your mind like brittle ice on puddles. *You have come.*

You stop. The thing before you is dying. You can see it in his green light, almost translucent, weaker than before. His body feels cool to the touch, his breath painfully slow, trapped in some sort of stasis. *Finwë?*

The body does not respond. *Our story . . .* his voice breaks into your thoughts. An exhalation follows, one that borders on his last. Cautious you feel for a heartbeat and find a low erratic thrub. The boniness of him reminds you of the dead in the chamber below the great hall. *. . . must not be lost.* Thin arms ensnare you, drag you rigidly to his face, his pasty mouth on your mouth, filling you with smoke.

There are words without words as Finwë enters you. His memories fill your head, leaving you nauseous but buoyant, placed into his dream.

There are trees and full sun. He is here, an unfaded glory. Another stands beside him, Finrod, his brother. There are dozens of their people, tall and healthy. Something in their angelic movements reminds you of the elves from your stories.

There are humans, men and women, skin soft brown, who greet the elves with reverent ceremony. It is a wedding. A steady drumbeat. A man and woman dance at a distance from each other, dance their past and future lives together. The village joins the couple; Finrod and Finwë, twin princes, are welcomed, then other elves enter the growing circle. The beat swells to unite them, man and woman, humans and elves, in one blissful dance.

Finwë exhales, his breath within you, the corpse relaxing its grip. You break away as the green light fails. A foreigner stretches inside, fills your hands and feet with its presence. *We must go;* his voice.

Within you, times change. *White men drive the Natives north; they are coughing the white man's cough. The elves watch from the trees, helpless, angry. More white men arrive. Trees are felled, forests reduced to scrubby patches.*

Small houses squat in the mud; everywhere fences and walls rise, dividing the land into unnatural squares.

You escape into the tight passage, your ankle rioting pain. Finwë's rapid memories overwhelm your senses as *the elven leader falls ill, fades into gray death. The two princes lead the procession, rows of elves rise to honor their fallen king, their fallen father. Finrod's anger directed at the little men, calls for retaliation. Finwë wraps his arms around his brother, reminds him it has been prophesized, they must accept fate.*

You collapse, gripping your ankle, coughing around the *flourish of white men, a small city emerges; drunk bawdy men and women fill muddy streets, dead animals carved in open-air shops, wild dogs tear at fly-strewn flesh. Finwë approaches as ambassador, looking to make peace between human and elf, as it has been in the past. He is captured, taunted, lowered into a pit filled with sewage. Men piss and defecate on him, laughing at their powerless captive. Finwë pales, trapped in the foul water.*

The voice within you urges you on, gets you back on your trembling feet, the images roll in faster than you can move. *Finrod leads a band of elves, taking up swords to attack, driving their points into bloated flesh. Men surround them, outnumber them by hundreds, elvish blood mixes with human's, Finrod barely escapes, Finwë remains.*

The map leads the way, you edge forward as the story unrolls; *a man lifts him out of the pit, washes him down, his white nudity blaring. He feeds the elf, treats his wounds, does this without speaking. Other men enter, brandishing fire irons, searing the elf's gentle flesh. They pour wine into his mouth and drag him outside, follow him under cover of darkness. Finwë stumbles back, leading the men into their village, dozens are slaughtered before they can escape.*

You slant up through ancient tunnels, slipping into exhausted sleep every few hours, crawling at last into the wet summer night. The heavy rain cleanses you of underworld odors, you open your mouth to receive heaven's gift while *the elves burrow into the ground, a secret warren; Finwë imprisoned beneath their great hall. The men move up the island, stripping it bare like locusts. The forest is plowed into farmland; wooden houses line cobblestone streets; houses eclipsed by massive brick buildings. Industry fills the sky with soot, the water with sewage. Fish lie dead on*

*the banks of the rivers. The elves vanish like the Indians, a slow creeping death
takes them. The dead are burned without ceremony.*

Above ground you become disoriented, the map no longer useful.
You roll across a larger garden, long sweep of muddy lawn. Large
trees emerge from the darkness in a symphony of raindrops on leaves.
A park, you understand, Finwë's thoughts sweeping over yours, *men
ripping huge wounds in the earth, uncovering the elves' tunnels, slaughtering
the alien creatures they find there. The passages are walled in, trapping them.
The city bloats, the horses give way to cars, cobblestones covered by asphalt,
bricks fall to glass towers spiraling into the clouds. The elves fade, their radiant
skin pales, their elaborately patterned clothes fall ragged, muddied, dying.
There is only hatred. Finwë lingers, a living corpse beneath them all.*

You limp along, the park sprawling in all directions. Hearing the
wet rush of traffic, you move in that direction to find a large stone edi-
fice. You run your hands along the edge, finding a metal plaque and
touching the letters, *Engineer's Gate.* Central Park. You cry, thinking
about the others, the procession of men and women enticed by
Finwë's invitation. Their bodies spiraling into the pit, left to rot and
decay.

Keeping the park on your right hand side, you totter down Fifth
Avenue toward the south end of the park where police are likely to be.
You must outrun Finwë's visions; they sweep down on you chaoti-
cally, their chronology now violent and random.

When you finally reach a policeman, you tell him you've been at-
tacked, that you need to get to the hospital. Finwë's thoughts spiral
down on his abduction, the stench of human waste fills your nostrils.
The policeman at first ignores you, treating you like some homeless
nut, then he is suddenly kind, awkwardly skirting your blindness.
Missing person. He takes you into a squad car and provides a dusty wool
blanket to warm you; its smell leading Finwë to remember the damp
of his tomb.

At the hospital the nurses take you in, strip away your soiled
clothes. They ask who they should call and you instantly say Jake,
give them his number. He arrives after your broken foot has been x-
rayed and sealed in a heavy cast and you are hooked up to a saline drip
to replenish fluids. You grit your teeth through the pain, knowing

that you survived. Somewhere deep within you Finwë shouts, wanting his story told.

Jake hugs you tightly; you hear the tension in his voice as he fights off tears. You kiss him. You don't have the words to thank him for coming, for being there always. Words are kept close and tight by the elf's ghost.

I thought you were dead. The door was broken, you were missing for days. Jake kisses the side of your head, thanking god for returning you safe and sound.

That doesn't matter now. You ask for paper and a pencil. You have to write something down before the painkillers kick in, get the swirling stories out of your head and onto the page. You listen to Jake hold his breath, exhale slowly, the wet rise of a smile. *All right.*

Jake returns with a spiral notebook and pencil purchased from the gift store. You take the pencil in hand; it feels right, a natural extension of your arm. You open the book to the first page, touch the edges with your fingers, judge where to begin. The letters begin to form, graceful sweeps and curls, the elf's words pouring out of your hand like lost magic. Finwë laughs, the sound emerging from your mouth, as his story spills onto the page.

doi:10.1300/5642_18

How Laura Left a Rotten Apple
and Came Not to Regret the Cold of the Yukon

Lynne Jamneck

Never did I think I would find enchantment in a place like the Yukon. Not that I didn't believe in magic. I just never thought I'd leave the city. Then again, I should know better. I surprise myself all the time. Besides—snow, you know. It's like that.

I left New York because it became too much of everything. Too many people, crowded beyond belief. Skyscrapers and cranes that endangered my sense of perception. Noise—the constant, grinding clamor that rendered me helpless to defend against the solid input of information. Unsympathetic concrete inflexible beneath my feet . . . and way too much daytime TV.

The last straw was receiving an irate flip of the bird beneath a ginormous sky-stealing DKNY billboard by a cabbie and not understanding the accompanying insult. At times like these, I was glad I didn't own the prerequisite New York accessory—a gun.

I packed the only three suitcases I owned and had a last stroll through Central Park. The Statue of Liberty remained her stoic self throughout our one-way conversation. I smoked a last Marlboro beneath her perpetually flaming torch. She didn't seem to think much about my confessions about quitting the habit. Maybe she missed France. I got the distinct feeling she didn't give a flying fig about my complaints. Really, who could blame her?

I caught a KLM flight from LaGuardia Airport and spent more than ten backbreaking hours in transit, before taking a chartered airplane the size of a mosquito to the small town of Poniwok in the Yukon Territory.

The weather was atrocious.

Well. Too late to turn back now. I'd never give that black Gotham the satisfaction.

Poniwok.
Population 4,500.
David Lynch's wet dream.

Mountie Sergeant Gwen Morrigan looked at me intently from above the rim of her steaming cup of diner coffee. Blonde wisps of hair spider-legged from beneath her chocolate-brown wool beanie. *Tuque,* as she had reminded me on several occasions. Rhymes with *took.* Beanie—what the hell? Americans, go figure. She made me nervous for all the right reasons.

I watched as she nestled the cup in its saucer and dumped yet more sugar from a squeezie bottle into the tar-black coffee. She never wore gloves, despite the mostly well-below-freezing-point temperatures. Tough cookie. I checked the mercury of the gauge on the wall: −6 Celsius. And I had grown used to this?

The sergeant swallowed her coffee as if it was strong drink and looked at me mischievously. The smell of butter tarts wafted from the diner's kitchen. The taste of pecan pies without pecans. I glanced briefly at the occupied booths near us. No one seemed the least bit interested in our conversation.

Morrigan weighed her words and asked: "Were you a rebel, Ms. Kane?"

I almost blushed at the inflection in her voice. "Well. Not too sure about that. I write stories for a living. That, at least, is my father's idea of rebellion."

How had we stumbled onto this topic of conversation? One moment she was asking me why a best-selling author had left the Big Apple for a small cherry, and then all of a sudden she was citing my apparent mutiny and I was feeling like a lovesick teenager.

I hadn't planned on fooling around with the local constabulary but there was something . . . *absurdly* alluring about Gwen Morrigan. And to find her in such a desolate, barren place as Poniwok was edging on the mysterious. New York had never offered up a gem such as this.

Gwen smiled at me knowingly. "You still haven't told me why you left New York."

I didn't want to say something pedestrian, so I simply pitched my shoulders dismissively. "Too much . . . New Yorkness." So I said something stupid instead.

"New Yorkness? Huh. And they say Canadians talk funny."

I swallowed coffee and kept my mouth shut.

"So what did your agent say when you told her you were taking off to a place no one had ever heard of?"

A sudden gust of ice wind howled wolfishly round the corner of the deli and made off down the road. "She nearly had a heart attack."

"I can imagine."

"According to her, I wasn't rebelling; I was making the biggest mistake of my life. She said that New York forgets people once they leave the city's perimeter."

Gwen smiled and signaled the waitress for more coffee. "We have no such qualms around here."

The first time I saw Gwen it was snowing, a rather habitual occurrence in Poniwok. I was trying my best not to look like a total dolt while lugging my suitcases off the chartered plane that had deposited me in Old Crow—population 260—about a hundred kilometers east of Poniwok.

She stood at the foot of the steps leading down from the airplane, snowflakes plowing furiously round her head, boots sunk down in the snow up to her calves. She didn't seem to notice.

When I finally got myself on the ground, Gwen had resolutely stuck out her hand for me to shake (no gloves) and I'd dropped everything to grab it firmly with both of my own. Curious . . . I remember feeling heat radiate from her, her bare hands warm through the padded wool gloves I was wearing.

I didn't give it a beat of thought at the time. I was suffering from a wicked case of jet lag and my period had started with subliminal vengeance just hours before. I chalked the experience down to a doozie of a hot flush.

Gwen said something but I didn't hear it over the din of the airplane's propeller and the howling wind. I smiled and nodded and she picked up two of my three suitcases without fuss and started walking toward the robust police pickup truck parked a couple of yards away. I didn't waste any time in following her. Was this the extent of the welcoming committee my agent had talked about? *Yes Laura, small isolated towns love welcoming New York celebrities to their communities.* She must have been sarcastic.

You think?

Ruth—bless her heart—had almost choked on her breakfast baguette when I'd told her on a sun-drenched Manhattan Monday morning that I was leaving New York. She just about had a coronary when I told here *where* I was going.

"Professional suicide, Laura!"

Drama queen. I told her not to worry—people liked it when writers did eccentric things.

"You're not eccentric Laura; you're pissing off to some . . . native Nowhereland!"

Her words now carved shrill noise in my head as I ducked down and struggled my way to the police truck. I felt wet, everywhere. The lamenting wind seemed to be whispering admonitions in my ears with icy lips.

I tossed the suitcase with the others already on the backseat and dragged myself into the passenger seat. Finally, mercifully, out of the snow. The inside of the truck wasn't much better.

The crazy woman without gloves was sitting behind the wheel, humming off-key to an old '80's song on the radio. My face felt numb. Was that a contradiction in terms?

"I hope you're Laura Kane," Gwen Morrigan said, looking at me with those dark, shadow-pooled eyes which seemed out of place in a place so white. "Otherwise I've gone and picked up the wrong woman."

In different circumstances, I would have recognized that right off as the come-on line I later realized it was. But I was tired and crabby and hungry and briefly contemplated getting right back on that horsefly of an airplane and risking Ruth telling me *I told you so.*

It was only later, drifting off to sleep beneath a tally of blankets that I remembered: I don't get hot flushes.

Esther Fromgard owned the Poniwok grocery store. In truth, that was too kind a description for the place, but it fitted my vocabulary. It really was more of a supply store where you were encouraged to buy in bulk. A box of canned tuna, a carton of instant pasta, ditto the coffee creamer.

Now Esther, she was a talker. Why wasn't that a surprise? She took a liking to me from day one. Or maybe she just pretended very well.

"Seeing as you're new here in town—let's see. You have one of them butterbean bags at half-price. You should eat. Just look at you. You're too thin."

I refrained from telling her that all the butterbeans would do was make me fart. Instead, I thanked her. She waved a liver-spotted hand. "New York City, 'eh?" She lit an unfiltered cigarette with a remarkably steady hand.

"Imagine that," I said, thinking of an old song.

"What on earth you doing here then?" The question was both curious and skeptic.

I took a bottle of unfamiliar but expensive-looking Scotch from a shelf. "I came to write a story."

"Huh. Not enough stories in New York?"

"Too many."

"Now that—that's true."

I wondered if Esther had been to New York but didn't ask. I took the Scotch—and the bag of beans I'd be eating through the remainder of the year—along with some fresh milk and eggs to the counter. Esther sucked her cigarette with devotion while scanning the contents of my basket. I had no idea what the items would come to. None of the supplies were price marked but, considering Esther was my only option I didn't see that it mattered much.

"What you think of our sergeant?" Esther asked, writing what I assumed was the accumulative total of my shopping on a notepad.

"Sergeant?"

"Our sergeant. Gwen Morrigan. Always thought that was a funny last name. Not Poniwok stock."

"Oh—Sergeant Morrigan!"

She looked up at me quizzically from the notepad. "What—no sergeants in New York City? Only them detectives?" She pronounced it *deh-tectives.*

"No, no, of course there are sergeants in New York." Esther's sly smile made me think she was having me on. "Sergeant Morrigan's not from here?" I asked, my curiosity peaked and wanting to cover my chagrin.

"Nope. Came to Poniwok couple of years ago. Damned if I can exactly remember when. Filthy cigarettes—make me forgetful."

That was a novel one for the Surgeon General to get his teeth into. "It was very nice of her to meet me at the airport."

Esther laughed out loud. "Airport! That's a real good one, Honey. Well, someone had to go and get you in that whiteout of a snowstorm. You'da ended up in Alaska without a proper guide. This place is like Brigadoon when the snow closes in 'round it. Here you go." She handed me a distended brown paper bag and some change. I was going to have to get used to carrying cash with me.

"The sergeant's a peach. She caught those baby-moose killers coup'la months ago with some fancy *deh-tective* work."

"Mr. Morrigan must be proud," I ventured.

Esther lit another cigarette. "No Mr. to speak of. That girl's too damn stubborn for any man. Too damn tough, too."

I smiled at Esther and pushed past the obstinate door back out into in the cold. Things were starting to look up.

Two months later, and the good sergeant and I were dancing round one another in the most magnificent and stupidly romantic of ways.

Hard as it may be to believe, the weather took a turn for the worse. Ruth phoned and asked when I was coming back to New York. I told her that I'd written twenty thousand words in one week. She reiterated that this was solely because it continuously snowed in Poni*wak* and Fifth Avenue wasn't a taxi drive away anymore. I told her hey—if it ain't broke . . .

Ruth countered by asking why I was so goddamned chirpy. I said because there was the distinct possibility that I was going to get laid very soon. Then I slammed the receiver down like a giddy teenager and promptly unplugged the phone.

It was Tuesday morning. I was just going to sit down with a charged laptop and frozen knuckles when a knock at the front door stopped me from starting a new chapter. Terry McKenna—the intrepid P.I. of my mystery series—would have to wait her damn chance.

I was expecting Koki, or Cookie, or whatever the hell his name was. Koki, an elderly Wiseman of unknown heritage, was a handyman of sorts. Jack-of-all-trades and master of all to boot. How did he do it? I had no idea. Electrical, plumbing, carpentry, whatever. Koki had a magical tool that could fix all.

This was great news to me since the last plumber I'd foolishly invited into my apartment back in the city had done such a spectacular job at being incompetent that my whole bathroom ended up getting a rehaul. I kid you not.

But I digress.

Koki was supposed to come and cast his keen eye on my generator. Most of the houses in Poniwok had one, but the place I was staying in hadn't been lived in for some time. The generator had already failed me once after the electricity went down during a snowstorm. I wasn't going to have it happen again. When the lights went out in Poniwok, things were as dark as a witch's nose hole.

I opened the front door, ready to try and understand as gracefully as possible the foreign dialect of Koki's accent. It wasn't him. Surprisingly, I didn't seem to care.

"Sergeant Morrigan." And again, without any gloves.

Gwen seemed pleased at my surprise. "You know you've got a gutter round back that's just about ready to hit the ground running?"

I stuck my head round the edge of the door to look but didn't spot the felonious trimming. "Koki's coming over; I'll ask him to look at it."

"Ah, actually, no. That's what I came to tell you. Afraid your generator and the gutter will have to wait."

"Why don't you come inside? I grow cold just from looking at you out there."

Gwen shrugged. "I'm tough."

"So I've heard. Come inside anyway."

In all likelihood, it could be attributed to the fact that Gwen Morrigan made me feel like a pining adolescent, but I swear . . . it's the queerest thing. Whenever she comes near me I smell bluebells. And maybe . . . peaches. And it wasn't her perfume, either. Nothing bottled smelled this fresh, this . . . alive. And it was as if the smell expanded outward to fill whatever room she happened to be in. Even outside, in the snow, in the wind, I've smelled it. She had the uncanny knack for making everything seem warmer somehow.

You're right, Laura, babe. Pining. Adolescent.

"I hope nothing's amiss with Koki," I said trying to get my mind back on track.

"Oh, hell no." The low, steady timbre of her voice held a tone of amusement. "Koki's just an impatient son-of-a-bitch sometimes who won't act his age. Seems he climbed up Slick Grayson's roof day before last an' slipped."

"Oh shit. Is he okay?"

"No doubt. Just sprained his ankle something good in the resulting fall. He won't be on that leg for a couple of days to come."

"Poor Koki." And damn his stupidity. What about my generator?

Gwen stepped closer, cutting the space between us. "I thought I'd ask if you wanted to come out to the creek. Going to see if those moose poachers have been foolish enough to come back." Her lips hovered. Was there something else? For how much longer would we be able to keep our hands off each another?

I had to say something. "You're not taking one of your constables with you?"

A risky spark glimmered in her eyes. "Nope. Scaller's got the day off and I need Doug to supervise. Got a cluster of fresh ones from Whitehorse in the Detachment office and I don't want any of them chafing away footprints. Besides, you're a much better conversationalist than any of them."

"Ha."

"Better looking, too."

"Oh—"

Kiss her.

Kissherforgodsake.

"I should get back to writing . . ."

"Yes, you should. So are you coming with me or what?"

How could I resist such an invitation?

The wind-chill factor rivaled the sharp edge of an untouched razor blade. Even in Gwen's macho pickup, I could feel it slither and creep in through the cracks, the ventilation gaps.

The snow had stopped. Before we drove out of Poniwok, Gwen made sure to check that the truck's snow chains were securely fastened. No shrinking violet by any means myself when it came to anything physical, I'd nevertheless been happy to stand aside and admire the way her hands worked the steel belts into submission.

The creek was a frozen-over lake of decent size, walled to one side by a crescent of black spruce and lodgepole pine forest. It looked dark in there. I didn't say anything because the thought of coming across vulnerable in front of Gwen made me wither.

We got out of the truck. Despite the fact that it had stopped snowing, weather conditions still seemed decidedly bleak all 'round. The chilling wind still had the ability to bear straight down into the core of my bones. Hesitantly, I closed the truck's passenger door.

"Come, on Laura. Toughen up."

I looked sideways across the bonnet of the truck and saw Gwen grinning smarmily. Then she turned around and walked off toward the sickled forest before I could save face with a clever comeback.

I set off after her, having by now at least mastered the art of walking through knee-deep snow. When I caught up, she was already standing at the edge of the forest.

Out of breath, I said: "I didn't know there was profit in killing moose."

"There isn't, really. It's cheap, illegal game. Tastes like beef and it's low in fat. Last I heard you could get a hind quarter for $150 in Sydney."

"That's awful."

"Mmm. The poaching thrives because there's been no concentrated effort to clamp down on the illegal selling of moose." Gwen's eyes narrowed as if she was scanning for something inside the drawn-out darkness between the trees. A stilted demeanor had replaced the easiness with which she usually carried herself. Resentment colored her face.

"I didn't think that sort of thing happened here."

Gwen's shoulders relaxed somewhat. She gave me a sideways glance. "Happens everywhere. Always has. People have forever had an uncanny knack for disturbing the natural rhythm of the world. Scarier still—they seem to be getting better at it all the time."

"Yeah." I couldn't think of anything else to say. Again, my God-given talents left me in the lurch.

"Come on." Gwen motioned me to follow. I was relieved to hear the lightness return to her voice.

"What exactly are you looking for?" Things became even darker as the first trees closed in behind us. The bare branches of the trees looked oddly petrified. "Surely you can't kill a moose with a trap?"

"Nope. Not kill. Seldom catch, either. But they hurt themselves something awful trying to break loose. Makes it real easy to track them down with a rifle."

"How very sporting."

Gwen's hand suddenly shot out and pushed back against my stomach. Adrenalin buzzed through my limbs. I stopped dead.

On the ground, right at the tips of my boots was a small, cleared piece of ground. A vicious looking spike trap nestled there, hidden by a makeshift barrier of stacked snow, its jagged teeth patiently waiting for something to snap on.

"Careful," Gwen breathed. Steam rose from her lips and wafted lazily out into the cold. "They trap writers from the big city up here, too."

"Holy shit."

"Here." She took the collapsible steel baton from her belt and handed it to me. "Be kind to a moose. Stick it in there."

I did. The trap sprung shut with a sadistic clang. There was a tight, rustling sound from inside the trees. I tried to stare through the black curtain of gloom but my eyes didn't seem to want to focus.

"Fairies," Gwen said. I looked at her and laughed, relieved at her attempt to break the tension and lighten the mood. She hadn't taken her hand from my stomach. I could feel the heat from her fingers radiate through my parka, crawling past the fabrics of my clothes beneath my skin and settling there like a restless animal. It was the most alive I'd felt in a long time.

A gun blast sounded suddenly, close, crackling like lightning through the cold air. A pierced, bursting sound that came from someplace between the thick brush of trees. Whiskey jacks shuddered and rose from the trees in a unanimous beating of wings.

The heat in my stomach suddenly became hot, disproportionate. In an untethered moment I remember thinking—

—*Gwen—what are you doing to me—?*

I looked up from the sprung trap to Gwen's face. Why was my vision blurry on such a crisp day? And things sounded . . . distorted . . . Were those birds?

The world shifted.

Gwen's face seemed superimposed against the gray sky. She was saying something, her lips moved, but I couldn't hear again. A high-pressure sound filled my ears, whistling—

Why did Gwen look so anxious? We disabled the spike—

Look at her strawberry hair thrashing about her face. I felt the pressure of her hand intensify. I looked down.

Something seeped slowly through her fingers and dropped blood red on the disrupted snow. It took me a moment to realize.

And then the heat began to hurt. My knees buckled. Seconds after I felt the clammy iciness against my scalp and Gwen's hands ripping open my jacket, buttons popping. Was that snow falling? Again?

"Jesus it hurts . . ." My voice sounded foreign.

"Look at me, Laura. Look at me—you're not going to die. Just relax. Look at me."

I did. Her eyes so calm . . . dark but somehow ethereal.

Everything became displaced.

Strange how I could feel things—hear them from a place where I wasn't quite sure where I was. Not sure whether the extreme brightness was snow or impending death hastening in for the kill, I decided to shut my eyes.

The brightness remained but was somehow calming. Someone spoke but the words sounded distant, muted.

Gwen?

Sounded like—

. . . *pissing off to some nowhere neverland!* Ruth's words echoed dully in my ears.

No feeling. Slipping away. . . should have stayed in New York . . .

Esther Fromgard? Leaning over me, looking down at the blood on my clothes. . . . What was Esther doing in the woods? Who was minding the store?

"He's dead," she said, looking away to her right. A crow cawed somewhere close.

Gwen's voice: "Should have killed him myself." My eyes blurred again.

Esther: "Not your job . . . won't stop, still. Others will come . . . think you've gone soft."

The rustle of feathers, something large. "Laura . . ."

The word drifted loosely.

Koki eventually came by to fix the generator. His ankle healed before my injured abdomen. I hadn't even been aware that he'd been at the house.

Esther told me. She brought me steaming chicken soup every day. I didn't dare move from the bed, save for the insistent calls of nature which were bad enough. My insides were torn, and I felt it. I reckoned a slug to the gut would do that. I also realized, with some pride, that maybe I was tougher than I thought.

"Lucky," Esther said to me between puffs of nicotine. "A hair's breadth to the left and you would have been crow's meat."

"Was it the poacher?" I managed to ask. Everything hurt.

Esther flicked her cigarette butt out the bedroom window. "Yes. A poacher." She didn't say what kind of poacher.

Ruth demanded that I move back to New York. I said no, but reminded her that a near-death experience would definitely make for good publicity. She was somewhat appeased by that.

Gwen visited. Always when I was asleep. Don't ask me how I knew. Maybe it had something to do with the crow that would come and sit on my windowsill when no one else was there. Even when it snowed. Especially when it snowed, and the world outside looked like a white, boundless battlefield.

It took me a good five weeks to get back on my feet. By this time I'd gotten pretty tired of chicken-soup-a-la-Fromgard, but at least I'd written another twenty-five thousand words. Terry McKenna was happy, I was happy. This was good.

A part of me obviously needed Poniwok. Writer's block had hit me with a vengeance after I'd finished the second book in the McKenna series. I'd come to the Yukon partly because I thought that, with fewer distractions, my mind would become clearer. Focused. The Big Apple was a master at telling its own tales. But she became jealous when other stories infringed upon her territory. Poniwok was brutally different. It invited tales to be spun.

On the fifth Monday morning after getting shot between the cedar trees I went down to Poniwok's Detachment Office. Dolly Matera, the receptionist clerk greeted me with churning enthusiasm.

"Dolly, it'll take more than an errant bullet from a poacher's rifle to keep me off my feet."

"That's the spirit!" Dolly chimed. If she had a bell, she would have rung it. I didn't tell Dolly that, no—it was mostly stubbornness.

"Damn . . . poachers," Dolly affirmed the sentiment I'd been thinking for the past five weeks with a faraway look in her eyes.

I asked: "Sergeant Morrigan, is she in?"

Dolly perked. "You know, she just popped out." She leaned closer and lowered her voice to a conspiratorial whisper. "I think the sergeant took up smoking again." Dolly had a gleam in her dark, almond-shaped eyes. Her face, framed by a wild head of hazelnut hair

that perfected the just-out-of-bed-look made her look like a mischie-
vous pixie bent on monkey business.

"Of course, you didn't hear it from me," she added innocently.
"The Morrigan's never been this hell-bent on impressing someone."

The Morrigan? Probably one of those horrid Americanisms. I read-
ied myself to leave. "You'll tell her that I was here? Just to show I'm
not completely pathetic."

Dolly gave me a chiding look. "Pathetic? Hardly. You did persuade
death to look the other way, after all. That takes some doing, believe
me. But I'll be sure to tell her anyway."

I was sure that just about the whole of Poniwok were aware of
Gwen's and my flirtation. No one seemed in the least bothered by it.
I was delighted. Being pleasantly surprised by people was still one of
my biggest fancies.

Back home I ignored the digital clock on my laptop that read half
an hour shy of noon and poured myself a double scotch. The liquid
went down ruthless and strong. It burned away the slight reminder of
a sting that had been plaguing between my ribs ever since I'd got
shot.

Laura, you were shot. Almost killed. It sounded like something that
would happen to Terry McKenna, not me for godsake . . .

As if it wanted to affirm my status in the land of the living, the
weather had turned conspicuously pleasant. Practically overnight, the
perpetual gray mass in the sky had become tattered enough to let in
short rays of sun and sketchily scattered patches of blue. It seemed a
bit extraordinary, this sudden change in climate. I decided to forget
about the peculiarity soon enough though and to enjoy the change
while it lasted. Who knew how long before it all dissolved into rain,
sleet and snow once again?

The crow hadn't been on my windowsill for two days. I was starting to miss its company.

Ruth would have a field day with me. *This place is making you superstitious, Laura.* I could just see her: black Stella McCartney suit, cell
phone glued to one ear, cigarette waving aimlessly in the other hand.
Well I say: what's wrong with a little superstition?

I was about to sit down and check my e-mails when a single knock on the door interrupted my flow. If that was Esther with more chicken soup . . .

Then a familiar voice outside said: "Come on, open the door. It's getting hot out here."

I smiled, shook my head. Only Gwen would find the sun annoying. My heart thumped double beats. I opened the door.

"Wow. Spiderman," Gwen said.

I'm unashamed to admit that I was momentarily distracted by her perfect breasts beneath the faded Mountie T-shirt. "Spiderman?"

Gwen indicated my own T-shirt. It had been a gift from my famous comic-book cartoon-artist brother. "Leaps tall buildings in a single bound?"

"I think that's Clark Kent. Superman?"

The atmosphere was charged with the stupidities of small talk and lust. Neither of us moved. I smiled, expelling a panicky laugh. Then Gwen came inside, pulling the door shut behind her and we were kissing even before I heard the latch *click* into its slot.

There it was again. Bluebells. And her mouth; her lips, her tongue hot and her hands as eager as mine. Jesus—my head felt like it was going to spin off my neck. Gwen's hands were warm on my bare skin as they slowly roamed up my back. Her touch was searing, relentless. I pulled her against me and thought I'd die a sensational death when her erect nipples brushed mine.

We made love on the flimsy couch in the living room. The thing had been there when I moved in. Previously, I'd thought it was probably good for nothing but taking up space. I was wrong.

Gwen was tough. In control. I couldn't stop touching her. The feeble couch protested a gratifying number of times.

Maybe you didn't run away from something . . . Maybe you ran toward something . . .

The words from a dream the night before, the only thing I could remember from my sleep upon waking.

The weather had clouded over again and viciously so. The police pickup shuddered and slipped as Gwen maneuvered it across the rocky road, past the creek, out into the open.

It had been three days after our initial tryst on the couch. At night, when I knew Gwen was sitting behind her desk in the Detachment Office, I couldn't sleep. She'd bewitched me. I felt restless whenever she wasn't with me.

Gwen slammed her foot on the brake. The pickup came to a jerking halt. Before I could ask what was going on she was getting out of the truck. I followed suit. I'd learned by now.

It was dark out. The night bled a deep hue of blue, reflecting mutedly off the snow-covered ground. Gwen pitched herself on the bonnet of the truck and looked up into the sky. A moment later she held her hand up, pointed at the stars and said: "It's starting."

I looked up. It was as if someone had taken a container of green and yellow paint and thrown it across the canvas of sky above us. Without a sound or introduction, the night was lit up by the extraordinary brilliance of the aurora borealis. It pitched and washed across the sky in slow ribbons of yellow and lime green, feeding the night sky's palette. Strands of red occasionally whorled and surged in between.

It was a magnificent sight. As if doors had opened between worlds. The strands of color shimmered and shifted across the sky in broad, open arcs. Some disappeared behind us, back toward the creek. Others hovered, altered color.

I looked at Gwen. She stared at the display of colors intently. From the corner of her eye I could see their dancing reflection.

"The *Tuatha De Dannan,* marching across the sky." The statement carried reverence.

"The fabled Faery People."

Gwen nodded, pleased at my recognition. "When they were defeated by the Milesians, some of them retreated underground, to live in the *Sidhe.* The Faery Mounds. Others ascended. To keep the balance. When they move across the sky like this, they bestow the blessing of the Faery upon Earth."

If I'd left New York only to see what I was currently experiencing it would have been worth the effort.

We watched the lights. Sometimes Gwen became silent. I detected a curious sense of longing in her at those times.

I don't know how much longer we sat there, entranced by the wizardry of the night sky, but as we got ready to leave, Gwen bent down to pick up something. As I opened the passenger door of the pickup she offered me a kiss spiced with promise and a full, blooming sprig of bluebells. I didn't ask where she'd found them. I never wanted to break the spell.

doi:10.1300/5642_19

Mr. Seeley

Melissa Scott

The house was empty when he got home. Emptier than empty, the kind of quiet that usually went with a long time away. Tully hesitated on the back porch, for a second almost afraid to call, then shook himself, and let himself in through the kitchen door. "Joe?" The counters were clean, the dishes not just washed but put away, and dinner not yet begun. "Royelle?"

There was no answer, not from the maid—who shouldn't be there anyway, it was dusk and long past quitting time—and not from Joe Farr, who should be. The flower shop had been closed when Tully came through town, and Joe usually came straight home after he'd locked up. Tully scuffed his feet on the worn bit of canvas just inside the door, and came all the way in, scooping off his cap.

"Joe?"

The house was silent. Tully hesitated, biting his lip. All the way down from Troytown, he'd been looking forward to seeing Joe standing in the kitchen finishing whatever Royelle had made, looking forward to him looking up with that smile on his face to ask Tully to stay to supper. *Royelle made too much again*, he'd say. *Can't have it go to waste.*

Tully scuffed his feet again, reached for the light switch, and changed his mind. He wasn't really supposed to be there, his place was in the room over the garage, but when Joe was here, he was more welcome than a mere employee ought to be. . . . He shoved the thought away, stuck his hands and his cap into his pockets. Probably he should head back to the garage; maybe when Joe came in, he could wander over, pretend he'd come to ask something about the day's deliveries. He turned to leave, and jumped as someone knocked at the door.

It was a colored boy—no, not a boy, a dwarfish little man, one shoulder hunched up and a grin that was all too simple to be trusted, a very black little man in pale cloth trousers and a dust-pale collared shirt.

"You Tully Swann?"

"I'm Mister Swann." Tully tried to look disapproving, but his heart was racing too hard. Jesus, the boy had startled him, coming up on the porch like that.

"Sister Farr sent you a note," the boy said.

Tully opened his mouth to slap him down—every white man in Nolan County might call Joe Farr "Sister," even the ones who didn't mean anything nasty by it, but no colored had any place doing it—and the boy plowed on as though he hadn't said anything improper.

"Mr. Seeley wants to see you."

That shut Tully up. Mr. Seeley was—Mr. Seeley. He'd been a judge, years back, then when Prohibition came in, he'd retired and bought land up on Irish Mountain, saying Nolan County was no place any more for a drinking man. They said he had parties up on the Mountain with women from far away as Memphis and even New Orleans, and you could see the lights of his house for miles. Even on a foggy night, you could glimpse them; Tully'd seen them himself, coming down County 9 with a load of bootleg liquor, gentle lights flicking in and out like the fireflies in summer.

"Give me the note," he said, and knew as he spoke he'd missed his chance to put the boy in his place. The boy knew it too, the knowledge sparkling in his eyes, but he handed over the folded sheet of paper without cracking a smile.

Tully opened the note, reached for the light switch to make the scrawled words come clear. The top part was written in scratchy blue: Sister's favorite pen, the one his mother had given him when he graduated from high school, the one he'd used ever since even though it never had written quite right. Just a few words in Joe's familiar looping hand, *Tully—please do what Judge Seeley asks—Joe Farr,* and then beneath it, in darker ink and a broader, bolder hand, a longer note.

Tully Swann. Please make pick up and delivery of goods to my house at Irish Mountain. Cal will show you the way. Auberon Seeley.

Auberon? Tully thought. It occurred to him he'd never heard Mr. Seeley's Christian name before. If you could call a name like that Christian. He looked at the boy. "You're Cal?"

Cal bobbed his head, almost a parody of respect. "Yessir."

"What goods does he mean?" Even as he asked, Tully thought he knew. Sister was a small-time bootlegger himself, selling liquor to the ladies of Troytown to supplement what he made at the flower shop. Tully had been driving for him since he was seventeen, and sometimes he branched out, worked for other bootleggers, carrying the goods up and down the mountain roads. He was getting a name for himself, had offers from bigger men, but so far he hadn't felt the need to take any of them up on their offers. Sister pretended he disapproved—or maybe it wasn't all pretense, he was a worrier—but at least since Tully'd been driving, Big Jake Montross hadn't been able to bully Joe into paying outrageous prices.

The boy bobbed his head again. "The usual, boss. Mr. Seeley says, you take his car."

Like hell, Tully started to say, but then he looked past Cal, out through the door to the yard, and saw the car. How he'd missed hearing it, he'd never know—maybe Cal had turned off the motor, let it roll through in neutral—but even in the scant light from the kitchen, the lines of it were clear and clean. A black touring car, with a long rounded hood like the newest Fords and a sweet-curved sweep of fender and running board; the back had a low trunk like a Buick roadster, but it wasn't either one. A little bit like a Packard, maybe—as expensive as a Packard, anyway—except Packard never made anything as smoothly curved as those fenders. A Peerless? Duesenberg? He'd never seen either of them except in the Hollywood newsreels. The radiator grill, black-painted like the rest of it, was empty of any badges. Eight cylinders at least under that long hood, he thought, maybe even twelve. Someone had picked out just the edges of the doors and the flanges with silver paint, barely enough to catch the star shine on a new-moon night, and the chrome-plated triple bumper was scrubbed to gleaming. There were headlights and fog lights and a third pair between them, and the spare wheels strapped to the running boards were as black and polished as the body.

"What the hell kind of car is that?" he asked. He hadn't meant to, but he couldn't resist, had to know, and Cal gave him a quick, unreadable glance.

"That's Mister Seeley's car."

"Yeah, but what make is it?"

"Mister Seeley, he had it built special," Cal said. "Ain't no other like it in the world."

Or at least in the county, Tully thought, but he couldn't master the skepticism he knew he should feel. "Wait here," he said, and stuffed the note in his pocket. Sister reluctantly owned a shotgun, kept it locked in a cabinet in the little passway between the kitchen and the dining room, but Tully had the key on his watch chain. He collected the gun, automatically breaking it and slipping shells into the chambers and another handful in his pocket, came back into the kitchen with it hanging in the crook of his arm. Cal blinked at the sight. Tully ignored the movement, gesturing for him to go ahead of him out the kitchen door, then followed the little man, closing the door gently behind them both. He laid his hand on the car's polished nose, feeling it cool as though it had never been driven, and knew he was going to take the job.

"So what kind of goods are we picking up?" he asked, and ran his hand along the edge of the driver's door. The window was open, and he slid the shotgun inside, setting it at a safe angle against the seat. "Or maybe I should just say how much?"

"I believe it's a full load, sir," Cal said, and his teeth flashed in the twilight.

"Open up the hood for me," Tully said, and stooped to check the springs. They were reinforced just like they should be, and the engine—twelve cylinder, twin sixes and clean as a whistle—looked solid. He stepped back to let Cal close and latch the hood, then pulled open the driver's door. Cal grinned again, and scrambled around to the other side.

"One thing," Tully said. "I'm going to need some help loading."

"They'll be folks there, I think," Cal said.

"So where we going?"

"We follow Highway 20 west, boss, til we get to the junction of County 12," Cal said. "Then I'll tell you where to turn."

It was almost full dark, the sliver of a moon just setting over the fields to their left as they turned onto the highway, and the fog was starting to rise from the ditches. Tully took a deep breath, and smelled, over the oil and gas and leather, the wet, dead-leaf smell that meant the fog would last. The headlights cut through the damp air, the pavement a sharp straight line, and he worked quickly through the gears. This was a car for racing, a car for overdrive, for a foot to the floorboards and all the cylinders bellowing. He grinned, reading their speed, and slowed reluctantly as they came up on the crossroads.

"Where to?"

"It's a right, boss," Cal answered. "Then straight on til we cross the St. Francis."

Tully nodded, swung the car right onto the county road. It was gravel only, crunching under the wheels and rattling the undercarriage: smarter to keep the speed down, on a road like this, but a part of him still wanted to floor it, send the stones spraying just to see what the car could do. This was Cahill country, the Cahills being both sheriff and bootleggers, and he hoped Mr. Seeley had squared this business with Pete Cahill. Otherwise. . . . He shut his mind firmly to that "otherwise:" he was not going to go to jail, not with Sister needing him, and not with a car like this under him anyway, because nobody in the county could catch him even in Joe's Franklin. It was still foggy here, that was something, maybe even getting thicker; he thought for a moment about trying the second set of lights, but decided against it. The road dipped once, then twice, and the posts of the St. Francis bridge loomed out of the dark. Tully slowed, the wooden slats noisy under the wheels, and Cal stirred beside him.

"'Scuse me, boss, but it's coming up soon."

"What am I looking for?"

"There'll be a track, off to the left, under a big poplar tree."

Even as Cal spoke, Tully spotted it, a road he'd never seen before, barely more than a pair of bare wheel tracks in the grass. He turned onto it, hoping the ground was harder than it looked, but the big car took it without hesitation.

The track wound with the river, following its banks, and the fog was heavier. Tully switched lights, slowed down, hunching forward over the wheel. Here and there the fog was like a wall, reflecting the light so he could barely see beyond the end of the hood; he held his breath, driving through, but each time the wall dissolved, whisking up and aside like a curtain at the movies.

And then at last he saw more lights ahead, an indistinct glow that resolved to more headlights, slurred and soft with fog, and he had his foot on the brake and his free hand resting on the shotgun before Cal could clear his throat.

"This'd be them, boss."

"I sure as hell hope so," Tully muttered under his breath. He kept the car in gear as Cal opened the door and walked forward into the fog. There was a mutter of voices, Cal's for once genuinely deferential, and then the boy came back into sight, beckoning him forward. Tully took his foot off the brake, slipped forward through a last bank of fog that closed behind him like a door.

They were in a clearing, a widening of the road, the river to his left and a stand of trees to the right. The other headlights belonged to a new-looking Oldsmobile, drawn up on a slant so that the beams of its lights cut across the road and were lost in the trees. There was a darker shape that might be a truck behind it, and three men beside the car, one of them tall and slim and wearing a well-cut suit. He was the one who stepped through the lights to lean in at the window.

"So, you're Auberon's new man." He had a voice like a movie star, not quite English, but almost, and a thin, fine moustache just like Errol Flynn. The hand on the window edge looked manicured, and for an instant the air carried a whiff of sandalwood.

Tully suppressed a shiver, telling himself it was the fog and not desire or fear. "Just for tonight," he said, and the stranger grinned.

"That's what they all say."

"Mister Tamlin," Cal said. "Mister Tamlin? You want we should start loading, sir?"

The fair man straightened, looked back over his shoulder, still with that same easy, superior smile. "All right, Cal. I guess Auberon's in a hurry?"

"He told me to make it quick, sir," Cal said apologetically. "Sorry, sir."

Tamlin shrugged elaborately. "All right. Come on, boys, Mister Seeley wants his liquor." He turned back to the car as the shadowy figures began to move, stooped again to the window. "What's your name, son?"

Tully answered with the first name that came to mind. "Jeff Davis. Cahill."

"Jeff Davis Cahill," Tamlin repeated, and Tully cringed. It didn't generally pay to lie, not where most everybody knew everybody else in the business, but with a stranger involved, it made sense. The man gave him the willies, anyway; he didn't trust the man, didn't want this too-sharp stranger knowing his real name. But he'd forgotten Cal, and now Cal could give him away. He braced himself to brazen it out, to denounce Cal for a lying ignorant fool, but the little man just looked at him, eyes wide in his dark face. "That's Jefferson Davis, I presume."

"That's right." Tully made himself meet Tamlin's mocking stare. *Goddamn Yankee,* he thought, and that seemed to break the spell. Tamlin straightened, looking over his shoulder at the men still hauling the wrapped bottles, and Tully clicked open the door.

"Excuse me," he said, and made his voice as insolent as he dared. "Got to be sure they load it right."

Tamlin stepped back, out of the light, and Tully reached for the flashlight he'd seen before, went around to the trunk. His legs were trembling; he stiffened them, let the light play over the burlap-wrapped bottles. Tamlin's men knew their stuff, but even so Tully waited until the last bundle had been stowed away before climbing back behind the wheel. Cal was there already, looking worried, and Tully pressed the starter. He backed the car, careful because of the soft ground at the river's edge, started back along the narrow track. The car felt heavier under his hands, but steady, the springs solid, and he took a deep breath, working his shoulders. There was something

about Tamlin that set his back up, beyond the fancy suit and the manicured hands, and he risked a glance at Cal.

"Who was that guy?"

"He's Mrs. Seeley's boyfriend," Cal answered. "So you don't want
to get on his bad side."

"Mr. Seeley puts up with that?" In spite of himself, Tully heard the
outrage in his own voice, and Cal shrugged uncomfortably.

"They go their own ways, Mr. Seeley and his wife. He's got a girlfriend or two of his own up on the Mountain."

That was true enough, or at least that was what the gossip said. It
just seemed strange a man as tough as a judge would let his wife get
away with something like that. "Where the hell did she find him?"

"I believe he used to be in pictures," Cal said. "Or so I heard."

"That figures."

"May I ask you a question, sir?"

Tully glanced sideways again, startled. "OK."

"Who told you not to tell him your name?"

"Nobody." Tully scowled at the track unreeling in the headlights.
"Why tell folks your real name if you don't have to? Besides, I don't
know the man. As far as I know, he might could be off to the sheriff
right now."

"It wasn't Mister Farr who told you?"

Tully shook his head, the back of his neck prickling. "Why?"

Cal looked away. "Coming up on the highway now, sir."

Tully hesitated, wanting to know more, but he could tell from Cal's
face he wouldn't get a sensible answer. He let the car bump up over
the last ruts and onto the gravel road, not bothered at all by the
weight of liquor in the back.

"Which way's best?"

"East, sir," Cal said. "And you can let her fly."

Tully couldn't help a grin at that, but he kept the car to a decorous
thirty-five until the intersection of County 9. That road was paved all
the way to the state line, thanks to the fact that the Cahill county
commissioner was tight with the Cahill bootleggers, and Tully shifted
into third. The car responded, surging forward, the twelve cylinders
rumbling like a distant storm. There was one more gear, and only

about ten miles to use it before 9 started its climb up to Moorton Gap, but the fog was still heavy, and he held himself back. Beside him, Cal looked more relaxed. Hell, Tully thought, Cal had sounded almost respectful there for a minute, almost like—almost like he'd passed some test he hadn't known was there. Though why anyone would make a fuss about him not giving his proper name to a strange bootlegger, he didn't know. But it had mattered. The fog lifted as they made the first long turn into the hills, and as it parted, Tully thought he caught a glimpse of Irish Mountain, the lights garish at its peak.

"How far up?"

"'Bout three miles," Cal answered. "You'll see another turn-off to the left. Watch for a white cut on a big oak tree, and then about another hundred yards."

The directions were better than the turn-off road. Tully winced as the big car pulled itself up the steep turns, jouncing over rocks and holes left after the rain had carved its own track down the mountain. In fact, there were times when it felt as though he was driving up a dry creek, not a road, but every time he thought he'd lost the track, the wheel ruts reappeared again.

"Mr. Seeley must not get many visitors," he said under his breath, and Cal cackled softly.

"We go up the back way, sir. Not so much notice paid."

Tully grunted, hauling on the wheel to avoid a bigger rock that loomed out of the darkness. It was a good idea, he supposed, but damn hard on the car.

The road tipped down again, swerved off to the left, and the fog thickened abruptly. The headlights swung and steadied, sparking off a shimmer of water that resolved to a wide, shallow-looking stream. A curtain of fog was rising from it, as thick as it had been by the river. Tully looked dubiously at it, and then at Cal.

"The boundary line, he calls it," Cal said. "You can drive on through."

Tully grimaced, but put the car in first. The water wasn't deep, not even up to the wheel rims, but he could feel big stones shifting under the tires, and the fog swirled close, blinding him for an instant. And then they were out of it, in clean air, and the road showed clear ahead, a wider, smoother track. He thought he could hear music, but the noise of the engine washed it away. There were lights ahead, and in spite of himself he pushed the accelerator, driving the big car a little harder.

The car wound its way up the track—almost a road now, beaten smooth—and came at last through a screen of trees into the clearing that surrounded Mr. Seeley's house. It was a big place, two stories, with every window lit up and more lights on the broad porch that ran along the front of the building. The music was very clear now, the kind of jazz you could hear on a still night when the air was just right and the radio could pick up the St. Louis stations. Thunderstorms always seemed to follow those nights, and Tully glanced up, but Mr. Seeley's lights turned the sky to empty velvet. There were a dozen cars drawn up to the porch, another dozen parked on the edges of the clearing, fancy roadsters with paint that showed cream and red and green in the headlights, and as he edged the car between them he spotted two custom Pierce-Arrows.

"Take it around the back?" he asked.

To his surprise, Cal shook his head. "Pull up to the steps there. Might as well make it easy."

Sure enough, half a dozen boys in white waiter's jackets had appeared at the end of the porch. Even before Tully cut the engine, one of them had opened the trunk, and they began hauling the liquor inside. He levered himself out from behind the wheel, blinking in the light from the porch. He was stiff, but there were so many people watching that he didn't feel right stretching. There were seven or eight of them, mostly men, but three women with them, leaning on the rail and on their escorts, highballs in their hands. They were dressed to catch the eye, in long dresses that had to be silk, like something out of the movies but twice as sheer and clinging. One of them had what looked like diamond clips in her wavy hair, glittering in the porch light; she saw him looking and gave him a lazy smile. There was interest in it, but contempt, too, and Tully was suddenly away of his work pants and shabby jacket. She turned away, laying her hand on the arm of a man in a dinner jacket, and vanished into the shadows.

"Where's Joe?" he asked, and when Cal didn't answer, caught the little man by the shoulder. "Joe is here, isn't he?"

Cal nodded, almost reluctantly. "But you better leave him be, Mister Tully. He—he wouldn't want you involved."

"What the hell is going on?" Tully kept his voice down, aware of the men on the porch above him, and grateful for the shotgun still half hidden in the front seat. It wasn't much—he'd bet money most of these guys were packing heat—but it would give him the advantage of surprise.

"So this is Joe's prodigy."

Tully looked up quickly, to see a man standing at the edge of the porch, both hands braced on the rail. He was tall, and slim despite his pure white hair; his dinner jacket fit just right, and he stood like a man who owned the world.

"Mr. Seeley."

"Tully Swann. Come on in, son. You earned it, as good a job as you've done."

"It was a favor to Joe," Tully said, stubborn, but walked up the steps like a man in a dream. Mr. Seeley put an arm around his shoulder, smiling broadly. Tully smelled tobacco and aftershave and whiskey, and pulled off his cap as Mr. Seeley walked him into the ballroom.

It wasn't really a ballroom, of course—or maybe it was, he didn't have anything to compare it with except the movies. There were easily a hundred people there, all in evening dress, plus dozens of waiters and a band on a little platform tucked in one corner. There was even a cigarette girl in short skirts and a perky cap, and Tully stuffed his cap in his pocket, repressing the urge to rub his shoes on the backs of his legs to shine them. Mr. Seeley's arm was heavy on his shoulders, and people glanced their way, curiosity turning to smiles that had something knowing in them. Tully shivered suddenly, a memory, something, nagging at him, and Mr. Seeley smiled.

"Someone's walking on your grave." He released Tully, beckoned to a passing waiter, who twirled like a dancer and presented a tray of cocktails. "Better drink up, son."

"Thank you." Tully took the glass carefully, the stem fragile between his fingers. "Is Joe still here?"

"Of course. But y'all don't want to leave yet, the party's just starting. Have something to eat, too." There was a note in the voice that brooked no disobedience.

"Thank you," Tully said again.

"Erasmus." Mr. Seeley lifted his hand, beckoned to an old, straight-backed black man who wore a silver key on a ribbon around his neck. "Make sure Mr. Swann has everything he needs."

"Yessir." The old man bowed, and Mr. Seeley turned away. "May I get you something to eat, Mr. Swann? Or perhaps something else to drink?"

Tully shook his head. "No, I'm fine. Thanks."

The old man nodded once, and backed away. Tully glanced around the room, searching, thought he saw Joe's familiar figure by the doors at the far end of the room. He started toward him just as the band ended its song, and the white-jacketed clarinetist announced a break. The crowd swirled away from the dance floor, blocking his view, and when he could see again, Joe was gone. He scowled, frustrated, and lifted the glass to his mouth. Before he could drink, someone bumped him, spilling the whiskey. He swore, and the young mulatto caught his arm, apologizing.

"I'm so sorry, sir, it's all my fault, I wasn't looking where I was going."

He was one of the musicians, a slim boy with marcelled hair and café-au-lait skin in a white shiny jacket with the bandleader's initial embroidered in gold on the lapels. He pulled a handkerchief from his pocket, dabbed expertly at the damp sleeve of Tully's jacket, standing so close in the crowd that Tully could smell his sweat.

"Don't drink nothing," the boy said, a fierce hiss. "And don't eat nothing neither."

Tully opened his mouth to ask what he meant, but the boy had already stepped back, tucking away the crumpled handkerchief. "There you are, sir, all fine. My apologies, sir."

"'S all right," Tully said, not knowing what else to say, and the boy slipped away, lost instantly in the crowd. Tully looked after him anyway, and saw Joe Farr at last, standing alone at the edge of the room, just outside the spill of light from the chandeliers. Tully breathed a sigh of relief and started toward him, ditching the empty glass on the first table he passed. Joe would know what was going on—and in any case, Tully wasn't fool enough to ignore that kind of warning.

"Hey, Joe."

"Tully." Joe Farr frowned, unhappy lines etching his smooth face. He looked older than was reasonable, and his usually perfect hair was mussed. "I'm sorry I got you into this."

"That's all right," Tully said. "You don't want to disoblige Judge Seeley."

To his surprise, Joe smiled at that, though the amusement didn't reach his eyes. "That's the truth."

Tully risked a quick glance over his shoulder, lowered his voice even though the nearest figures were out of earshot. "What the hell's going on, Sister? I get home from making deliveries, and there's this weird hunchback colored boy waiting for me with a car like I ain't never seen, and a note from you—"

Joe lifted his hand. "Not here."

Tully bit his lip and waited. Joe's eyes darted from side to side, obviously looking for someone, and it was all Tully could do to keep from turning to look himself, though for what he didn't know. Instead he watched Joe Farr, the smooth-cheeked face that saw the barber more than twice a week, the clean, neat-nailed hands that were as soft as the summer wool suit, and wondered if that was fear he saw in the older man's eyes.

"Outside," Joe said abruptly, and Tully followed him through the French doors onto the porch.

One step to the left took them into shadow, away from the lights that spilled out of Mr. Seeley's house. The people who had been on the porch before seemed to have found other amusement. They were alone except for a man in a tuxedo slumped in a chair with his head back and his legs stretched out, asleep or dead drunk.

"So what's going on?" Tully asked again, and wondered if he really wanted to know.

Joe clasped his hands at the small of his back, leaned gingerly against the rough shingles. "I told you, I owed Judge Seeley a favor."

"It's a hell of a favor," Tully said.

Joe's eyes dropped. "Yes. It was."

There was a little silence. It was clear Joe wasn't going to say more, and that meant trouble. Joe'd spent time in Memphis, or so the ladies said, come home in a hurry. . . . A morals charge was the kind of scandal that could drive Joe out of Troytown, and there'd never be a better place for Joe to live than among the folks who'd known him since he was a child, and knew he was a good and harmless man. And I don't want to leave Troytown either, Tully thought, and only then wondered if Joe would want him to come along. He licked his lips, said in a voice that came out only a little wrong, "Well, anyway, you done your favor. I got him his liquor. Cain't we go home now?"

Joe shook his head, still not meeting the younger man's eyes. "It's not that easy."

"I know he's a judge, or used to be," Tully said. "And I know he likes his liquor. But, hell, we're not the folks to be providing for him. Place like this, it'd take Big Jake to handle what he needs, and it'd be cheaper buying from him directly."

"That's not what he wants."

"You better tell me," Tully said, and hesitated. "Please, Joe."

Joe took a breath, pushed himself almost upright. "My mother said—she said Mr. Seeley was one of the Fair Folk, said her family knew their kind when they saw them, looked right through the glamour and saw what was really there, and she told me to stay well clear of him. But then, when I had my trouble in Memphis, he took care of it, found witnesses for me, and all because he liked knowing that we were under an obligation to him even though we knew who—what— he really was. After Mother died, he called occasionally, made me find him some fancy brandy, French wines, things like that—something that made me sweat but not something I couldn't handle. But now . . ." He shook his head. "Now he's heard about you."

"What do you mean, he's heard about me?"

"You're the best driver in the county," Joe said simply. He dredged a smile from somewhere. "I still remember when you were sixteen, the first job you did for me, the way you just drove around Billy Cahill. I'm plain lucky you're still willing to work for me." The smile vanished. "Judge Seeley could use a man like you. They all could, all of the Fair Folk. You could bring them—anything."

Tully stared at the other man for a long moment. The one thing was true, he was a good driver, probably the best in the county and maybe in the state, but the rest of it. . . .

"The Fair Folk," he said, slowly, and Joe scowled, flopped back against the wall.

"I know, you don't believe me. Well, you don't have to, I'll figure something out."

"I didn't say that," Tully said. There were stories—hell, everybody'd heard them, tall tales and ghost stories, saved from long ago, but they fit what he saw on Irish Mountain. More than that, they fit the feel of it, the haughty women and the knife-blade men, Mr. Tamlin with his almost-English accent, Auberon Seeley playing king of creation, and the walls of fog that separated them from the rest of Nolan County. They fit the test he'd been set that he hadn't even known was there, fit the look Cal had given him when he asked after Joe. They fit the boy who'd told him not to drink or eat, and the chill he'd felt when Mr. Seeley laid a hand on him. He shook his head. "I didn't say that at all."

Joe looked up, momentarily alert, but then he shook his head in turn. "I'm sorry, Tully. I never meant to get you into my troubles."

"Why can't we just walk out of here?" Tully asked. He was trying to remember the stories, but came up with a muddle of disjointed pieces, and shoved that thought aside. "OK, not walk, but, hell, the car I came in's right over there. We get in it, drive down the Mountain—what the hell can he do to stop us? Tell the sheriff we didn't fulfill a liquor contract?"

"You don't know," Joe murmured. He was looking past Tully, at something only he could see, and Tully clenched his fists in frustration. We can't just give up, he wanted to say, can't just sit here and do nothing and let Judge Seeley roll doom over on us. The words wouldn't come, stopped by the tired, dead look in Joe's eyes.

"Damn it, Joe," he said, and leaned forward, kissed the other man full on the lips. They'd made love before, twice, up in Joe's spare room with all the curtains drawn and no word said after, but their mouths had never met. Joe twitched, eyes flying wide open, startled and afraid and then utterly astounded. Tully pressed him back against the shingles, forgetting everything in the touch of bodies, and Joe shook his head, pushed him away.

"Wait."

Tully caught himself, heard his breathing ragged, knowing Joe was right.

"Wait," Joe said again, and straightened his jacket. "Do you mean it?"

"Would I do that, here and now and under Auberon Seeley's eyes, if I didn't?"

Joe made a noise that was almost a giggle. "Probably not." He straightened fully, smoothing his hair to its usual sleekness. "Is the car still there?"

Tully glanced along the line of the porch, saw the grille and the headlights looming in the dim light. "Yeah. We got to try it, Joe."

"Let's go."

They walked the length of the house, skirting the parked cars, the light from the porch splashing at their feet. Inside, the music started up again, and Tully hoped that meant everyone's attention would be elsewhere. The man on the porch shifted in his sleep, sliding down further in his chair, but there was no other movement. The car loomed, sleek and black and ready, and Tully set his hand on the door.

Cal was sitting in the driver's seat. He'd been sleeping, but woke instantly, and Tully froze, all the clever lies gone from his head. Cal looked at him, and then at Joe, and Joe said, "We're leaving, Cal."

"Mr. Seeley know?"

Tully shook his head. "Come with us," he said. It was a weird feeling, like he'd just skipped over a whole page of conversation—Cal protesting, them arguing, bargaining, offering—and even weirder when Cal nodded, like he'd heard every word of it.

"Thank you, sir." He slid across the seat, and Tully frowned, intending to order him into the back seat, but Joe touched his sleeve.

"I'll ride in back."

There was no point in arguing, and no time, anyway. Tully slid behind the wheel, closing the door as softly as he could, and pushed the starter. The car rumbled to life, and he backed it away. There was no movement from the house, and he swung the car around, keeping it in first as he threaded his way between the rows of cars. Time for speed later, he told himself; slip away quiet now, and maybe they won't notice you're gone. The opening loomed in the trees, the turn onto the track that was the back way up the Mountain, and in the narrow mirror he saw someone silhouetted against the lights of the house.

He hit the accelerator, and the car leaped forward, sliding down the rutted path. From the porch, he hoped it would be barely visible, just the flash of taillights and the dark body vanishing into the trees; and there would be confusion, too, or at least he hoped there would be, Mr. Seeley not believing they'd gone, and time wasted looking. He put the car in second, let it skid around the first turn. A flatter section ahead, and he took third gear, heart thumping as the wheels slid and caught and slid again. The trees seemed to reach for him, branches scraping the hood, clattering against the roof. There were rocks he didn't remember, boulders popping up out of the ground. A huge oak loomed in the middle of the road; he jammed on the brakes, swearing, then realized the track swerved around it and then down a steep incline. He barely got it into second, cursed again, and looked in the mirrors.

Mr. Seeley's house was out of sight, but he could see headlights now at the top of the hill: someone, several someones, were coming after them. "You got that shotgun loaded, Cal?" he asked, and barely heard the murmur of agreement. "Joe—"

He looked in the mirror again, not daring to take his eyes off the road, caught a glimpse of a white, seamed face, an old man's face, tired and sick and hurting. "Joe?"

"Don't look back," Cal said, swiftly. "Whatever you do, don't look back."

That was another warning, another test. Tully caught his breath, concentrating on the driving. A tree leaped into the path; he twitched the wheel, felt a rear tire wobble on the edge of nothing as the loose dirt crumbled away. He knew better than to gun the motor, time stretching so that he could feel each separate movement: the car starting to dip back to the left, the right wheel pushing, his own hands turning the wheel half an inch to the right, and then at last the left wheel rolling up onto solid ground and the whole car jumping forward. All over in a heartbeat, but he looked in the mirrors to see the headlights coming closer.

He could still see Joe's face in the mirror, too, quick, nightmare flashes: an old man, a sick man, white-lipped like a TB patient, bruised blue like a drowned man. There were coins on his eyes, and stitches holding his mouth shut; great red patches of fever flush on unshaven cheeks, then skin like paper curling on a grinning skull. He looked toward Cal, wanting to know what, why, and a monster looked at him out of the dark, fangs gleaming in a grinning drool-wet mouth, clawed hands curled around the barrel of the gun. In the mirror the headlights flashed again, great bright wedges sweeping through the trees.

There was nothing left but driving, left hand locked on the wheel, feet dancing on the pedals, the engine telling him when to shift, where to throw the power to the wheels and when to hold it back. Maybe Joe was dead, dying, lost, maybe Cal was something not human, never been human, but that didn't matter. Nothing mattered but to get down the Mountain. The following cars were closer now, impossibly so—but then, a voice whispered, Auberon Seeley wouldn't have anything but the best, and he wouldn't give that best to a white trash bootlegger's boy. The road swung hard right; in the headlights' beams, Tully saw a second track, barely a break in the trees. He took it, knowing instantly where it had to go; the car lurched, swayed drunkenly on the stiff springs—in the mirror, a dead man wept tears of blood—and cut straight down the hill. Beside him, a monster swore in terror; the road loomed again, and he hit clutch and wheel, skidded back onto the smooth track. He'd gained a thousand yards by cutting off the switchback, and scared them, too, seeing him disappear over the edge. They'd figure it out quick enough, but it'd slow them down. He clung to the thought even while his heart mourned what he feared to see in the mirror, and put his foot down as though the engine roar would save them all.

And then they were at the stream, the fog more like a wall than a curtain. The river sound was louder, too, as though the water had risen, but it was too late to stop. He could see the headlights starting to close in again, and he let the car plunge into the stream.

The water was deeper, up to the running boards. A cylinder faltered; he swore, feathered the throttle, and felt stones rolling under the wheels. But the fog was parting, reluctantly, and the ground was easier, rising almost gently out of the water. Tully gunned the motor, knowing Mr. Seeley was close now, and swung the wheel over hard, pulling the handbrake to fling the car around to face the way they'd come.

"Gimme the gun, Cal."

"Take these."

He almost didn't dare look, but the hand that met his, fumbling hand-wrapped shells into his palm, was normal again. He flung the door wide, stepped out to face the oncoming lights. He closed his eyes, and fired both barrels into the invisible sky. The blast split the darkness, brighter than lightning; even behind his eyelids he saw red and yellow streaks, and struggled to reload.

"What's in the shells, Cal?" That was Joe's voice, mercifully normal, but Tully couldn't spare even an instant to look at him.

"Iron, sir," Cal answered, and his voice rang loud even in the foggy air. "Cold iron."

The fog closed in again, and Tully braced himself. The first car that came over, he'd blast it right through the windshield—

"Mr. Swann." That was unmistakably Mr. Seeley's voice, but he sounded more amused than angry. Headlights swam behind the fog, turning it gold streaked with thicker gray and white. Out of that curtain walked Mr. Seeley, white hair gleaming even in the murky air. "I trust you won't shoot."

He stopped at the edge of the stream, glanced down, and stepped fastidiously away from the muddy patch where Tully's car had gone into the water.

"Not unless you make me," Tully called back. "Now listen here. I did what you wanted, and we're going home now. You can send one of your boys for the car in the morning."

Mr. Seeley laughed aloud. "You can keep the car, Mr. Swann. I don't have any more need of it."

Tully shook his head. "I don't want no debts between us, Judge."

"No," Mr. Seeley said. "No debts. You earned what you have."

It was another test, Tully was sure of that, as sure as he'd ever been of anything. He racked his brain, snatches of songs and stories roiling through him. "Do I have your word on it?" He didn't know where the words had come from, but he knew in his soul that they were the right ones.

"You've taught him well, Joe," Mr. Seeley said.

"No." Joe stepped to Tully's side, and Tully slanted a nervous glance at him. Joe looked—himself again, a bit tired, maybe, and who could blame him, but the visions in the mirror were gone. "I didn't have to tell him."

"You're a very lucky man, Joe Farr," Mr. Seeley said. "Very well, Mr. Swann. No debts between us. You have my word on it."

Tully lowered the shotgun, but kept it ready, just in case. Mr. Seeley nodded once, a polite good night, and turned away. The fog swirled back around him, and a moment later, the first set of head-lights swung away. A second followed, then a third and a fourth. Their taillights glowed red, and slowly disappeared into the fog, the engine noise fading with them like an echo.

"Well, now," Joe said, on a sigh, and Tully touched his shoulder, glad to feel solid flesh and bone beneath the fine wool. Cal leaned on the roof of the car, head down for an instant like a man praying, but then he straightened as much as he was able.

"Getting toward morning, sir."

Tully nodded. "Let's go home."

doi:10.1300/5642_20

Year of the Fox

Eugie Foster

In the lush countryside of the Middle Kingdom, a family of *huli jing,* fox spirits, hunted, danced, and barked their musical laughter. One night, as Master Sun turned his face away from the land, and Mistress Moon drew a glittering veil of clouds and stars over herself, Mother Fox sat her children down to explain to them the way of enlightenment.

"Foxes are by nature a bit wicked," she said. "We delight in tricks and thefts, for our paws are silent and our minds quick. But it is one thing to charm a bird into one's jaws and quite another to revel only in mischief. For while we are greatly tempted, likewise great is our reward if we are virtuous."

Mei, the vixen cub, sat with one ear swiveled to Mother and the other distracted by a fearless moth. "Mama," she said, "what kind of reward? You mean a juicy rabbit or succulent egg?"

"No, no. A reward better than earthly delights."

Jin, the male cub, chewed at a burr caught between the pads of one paw. "What could be better than an egg?"

Mother barked, high and sharp. "Listen, my children, for you are almost grown! Enlightenment is your reward for being good foxes. It is the pathway into heaven whereupon we escape this wheel of mortality. Otherwise we are doomed to return again and again after we die, redressing the wrongs we have committed."

Mei leaped up, her jaws snapping shut around the moth. She licked her muzzle. "I'm hungry, Mama, when will we go hunting?"

Mother cuffed her. "Pay attention, cub. Have I ever taught you wrongly? Was it not I who showed you how to listen for mice tramping about underground?"

Mei sulked. "Yes, Mama."

"And was it not I who taught you to find crunchy beetles among the rotting logs?"

"Yes, Mama."

"So heed me."

"But my belly rumbles," Mei whined.

"You must learn to rule yourself, or you will never earn enlightenment."

"May we not earn enlightenment on full bellies?" Jin asked, rolling on his back to show that he was an obedient son.

Despite his display of respect, Mother growled. "Very well. I will bring something back to stuff in your greedy maws. But you must wait here so your clumsy paws do not prolong the chase."

Both cubs meekly bowed their heads.

Mistress Moon trod the arch of heaven, her veil sometimes modestly concealing her face, and sometimes slipping shamelessly. The fox cubs, peeping from the entrance of their den, watched her erratic display unperturbed, for they knew she was inconstant and fickle. But she seemed particularly leisurely that night, dawdling to gossip with the celestial fires and flirting with the wind.

"Where is Mother?" Jin finally asked. "My belly is so empty I think it has started eating itself!"

Mei rose to her paws. "She has been gone too long. If we wait much longer, I will surely die."

Without Mother's guiding nips and sharp eyes to curb them, the cubs grew giddy with freedom. They frisked beneath the stars, admiring how Mistress Moon turned their russet fur silver, and splashed in winking streams that trilled songs of adventure and secrets in the burbling language of *shui,* water.

Laughing, her tongue lolling to the side, Mei froze mid-bark, all four paws rigid in the earth. A familiar scent had darted past her nose—one of comfort, warmth, and home. It drew her, straight as hunger, to a still puddle of softness, hidden beneath a leering hedge.

"Jin, I found her! Mama, Mama, we've been looking for you!"

But Mother did not move. She did not yip a welcome, even when her cubs scampered to her side.

"Mama?"

She lay at a strange angle, most unnatural. Her neck bent backward and the smell of blood was thick in the air. Mei nudged her with her nose. She saw in the moonlight a shining glint that encircled her throat. It cut through thick fur and flesh. Leaning close, she saw that Mother's back was broken, and most horrible of all, where her tail had been, proud and lush, there remained only a bloody stump.

Mei skittered back, rubbing her face in the cool earth, as though that would cleanse the sight from her mind. "We need to leave here. It is a place of death."

"What do you mean? Mother is asleep."

"She is dead. A fox hunter's trap ended her life, and a fox hunter's knife took her tail."

A trembling seized Jin from ears to paws. "Dead? No, she cannot be dead. Just this night she was lively and spry."

"Much can happen between twilight and dawn. Come away."

Jin began to cry, his howls piercing the night. Mei tilted her head back and joined him in his fox song of mourning.

Brother and sister lived together for a while in a shallow scrape, a burrow they had stolen from a family of rabbits after spreading panic and havoc through their community. There they plotted revenge with eyes that glowed yellow in the night.

"It is humans who killed her," Jin said. "A senseless, cruel death. They did not wish for her flesh to eat, but rather coveted her fine tail."

"Foxes may be wicked, but humans are evil," Mei agreed.

"I hate all of them. I will bring them down in their pride and folly. In the name of our mother, I swear it."

"I too," Mei said. "We will wreak madness and despair upon those who dare to think foxes may be conquered by cowardly snares!"

"I will turn myself into a handsome youth," said Jin, "and lure a holy monk from his sanctuary with cries for help. Then I will trick him with my magic into thinking a goat is holy. He will anoint it with precious oil and bow down before it. How I will laugh when I clear the magic from his eyes and he learns that he has been worshipping a foul goat!"

"That is nothing," Mei said. "I will turn into a beautiful maiden and make some unsuspecting man fall in love with me, or better yet, some unsuspecting lady. Think how dismayed they will be when I reveal my true fox shape!"

Jin bared his teeth in glee. "Such wonderful sport. We will prove ourselves to be the most cunning, the most sly foxes in all the Middle Kingdom. It will make our mother laugh as she watches from the lap of Buddha. Let us meet back here in a year to share the tales of our adventures."

Mei watched as her brother used *huli jing* glamour to shed his red-gold fur in lieu of a silk robe of malachite green with wide sleeves that swept the ground. Tawny streaks of embroidered lightning criss-crossed his back, outlined in gold and carmine threads. His face, without its fur, was still pointed, with a sharp chin and tapered ears. His eyes were wide and dark, as mysterious as the night sky, and they glowed, giving his fox nature away.

"Better avoid their torches," Mei said. "Or they will realize you are not one of them from the fire of your gaze."

Jin frowned, displeased that his disguise was less than perfect. "Aren't you going to change shape?"

"I will choose my form after I have stalked my prey," she said. "To better savor the joys of the hunt."

"As you will." Jin lifted his arm in farewell as Mei dashed away. "Remember, one year from today!"

Mei flicked her tail in acknowledgement.

The maiden wore a coarse, roughly woven *shen-i*. Her name was Lian, which meant "graceful willow." Mei thought it was a most fitting name, for though her tunic was drab brown hemp belted with a simple cord, and the skirt was tattered and threadbare, Lian might have been wearing the finest brocade. She moved as though she were a princess in the imperial palace, each step as lithe as a dancer's, with a calm serenity that rivaled a priest's.

She lived with two elderly servants, Chen and Ping, a man and woman so ancient the only indication of their sex was their attire.

Whether sewing, cooking, or weaving, Lian went about the day's chores with a glad and merry heart. At night, when the lanterns blossomed to life, she read aloud from slender books of poetry and proverbs, or practiced calligraphy.

Mei watched her from a nest of bamboo in the forest that surrounded the mud and straw hut. When she hungered, she stalked mice and beetles, swallowing down the tiny sparks of their lives in a fierce snap of her jaws. Though Mistress Moon and her attendant stars tempted her to dance beneath them, she stayed still, not wishing to alert her quarry that *huli jing* lingered near.

A pure soul such as Lian was fine game. Foxfire visions to trouble her dreams would strip the tranquility from her mien, and barking demon shapes with dripping fangs that lunged and tore at her from the shadows would shatter her composure. Mei grinned.

One night, as the vixen contemplated the particulars of her strategy, she heard rustling in the bamboo forest. Curious, as all foxes are, she looked to see who approached.

The stench of the interloper assailed her delicate nose. He was unwashed and rank, smelling of night soil, fermented rice, and blood. Over his shoulder was a dingy sack with many rents in it, and in his hands, a curious curl of wood linked at the ends by sinew. A long fang lay upon the string. Mother fox had taught her about human surrogate teeth so Mei understood its purpose, although she found the details of its operation perplexing.

She crept from her hiding place and joined herself to the man's shadow.

It was obvious this man was a villain, a bandit who preyed upon the unsuspecting. The vixen fretted. All her planning would go to naught if this man despoiled Lian in her stead. Still, the world was wide and full. Would it not be easier to find other prey to torment than to intervene?

While Mei vacillated, the bandit pushed open the hut's flimsy door. He drew upon the sinew with its long tooth until it sang with tension. At that moment, his sack shifted, and a portion of what it contained spilled out: a fox's tail.

This man was both a bandit and a fox hunter!

Mei barked in fury. At her outcry, she heard stirring within the hut. The man swung to Mei, his fang now pointed at her. But she had seen how he moved and was confident she was quicker. She leaped, sinking her teeth into his leg, and the next moment, his false tooth hurtled faster than Mei thought possible. It tore into her side. She had scarce moments for surprise before night slammed his fists closed around her.

As the world spun away, Mei wondered what Jin would do when she was not there at their appointed meeting.

Mei had not expected to open her eyes again, at least not in this world, perhaps on celestial Mount Tai where souls ascended after they died. So she was surprised to take in Lian's room. She lay on the maiden's bed, bundled in a straw blanket. She recognized the low table with its calligraphy brushes and the thin books stacked beside it.

Mei's side was wrapped with clean bandages and smelled of herbs and medicine. It pained her greatly. The blood flow had stopped and there was no scent of corruption from the wound, but she was weak as a newborn cub. She could barely swivel her ears.

She wasn't dead. Why?

As though in answer, Lian entered, pushing aside the ragged curtain. The maiden bowed when she saw Mei's eyes upon her. She held a bamboo tray upon which sat a bowl of clear water and a bowl of *congee,* rice porridge.

How, mused Mei, *could a creature with only two legs move with such grace?*

"Mistress Fox, I see you are awake. Please be at ease, exquisite one. You are not well and should lie still." Lian folded to her knees beside the bed. "You must be hungry and thirsty. There is a little fish in the porridge, and the water is fresh. It would do you good to eat and drink."

Lian set the bowl of *congee* under Mei's nose. The savor of clean, sweet rice and the delicate aroma of broiled fish made her mouth moist with yearning.

The maiden lifted a pair of chopsticks from the tray and used them to offer Mei a ribbon of fish.

The vixen accepted the tidbit. It was delightful. Her belly clamored for her to gobble the whole bowl as fast as she might, but she had better manners. She let Lian feed her, and forced herself to chew each mouthful slowly before swallowing. Between bites, Lian offered Mei sips of water from the bowl.

"You are a most mannerly fox," she said. "Chen and Ping said you would growl and snap, but I knew you would be courteous. After all, why would you save us from a bandit one moment and then bite off my hand the next?"

Mei was strangely reluctant to disillusion Lian of her courtly fox notions, so she accepted the water without baring her fangs, and she let Lian run her fingers through her coat. And when the maiden cuddled Mei in her arms, soothing away fever and cold with the comfort of her body, Mei did not even contemplate nipping her.

One night, when the moon was a sickle of silver shining against the darkness, Mei waited for Lian's breath to slow in the deepness of Lord Sleep's realm. Her wound no longer troubled her, and she was shamed she had allowed herself to fall into the care of her enemy. She ran from the hut on secret paws and hid herself in a thicket of bamboo.

That night, Mei plied the stuff of spirit glamour, taking upon herself the shape of a noble lady. She gazed with pleasure upon the smooth skin of her white hands, delicate as nesting doves. A *pien-fu* took the place of her lustrous fur. Its loose folds of crimson wrapped her body, secured with a rippling, pink sash. The tunic of silk spilled to her knees, and the matching skirt was modest, long enough to conceal her tiny feet. A tasteful pattern of storm clouds adorned the cloth, embroidered with cream threads, highlighted in damson.

Conjuring false tears as easily as her false shape, she stumbled to Lian's doorstep.

She beat at the flimsy barrier and called piteously. "Help me, oh, help me! Won't someone have mercy on me?"

Immediately, Mei was rewarded by the sound of commotion from within. Lian herself swung open the door, and Mei dropped to her knees. She let the curtain of her glossy, jet-black hair fall so it covered her face.

With fox-born artistry, she allowed Lian to spy the liquid gleam of her eyes through the cascading strands of darkness. From such mysterious gazes, Mei knew, were human hearts beguiled.

"Oh, kind mistress," she wailed. "My escort was ambushed by a band of rogues. They killed my servants, and I had to flee for my life. I have been lost in the forest. Please help me!"

Without waiting for Lian to reply, for she knew the maiden would never turn such a pitiful traveler away, Mei crumpled in a pile at her feet.

"Chen, Ping!" Lian summoned her servants to help her carry the swooning lady inside. They arrayed Mei on Lian's bed (a familiar establishment for the vixen), and Chen and Ping fluttered about, brewing tea and lighting incense.

Lian dabbed cool water on Mei's wrists and forehead. When Mei sensed her bending near, she opened her eyes.

"Beautiful maiden," she whispered, "you are my savior. I am forever in your debt." Mei bridged the tiny space between them and pressed her lips to Lian's.

The girl pulled away in surprise.

Mei hid her face in the voluminous folds of her sleeve. "Did I offend you?" She peeked one eye out, and was pleased to see Lian's face was soft with wonder.

"It was only—unexpected. You are safe now, mistress. Please do not be afraid. Although there are evil men about, we are smiled upon by good fortune."

"Do evil men come here often?" Mei pretended to quail behind her sleeve.

"Not at all. In the many years I have lived here, a bandit has only threatened once."

"What happened?"

"A fox protected us."

"A fox?"

"Indeed, she barked and bit the rogue. While he reeled about with her jaws upon him, I hit him on the head with a saucepan."

A saucepan? Mei pushed aside the laughter that threatened to bubble from her chest. "You are so brave. I feel so feeble beside you."

"You are a refined orchid, mistress. The notion of bandits sullying you with their stinking presence makes me wish I might have more than a saucepan to fight them with."

Mei flung herself into Lian's arms. "You mustn't call me 'mistress.' You are as a sister to me. Call me Mei."

Lian clasped the vixen close. "I am Lian, Mei, and I have always longed for a sister."

In the following days, as she lay, ostensibly sick and wan, Mei found ways to display glimpses of her white flesh to her hostess: an ankle slipped from beneath her hem, the alluring shadow of her breasts covered by thin silk. At these exhibits, Lian always discreetly lowered her eyes, but Mei knew she had fascinated her. She spied Lian many times gazing rapt beneath the fan of her eyelashes.

"My sister," Mei said one day, "Why do you insist upon sleeping on that thin straw mat on the floor? I know I have usurped your bed, but surely you do not think me so corpulent that we cannot share it?"

Lian laughed. "You are as slender as a young beech tree!"

After that, maiden and vixen slept in the virgin-narrow softness of Lian's bed. It reminded Mei of how Lian had warmed her in her arms when she had shivered with fever in her fox shape. But after all, if it hadn't been for Lian, she would not have been hurt in the first place.

She plied the maiden with tender kisses as she slept, teasing desire from her like water from ice. Mei fed upon her sighs, feasting on stolen ardor, mounting desire, and passion. As the nights passed, Lian soon found excuses to linger by Mei's side, letting chores go undone, where before she had always been diligent. She even set aside her poetry and calligraphy, preferring to sit and gaze upon Mei's beauty.

Time passed, dancing the seasonal steps of darkness and light. Every night, Mei drank a nectar of energy and passion from Lian's lips, and curled herself into the warmth of the maiden's body. When the days began to trip over themselves in haste, and the nights to lumber along like lazy donkeys, Mei grew bored enough to toy with Lian's brushes and riffle through her books.

"Where did you learn to read and write, my sister?" Mei asked.

"My family is descended from a revered heritage of poets. Hard times plundered the wealth we had, but as long as I have my books and my ink stone, I am still rich."

"I wish I could understand the characters you paint," Mei sighed.

"You cannot read?"

Mei shook her head, oddly bashful. "My mother never taught me."

"Would you like to learn?"

"Could I?"

So Lian demonstrated the correct way to grind ink and hold a brush. She taught Mei the characters for the five elements, *jin, mu, shui, huo,* and *tu,* and the character for soul, *ling hun.*

"You know so much," Mei said. "You belong in elegant palaces, not out here where there is only dirt and rocks."

"I have seen the inside of palaces. When my family was high in the regard of the emperor, I walked on jade tile and wore ivory combs in my hair. But when the fates and some politicians conspired to dishonor my family name, I found I did not miss those things." She tapped the spine of one of her books. "Learning is a treasure that follows its owner," she quoted.

"But what of the glorious gardens and fountains?"

Lian laughed. "A book is like a garden one may carry in one's pocket."

"And the men who plotted against you?"

A look drifted over Lian's face, bringing distance and a hint of clouds to her eyes. "The Buddha extols us to forget injuries and remember only kindness. Who am I to rail at the wheels of fate? Perhaps I wronged them in a previous life and they are only righting the balance." Lian winked, the far-off look erased. "Or perhaps I shall redress what has happened in another life."

"You are a follower of Buddha?" Mei asked. "My mother once tried to instruct me on his wisdom, but I was impatient with her lectures."

Lian put down her brush. "I am not a monk or a wise man, but I know Buddha taught that what we undergo in this life is a result of our previous actions. Nothing is permanent in this world, and it is a place of suffering. But if we live as best we can, one day we will achieve bliss and end our time on the eternal cycle of rebirth."

That night, as the stars gazed in the darkness upon the Earth, Mei could not sleep. Her thoughts were jagged, fierce things, troubling her with their sharpness.

Was Mama's death due to the inherent evil of humans, or was it merely a turning of the karmic wheel? What if Mama, in a previous life, had wronged the fox hunter, and so it was mete she die in his wire? How then could it be virtuous to wreak havoc upon all humans in the name of vengeance?

Because foxes are natural liars, it was easy for Mei to tell herself falsehoods. But also, because of her natural affinity with lies, it did not take long before she scented her own pretense and knew it for what it was. More than the nature of enlightenment, the very thought of harming Lian pained her worse than any thorn in her paw or burr in her coat. She could no more contemplate undertaking her planned mischief than she could will herself another tail.

Embracing this truth was like a foretaste of enlightenment to the troubled vixen. It freed her from her restlessness, and she fell away into a chasm of dreams.

When the new dawn spread garlands of light through the hut, Mei found herself watching Lian with new eyes, ones opened by newfound tenderness. And with them, she saw something she had not noticed before.

"When did you become so thin?" she exclaimed.

Lian's cheeks, once as bright as spring peaches, were sunken. The maiden was pale, and her eyes seemed too large for her face.

"It does not matter," Lian replied. "For I rejoice that you grow stronger every day."

It was true. Mei felt more vigorous than she had ever been. She realized with rising horror she was so energized because of what she had taken from Lian. In the night when she plied the girl with secret touches and kisses, the delicious flavor she tasted was nothing less than Lian's *chi,* her vital energy.

At once, Mei vowed to stop her nightly caresses.

But despite her best intentions, Lian continued to fade. With sorrow heavy in her breast, Mei realized she must leave or risk irreversible harm upon one that had only shown her kindness and generosity.

Only the power of time and the incisions of distance would sever the connection between their energies.

That morning, while Lian listlessly toyed with her breakfast *congee,* Mei hid her face in the shadow of her hair. "My sister, I think it is time our paths divided."

She heard Lian inhale, a gasp of distress. "Y-you wish to leave me?"

The vixen could not bring herself to meet the maiden's eyes. "It occurs to me that I have dishonored my family by evading my nuptial responsibilities. I may no longer face my ancestors if I do not return to my duty."

"But what of the bandits? And the nights grow cold. You must wait out the winter here, at least."

Mei's eyes burned with anguish, but she only shook her head. "I will embrace my fate, as I should have months before. Tomorrow I will set out."

"Tomorrow is too soon!" Lian's voice was ragged with distress. But no matter how she pleaded, Mei would not change her mind.

The fox maiden rose early to find Lian's shadowed eyes upon her. They did not speak while Mei dressed, nor when Lian bundled a rice cake into Mei's pink sash.

Outside, in the pre-dawn chill, they stood, not touching, avoiding each other's gaze.

"Be well, my sister," Mei said at last.

"May Buddha guide your steps," Lian whispered in reply. She burst into tears and fled inside.

Mei stood for many seconds before the hut's door, warring with herself. At last, she turned and walked into the forest. Buddha said that suffering was caused by craving. If she did not crave Lian, then neither of them would suffer.

When she had traveled a hundred paces, Mei shed her human form. Her fox body felt uncomfortable to her, stiff and unwieldy. It was strange to run on four paws, and she grew confused and giddy at the wealth of scents that beset her nose. She had spent so long as a woman she had all but forgotten what it was to be a vixen. And yet, she swiftly learned to once again savor the feel of the breeze in her whiskers, and revel in the splendor of her tail as it furled in a banner behind her. It was, after all, high time she walked the ways of a fox once more.

Mei worked to clear her mind, embracing the fullness of delight which was paws upon the earth, night song in her ears, and the breath of sky through her fur. She meditated upon the shape of trees without their covering of leaves, and upon the fragility of snowflakes as they drifted from the heavens. And when the winter frost grew bitter and food scarce, she accepted the chill of her limbs and her hollow gut with philosophic grace.

The crack-crack of the thawing river occurred in the completeness of time, and new-green buds dotted the skeletal trees. With a full belly once more, Mei contemplated the warm skies and delicate blossoms of spring with wonder.

Then, one night, she heard a tendril of fox song in the darkness. She recognized the voice, though it was deeper and stronger since the last time she had heard it. A year had waxed and waned; Jin had returned.

Atop the hillock where they had romped as cubs, sister and brother met with joyful yelps and yips. Jin had grown, his slender body wiry and quick. In the year's passage, he had shed the last of his cub uncertainty; he blazed with vitality.

"Your voice thrills my ears," Jin said. "My eyes delight in your image!"

"Nose meets nose with happiness," Mei cried.

With the jubilation of their first greeting behind them, Jin sat, curling his tail around his haunches. "Now tell me, my sister, a year has passed. What magnificent trickery have you wrought?"

Mei flicked her ear, suddenly coy. "I am certain your adventures are more worthy of exultation."

"I hardly know where to begin. Why, more monks, priests, and magistrates than I have pads on my paws have been brought low by my cleverness. And the maidens I have dishonored! I suspect there will be many half-fox children before long."

Mei found it difficult to maintain her pretense of enthusiasm. "Oh?"

"But before I tell you of all my adventures, let us hunt together, as we did as cubs."

"Are you hungry?"

Jin barked in laughter. "Yes, for mischief! As I journeyed to our appointed assignation, I saw a virtuous maiden who lives with her elderly servants. She is called 'Graceful Willow.' Think how exciting it will be to corrupt her and bring her low."

"I do not think—that is—"

"What is the matter, sister? Such recreation so nearby and you hesitate?"

"I have come to the belief that it is better to eschew wickedness," she admitted.

"So it is true."

Mei was startled to hear the rage in Jin's tone. His molten eyes seethed with suppressed anger.

"The birds gossip and the trees whisper of the foolish fox who loves a human," Jin growled. "It could not be my Mei, I told myself, for we have vowed havoc upon all humankind. No sister of mine could be so treacherous as to dishonor the memory of our mother."

Mei trembled, but only said: "A clear conscience does not fear devils at the door." It was a proverb from Lian's books.

Jin snarled. "Silence! I must clear this smear upon our family honor."

Mei cowered, tucking her tail low between her legs. "What do you mean?"

"I will attend to this human who has corrupted you. When I am through with her, you will be free of her."

"No! You will not harm Lian. I forbid it."

Jin screamed in rage, a high-pitched shriek that ripped the night. In a blur of claws and fangs, he launched himself at his sister and pinned her beneath his weight.

"Shameful bitch," he growled. "You dare to forbid me? You who have broken the oath we made."

"It was a cub oath," Mei whined, "made in haste and ignorance."

Faster than she could blink, Jin bit her tail, his keen teeth severing it with brutal force. He threw the bloody trophy to the ground.

"Your loss of face sickens me," he snarled.

Mei muffled her shriek of agony, clamping her paws over her muzzle. Through a haze of anguish, she watched her brother bound away into the forest.

Her tail, her beautiful tail! Jin had disfigured her so her disgrace was transparent to all. Every fox, badger, and dog, every squirrel and bird would see her shame. They would mock her misery, pointing at her dishonor.

She slunk to where her once-proud tail lay in the dirt. The twin clamors of humiliation and anguish deafened her, but she did not have the leisure to lament. She must protect Lian from Jin's wrath.

What was once as easy as running was newly painful. Mei suffered in silence, changing her shape once again to become a human maiden. With her transformation, the bleeding ceased. The ache of it still worried at her, like a festering boil at her back, but her life no longer trickled from her with each thrum of her heart. Her fingers trembled as she picked up her severed tail and tucked it into the sleeve of her *pien-fu*.

Each step was like treading a roadway of blades. Every part of her was thinner and more vulnerable as her fox magic tried to stretch less flesh to cover the same sized frame. Pebbles in the road that her rugged fox paws would not have noted ripped the silk of her shoes, and then bit into the soles of her feet. Soon she left a trail of blood, dark and wet, behind her.

Better to run as a fox, then. But she doubted she would have the vitality to change again to a woman, and surely Lian would not heed the ravings of a fox.

She wavered, weakened by blood loss and pain. She stumbled over a length of bamboo, felled on the ground.

"A clever fox knows good fortune disguised as bad," she said, picking herself up. The bamboo was a stout branch, jagged where it had snapped from its base, but dry and hard, an admirable cane.

Mei began to run, a hobbling, shambling sprint. She ignored the pain lancing like teeth at her feet and let her breath fill her consciousness.

The acrid taste of smoke drifted on the wind, caught even by her clumsy, human nose. Tendrils of grey and black curled in the sky. And then, like a counterfeit sunrise, glints of living vermillion flickered, bright as spirit dreams.

"Lian!" Mei shouted. "Your house is on fire! Get out! Run!"

As she lurched into the smoke-thick clearing, she saw vines of fire swathing the thatch roof. The door crackled like dancing devils.

"Lian! Chen! Ping! Awaken and escape!"

A whip of smoke, tipped with sparks, slashed at her eyes, blinding her. Eyes streaming, Mei rubbed at them with the edge of her sleeve.

When she looked up, the hut was surrounded by foxes. A hundred Jins barred her way, identical white fangs bared in anger, two hundred glistening eyes fixed upon her.

"I have wrapped the hut in a labyrinth of smoke," he said from a hundred fox mouths. "Even if the humans heard you, they cannot escape."

Mei swung her bamboo cane at the nearest Jin. He faded into the milling throng of foxes, eluding her with ease. A pack of Jins enclosed her in an ever-moving, dizzying fence of bodies. When she tried to strike at them, her bamboo passed through fox bodies as though through shadows.

A cackle of mocking laughter warned her, but not soon enough. Fresh pain, hot blood, and a ragged gash in her sleeve told her to beware of the one real fox in the roiling morass.

But how to know him?

She swung her bamboo, and behind the cover of the whistling stalk, she scrutinized each fox, hunting for the different one, the unique one.

An impact of paws at her back brought her to her knees. She thrust her cane wildly at phantom images that smirked and taunted her.

There. Was that a shadow in one fox's eyes—a film of madness, a veneer of lust? Jin did not comprehend his own madness, so did not create it in his duplicates. As before her brother's eyes had given him away in the shape of a youth, so again they gave him away as a fox.

Feigning weakness, Mei slumped, half-sobbing and half-whining. "Stop this. Do you mean to kill me as well? Do you have no mercy for your sister?"

She let her hair swing over her face, a mask of darkness. But she kept one eye clear, and with it she tracked her brother. She lured him closer, letting the bamboo hang limp in her grip as she continued to wail and sob.

He was drawn to her suffering, as she had hoped he would be. Her human disguise was finer than his, and he loved the noise of human misery. He fed upon it, as she had once fed upon Lian's love.

He crept near, his tongue wet with anticipation, his nose eager to scent the tang of despair upon her breath. Mei gauged it carefully, for she would have but one chance. When she could feel the radiant heat of his body battering through the thin silk of her *pien-fu,* she struck.

Throwing the force of her body behind it, she thrust the bamboo pole into the yipping demon before her. She was rewarded by the solid impact of the jagged point hammering into her brother, piercing him through.

But he did not die immediately. So close was he to her that it was but a jerk, a twitch of malice to clamp his teeth around her wrist. He severed the pulse that rushed there, and a spray of red decorated his muzzle.

The shock of it forced the last will from Mei. Her maiden form shrank away, overwhelmed, replaced by her bleeding, tailless fox shape.

Jin released her. "Do you think she will love a fox?" he snarled.

The hut door thundered open. Lian reeled out, supporting Chen at her side, with Ping draped over her shoulders. The three fell in a coughing, gasping pile, their faces and clothes grimed with soot.

"It does not matter. She is safe from you. It is enough." Mei spoke to an empty husk. Her brother's soul had fled.

Lian rushed to where the two foxes lay—one dead and one on death's threshold. She cradled the bleeding, trembling fox in her arms.

"Mei, I heard you calling, but I could not find the door. It was as though some demon hid it. We found only wall and wall and more wall."

"You know me?" Mei whispered. "Even as a fox?"

"Do you think me a fool? Of course I know you. I have always known you, whether you wore a beautiful red coat, or the red silk of a *pien-fu*." There were tears in Lian's eyes. They fell like brilliant gemstones to anoint Mei's muzzle. "Besides, how many ladies with sharp teeth and burning eyes do you think come to my door?" She bowed her head. "I loved you, my fox spirit, when you came to me on four silent paws and watched over me with eyes that glowed in the darkness, and I loved you when you were soft hands and a waterfall of hair in the night."

"My last fear was that you would not know me," Mei whispered. "Now I may greet my next life with peace."

"Do not leave me! Do not die!"

"I see a road," Mei whispered. "Oh, how sweet it is, with the grass so green, and the sky so clear." She lifted her head and brushed Lian's face with her tongue. "Do not cry. Did not Buddha teach us that life is but a dream of walking? I am going home."

"I will meet you there, my love." Lian hugged tight the soft-furred figure as it grew lighter by the weight of a single, shining soul.

doi:10.1300/5642_21

Ever So Much More Than Twenty

Joshua Lewis

She was called Jane, and always had an odd inquiring look, as if from the moment she arrived she wanted to ask questions. When she was old enough to ask them they were mostly about fairies. Her father, Michael, began to tell her fairy stories when she was very young indeed—abridged and expurgated tales of the fantastic, in which evil lost and good won, in which there was violence without blood and romance without sex, and in which monsters were always outwitted and children were always saved. Later, when she was older, he told her the real versions. It was always their private world, their place that they shared, Jane's whole life.

In turn, Jane was Michael's world—except for George, of course, and now George was gone.

George had been "gone" for a long time, of course, grown distant and disconnected, and Michael had felt George's different aspects leave him and Jane slowly over the last few years. In fact, George's physical presence had been about the last thing to go, and it had been a year since then, and only now had it really sunk in.

When people asked Jane, she liked to say, "I don't see Pop any more. He's gone back in time," and Michael thought that was pretty accurate. Fifty was not an age that agreed with George. Or perhaps he didn't agree with it. Somewhere 'round about thirty-eight he'd decided he wanted to age backward, like Merlin. He dressed like a man half his age; he started frosting the tips of his hair again; he spent hours and hours in the gym. When Michael had first known him, the hours he spent in front of mirrors had been pure delicious adolescent vanity. But eventually, accompanied by a constant worried moue, it became a careful cataloging of defects–the inevitable creasings in his face, creams and unguents notwithstanding; the slightly, slowly widening forehead; the slow cruelties of gravity.

During which time Michael usually sat in his armchair, graded papers, and quietly aged.

The fights started, escalated slowly over the whole of Jane's teenage years. What began as gentle teasings ("oh, sweetie, we're busy this weekend; your dad needs ironing") and friendly suggestions ("just try a little of this on the sides of your eyes—look at me, no crow's feet here") gradually became colder, harsher. If George couldn't stand the thought of his own aging, how could he share a bed and a life with the ever-aging Michael? As the years went on and George poured more and more time and money into what Michael called his "Dorian Gray project," Michael became his portrait, a reminder of time and its power.

The last day, the day George finally packed a bag and left and didn't come back, the fight started, as most truly significant fights start, with a tiny insignificance, a trifle. It was a typical early evening—Jane ensconced in her room doing homework, Michael sitting at the table writing lesson plans, George trying his best to distract him. Eventually Michael found him tickling his fingers gently down Michael's cheek as if he were searching for something. Michael did his best to evince no reaction whatsoever. And if George noticed that Michael was holding his breath, he didn't say anything.

"You know," he said. "You know, when I look at you, I don't see a fifty year-old man."

"Forty-eight," said Michael automatically.

"That either. I see the twenty-eight-year-old boy I met years ago. He's in there. I can just barely make him out—he's run talc through his hair, and disguised himself with actor's putty. So now his cheeks droop a little," tracing the shape with his hand, "and that stubble I found so sexy is a dull grey. . . ." He took his hand back self-consciously, and gave Michael a little half-smile. "You're still that twenty-eight-year-old boy," he said. "You're just wearing a fifty-year-old-man costume."

"That's funny," said Michael. "Because you're a fifty-year-old-man wearing a twenty-eight-year-old boy costume."

A little while later, when they were all shouted out and George had driven off—*and not even said goodbye to Jane,* Michael thought—he wondered if perhaps he should have been less mean. George's tone had been kind, and he had probably thought he was *being* kind. He decided to go and find Jane.

She was in her room, of course, flopped on her bed, of course, some well-worn paperback propped on her pillow, of course. "So," she said, not looking up, "how did that go?"

"You know, you're as long as the bed now."

"I grew," she said, in that voice that children use when they are embarrassed by their parents' affection and would prefer they stop right now, please.

"Lying on the bed like that, you could be—well, you could be seven or you could be seventeen. You've been doing that all your life."

"I'm seventeen," she reminded him. "And I always read, but it wasn't always because I was tuning out the fighting."

"You tuned it out?"

"No," she said. "Of course not." She flipped over onto her side. "So, not so good, huh?"

"Oh, it went great," Michael said. "Just great. You know, some mutual insults, a lot of things we don't mean and will later regret . . ."

"Do you regret them yet?"

"No," he admitted.

"Well then," she said, and left it at that.

"Sometimes, Jane, you seem a lot older than you are," he said.

She rolled her eyes. "*Daaad.* I'm seventeen. That's old! Old old old."

"Old old old," he agreed. "Old as the hills and the fairies in 'em."

"When I was a boy," began Michael, maybe a year later. He was sitting on Jane's bed, where he'd sat and told this story a million times before. Jane was just about to finish high school, and the summer stretched in front of them both like a deep breath. He used his story-teller voice, and Jane gave him a little smirk for it. "Hey, did you ask for the story or didn't you?"

"I did." Jane was all mock contrition.

"Right," he said. "Now, be a good listener, or I'll tell all your new friends at college that your daddy still reads you stories at night. Okay?"

"Tell the story," she said.

"Okay. Once, I was a boy, not much younger than you."

"That's not how it goes! It's 'not much older than you.'"

"You," said Michael, "have grown. So. I was a boy. Can we at least agree on that?"

"Long, long ago," Jane intoned. "In a galaxy far, far away."

"In *New York.*"

"Whatever."

"Once, when I was a boy," Michael glared. Jane giggled. "We used to go, Grandma and Grandpa and I, to this house, upstate. It was on a big lake—well, not that big. Medium. You could row across it in, I don't know, half an hour, and they stocked it with trout, and there was a diving platform, and your Uncle Johnny used to row out to the middle and drop a fishing line in the water with no bait, and blast Dean Martin tunes so you could hear them clear to Syracuse, and fall asleep with no shirt on so he turned red as a lobster."

"Dad, I'm warning you—"

"Okay, okay. On the *other* side of the house from the lake were woods."

"Magical woods," said Jane.

"Sure, if you want. And I, not liking Dean Martin and finding fish to be kind of slimy and disgusting, used to go for these long walks in the woods. I used to love my long walks in the woods."

"Also, pina coladas. And getting caught in the rain."

"Shhhh. Telling a story here. So where was I? Oh, right, walking in the woods. And then one day I met a strange boy there."

"What did he look like?" prompted Jane.

"He was tall, but not quite as tall as me," recited Michael. "But quite a lot taller than you!"

"Not anymore," laughed Jane.

"No, not anymore. And he had beautiful smooth skin the color of oak bark, and what color were his eyes?"

"Eyes the color of acorns," Jane said firmly.

"Exactly right, but the strange thing about him was his hair. His hair bedded in thick curls, tangled and wild, but what was the strange thing?"

"It was green. Like fresh moss."

"That it was. Anyway, I was surprised to meet anybody in those woods at all, so I said, 'hello,' and he said 'hello,' and—"

"Skip to the great love!" cried Jane. "You had a great love!"

"We had a great love," admitted Michael, "but not, uh, right then."

"Ew," said Jane with feeling.

"So with Piaras as my companion—"

"—for that was his name—"

"Who's telling this story?"

"I'm just postponing the tragic ending."

"So I spent that summer, and the summer after, and the summer after, by Piaras's side, every day, if I could. He was—"

"You skipped the part where he was a fairy," Jane complained.

"I thought it was obvious from the green hair."

"He was a fairy."

"He had green hair!"

"Fairy!" demanded Jane.

"And one day, that first summer," said Michael, as if nothing had happened, "I asked Piaras if he could ever visit me at home during the fall or the winter, and he revealed to me that he was a fairy, a nature spirit, bound forever to that one magical wood."

"Now, you knew about fairies," said Jane.

"Now, I knew about fairies," repeated Michael, "because I'd always been interested in them and I'd read Irish fairy tales and I'd had endless fantasy novels and fairy field guides and who knows what all on my bookshelf since I was a little kid. So when Piaras told me he was a fairy, I knew a few things right then. I knew that I was very lucky, because earning the love of a fairy was an unusual thing, and a magical thing, and not likely to ever happen again. I knew that he could not lie, but also that I had to treat him well, because his anger could be an unstoppable tempest. And I also knew that Piaras would never grow old, not ever—that he would remain a sixteen-year-old boy forever, and forever he would live and play in those woods. And when *I* was sixteen, I thought I would come back to those woods every year for the rest of my life, and our great love would keep me, and keep me young."

"How great was your love?" Jane said innocently.

"Oh, our love was great and pure," said Michael. "Well, maybe not that pure."

"Spare me the details."

"It wasn't just that Piaras was beautiful, and full of life, and took me on great adventures through the caves and treetops of that wood—"

"—though he did—"

"—though he did. We spent hours and hours and hours talking, laughing, thinking out loud. He had the most wonderful things to say about the world, and lots of questions about what my life was like, and I had lots of questions for him. And lots of lofty plans, and he thought they were fascinating, and he had all sorts of gossip and stories about the fairy courts, and I thought *they* were fascinating, and we just . . . got along very well. It was a perfect friendship. And a perfect romance. At least for a sixteen-year-old."

"Thank you for sparing me the details," said Jane.

"You," said Michael, "will never get to hear *those* details."

"I," said Jane, "never, ever, ever, ever want to."

"So then a few years passed," Michael continued. "And I was going off to college in the fall, just like you are now. And at the end of the summer, I said goodbye to Piaras, just like I always did, and I said, 'See you next summer,' just like I always did, but I think we both knew I wasn't coming back. We cried a little, and we stayed out later than usual. And when I absolutely had to get back, Piaras kissed me, once, very deliberately, like a gift. Like to say, 'here is this kiss.' But what he actually said was, 'You are bound to the fairies now. That tie can never be unbound. You will return. Promise that you will not grow up until you are beyond the fairies.'

"And I promised. But that was wishful thinking, if fairies could be said to have wishes. The next summer I had an opportunity for a great job far from New York, and the summer after I backpacked in Europe, and the summer after I lived in an apartment in the city with friends, and so on, and then Grandma and Poppy sold the house on the lake, and that was that. I never saw Piaras again."

"Do you ever hear his voice?" said Jane eagerly. "On the wind?"

Michael knew the answer to this, and hated that the question made him sad now. He felt suddenly heavier; a weight dragged his cheeks down, furrowed his brow, lowered his eyes. Smiling would be like hefting an impossible weight. "I used to," he said honestly. "But eventually I got too old to listen for the voice of a beautiful sixteen-year-old boy."

Jane must have caught the bitterness in his voice, because she said, "Unlike Pop."

Michael sighed. "I'm sorry."

"It's okay," said Jane.

"No," Michael shook his head. "You should still get to be a girl. You don't need to be 'it's okay'-ing me yet. I'm okay. Just lonely."

"Because he's gone?"

Michael thought. "I think I was lonely way before he actually left."

"I know," said Jane. They sat in silence for a moment.

"Do you miss him?" said Michael finally. "I mean, when you don't see him?"

Jane rolled onto her back and put her hands behind her head. She stared at the ceiling. "Sure," she said. "But even when I'm with him, mostly I miss who he used to be."

"Yeah, well," said Michael. "He's living in his past and we're in his present." He waited a moment. "Do you want to hear the end of the story?"

"Sure." Jane sat up again, leaning back on her hands.

"I never saw Piaras again," he repeated, "but I dated other people, and eventually I fell in love with a boy named George, who was very different from Piaras but who was very right for me, then. And we settled down, or something like it, and after a while we decided we would like to have a child, so we adopted a girl named Jane. She was a beautiful baby, with skin like a white peach and black rabbit eyes that were always looking around. And she grew up like a reed, pale and slender, and she had a pretty long face and straight black hair in a ponytail halfway down her back." He smiled and reached around behind her head to tug at her ponytail.

"And her dad used to tell her stories all the time."

"That's right. About ghosts and monsters and angels."

"And fairies."

"Them too. And she had a first-edition of *Peter Pan* that was her prize possession, and he taught her how to take care of it so it would last, but she knew it was too wonderful a thing to put in a case and just look at. She had to open it, again and again, and read it, again and again."

"And she was really hot, right? And talented and brilliant?"

"And she was my beautiful girl," said Michael, and he kissed her on the forehead. "I should go to bed," he said, getting up.

"Thanks for the story," she said.

"I'm sorry it was sadder than usual."

"*I* think it has a good ending. It ends with me!"

He grinned and said good night.

They slipped imperceptibly into summer, with nothing to do. Michael walked around the house day after day, like he'd lost something and didn't know where to start looking. Jane sat on the screen porch and dully tapped at her laptop, looking for summer jobs in the online listings, her elbows sweatily stuck to the pollen-coated vinyl tablecloth. When they talked, they talked idly about going away for a few weeks, or a month, but they didn't have any place in mind to go. George had always planned the vacations and it seemed strange to co-opt his role, even a year after his exit.

Jane found the house listed on some real estate Web site. She had to go get a box of her father's letters down from the attic and check the address, but yes, it was *the* house, near *the* woods. Its owners had died and their kids were selling the place off. It didn't look to be in great repair, but it was going pretty cheap. She found herself realizing that she wanted very much to go there. No: she wanted very much to *be* there. She felt the pull of the house even through the photo on the screen. She printed the listing out and just left the paper in the printer, knowing Michael would find it.

Michael bought the house almost reflexively. He realized that Jane must have found the listing, but he didn't mind the suggestion. It was a good suggestion. He'd been having a hard time knowing what to do with himself, and sometimes, he thought, others might know better. Maybe buying the house was an act of self-affirming spontaneity, the kind of thing people do when they are single and enjoying being single and want to do something without asking anyone else to prove that they can. Maybe it was a frantic unconscious grasp toward something familiar and good. It was about a week before he even thought to mention it to Jane, who smiled like it hadn't been her idea.

When they arrived at the very beginning of the summer, the house felt strangely untouched, as if it had been preserved for these many years. There must have been several owners in the twenty-odd years since his parents had sold it, but so much seemed to have been untouched—the wallpaper, the painted kitchen floor, the door knocker in the shape of a Celtic knot, the hill down to the lake, the only dock warped. There was no rowboat there anymore, but he didn't exactly miss it.

The movers showed up a couple hours later, and it took Jane about twenty minutes of watching them unload furniture and boxes to get utterly distracted by the woods across the road (now paved, Michael noted). "We should go for a walk," she said. "So you can point out all the landmarks from the stories."

"We should," said Michael absently. But of course that day they moved furniture around and unpacked clothes and stocked the kitchen and dusted cobwebs out of corners, and they were tired, and read books on the overstuffed red sofa Michael had bought for the musty living room, Jane's stocking feet propped up on Michael's lap as she paged through the first of a trilogy of extremely terrible werewolf detective novels she'd brought with her.

The second day he fetched a rusty ladder and examined the state of the roof and gutters, and then he started the long process for scrubbing the painted wooden floors. Jane took a book and disappeared into the woods. She called Michael on her cell phone a couple of hours later to report that she had not yet seen any fairies but that she had found a very nice tree to sit against and was reading.

"How strange," said Michael, "that cell phones work there."

"You thought, what, the magic would disrupt the signal?"

"Well, kind of," he said. "I don't know how it works."

"If I meet Piaras I'll ask him."

She came back a few hours later, and he greeted her with, "So, what kept you so long? Did you meet a boy?"

"Daaaad," she said, whacking him in the shoulder playfully with her book. "Noooo. But the woods are very pretty. It must've been great to be a kid here. We should go for a walk together tomorrow."

"We will," he said absently.

Lying in bed later, Michael wondered where Piaras was. These were his woods, and he was their youthful champion forever. He must be there, somewhere. He must have known Jane was there—every tree would have told him. Did he know who Jane was? Could he recognize her connection to his love of thirty years back?

Perhaps I've been forgotten entirely, Michael thought. Thirty years are like a moment to a fairy—perhaps many have come and gone since.

"Am I the first?" he had asked Piaras one afternoon, lying half-naked in late morning sunlight, arm blocking his eyes from the glare. Piaras had been sitting on a rock next to him, chucking pebbles into the brook, and he'd glanced over with a wry smile.

"Well, no," he'd said. "No. But if it makes you feel better, you're the first in a long time."

"So you're shy?"

"Shy?" Piaras had said as if slighted. He'd leaned back and rolled off the rock on top of Michael. He'd planted an extremely sloppy kiss on Michael's lips, and while Michael spluttered Piaras had laughed and said, "Selective!"

Michael realized with a start his overwhelming relief that Jane hadn't met Piaras out there, and then felt guilty about that relief. There would be *nothing wrong,* he told himself, with Jane meeting Piaras. He'd raised her, almost without thinking about it, to be a friend to the fairies. In fact, there was a way in which she *deserved* to know Piaras—deserved it more than Michael himself, really, who'd just been a stupid kid who'd happened to catch Piaras's eye. And Piaras was such a part of his history—it was like keeping part of himself from Jane.

Perhaps that was exactly it. Piaras was *his* youth, *his* memory, like a character in a beloved book. Let Jane enjoy her wild youth, he thought, just let her enjoy it in some other woods.

But then why had he come back? They were woods of childhood. They could no longer be his.

"Piaras, Piaras, always Piaras. You won't shut up about Piaras," said George scornfully in his mind. "Look at you—you think he wants someone who gets winded like you? With bags under his eyes like you?"

Michael rolled over. He had to at least try to sleep.

Jane was what people politely called an introvert, certainly—she craved and enjoyed her time alone—but after a couple of weeks Michael wondered why even he was too much company for her. She'd taken to leaving just after breakfast for the woods, and often she didn't even take a book with her—she would bring a sandwich and come back around twilight. Or she'd spend the day at home but then disappear after dinner for hours with a flashlight.

She'd never been the kind of teenager who'd kept things from him, so he wondered what was going on. He liked to think that if she had a boyfriend—or a girlfriend—she would tell him. But was that even feasible? Who was around? There were only a few houses in walking distance, and none of them had anybody under the age of forty in residence. Maybe somebody's nephew or niece had decided to come for the summer? *Not Piaras, don't let it be Piaras,* he thought. Maybe some other fairy, someone he hadn't heard of. And that Piaras had never mentioned. Would she tell him if it were Piaras? Would she be embarrassed, nervous? *If it is Piaras, I don't want to know.* He paused. *What a liar I am,* he thought. *Of course I want to know.*

In any case, Jane was so shy, he didn't want to press. He trusted her. It was, after all, sometimes hard to tell people things. He remembered how hard it was to tell George about Piaras, how surprised he was when George believed him and took it well.

He wondered now if George just thought of Piaras as an extended metaphor. He couldn't reconcile the young man who'd found Michael's stories delightful with the middle-aged man desperately grasping onto modern technology to keep him young and sneering at Michael's own natural aging.

When he spent time with Piaras, he could tell him anything. Anything. It was not so much that Piaras understood—after all, much of Michael's American teenagehood was completely inexplicable to a fairy—as that Piaras *listened,* always intently, and in those moments he seemed much older than the laughing boy of minutes earlier.

"Are you *sure* you haven't met someone?" Michael asked Jane at dinner the next night. He kept his voice carefully teasing.

Jane looked up in surprise and said, "Who would I meet? I've just been taking walks. You should come with me tomorrow—it's so pretty and all the renovations stuff can wait a day."

"Sure," he said distractedly, hating his suspicion, hating the gap between them. Maybe this is what it means to have a daughter grow up, he thought. Maybe this is the leading edge of a wedge that will keep us forever on opposite sides of some gulf. Am I turning into George, eaten by my own jealousy of youth? Am I finally so far gone that I envy even my own daughter? I've never been jealous of youth before, he thought. I don't want to think of Jane as some symbol of youth. I just want to think of her as Jane.

The next day Jane left in the morning, and he repainted the fence in the backyard.

The house had a sharply gabled study on the upper floor, almost an extra room tucked into a corner—unusable as a bedroom but perfectly suited to a writing desk and (once upon a time) some candle sconces and a window above spreading light like butter on the dark wood eaves and the surface of the desk. Michael discovered that when he stood on the chair and pulled down the top pane of the window, he could see clearly into the shallow part of the woods across the street, when it was day or when there was enough moon. He must have looked ridiculous standing there, but no one was around to see him.

He saw Piaras on the third night. Piaras tended to blend in, of course, being generally the same color as the trees, but even thirty years later he recognized that distinctive gait, the natural way he dodged and gamboled over the rocks and under the branches. Behind him was Jane, following like a ghost, light blue dress highlighted by the full moon. A knot tightened in Michael's bowels, and he stepped down quickly. He sat down on the chair and stared at the surface of the desk. He turned the desk lamp off, and then back on. His mind raced blankly.

A few minutes later, he was across the street, in a hastily donned coat. He thought, *Piaras is mine.* He thought, *Piaras isn't anyone's.* He thought, *Jane deserves a summer romance just like I had.* He thought, *Jane is mine.* He thought, *are fairies always bisexual?* He thought, *once I was Piaras's, and once I was Jane's, and now they are each other's and I am neither of theirs.*

He walked blindly through the woods. Years-hidden memories pulled themselves into consciousness out of sheer survival instinct, and he walked unmarked trails the way he once had, through reflex. He called George's cell phone number and to his surprise, George picked up. "Hello, Michael."

"George," said Michael. "I . . . I . . . just wanted to let you know that . . . Jane has a boyfriend."

There was a pause. "Well," said George slowly, "that's great news! I mean, she's so shy, I worried she wouldn't let anyone get close to her . . . isn't it great news?"

He was being good, thought Michael—he is being polite, as the saying goes, for the sake of the child.

"It is," said Michael in a tone of utter despair. "Great news."

"Michael," said George, "are you all right? You don't sound all right."

By your lights, I haven't been all right since my hair started going grey, thought Michael, but he didn't say it. Nor did he say— *well, you see, Jane's new boyfriend is my old boyfriend*— as that sounded creepy. Instead, he said, "It's like she's gone. I've lost her." *And you.*

There was a long pause, and when George spoke, his voice was kind, as kind as it had been that day a year ago when they fought. "She was never yours, Michael. Or mine. Children are children, and we are grown up."

"I feel like saying, 'Old man! Old man, get out of me,'" Michael said.

George was silent. There were many things he could have said, and Michael was grateful that he did not say any of them. Instead, Michael got hold of himself, ended the conversation, and stumbled his way back to the house in the dark. When Jane got home, she found him already asleep.

The next day at breakfast Michael said, "I really miss spending time with you. Let's spend the evening together, just us, the way we did that first night here. Will you stay home at the house, and just hang out?"

Jane looked down. "I'm sorry I've been gone so much," she said. "I'll stay home tonight, definitely. In fact there's something I want to talk to you about."

She said it with innocence, but Michael found himself without any appetite. He nodded and got up from the table. "It's a date, then."

"So, look," he said, when they'd finished the dishes, and Jane was drying her hands on the other side of the room, "I've been thinking. And you deserve a romance as much as anybody."

She turned, looking honestly puzzled. "What?"

"I mean . . ." He trailed off, and then sighed. "There's no reason for you to feel bad about . . . anything . . . or secretive . . . about what you may have been up to. . . ."

"Dad," she said, looking concerned, "can we go into the living room before we have this conversation?"

"Sure." He followed her in, but before she'd even sat down, he said, "I mean, this is the way of things. Our generations go by—I get older, and, and, you grow up."

"Dad," said Jane again, sounding more desperate, "can you just wait a couple of minutes?"

Michael, however, was on a roll. "The fairies, though, they're constant; they're here forever as far as we're concerned, and it's the natural way of things that my time has passed and yours has come."

"Just a few minutes," she pleaded, glancing at the windows. "Wait."

"You know, Jane," he said, settling down into his chair, "most people never even slightly encounter immortality. We live short lives and we rush to fill them before they go, and for most of us, the only way we can fill them is to spend time with others like us—blind and short-lived, with no magic at all.

"So when you do find magic, you should be thankful for it, every day—every day, and you should never give it up. You should never give up any magic you find. Never."

"Are you saying you did?" said Piaras, and then he was standing outside the huge bay window, and then he was climbing through, and then he was standing in the living room. He towered over the furniture to Michael, the way the trees towered over him. His voice was as soft and even as it had been.

Michael struggled to find his own voice. "You always did know how to make an entrance," he managed to cough out.

"Your daughter and I have been spending a lot of time together," Piaras said, smiling.

"I know," said Michael. "I saw you through the tower window the other day."

Piaras nodded absently, as if he'd already known. "You know," he said thoughtfully, "this is actually the first time I've ever been in the house." To Jane, "I could never come in before—your grandparents would have been put out."

"Look, Piaras," said Michael, struggling to take hold of the conversation, "I guess you've come to tell me that you love Jane, and Jane loves you. And I've been thinking about it a lot, and yeah, I'll be honest, it sort of hurts, but I understand. One generation passes—"

"Oh, you silly, silly man," said Piaras softly. "You jump and leap and gambol at conclusions the same way you did when you were a boy."

"I jump and leap?" demanded Michael.

"Michael," said Piaras, "Jane and I are not in love. I love her, surely, as of course I would love any of your family. She is like you in so many ways. We have been talking, as I said. Well, mostly I have been talking."

"He's been telling me stories," said Jane. "About you—when you two used to be together."

"You aren't in love with Piaras?" said Michael.

"In love with my dad's ex-boyfriend? *Ew,*" said Jane, with relish.

"She invited me here," explained Piaras, "because one of the things we've been talking about is how you've stayed cooped up in this house these weeks. I knew you'd come back the moment you arrived, and I was happy, and I was waiting for you. And then you didn't come. I thought you must have forgotten about me.

"But then I met Jane, and she knew so much about me, I knew you must have told her, many times. And I couldn't figure out why you hadn't come to find me. I bet Jane that you had forgotten, that you hated me. She bet that you hadn't. And I remembered that you were a proud boy, and now maybe you are a proud man. So Jane convinced me, and I have come to ask: will you come away with me? Will you come walking in the woods like you once did? Have you kept a fire in your hearth for me?"

Michael sighed. "My dear Piaras," he said. "Here you are in front of me again, and you are exactly the same. It has been so long, but it also feels like yesterday. How time flies."

"Does it fly the way we did?" said Piaras artfully.

"Do you know," said Michael, "I sometimes wonder whether I did fly."

Jane interjected. "Dad, he's really sad. All these years you've talked about your great love, and now here he is to take you back with him, and it's the most romantic thing I've ever heard, and you won't go?"

"Oh, Piaras," sighed Michael. "I can't. Maybe I need to turn up the lights, so then you can see for yourself."

Piaras twisted his mouth into a wry smile. "See what, my dear?" He sat himself carefully on the rug in front of Michael, and then he took Michael's hand and gently placed it in his green curls.

Michael let his hands play in the hair of the boy and smiled, but it was a wet-eyed smile. "I am old, Piaras," said Michael. "I am ever so much more than twenty. I grew up long ago."

"Did you?"

"Don't you have eyes?" said Michael. He ran his hands roughly through his hair. "Don't you see the wrinkles on my face? Don't you see how I've become old and slow? How my hair is the color of iron?"

"But you've also turned wise," said Piaras.

"What good is wisdom to youth?"

"Michael," said Piaras sharply. "I am a fairy. I am many things, but I am not young."

"You are too young for me," said Michael with despair.

Piaras looked at Jane. "Are you hearing this? Didn't you say your father gave you a lot of fairy books when you were little? Did *he* read them?" He turned back to Michael. "My dear man, I have seen the earth when it was young and new and fresh. I have presided over these woods since wild nature was truly wild, before this house, before that road, before you or anyone you could remember. I am not the oldest of fairies, nor am I the youngest, but *me* too young for *you?*" He laughed aloud. "Michael, you could live to the ripest age a man has ever lived, and you would still, always, be far, far, *far* too young for *me*."

There was a long silence. Michael didn't know what to say.

"I've read a lot of fairy stories," said Jane, "and you know, there are two kinds of people who get to be with the fairies in them. There are the young and free, the spirits who are like fairies already, almost, and the fairies come to them, and they run, um, 'not yet bound to the world,' I think one story says."

Michael and Piaras both stayed silent, and she pressed on.

"The other kind are the wise kind—the grown-ups, the men and women, the wise uncles and grandmothers, who walk with the fairies, who know their ways, who have their knowledge of the land and the plants. They are the ones in the stories who know how to heal, and how to ensure a good . . . you know, crop, or whatever.

"So they had to get there somehow, right? It's not like they could have lived their lives without any magic for years and years and then one day some pretty elf shows up and bang, they're aged and wise. And I wonder . . . I wonder if the wise men who walk with the fairies are the same as the spirited boys who frolic with them. Just, you know . . . years later."

There was another pause, which Michael broke by clearing his throat. "Well," he said tentatively, "that sounds good to me."

"I would like that too," said Piaras softly.

"Would you?" Michael pressed.

"I'm a fairy, Michael, and fairies are inconstant as weather. Yesterday, I wanted a young boy to run with, to kiss in the meadow. Today, I want a wise man, to walk with steady steps next to, to discuss the things of the world.

"Will you walk with me, my good man?" said Piaras, extending his hand in a formal gesture. Taking it, Michael pulled himself up and out of the armchair.

"Now?" he said. He looked to Jane. "I asked you here because we haven't spent enough time together, and now I'm leaving without you?" Jane appeared to ponder this carefully. "Well," she said, "I don't know. You might make it up to me by coming into the woods tomorrow with Piaras *and* me."

Piaras reached up and pulled Michael's head down to his, and kissed him. Piaras's mouth was a memory to Michael, a warm remembrance of youth, and it was immediate, present, a warm flood of love through him. It was both at the same time.

Breaking the kiss, Piaras turned to Jane and formally bowed low. "Ms. Jane," he said, "may I take your father away for the evening? He and I have much to talk about."

"I don't know," said Jane. "I like seeing Dad smile like that. I'd like to see that some more."

Of course in the end she let them fly away together. Michael's last glimpse as he followed Piaras showed her at the window, watching them receding into the night until they were as small as stars.

doi:10.1300/5642_22

Mr. Grimm's Faery Tale

Eric Andrews-Katz

William Grimm sat behind the desk in his office. He tried not to breathe while the previous client's unwashed body odor began to diminish. It made his stomach tighten and he wrinkled his nose from under his wiry glasses. Trying to shake his mood, he subconsciously took a deep breath and immediately regretted it as the stench invaded his nostrils. His mind drifted back to the hospice where another of his close friends was very ill. He had seen three friends in as many years fall under the virus' curse and struggled as their minds faded into sickness and darkness. He felt helpless.

"I wish . . ." William muttered and sighed heavily. He shook his head to clear it and brought himself to his present task. He reached an arm out and with a small hand, picked up the next file of the next unemployed person of the next appointment seeking job assistance and/or placement.

Grimm was about to review the applicant's résumé when a scent of freshness crossed his desk. He sniffed trying to place the smell. It reminded him of lush, green forests or an early-morning meadow spotted with wildflowers. Maybe laundry softener. From the corner of his eye, he saw a bluish blur glide into the seat across from his desk. He glanced over the name on the file before looking for the person.

"Good afternoon, Miss, ah, Mary Weather." It was almost a question. He tried to speak with disinterest to make up for the softness in his voice. He believed it suggested authority. William lifted his head and blinked. Only a blue peak could be seen. It reminded him of an upside down ice cream cone. Slowly, he slid forward and looked over the desk's edge.

Mary Weather was dressed in blue—electric, bold blue to be precise. No taller than four feet, she wore a dress that billowed out around her much like a hoop skirt of the Ol' South, but it folded nicely over her knees. She wore a French Blue conical hat, but instead of a wide brim, it had two lighter cloth ribbons that tied below her chin and kept the hat in place. Her chipmunk cheeks with red pinches gave her a kind, elderly, granny-type of look. The soft wrinkles of her face added to the comfort she seemed to naturally offer. The woman's hair was black with gray strands liberally strewn throughout.

But it wasn't her gentle face or the woman's height that caught William's attention. Neither the matronly demeanor, nor the boldness of color made his lips mold into a perfect "O" as he raised a single eyebrow. Held delicately in a feminine, almost childlike hand was a wand. Mary held it erect like a conductor's baton ready to fly into action. Sitting atop the shaft, a bright yellow star dimly glowed. Tiny lights like snowflakes fell from the star, transforming from translucent white into blue specks before disappearing.

William took a moment before snapping his mouth shut. He pulled himself back using only his neck and shoulders until he sat against the chair's backing and both feet were firmly planted on the floor. He felt his chest and buttocks clench. William started to say something several times, but each attempt was unsuccessful and frustratingly ended before beginning. He didn't know where to start.

Eventually, William took a deep breath and slowly spoke. "How may I help you, Miss Weather?"

The tiny matron sprung to life like living animation. She jumped up and stood on the chair creating the illusion of an eye-level, even pegging.

"Oh," she said with a chuckle, "that's me. Yes, I'm Mary Weather." She cupped her free hand to her mouth and giggled. "It's not like I don't know my own name." She glanced at the nameplate on his desk. "You're Mr. Grimm." She frowned at the name a moment then clenched her eyes. "And, I'd like a job, please." Her eyes opened and she nodded with enthusiasm. The vibration caused the wand to tremor.

William kept his eyes on the sparks that fell. His words were slow, distracted by the sound of tiny bells. "What kind of work are you looking for?"

The woman spoke rapidly. "Anything will do really. I'm kind of a Jack-of-all-Trades." She covered her mouth again and giggled. Her tiny shoulders rocked. "I guess I mean Jill-of-all-Trades." She laughed passionately. Her hand provided little barrier from either the sound or the traces of spittle that flew out.

"What kind of skills do you have?" William asked. Discreetly, he wiped the side of his cheek. He dismissed the visuals with a shake of his head. This was going to be an extreme case. Either it would be quick and easy or he was in for long and slow pain. He hoped his head wouldn't start to hurt.

"Well," Mary said. She closed one eye in thought and tucked her free hand under her chin. "I can change the color of things into the color blue. I like the color blue." She leaned in and supported herself on the desk with both hands. She whispered a secret: "It's my signature color." She nodded confidingly.

She returned to standing upright on the chair. "I can make little things appear and vanish. I can hide princesses in the forest, turn puppets into real boys and grant kitchen wench's wishes." Her eyes grew wide with delight. "Did you hear that? It sounds like 'The Twelve Days of Christmas.'" She began to sing, "kitchen wench's wishes, fiiive goollddden riinnngggs!" She laughed and clapped her hands. Iridescent lights fell from the wand. "I'm sorry, sometimes I just can't help breaking out into song."

William kept his neck very still. The bottom of his head began to vibrate beginning at his chin. He puckered his lips biting the inside of his cheeks. He heard bells again. They were creeping him out. He shifted in his chair looking for their source.

"Is something wrong?" The petite woman imitated William's awkward shuffling. "What are we looking for? Besides a job for me?" She giggled, reached out and grasped his arm giving it an affectionate squeeze.

"I'm sorry. I keep hearing tiny bells ringing. It's distracting."

"Oh that!" Mary laughed and gently shook her wand. The tiny lights that fell rang gently through the air before vanishing. "Sorry, it was either the bells or the 'Mexican Hat Dance.' All the good sounds were taken." She waved the wand again. Dancing light arched over the desk. "I wanted the theme to *Bonanza,* but it was already gone." She leaned back and rocked on her heels in amusement. Then she saw William's stern look and calmed down. "I'll just place it right here so it doesn't distract you." She set it on the desk's closest edge.

William looked at the wand and slowly reached toward it. It was beautiful and alluring and he just wanted to run his fingers over the intricately carved designs. As his hand approached the glowing ball around the star, his fingertips began to warm. In a flash of blue lightning, the wand was snatched away.

Mary raised the wand but kept it out of the reach of William's hands. Her index finger on her free left hand raised in caution. All trace of gaiety had left her and those motherly eyes widened with warning. Aside from a raised, painted on eyebrow, only her lips moved.

"There will be *no* touching of the wand."

William sheepishly nodded more in surprise than concession. Her voice held an edge, a high sound like the recording in an old talking doll. "Kiss me goodnight," "Pick me up," "Touch the wand and I'll kill ya!" all spoken with the same saccharine robotics.

Mary began to lower the wand and then snapped back into a defensive position. She waited in warning and then rested it against her shoulder.

"We'll just keep it here for now," she patted the glowing star. "No bells, but you can still see it."

William sat back in his chair and Ms. Weather made a grand production of folding her arms, watching him. They stared at each other for several moments of silence.

"Let's start again," William said professionally. "What did you do at your last job?" He shuffled in his drawer for a notepad and pen. With a blast of indigo, a blue tinted pad and pencil appeared neatly on his desk. On the pencil's erasure was a tiny troll doll with wild azure hair. "Thank you," William mumbled, taking the pencil in hand.

"My last job," Mary burst forth, "was for King Stephan. I took care of his daughter, Briar Rose. Lovely girl. Lips as red as petals and skin as soft as daylight. She always walked with a song in her heart." Her voice broke with tears. She pulled a cornflower-colored, lace hanky from her sleeve and dabbed at her eyes before blowing her nose loudly, sounding like a cartoon foghorn. "Rose grew up and a hundred years later got married. Then there was no need for me. Mission accomplished." She sighed heavily before snapping back into full animation. "Wanna see some pictures?"

"I'm sorry," William said. He politely and pointedly blinked several times. "Did you say, 'one hundred years later'?"

"Oh that," the tiny woman laughed as she folded up a row of snapshots preserved in plastic covers. She snapped her fingers and they disappeared. Her arms moved as she spoke, lifting the wand. Lights fell and the bells returned. "I bet you're thinking; 'my goodness! One hundred years, that's a long time,' but I tell you, it would have been sooner if it wasn't for that whole evil spell."

"Evil spell?" William wasn't sure if he should be amused or ring for security.

"Yeah, yeah, yeah," Mary related, "there was this evil faery you see and she cast a spell. Briar Rose pricked her finger on a poisoned spinning wheel's spindle and died."

"She died?" William repeated. He was stunned. His finger began to reach for the security button under his desk.

"Well, almost," Mary barreled on. "But I ask you: should one bad prick really kill ya?" She quickly puffed herself up proudly before continuing. She nodded and stuck her thumb into her chest. "I saved the girl. I changed death into sleep. That would be the whole hundred year's thing. Goodness triumphed in the end when true love's kiss woke her." She pulled out the hanky again. "One good kiss and all was as it should be." She smiled with melancholy. "That was a good job." She nodded enthusiastically and rubbed her fingers together. "A *good* job, ya know what I mean?"

The wand flashed and a tiny cash register appeared. It rang with a "ka-ching" and the words *Major Sale* appeared in the window. It disappeared a moment later with a puff of smoke.

"So . . ." William was at a short loss for words. "Let's start with your interest in children."

"Not so much anymore," she was quick to correct. "Ya see, before King Stephan, I worked in France with my cousin, Dente. She has this huge business. Trade and commerce. Whenever a kid put a tooth under his or her pillow, I would slip in and leave a shiny quarter. Sweet deal for the kid, eh? Free money for a tooth?" She giggled.

"What did you do with the tooth?" William asked. Under his desk his finger circled the red security button without ringing it.

"Did I say there was going to be a question-and-answer period?" She snapped harshly. In a flash, she broke into a huge smile. "Just kidding!" Mary chortled and lifted off the chair, spinning like a blue and white dreidle. Sparkles shot off of her like exhaust fumes.

William noticed the heart-shaped, sapphire gossamer wings that wafted the woman back to a standing position. They also rang with tiny chiming.

"I'm sorry." Mary slowly calmed herself down. Noticing William's shiver and renewed search for the bell sounds, she pointed to the wings and then the wand. "They came as a set. One sound fits all."

He only smiled back. His head was already hurting.

"As I was saying, I worked with my French cousin, Dente Fey, and my beat was this little village. The king of the village had two sons. Well," she clutched at a lapis necklace around her neck, "the younger son was a wisenheimer, ya know what I mean? The older prince was definitely charming, but the younger one was a little monster. You should have seen the dreams he had!"

She whirled her fingers around her ears in opposite directions and stuck out her tongue. It was colored like a purebred chow-chow dog. She winked with much exaggeration.

"He woke up and caught me leaving the money and that's definitely not allowed in the rule book, so my night was not going well." She took a deep breath and pulled on an angry face. "To make matters worse, he wanted me to grant him three wishes or he threatened to tell his parents!" She put both fists on her hips in mock indignation. "I told him, 'This is a wand, not a lamp!' Then I said, 'if you are going to act like a beast, be one!'" Her fingertips covered her lips with faux repentance. "I guess I waved the wand and the next thing you know. . . . Oops! He's on all fours, covered in hair, howling at the moon!" Her eyes rolled off to one side and she shrugged her shoulders. Mary shook her head to insist on her innocence. "It's not like it didn't work out for him." She leaned forward and whispered, "He lives in a castle and gets his freaky-freak on in a three-way with an enchanted French candelabra and an English teapot." Her face was long and her eyes were wide. She nodded knowingly. "Can you imagine?" She tightly shook her head with a distinctive "Tsk, tsk, tsk."

"Ms. Weather," William began. His hand slowly receded from the panic button and he knotted his fingers together on top of his desk. "This may sound like a silly question but . . ."

"Oh," she giggled, "call me Mary. You're like an old friend, now. And there's no such thing as a silly question if one can learn from it."

"Yes," William drew the word out with a snake's breath and frozen smile. "Since you are gifted shall we say with 'extra abilities,' why do you need a job at all? Couldn't you just conjure what you needed?"

"Oh, no. Noo, nooo, noooo." Mary sounded like a shocked owl. "I can't use my powers for self-profit." She chuckled. "That would be cheeaatiiinnng." She sang the last word. "Besides, that's something only an evil faery would do." She reached out to pat William's hand. "Or a politician." She broke out into hysterical laughter. "Get it, self-profit, politician?" She laughed heartily and spun off the chair floating back downward. "Sometimes I just slay me like a princess-guarding dragon."

"There are evil faeries?" William asked. His hands clutched each other tightly, his patience reaching new limits.

"Oh sure," Mary answered. "There's Maleficent, the Banshee, the Sluag, Roy Cohn . . ." She erupted in gales of laughter patting her hand over her heart. "There I go again!" She slapped the back of her own hand, "Bad Mary! Bad fey! No biscuit!" Her hands flew wildly about as her laughter began to subside. She calmed down with a sigh.

"So you've never done anything bad?" William asked. He had to admit, he had begun to like her. Once the initial shock of her gregariousness passed, it was hard not to. He felt his breath become regular and his back started to relax.

"Well, bad is actually a relative term," Mary replied. "And if you want bad relatives, you should meet my sister! Talk about a howling banshee! No, seriously, it depends on how you define it. I had this one client named Gepetto." She put her hand to the side of her mouth and whispered behind it. "Dirty ol' bugger, but I didn't know it at the time. He fell in love with the puppet he created." She lowered her hand. "Since my great, great, great grandmother did such a wonderful job on one of her clients—Pygmalion (what a name!)—I thought I'd help poor Gepetto out and bring his work to life. What a mistake *that* was!"

Mary looked to both sides of the room and focused her glistening, blue topaz eyes on William. "I won't tell you the details," she related in a stage whisper, "but I got to little Pinocchio just in time to change him back and give that lecherous father of his some nasty splinters!" Mary's eyes went wide with false shock and her mouth opened in mock surprise. She giggled wickedly. "Robin Goodfellow and I laughed about that for days!"

"Who?" William asked.

"Robin Goodfellow." Mary seemed shocked by the lack of recognition. She winked exaggeratingly. "I'm telling you, Titania named him 'Goodfellow' for a reason!" She ran her tongue slowly across her lips. "Hubba-Hubba Zing-Zing!"

William watched her turn color with embarrassment. Or perhaps from great satisfaction, he wasn't sure. He didn't want to know and blocked the implied visual before it took complete form. Red color crept up the woman's face, mingling with all the blue surroundings and created a rich, purple blushing.

"So you were fired from that job?" William asked.

Mary smoked a cigarette that he had missed her lighting. She exhaled a rose the color of a Confederate uniform, as easily as someone would blow rings.

"Yeah," Mary replied with a heavy breath, "but it was worth it!" She waved her wand causing both the cigarette and the smoke flower to disappear.

"Okay!" William snapped. He lowered his falsetto voice to a low rumble. He paused between each word to make sure there was no misunderstanding. "The bells need to go! Can we put that thing on mute?"

She tucked her mouth tightly behind closed lips. Her eyes were round dark oceans and her painted-on eyebrows were raised in defensive arches. "Sure." She said it as if the word was hot. Her delicate hand reached up and snapped. A low sound of descending xylophone scales deflated in the air. The glow around both the wand and the wings dulled. Mary kept her hand raised and put it into a fist. She mumbled while keeping her eyes focused directly on William, "if you want to take away some of the *fun*." She turned her head away and breathed heavily, pouting.

"It's distracting and giving me a headache," William said in a softer voice.

"Oh your head hurts?" Mary clicked into action; all traces of hurt feelings apparently vanished as a smile crossed her face and the rose color in her cheeks blossomed. "Let me have your hand and I'll take care of that!" Her sing-song voice returned. "I know just the cuuureee!" She ended the word with a playful purr.

Hesitantly, William turned his head slightly and slowly lifted his hand out to her.

"Would that be a spoonful of sugar?" He asked hopefully. The glowing lady bounced upon the chair.

"No." She took his hand into hers and began to knead it. "It's acupressure. Now close your eyes and take a deep breath in."

William did as he was told. He let go of his inhibitions and closed his eyes, giving into trust. Slowly, his lungs filled with a deep breath. He smelled the forest and earth's freshness. *No,* he thought, *it's definitely Bounce.* The tightened band in his head slowly ebbed away. It faded and the pain was gone. He took another deep breath, feeling the freshness clear his mind and begin to flush away the tension in his neck and muscles. In his mind it was twilight and the color of the sky welcomed him. Something glistened there and it came forth from the evening's cloak.

"Boo!"

William's eyes bolted open. The word still thundered in his ears as Mary's face appeared nose-to-nose with him. He pushed himself back from the desk. The chair rolled backward until it crashed into the office wall behind him. His heart pounded. His breathing short and heavy as he held his arms aloft in front of him defensively.

Mary laughed wildly as she lifted herself off the chair and knocked it backward. Flying head-over-heels in a rolling motion, she looked like a single colored ribbon in a badly repetitive rhythm gymnastic routine.

"What the hell?" William barked out in between heavy panting. "I have a headache, not the hiccups!"

"Not anymore," Mary cried out. She stopped rolling and righted the chair with a wave of her wand before sitting back down, holding her stomach. Cobalt tears flowed down her cheeks. "Your headache is gone."

William stopped to think about it. His heart began to slow down to a normal pace and his breath evened out. The pain in his head had vanished. "You're right." He whispered and gave a nervous laugh.

He looked across the desk and saw Mary holding a box of laundry soap imitating a television commercial.

"Ancient Chinese Seeecret." The box disappeared.

William's smile grew and then froze. An idea raced through his mind. He felt color rush into his cheeks and warm his skin. He shot forward crossing his arms and leaning over the desk. He delightedly studied the petite woman on the other side.

"How would you like to work with people who are ill?" he asked.

He could tell from her expression that she was contemplating the proposal. A warm feeling started within him. His business intuition assured him she was perfect for the job. He waited until she returned his smile and watched as she happily nodded.

William sat back in his chair and turned to his computer screen. His fingers clacked away and a fleeting flash of pictures went by until a listing of referrals appeared in the cyber window before him. He put his finger against the screen to hold his place on the desired entry.

"Bailey House is a hospice for people who are dying as a result of HIV infection." There was eagerness in his voice. "And they need staffing."

"I can't stop death, only transform it," Mary replied. "Helloo, I thought we already went through this. Remember? The whole finger-pricking thing?"

"I remember," William said. His smile and enthusiasm remained intact. "A lot of these people suffer from dementia. Some of them are asleep and won't wake up before they die." William bit his bottom lip. He held his breath before continuing with guarded hope. "If you have the power to bring some ease to them, it would give them some light to look toward in a very dark place. I'm sure you would be able to help them in more ways than you could possibly imagine."

Mary glowed brightly. She clapped rapidly and a powder-blue globe of light formed around her hands to warm the room. The more she applauded, the brighter the illumination became.

Suddenly, she froze and peered through the light ball at William, a graven look on her face.

"There won't be any problem because I'm a faery, I hope?"

"You'll fit right in once you have a uniform."

Mary whirled the wand over her head in a spiral motion. The lights surrounded her and sparkled. Before they faded, she stood dressed in the traditional nurse's outfit, except colored a pastel, sky blue. She spread her arms and bowed.

"Muuuch better." William could barely contain his laughter. "You'll be fine."

William leaned back and scooted the chair comfortably up to his desk. He bent his head downward and took the furry troll-topped pencil back in hand, rubbing it between his palms to get the wild blue hair as fluffed out as he could. He scribbled a name and address on the aquamarine-colored notepad. In a single action, he tore the paper from its stack and slid it across to the woman in front of him.

"Go to this address and ask for Mr. Anderson. I'll give him a call and tell him to be expecting you." He offered her a warm smile.

"Thank you," Mary said. She took the paper and looked over the address.

"If you need me to, I can draw you a map. It's only a short bus ride."

"Oh," Mary smiled and cocked her head. "I'll just call the Pumpkin-Coach. Their driver will know how to get there." She nodded assuredly. "He's a smart mouse."

"Well, Ms. Mary Weather," William stood and reached over to shake the petite hand. "Good luck, and it's been a pleasure to meet you."

"Thaaannnk yooouuu," she sang and vigorously pumped his arm. She hovered over his desk to not offset her balance. She then let go and glided around to the floor. She half skipped and half trotted to the doorway. Before leaving, she stopped and turned around to face him one more time.

"I just have to say it," she called out.

William lifted his head from the notes he was making on her file. He shook his head and shrugged his shoulders waiting for her to explain.

"If you smiled a little more," she paused, "maybe you wouldn't be so Grimm!"

Mary Weather threw her head back and erupted in ringing laughter as she turned and left the office. The glockenspiel of ringing echoed behind her.

William smiled broadly. He shook his head at the crazy, delightful woman that just left his office. Without looking for it, his hand reached for the phone and he dialed a very familiar, seven-digit number.

It rang three times.

"Hello," he said to the receptionist on the other end. He used his best and most professional phone voice. "May I speak with Mr. Anderson, please? Thank you." He waited, letting his eyes roam over the notes he made. "Christian! It's William at Pantheon Placements." William instantly relaxed into friendly conversation. "I'm sending over a potential . . . no, she's not a nurse, but I think she will do very well helping out . . . What? No, more like a candy striper but she's to be paid. Trust me, even those with dementia will react positively with her. She's an eccentric. . . . If I meant freak, I would have said freak, she's eccentric." He continued mumbling to himself more than anything else, "and she has a fetish for the color blue. What? Oh, nothing. Never mind. Yeah. Yeah. Yeah. Let her grow on you. She has a way to make everything feel all right. I have no doubt she'll do an excellent job. Yeah . . . no, really no problem. You can buy me a drink later, how 'bout that? Okay, 'bye."

William hung up the phone. An intimate smile lingered on his lips as he filed away the notes and put the folder in the "Placed" file bin. He had a gut feeling that Mary would be able to at least brighten the haunted dreams of those souls in that hospice. It warmed him to think that with a wave of the wand, maybe, just maybe, those who were suffering could still have a Happily Ever After.

doi:10.1300/5642_23

ABOUT THE EDITOR

Some of **Steve Berman**'s fondest childhood memories involve books, so it's little wonder he grew up wanting to be a writer. His own queer fey story can be found within the pages of *The Faery Reel* (Viking Press) and more tales can be found in his collections, *Trysts* and *Second Thoughts* (both from Lethe Press). He has also written the young adult novel, *Vintage* about boy, ghosts, and New Jersey, where he happens to live. Steve is a Lambda Literary Award-nominated editor.

doi:10.1300/5642_24

CONTRIBUTORS

Eric Andrews-Katz has been writing since he could hold a pen. He studied journalism at the University of South Florida and eventually moved back to Gainesville where he attended the Florida School of Massage. He has a successful, licensed massage practice, and currently, with his partner, Alan, calls Seattle home. After three years of writing for a Web site (under the pen name Michael Young) Eric has finished his second book, *Magdalene,* and his second novel, a spy-parody called *The Jesus Injection.* His work can be found in *Charmed Lives: Gay Spirit in Storytelling,* and *The Best Date Ever.*

Christopher Barzak's stories have appeared in venues such as *Year's Best Fantasy and Horror, Trampoline, Salon Fantastique, The Coyote Road,* and *Nerve.* His first novel, *One for Sorrow,* described as *Catcher in the Rye* meets *The Lovely Bones,* the story of a fifteen-year-old boy haunted by the murder of one of his classmates, has been published by Bantam Books. He spent two years living in Japan, teaching English in a suburb of Tokyo, and now lives in Youngstown, Ohio, where he teaches English at Youngstown State University.

Holly Black is *The New York Times'* best-selling author of several contemporary fantasy novels. Her books include *The Spiderwick Chronicles, Tithe, Valiant,* and her most recent release, *Ironside: A Modern Fairy's Tale.* She resides in a century-old house in Amherst, Massachusetts, where she is hard at work completing a graphic novel series of suburban fantasy.

Richard Bowes has lived in New York City for almost four decades and done the things one does there. Over the past twenty-plus years he has published five novels and two short-fiction collections. His stories have appeared in *The Magazine of Fantasy & Science Fiction, Scifiction, Bending the Landscape,* and elsewhere. He has won a World Fantasy and a Lambda Award. His most recent novel is *From the Files of the Time Rangers* (2005) and his most recent collection is *Streetcar Dreams and Other Midnight Fancies* (2006). Recent short-fiction appearances include *Helix, Nebula Awards Showcase 2005, Postscripts #3, The Coyote Road,* and *Scifiction.*

Tom Cardamone made his first attempt at reading in public while sharing the stage with Steve Berman. After nervously auditioning "A Faun's Tale," an excerpt of an erotic novel-in-progress, Steve offered him the best encouragement an author can get: publication! The completed novel, *The Werewolves of Central Park,* is now available. Tom also has several short stories in current and upcoming anthologies, with new projects, both fiction and nonfiction, on the horizon. You can read more of his stories at pumpkinteeth.net.

Cassandra Clare lives in New York City with her boyfriend and her cat. She is the author of the dark fantasy young adult trilogy, *Mortal Instruments,* and is currently working on the third book, entitled *City of Glass.* She has a new short fiction in the forthcoming anthology *Magic in the Mirrorstone.*

Ruby deBrazier is a talented physician and poet living in New York City. This is her first published short story.

Eugie Foster calls home a mildly haunted, fey-infested house in Atlanta that she shares with her husband, Matthew, and her pet skunk, Hobkin. Her fiction has appeared in *Realms of Fantasy, The 3rd Alternative, Cricket, Paradox,* and *Cicada.* She also pens a monthly column, "Writing for Young Readers." Visit her online at eugiefoster.com.

Carl Vaughn Frick first found fairy space in the heart of the 1980s. He has lived in Seattle, San Francisco, and now resides in Portland, Oregon. Vaughn has worked as a cartoonist, illustrator, newspaper art director, photographer, ceramicist, woodworker, set designer, and in 1987 was co-chair for Seattle's Gay/Lesbian/Bi/Trans pride parade. For five years he wrote and drew an environmental comic strip called

Cascadia that appeared in various newspapers. Vaughn's cartoons and illustrations have been printed in *R.F.D. Magazine* and many other odd and quirky publications across the spectrum of imagination. Vaughn is currently working on two books: *In Transit,* stories of adventures from working for Portland's public transportation system, and *The life of Stan Stone,* the complete comic strip life of a character he began drawing in the pages of *Gay Comix.*

Craig Laurance Gidney has had fiction published in the following venues: *Spoonfed, Say . . . Have You Heard This One?, Ashe,* and the forthcoming anthology *Magic in the Mirrorstone.* He lives in his native Washington, DC.

M. Kate Havas earned her BAs in English and Art History from Wesleyan College. Aside from writing fantasy she enjoys costuming and dressage, and currently lives in Georgia with her horses. "Touch" is her first published story.

Lynne Jamneck is a South African writer currently living in New Zealand. Her fiction and nonfiction have appeared in various markets and anthologies including *Best Lesbian Erotica 2003, H.P. Lovecraft's Magazine of Horror, The Good Parts, Harrington Lesbian Fiction Quarterly,* and *Hot Lesbian Erotica.* Upcoming work includes stories in *Call of the Dark: Erotic Lesbian Tales of the Supernatural* and *Taste of Midnight.* Her first mystery, *Down the Rabbit Hole* is available from Bella Books. She is also the creator and editor of *Simulacrum: The Magazine of Speculative Transformation.*

Aynjel Kaye began life firmly rooted in Normal and has escaped. She is an angst-queen in exile holding court in Seattle, Washington, where she is plotting to retake her throne. She may or may not be a chocolate lover, a goth, a punk, and less harmless than she was before.

Joshua Lewis is a recovering computer geek. He is stumbling toward a postgraduate degree but is not quite sure what kind yet. He spends his days in New York working for a mysterious corporation and thinking a great deal about artisan cheese.

Catherine Lundoff lives in Minneapolis with her fabulous partner and a small herd of cats. Her short fiction has appeared in such anthologies as *Such a Pretty Face, Taste of Midnight, Cherished Blood, Blood Surrender, Simulacrum, Kenoma, The Mammoth Book of Best New Erotica 4* and *Best Lesbian Erotica 2005*. She has published two collections of lesbian erotica, *Night's Kiss* (Torquere Press), and the recently released *Crave* (Lethe Press).

Laurie J. Marks is the author of *Dancing Jack, The Watcher's Mask,* and the *Children of the Triadâ* series, among other works. Her essays and book reviews have appeared in the *SF Revu* and other journals, and she teaches composition, creative writing, and science fiction at the University of Massachusetts, Boston.

Laurie has caused a stir in the fantasy publishing world with her unfolding Elemental Logic series. The first book in the series, *Fire Logic,* won the 2003 Gaylactic Spectrum Award; the second book, *Earth Logic,* also garnered raves from professionals in the field and was nominated for the 2005 Gaylactic Spectrum Award. *Water Logic* released soon from Small Beer Press, and *Air Logic* will follow. She is also planning a non-series fantasy novel tentatively titled *The Cunning-Men.*

Sean Meriwether's work has been published in *Lodestar Quarterly, Skin & Ink,* and *Best of Best Gay Erotica 2.* He is the editor of *Velvet Mafia: Dangerous Queer Fiction* (velvetmafia.com) online, and *Men of Mystery.* Sean lives in New York with his partner, photographer Jack Slomovits. Stalk him online at seanmeriwether.com.

Sarah Monette's stories have appeared in *Alchemy, Strange Horizons,* and *Tales of the Unanticipated,* among others. "Three Letters from the Queen of Elfland," originally published in *Lady Churchill's Rosebud Wristlet 11,* won the Gaylactic Spectrum Award for Short Fiction in 2003. Her fantasy novels, *Melusine,* and its sequel, *The Virtu,* were released from Ace Books.

Elspeth Potter's stories have appeared in *Best Lesbian Erotica, Best Women's Erotica, Tough Girls, The Mammoth Book of Best New Erotica,* Fishnet.com, *The MILF Anthology, Alleys and Doorways,* and *Sex in the*

System: Stories of Erotic Futures, Technical Stimulation, and the Sensual Life of Machines.

Luisa Prieto attended the Odyssey Fantasy Writer's Workshop, where she studied with Jeanne Cavelos and Charles DeLint. She currently lives in Campbell, California.

Melissa Scott was born and raised in Little Rock, Arkansas, and studied history at Harvard College and Brandeis University, where she earned her PhD in comparative history. In 1986, she won the John W. Campbell Award for Best New Writer, and in 2001 she and long-time partner and collaborator Lisa A. Barnett won the Lambda Literary Award in SF/Fantasy/Horror for *Point of Dreams.* Scott has also won Lammies in 1996 for *Shadow Man* and 1995 for *Trouble and Her Friends.* Her first work of nonfiction, *Conceiving the Heavens: Creating the Science Fiction Novel,* was published by Heinemann in 1997, and her monologue, "At RaeDean's Funeral," has been included in an off-off-Broadway production, *Elvis Dreams,* as well as several other evenings of Elvis mania. A second monologue, "Job Hunting," has been performed in competition and as a part of an evening of *Monologues from the Road.*

Delia Sherman was born in Tokyo, Japan, and brought up in New York, where she has returned with her partner Ellen Kushner. She spent much of her early life at one end of a classroom or another, first at Vassar and Brown University, where she earned a PhD in renaissance studies in 1981, and later at Boston University and Northeastern, where she taught freshman composition and fantasy as literature. Her first novel, *Through a Brazen Mirror* (Ace, 1989), was published as one of the prestigious Ace Fantasy Specials. Her second novel, *The Porcelain Dove* (Dutton, 1993; Plume, 1994), won the Mythopoeic Award for Fantasy Fiction. Her short fiction has appeared in *The Magazine of Fantasy and Science Fiction* and many anthologies. Her most recent book, *Changeling,* may have been written for children but can be enjoyed by all. She is a member of the Motherboard of the James Tiptree Jr. Award Council.

Kenneth D. Woods lives in St. Louis, Missouri, with his partner Chris, and holds down a day job as a software developer. He spends his evenings and weekends writing short stories and novels. He belongs to a pair of Italian greyhounds, Fiona and Maggie. They run a tight ship.

doi:10.1300/5642_25

ACKNOWLEDGMENTS

The inspiration for this book falls to the marvelous editorial team of Ellen Datlow and Terri Windling. I would have never envisioned *So Fey* if I had not been involved with *The Faery Reel.* Terri also helped by suggesting several authors she felt would be perfect contributors and many of them ended up in the pages of what you are holding.

My editor, Greg Herren, encouraged me with the book from concept to end result and has earned my respect for his endless patience.

I appreciate all the submissions I read for the project and doubly appreciate the patience of the authors picked for the book. I can honestly say that each and every one was a pleasure to work with.

I'm reminded of my childhood and the debt to the elementary school nurse who discovered my love for fantasy (and monsters) and allowed me to skip classes and read her son's *Dungeons & Dragons* rulebooks in her office. Thanks, Ms. Schulman, wherever you are.

Most importantly, I need to offer special thanks to my family: my mother who has always believed in my writing, my father who taught me the whims of deal-making, and my sister, Susan, who has always been there with a friendly ear and helpings of milk and warm, home-baked cookies. Without their love, I would be lost and this book would never have happened.